ONE

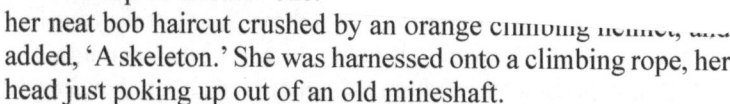

'We found a body.'

DS Tony Milburn respo

'On top of another one.

her neat bob haircut crushed by an orange climbing helmet, and added, 'A skeleton.' She was harnessed onto a climbing rope, her head just poking up out of an old mineshaft.

Detective Constable Meredith had been trumpeting her new qualification to work using climbing gear all around the police station for several months, but this was the first chance she'd had to show off that training in the field.

Tony shifted his weight. He stood on a metal grate that they had found hinged right back over on the grass. It should have been padlocked to prevent access to the vertical shaft, but they had found the broken padlock a couple of metres away. The grating had then been pressed into service as a belay support for the rope, and although its foundation was solid, he had decided to stand on it to be extra certain.

The detective sergeant looked away, the bright reflection from Meredith's helmet a strain on his eyes, even through his sunglasses. Staring over the grassy field, back down the hill that they had struggled up in the heat, he looked again at the missing man's grey Astra neatly parked in a lay-by.

'But, is it him?'

Meredith could annoy him at the drop of a hat, and with sweat itching his back, he was tetchy. Around him, the hilltop grass was steaming slightly. After a cold night, the sun now lounged on a blue sky picnic blanket, evaporating the remaining dew.

Tony showed her his phone screen with the photo that they'd been given by a distressed wife who had reported her husband missing. Meredith had dispensed with her own designer sunglasses in order to go down the mine with CSI Johnson, and she struggled to look up at the image. 'No, we can't tell: his face has been smashed in.'

1

Tony leant forward to peer past her down the stone-lined pit. One foot wobbled, slipping on the metal bars. His arms shot out sideways for balance. 'I'm not surprised. I can easily imagine him leaning too far and falling down there. And hitting your face on those rock walls would probably do a fair bit of damage.'

Below her, another orange helmet moved about, dangling on the rope too. The new crime scene investigator, Alfie Johnson, had encouraged her to join him in exploring the depths of the mine, once they had seen the broken padlock and half a dozen possessions scattered around the opening. He called up, 'Yeah, it's about ten metres deep, so plenty in here to make those injuries, even from simply falling.'

Tony spoke loudly so the conversation included Alfie. 'And there's also a skeleton down there?'

He remembered the somewhat over-familiar handling of his female colleague by the handsome new CSI as he had helped her into the hole. This new member of County Durham's forensics team was large, well-built, with a big, square jaw and a head of slicked-back, blond hair. There was a strong sense of Viking in his appearance.

He had wondered initially if he might need to report the man, or at least have a quiet word with him about interpersonal space and the needs of a professional workplace. Then he'd seen her smiling and laughing and giving the trademark flick of her brown bob. Her responses had given him the realisation that this new guy was probably the one in harm's way. New meat for Meredith.

Johnson replied, 'A coincidence, I'm thinking. That skeleton has been dead for at least fifty years. We'll need to take it back to the lab to work that out exactly, but the top corpse is freshly dead. Probably early this morning judging by the state of the congealed blood.'

'Coincidence?'

Meredith answered, 'Yes, probably. As you said, easy to fall down here. I think this pit was abandoned way back, like in

Published by Penfold Books
87 Hallgarth Street
Durham DH1 3AS
England

Author's website:
mileshudson.com

ISBN: 978-1-83812-581-3

Printed and bound by CPI Group (UK) Ltd, Croydon, CR0 4YY

Exclusively Human Authored.

Acknowledgements

Many thanks are due to:
Jo Colling; Kirsten Crombie; Chris Donald; Andy Dowson;
Durham Miners Association; Friends of Durham Miners' Gala;
Jane Hamilton; Trudy Hamilton; Carol Hudson;
Kirsty Parkinson; Neil Terry; Phil Vaughan;

About the Author

Miles Hudson loves words and ideas.

He's a physics teacher, surfer, author, hockey player, inventor, backpacker and idler.

Miles was born in Minneapolis but has lived in Durham in northern England for nearly 40 years.

By the same author

Penfold Detective Series

The Cricketer's Corpse

The Kidney Killer

Burns Night Burns

By Miles M Hudson

Audiopt Surveillance Series

2089

The Mind's Eye

The Times of Malthus

Penfold and DS Milburn
investigate The Case of

Saint
Cuthbert's
Curse

M M Hudson

Ⓑ PENFOLD BOOKS

Victorian times, but there's the odd bit of coal down there. Wouldn't surprise me if people fifty years ago were still collecting bits and pieces for the fires in their own houses.' She raised an arm out of the hole to point down the hillside the other way, towards Tudhoe village. The nearest houses were only about two hundred metres away.

The crime scene investigator's voice echoed up again. 'Can you pass down the body bags, and we'll get them raised up. I reckon we've got enough video footage from the bottom now to be able to move the bodies. I've taken soil samples and so on as well, but it's pretty cramped. I can't really process the bodies. The tunnel's too tight and dark.'

Five metres from the opening, they had erected a white crime scene tent. It hung open, and the trestle table inside already had a number of Johnson's tools laid out. His cantilever toolbox had several layers extending outwards, as the man had gathered some items to take down the pit.

'I can see your toolbox. Where are the body bags?'

'Oh yeah, sorry, I left them in the back of the pick-up. Box marked *BB*.'

CSI Johnson drove a beast of a vehicle: a brand-new, jet-black Ford pick-up truck. It had a big four-door cab, and a large truck bed, kitted out with numerous lockers and cabinets. He had bounced, off-road, right up the hill and it was parked beside the white tent.

Tony stepped off the grate and the rope creaked slightly. He jumped back, but it had settled safely enough, so he cautiously released his weight from it again. Clambering up on to the back of the truck, he discovered that, parked up here on top of the grassy hillock, Johnson's pick-up served as a great vantage point.

County Durham's countryside in full leaf was a glory to behold. He wondered how long the hot, dry weather could go on before everything was parched brown.

At about a hundred metres' distance, Tony's eye passed over his own unmarked police car, a nondescript, black VW Golf. It was parked a few metres in front of the grey Vauxhall Astra estate that had been called in by a local panda car patrol after the missing man's details had been broadcast.

He observed his gangly boss, who had chosen to remain with the vehicles and let the less senior detectives do all the hiking and climbing. Detective Inspector Godolphin Barnes stooped to try and look in through the driver's window. Even at such a distance, the man was so tall and thin that his bending over was comically obvious.

Tony rubbed a hand over his sweaty scalp and squinted up to the blue sky. He wondered if his barber had cut it too short for the blazing sunshine. The hairdresser had been about to disappear on a rugby tour to Argentina for several weeks and had shorn much closer to his scalp than normal. The last thing he needed was a sunburnt head.

Meredith appeared at the side of the vehicle, and he passed over two rolled up white PVC bags. Combining a sort of sliding and rolling action, he managed to reach a foot to the top of the rear tyre and step down. The little shadow offered by the side of the truck was a blessing. He crouched on his haunches to hide entirely from the sun.

As she walked away, he wondered at her outfit. As a plain clothes detective, Meredith normally wore a business skirt and blouse. The weather was extremely hot, but today she sported dark cotton trousers, currently covered by the climbing harness around her waist and bottom. Her upper body filled out a tight, navy T-shirt, and on her feet, he saw blue hiking shoes, with lighter blue branding stripes. It was as if she had somehow guessed she would need to join Johnson in their rope expedition down the pit.

She knelt at the ledge of the opening and passed down the body bags to a beefy hand that appeared. Her orange helmet was discarded near the scene tent, but her hair seemed to have been unaffected by the hour spent wearing it. Every fine, brown strand knew its place and the hairs shimmered and wobbled in perfect harmony.

It would take the CSI quite a time to carefully encase each corpse in its own bag for elevation to the surface, but the space at the bottom was too cramped for Meredith to be any help down there. She waited, kneeling and chatting down to her interesting new colleague.

Tony continued to marvel at the old growth trees and stared at a bird slowly circling in the distance, white down against the bright blue. He failed to notice the DC step over to talk to him.

'Are you listening?'

Behind his sunglasses Meredith wouldn't be able to see that his eyes were scanning the woods across the valley. She held up her phone, waved it at him with a scowl and swiped through several photographs taken in the almost pitch blackness of the small underground space below.

Tony stood up again to view the phone, and he wondered about what the two might have been doing together down there, rather than concentrating on the pictures. He smiled inwardly at the idea of calling the man CSI Hunk but returned to seriousness at the image in his mind's eye of Meredith calling the man that. He needed to warn Alfie.

'What do you reckon?' Meredith interrupted his inattention.

'Erm.' He paused to get a grip on what he should be thinking about. 'How do you think the bodies came to be down there?'

'Skeleton looks like it's been there for years. The new one though: he's fallen down there recently. I don't know if they were trying to climb down or what exactly. The blood on this guy's face is not running wet still, but it's fresh. I agree with Alfie: he fell down there this morning.' She supplemented her words with a gloved finger pointing at a large, bloody hole in the man's cheek and eye.

Although the July daylight would have started at about four o'clock in the morning this far north, Tony still wondered how the walker …? farmer? jogger? could have come to fall down there so early that he and Meredith were wrapping up the initial scene response before lunch. More though, why would he have spread his belongings out around the place and smashed open the access cover.

'Any obvious shenanigans? Drug paraphernalia, trousers round his ankles, anything blatant? Did he really just fall in?' Milburn spun round in fright. Detective Inspector Godolphin Barnes was leaning on the pick-up's tailgate, face pinched as he asked his usual level of inappropriate question. The DI had ghosted up the hill silently and must have been listening in as Meredith presented the photos.

She shrugged and kept on looking at Tony. He widened his eyes in response, wondering how the senior detective on scene could think this was what he should be asking.

Without waiting for an answer DI Barnes wiped a long hand down his suit chest and dismissively said, 'Actually forget it, it doesn't matter. I'm on holiday from this afternoon, and I think I'm going to have to go back to the station right now so that I can sign out in time to get to the airport.' He walked away without looking back. His lanky six-foot-three height meant those long legs sped him down the hill at quite a lick.

Tony felt a pained expression cross his face, his feelings conflicted. It was always difficult working with his boss. The man was annoying and confusing in equal measure, so his departure for a three-week holiday in Australia was good news. The bad news was that they had just found two dead bodies and were going to be a senior detective short in the investigation. Barnes rubbed people up the wrong way, but they were often riled up enough to give out useful information. At the very least he was another body to read documents. Budget cuts had just lost them their main civilian investigator. And Godolphin loved paperwork: a hundred case documents to review, feet up in his office, was the inspector's idea of a great day's work.

Tony looked back towards Durham City, squinting, the bright sunshine over-saturating everything, in all directions. The inspector slinked alongside the Volkswagen Golf in which he and Tony had arrived, yanked the door open and folded himself into the driver's seat.

As Barnes drove off, Tony realised this meant he would have to return to the police station in the car that Meredith had brought. They worked together regularly now, and he never enjoyed being in an enclosed space with the woman.

He looked back to her face. Her skin was flawless. Her hair still seemed perfect, despite the best part of an hour spent at the bottom of a tight mineshaft with a hulking great forensic examiner. She was objectively beautiful. Was the tingle in his spine one of attraction or trepidation? He hated the fact that he couldn't be sure himself.

Two

At the lay-by below, the morgue van pulled in. County Durham's most senior pathologist, Philip Gerard, dropped lightly from the footstep and headed up the hill. Under one arm he held his pack of forensics coveralls, and in the other hand carried a toolbox more like a plumber's than a doctor's bag.

'Do you want to look at these then?' Meredith was waving her phone more insistently, the screen pointed towards Tony.

'Not right this second. Is there anything else? What do you think was the cause of death?'

'Well, it's pretty clear that he died from blunt force trauma to the skull. I'd guess while falling down the shaft.'

'What about the other body?'

'Yeah, no idea. It's clearly been there a long time. I mean it's pretty skeletal and clothing looks quite old. It's muddy at the bottom, so it's been difficult to see any injuries, but it wouldn't surprise me if he suffered the same fate fifty years ago.' Meredith held her hands open, to indicate her lack of certainty, and then swiped her phone to show an image of the skull of the older body sticking out from underneath the newly deceased victim.

They turned at the sound of another vehicle stopping. Dr Julia Sedgley had arrived in her white BMW, and Tony realised that they should have already cordoned off the grey Astra. Sedgley was the crime scene manager and she would co-ordinate forensic investigation.

He guessed that they could make a reasonable claim that no evidence had been changed on the missing man's car since he'd arrived, despite there being no blue tape or official cordon protecting it. Tony jerked as the thought hit him that the Astra might not belong to their new dead body. On cue, the car's indicators flashed. Even at a distance, this made Tony jump. DC

Meredith pressed the key fob again, through the plastic of the evidence bag she held it in, and the car boot popped open.

Sedgley's big head of dark, curly hair emerged from the driver's side of the BMW, followed by the rest of her, lifting out another of the forensic toolboxes. She walked briskly to the now open car boot, and after a brief scan inside, she turned to look up and down the lay-by, then across the road, and further along it towards the village.

'Give me that!' Tony swiped the bag from Meredith's hand and set off striding down to meet Julia. As he walked, he phoned the scene manager to apologise. 'Up the hill to your left. Sorry, that was Diane messing about. Well, she was checking we had the right keys for that car so you can process it, but, well, sorry. I'm coming down to meet you and I've got the keys.'

She turned to watch him heading towards her. Theatrically, she pulled out a nitrile glove, waved it around to open up the fingers, and used it to slam the boot lid shut without touching the metal herself. 'Honestly, Detective Sergeant. Messing up my crime scene – when will you ever get control of your subordinates?'

Dr Sedgley was poking fun, but as he watched his footing, stepping through thick grass and tussocks, he thought, *Get control of Diane? You're joking aren't you? You're a scientist, when exactly* will *hell be freezing over?*

As Tony was on the phone when they passed each other, old Gerard simply nodded, with a cheesy grin adorning his tanned face.

Tony passed the evidence bag over to Sedgley. When she took it, he saw her nails were painted black, matching her dark eyebrows. She double-checked the opening and closing of the car door locks but wasn't ready to process the car for evidence. It wouldn't be necessary until they confirmed that there had been a crime associated with this vehicle. Maybe the owner was actually just on a walk in the fields thereabouts and had dropped their keys.

He pointed up the hill to the scene examiners' tent and explained how the bodies would be pulled from the ground and lie in state inside the small gazebo. Both would then have to go to the morgue at the University Hospital of North Durham, but he had not yet spoken to Gerard about post-mortem timings.

He turned, so the warming sun was at his back, and wondered if he could see the hospital uphill at the back end of Durham City. Looking north it was pretty much flat, across fields towards the city. Visibility was about as good as it could ever get, but they were five miles away. Squinting, not into the sun but into the bucolic distance, he reckoned he could identify the four points at the top of Durham Cathedral tower, but maybe they were actually just four distant treetops.

The lay-by was close to a livery stable, and the earthy smell of the countryside coalesced with equine odours – horse sweat and more. Just over the hedge across the road, a dark brown pile the size of a single-decker bus blocked the view in the opposite direction away from the white tent and across the next field. Tony decided he didn't want to know exactly what substances formed the pile.

He walked over to stand beside Dr Sedgley at the passenger door of the car. 'Given that we've got the keys for the car, would it hurt to have a look around inside?'

The scene manager leant forward so that her head was adjacent to Tony's and peered in the window in the same way he was. There was nothing obvious within the vehicle – it was spic and span. Unless one was to start getting out the fingerprinting kit or other more complicated forensic analysis tools there wasn't anything obvious to be examined inside. 'As I said, Tony, just cordon it off, get a uniform out here to look after it, and Alfie and I will go over it after I've been down the hole. The bodies are my first priority.'

Tony could feel his mobile phone vibrating in his jacket pocket, and when he looked at the screen, he immediately turned his gaze back up the hill to see the pathologist waving at him while holding his own mobile phone.

'Shall we?' His colleague from the forensics team indicated back up to where Meredith and Johnson appeared to be wrestling a mummy out of the ground.

When they arrived back at the gazebo, Meredith held up other evidence bags containing a wallet, a mobile phone and a canvas satchel. She explained that these were all either from the newer corpse or had been lying up there on the grass. They had not removed any evidence from the skeleton underneath.

Sedgley said, 'Well, don't get them mixed up. Make sure we've got the locations where they were all found secured exactly.'

Meredith replied dismissively, 'Of course. Alfie took photos of them all in situ, with the yellow number tags, and a view of the entire area with all the number tags visible. Don't you worry, Julia, we've got it all in hand.'

Tony looked at Meredith: his legs often still felt like jelly around her. He shook it off immediately and pursued a question for Sedgley's benefit. 'What do you think, Constable? Is there any foul play here or is this just a straight accident?'

Meredith put her hands on her hips, three large transparent plastic bags resting against her right thigh, and pouted. A look both sultry and seductive, devastating to any man nearby. She said with a tone of sarcasm, 'Well, I think we probably better wait for the post-mortem, hadn't we?'

Pathologist Philip Gerard was sufficiently senior within the county medical service that he didn't consider it necessary to agree to be lowered down a narrow mineshaft. CSI Johnson had promised he would take as much care of the skeleton as was possible. He used a body bag, but the fact that it had been pulled vertically upwards meant that by the time it reached the gazebo

11

tent, any skeletal structure had been lost, and it was just a rattling bag of bones.

Before Gerard could lose his charming demeanour, Meredith reassured him, 'You needn't worry either, Philip, we took plenty of photos at the bottom so you can re-organise all the bits on your steel table in the pathology lab.'

He nodded. 'Well it won't be me. I know that Jan loves a puzzle.'

Tony managed to twist Gerard's arm enough to convince him to open the bag there and then and have a look at the broken bits to see if he could make any guess as to how the person might have died.

With the body bag open on the ground, Gerard moved a few bits and pieces backwards and forwards. Bones had collected within the clothing, but the skull was the first thing the pathologist went for. As he turned it over in his gloved hands, everyone could see a significant hole in the occipital bone at the back. Gerard looked up at the two detectives from his squatting position, offering the injured skull for them to view. 'I'm gonna stick my neck out and suggest that maybe this killed him.'

They nodded in agreement, but Tony asked, 'OK, so did the fall do that? Or did something else hit him?'

Gerard shook his silver-haired head. The sun caught his tanned face, and the man looked like an ageing Hollywood star incongruously cast as Hamlet. 'Alas …' Nobody caught on to his joke, so Gerard placed the skull back on the notional top of the body and zipped the bag back up. 'That is beyond what I can tell from this initial visual assessment. You'll have to wait for the post-mortem.'

Meredith called down the mineshaft to CSI Johnson. 'How's it going down there, Alfie?'

Tony looked into the hole, a charcoal grey, rocky square that quickly became dark barely a metre down. He could hear the man's voice quite clearly, echoing up the stone column. Closing his eyes, he raised his cheek to absorb the warmth of the sun and listened to what the scene investigator had to report.

'There's really not much to see down here even with my bright light. I've taken full video and a lot of still photos, and I'm going to gather up anything that doesn't look natural.'

Meredith stood beside another three large plastic evidence bags containing a climbing rope and some other equipment: carabiners and pitons. One bag held a notebook with some loose papers sticking out of the edge. Julia Sedgley knelt beside Meredith and held up the bags one by one to look at their contents.

The crime scene manager leaned forward to look down the hole, and almost toppled in. 'Oops.' Her near accident gave her pause, and a line of thinking. 'Well, um. Well, I'm going to speculate that before he'd togged up with all the mountaineering gear, he leaned over too far and slipped. Maybe twisted around in a last ditch bid to avoid falling. Failed, fell into the hole and landed on the other body, the skeleton. Who'd probably done the same thing years earlier.'

Tony stared beyond his detective constable and the forensics manager, eying the contours of the grassy field as it curved down towards Nickynack Beck. He tipped his head slightly to the side and focussed back on Julia. 'But why? What were they doing here? What did they want inside the mine?'

THREE

'Please! Is this really supposed to be a treasure map?'

DC Madeline Aria looked across the table at Diane Meredith, with a slightly wounded expression. Aria protested, 'Well, it has a label saying *St Cuthbert's Treasure, 1943* and an "X" at the Tudhoe mine, where we found the bodies.'

'X marks the spot? Are you kidding me? This is bullshit.' Meredith carelessly pushed the journal, with a map unfolded from its central spread, back across the desk towards Aria.

'Careful! It's fragile; we mustn't damage it.'

Meredith just shook her head.

Aria continued, 'More importantly, it's evidence.'

'Evidence of idiocy. I often wonder how it is that men have all the power in the world, when they're so pathetic. Look' – she leant across to point at a marginalia scrawl on the edge of the open map – 'I mean, please. *Beware St Cuthbert's Curse!* Infantile. It's not in the least bit surprising he fell down the pit.'

'Succumbed to the curse, you mean?' Aria sported a pleased smile.

The Major Crimes Team's main workroom contained eight desks, mostly empty apart from ubiquitous computer screens and keyboards. Three desks had been commandeered to hold large fans. The hot weather outside manifested as stifling, still air in the second-floor office space, and the two women had surrounded themselves as well as possible with any available ventilation.

Meredith leaned over and flicked the notebook to the inside back cover. 'Look, have you seen this? He made a wish list of what he'd spend all the money on when he found the treasure. He's even written *Treasure* with a bloody dollar sign for an "S".'

DS Tony Milburn cleared his throat theatrically to let the detectives know he had heard Meredith's diatribe. Their heads jerked towards him leaning against the doorjamb of his office. DC Aria looked mortified. Meredith looked proud, defiant. 'Can you gather all the evidence from the mine scene and bring it into my office – H is coming down for a briefing in a few minutes.'

Despite her protestations about the patriarchy, Meredith dutifully did her share of re-bagging the various possessions they had found on the two bodies in Tudhoe mineshaft. She gathered everything up, including the items Aria was holding, and carried it all into the partitioned office at the end of the MCT – Major Crimes Team – open plan office area. Tony had occupied the office since Harry 'H' Hardwick's promotion to DCI had seen him move upstairs.

In theory, the pecking order should have put the inspector, Godolphin Barnes, into the main MCT office. However, he had magnanimously offered to stay put in a smaller space down a flight of stairs on the first floor of the old Georgian building. Its original stone structure was historically beautiful, as per the whole of Durham City, but it led to some odd architectural situations inside. Most detectives assumed that Barnes had maintained his smaller office away from the MCT's to avoid work. The upshot, though, was the elevation of Detective Sergeant Milburn to the 'big' office.

Meredith passed him in the doorway, turning, ostensibly to squeeze through. The gap was not too small for her and the armfuls of evidence she carried, but her bottom managed to brush slowly against his hip nonetheless. He was certain he heard her expel the quietest gasp as it did so. She started to arrange the evidence bags on the desk for the forthcoming show-and-tell with the top boss, and, again, he was convinced she was leaning over the desk in an unnecessarily provocative way.

At that moment, Hardwick bustled in through the main door and strode up the gap between desks. His one good eye was focussed on the office chair he was heading towards, while his dead one appeared to be making eye contact and fooled Tony, as ever. The career copper was squarely built and a similar height to Tony. A horse-kick to the side of the head twenty years earlier had damaged all the nerves to his right eye.

Tony nodded at the DCI, who ignored him – hadn't seen the nod – marched straight past him and sat down in the comfy, almost bouncy chair. Meredith was standing, straight and demure, by the obligatory, but mostly defunct, filing cabinet. Tony had not moved from his sentinel position at the door.

'Can you give us the room please, Meredith.' The chief inspector's words were not a question, and he reinforced them with a trademark dead-eye stare.

She said nothing and made a show of how tightly she had to squeeze back out, despite the fact that Tony had left her plenty of space to walk past. Audible only to him, she exhaled another little gasp as she exited. He shook his head as he went in and closed the door.

Large, both physically and in presence, DCI Hardwick fingered the evidence bags and pulled a couple of objects out. The scene reminded Tony of days gone by when he had been called into this office to argue with H about how to deal with Meredith the stalker. She had been a uniformed constable in those days, working from the shift offices on the ground floor. Now, she watched them through the large window in the office partitioning.

He'd always thought the back of the room looked like a face. Remembering back to those days, the two small square windows high up on the back wall were the eyes. Centrally placed beneath these, the bulk of Harry became the bulbous nose, and the desk in front of him was the mouth. Today, the littering of objects on the desk appeared as poor dentition in that mouth: a line-up of misshapen and skewed teeth, in an assortment of colours.

Through the room's left eye, Tony could see the cathedral's rose window glittering in bright sunshine. It was perhaps two hundred metres away as the crow would fly, up and over the River Wear.

'Right, what have we got?' H looked up at Tony, who turned his gaze back from the window.

He started on his iPad, showing scene photos from down the mineshaft. 'Victim one here is Michael Dooley. It was his wife that called us in. She had his phone location, and it hadn't moved all night, and he hadn't come home from heading out with all his gear the day before.'

'All his gear?'

Tony grimaced at the explanation he had to impart. 'She reckons he's some sort of explorer of abandoned mines.'

'Oh yeah, I know the sort of thing. They post videos online of what it's like down there now. Sounds boring to me, but whatever floats your boat, I guess.'

Tony nodded along. 'The wife says he's been on some sort of treasure hunting kick recently. Got all sorts of climbing gear for getting down into deep holes.'

'Treasure hunting?'

Tony leant forward and unpacked the journal with the folded map in it. 'The journal has a lot of what looks like research notes about something referred to as "St Cuthbert's Treasure".' He pointed at the "X" on the map, and DCI Hardwick scowled.

Tony continued, 'Now, that seemed a bit …'

'Stupid?'

'Um, OK,' he laughed. 'I was going to say "out there" but, yes, "stupid" works. Until I show you this one.' From another clear plastic bag on the desktop, he pulled a different notebook. It was older and thinner than Dooley's. He opened a random page and the paper was tightly covered in neat, inked handwriting. 'This book was found on the other body, who was directly underneath victim one. It's a very similar journal of research and notes about searching for St Cuthbert's Treasure.'

H interrupted, 'Sorry, is this our Saint Cuthbert, from Durham Cathedral?'

'Don't know, but you'd imagine so. I mean how many Saint Cuthberts are there?' The question was rhetorical, and Tony carried on. 'This one has sketched maps, hand drawn, that look to marry up exactly with the one in Dooley's notebook.' He stepped around the desk to show his boss both maps, side by side.

Having laid the book down, Tony's eye was caught by Meredith glaring through the glass at them. He pointedly ignored her and went back to the iPad pictures.

'Both men died from head injuries. For Dooley, it looks very much like he hit a rock, or rocks, jutting out of the side as he fell down the shaft.'

'How deep is it?'

'I'm not sure exactly. Between ten and twenty metres, at a guess. The forensics report should be through later today. I'm sure Johnson will have measured it – he seems really on the ball. And Gerard promised us the post-mortem report by close of play too. Although only on Michael Dooley. The other victim is going to take a fair bit longer. Properly old – skeletal – going to need forensics as well as pathology to sort out who that one is. There's a name and address in the notebook, but they don't match the current database; the book is dated 1958. The major news though is that that one's skull was really stoved in. As much as he'll ever be drawn when outside his pathology dungeon, Philip did say victim two is a likely murder.' He supported the last statement with a finger pointing at another photo on the iPad, but the DCI was distracted.

'Jeez, really, post-mortem report today? How the hell did you get him to work so quickly? They usually take a week at least.'

Tony looked again at the staring Meredith and jumped at the chance to set out the landscape on his terms. 'He doesn't like Meredith, so I assume he didn't want her going up to the hospital to watch the pm.'

Hardwick leaned back, pushing his white hair against the comfortable headrest. The chair groaned. He frowned and gave Tony a half-hearted dead-eye stare. 'I'm glad you mentioned her. First on scene, right?'

'After a fashion,' Tony conceded.

'With Godolphin off on his jollies, you're going to be SIO on this.'

'Me as SIO? OK.'

'And we need somebody with the authority to move things forward as they need to.'

'Right.'

'So, I'm also putting you on an acting-up promotion to DI.'

'What?' Tony was genuinely surprised. He'd been Senior Investigating Officer several times previously, as DI Barnes was so regularly absent. However, the promotion to detective inspector, albeit acting DI, would give him the freedom to organise things, without constantly having to run to H to authorise the funds for overtime and forensic tests and suchlike.

Without any obvious trigger, Tony had a vision of his surfer buddy, Penfold. The New Zealander was a civilian who had helped out on a number of investigations, sometimes with the authority of being officially contracted as a consultant, but mostly off his own bat, with Tony turning a blind eye.

He wished Hardwick would use his actual blind eye more often, as Penfold was a brilliant investigator, but H couldn't stand having the man involved. Tony's mind wandered, remembering Penfold's help on the "Case of the Drunken Fifty Pound Notes". *He doesn't even charge us any fees.* But, he realised, an acting DI as SIO would be able to engage Penfold's help without running it by DCI Hardwick.

H had let Tony's thoughts run long enough, and he restarted the conversation. 'However, I'm going to allocate your staffing. You know what a mess the budget is right now, and worse than that is the lack of available manpower, so I'm going to have to organise personnel across all our operations right now, and I'm afraid you're just going to have to accept whomever I allocate.'

Tony felt like the boss had handed him a gift and then taken it straight away again. However, what H was concerned about was not a surfing Kiwi who had his own forensics lab in his basement, but the working relationship, or lack of one, that Tony had with DC Diane Meredith.

'We're not yet certain this is a murder case, or cases, so for now you get Aria and Meredith and a couple of uniforms as and when you need door knockers. And you, and that's it.' The DCI held up a hand to halt any protest before it began.

Tony was reeling and not even ready to start to argue. All thought of sticking up for Penfold had rushed from his mind as he looked through the office window to see Meredith staring back, the faintest hint of a smile playing at the corners of her mouth. Did she know what H had just said?

Hardwick expanded on his bid to make Tony's life difficult: 'These staffing problems just get worse and worse. We're gonna be about a dozen officers short for policing the Miners' Gala a week on Saturday.'

The connection did not seem obvious. 'Um, well I don't know where we'll be with this case by then, but I volunteered to be on shift on the day.'

The DCI grunted. 'There's no real volunteering these days – everyone's got to work the Gala. We're really going to struggle if anything kicks off. Now Barnes has gone, you're going to need to be Silver Commander.'

Tony's stomach dropped. 'Really?'

'Needs must, I'm afraid, Tony. I assume Barnes liaised with you before heading off Down Under. I need a safe pair of hands in charge, on the ground through the day, and that's you.' He paused to address any objections, but Tony couldn't think of a reasonable excuse quickly enough.

Barnes had mentioned it months ago but had not followed up, so Tony had presumed that an alternative Silver Commander had been appointed. If truth be told, he hadn't really thought about it at all, as nobody had said anything to him. He certainly hadn't been briefed, but this held no sway with Hardwick.

'You know how good Godolphin is with planning – he'll have left you a comprehensive set of procedures to follow. I'll ask you straight away to meet with their Gold Commander and try to get caught up on what Barnes has already cooked up with them. I'm our Gold Commander, so if you can confirm the overall plan and submit it to me, I'll sign it off for you. Critically though, listen to what they say and get everyone deployed to the most likely flashpoints.'

Tony laughed. 'Two hundred thousand drunkards wandering around the city, and you think there's likely to be predictable flashpoints?'

Harry was a pragmatic man. 'It doesn't really matter. As long as we've asked them where they expect the hotspots to be, and we cover those, we've supported them to the extent they're paying for.'

'What if they say more locations than we have people to cover.'

'That's why I'm appointing you as chief liaison – make sure they don't.' H flashed Tony a smile. 'This year the principal organiser is a bloke called Barry Black.'

FOUR

Tony woke at 6.13 a.m. to the buzz of his phone indicating the arrival of a text message.

Prodigal surfer returns Saturday, spent, energised.

When he wasn't writing in haiku format, Penfold's messages were usually composed as six-word stories. To Tony this meant they were mostly cryptic riddles. He felt the clarity of messaging became lost through Penfold's crowbarring of information into specific genre formats.

The tall New Zealander had been to Thurso in Scotland for a week, as the summertime waves in Hartlepool were "banal". Tony wondered how much headway they might make with the two mineshaft corpses in the next twenty-four hours, and whether Penfold would actually make any useful contribution. He fully expected to hear about "pumping overheads" and "three-sixties" and other surfing jargon that Penfold often spouted after his frequent campervan trips around the country.

The master bedroom in Tony and Kathy's house was light, despite the thick cream curtains. In summertime daylight in Durham extended from the small hours right through to ten or eleven at night. He brought his girlfriend a cup of milky coffee and kissed her gently.

She woke vaguely, but her eyes remained closed, and she murmured, 'Time 'zit?'

'Early. Keep dozing. At least an hour before you need to get up.'

She opened her eyes and slid up to sitting in the warm bed. The light through the curtains indicated another very sunny day was starting. Kathy cupped the coffee mug in her long fingers and watched Tony putting a tie on.

'Important meeting?'

'I don't know about important, but I'm going to Redhills to meet with the Top Marra of the Miners' Gala. H put me in charge of liaising with them about next Saturday. Barnes has gone on holiday again.'

'Top Marra, eh?' She chuckled quietly.

'Quiet, you. Our force doesn't have a big football club in the area – this is the biggest policing event we have to deal with.'

'But the whole essence of the word *marra* is about equal standing, friends and colleagues, with no sense of hierarchy at all. The phrase "Top Marra" is an oxymoron.'

'Apparently, once you meet the guy it all becomes clear. Old Bob Smith reckons he's a piece of work – styles himself after the union leaders gone by: grandiose about his standing, with as much political ambition as the mine bosses they fought against. So that's not his actual title – it's what people call him behind his back: "Top Marra Barry Black". Can't wait to meet him! But I'm sure one man – even the main Gala organiser – won't be able to undermine the fraternal tradition.'

'I know. I love it all. The celebration of mining heritage and working-class culture is brilliant. I guess the very fact that it's so long running means that bits of it are always going to seem antiquated. Are you going to be able to catch up with whatever Godolphin's left behind?'

'That's why I set up a meeting straight away. God knows what nonsense he'll have promised the bloke, safe in the knowledge that somebody would have to pick up the pieces when he's away.'

'You know they've dumped three shipping containers on Palace Green.'

'Who?'

'The Miners' Gala. They're all beautifully painted up with murals and stuff, but they're still giant metal boxes right out the front of my windows.'

'Oh, they're your windows now, are they?'

'Just double check they'll be taking them straight away afterwards, please.'

'Sure thing, will do. How's your day look?'

Kathy swept her hair behind a shoulder, sipped at the coffee, and answered, 'OK.' She shrugged. 'I mean I'm not meeting any top vegetables, but I've got some more special collection materials to review.'

Tony and Kathy had lived together for over three years, and in that time she had moved up through the Durham University Library service ranks to a top position. She had been in post for less than a month, as curator of the special collections at the university's archive library.

'What's your favourite so far?'

'Favourite? God, I don't know.' She paused and took another sip of coffee, before staring at the ceiling. 'The letter from second century Egypt is pretty impressive, but I think the one I fell in love with as soon as I saw it is the map of Nuremberg from the late fifteenth century. I mean, it's not even a map, more a sketch of all the buildings in the walled city. It's beautiful. But there's so much beautiful stuff. I can't believe my job is to look through all the most incredible books and documents the university owns, learn their history, and then decide how best to show them off to the public.'

She swapped her coffee cup with her phone from the bedside table and showed him her newly chosen wallpaper on the lock screen. It was a sketch of a bunch of small stone houses huddled together behind a wall, with a gateway entrance on the left, and a river flowing out through another arch in the wall on the right. Above the town was a flowery and olden style set of letters that spelt out *Nuremberg*.

'Aren't you supposed to look after them too?'

'Yes, of course, but that's a fairly well-worn path. I won't be inventing anything special there, maybe having to make difficult decisions with limited budget. But maybe if I can get more people through the door to look at the collections, we'll have more ticket money that I can spend on better conservation measures.'

With a smile, he said, 'I meant security, actually. But I guess that's how our different jobs give us different views on life. My head goes straight to their rarity and value, while yours goes straight to their beauty, fragility and literary importance.' Tony was at her side, and he leaned over and kissed her on the forehead.

She smiled too and grabbed his neck, holding him bent over to get a kiss on the lips before he left.

The city police station was about two kilometres walk down the long hill of Gilesgate. Tony basked in the early morning sunshine as he strolled, taking in the beauty of the city spread below him. The castle and cathedral stood out larger, at the centre of everything else, glowing almost golden in the morning light.

Looking down from his vantage point on the medieval World Heritage Site, he could see the many disparate buildings spilling on to the rocky peninsula that stuck up from within a full hairpin bend of the River Wear. The map of Nuremberg could easily have been a picture of Durham from history.

When he arrived at the office, the fans in the MCT office were already rattling away at full blast. DC Diane Meredith stood over a pair of desks that had been shoved together to form a big space to lay out the personal possessions of the two mineshaft victims. She unfolded the map stuck in one journal and slid it sideways. As Tony watched, he imagined Kathy laying out old folios, pictures and books and sliding them around to best organise the collection. He shuddered at the very thought of Meredith reminding him of Kathy.

Meredith turned at his arrival and talked him through what she had achieved in the previous hour, all of which was related to treasure hunting. She went back through the notes of phone conversations with Mrs Dooley, the wife of the man they were calling victim one.

Her husband had been prolific in his use of social media message boards, aimed at all manner of treasure hunting folk. His research of each trending treasure story was all-consuming. The woman was well versed in the specific names of these various online sites, and Meredith imagined her suffering over every meal as her obsessed partner recounted the latest rumours and mad ideas that he had read.

Regularly, Michael "Mick" Dooley would head off, across the north-east, to search some ancient woodland in Northumberland or a secluded seaside cave on the North Yorkshire coast. He had metal detectors, digging tools, all sorts of camping, lighting and climbing gear, along with a vast array of detailed maps of the area, some dating back two hundred years.

She said he had especially ranted about the Tudhoe mine, and the fact it was so close to their house and yet, of all the riches he'd chased after, this treasure was the most likely to be there.

Meredith had spent an hour, before anyone else arrived in the office, searching through some of these websites and discussion groups. The most comprehensive was a blog called "MaidMarionettes". The author, pictured on the website's header in full Sherwood Forest costume, looked like a Hollywood-style beauty. When she showed the screen to Tony, he wondered if the photo had been pinched from some Robin Hood movie website as a phoney byline image.

Meredith pointed out the menu options on MaidMarionettes. 'Look at all this: Coastal Shipwrecks, Shipwrecks in Onshore Waterways, Roman Hoards, Viking Hoards, Anglo-Saxon Hoards, Victoriana, Religious Treasures, Abandoned but Workable Mines, Abandoned Archaeological Sites, Abandoned Buildings. I mean this woman must do this full time, every one you click on has masses of information from all over the country. There's even an international section, which is huge. And

Dooley's got most of them bookmarked on his phone's browser.' She held up the device, its evidence bag empty on the desk.

Tony turned to look at Meredith rather than the screen. 'How did you get into his phone? Did his wife know the passcode?'

She smiled broadly. 'Alfie guessed it. The wife didn't know it but told me some useful dates that might help us to guess.'

'Anniversary?'

'Nope. His own birthday.'

Tony leaned down to the computer showing the MaidMarionettes website. He clicked through a few random pages and read some bits and pieces but mostly looked at pictures of trowels digging in soil and ghostly mine workings with narrow rail tracks leading into darkness beyond the flash's illumination. 'People never cease to amaze me.'

Something clicked in his brain, and he looked back up to Meredith, who was watching him. 'When was CSI Johnson here?'

'No, no, he had dinner at my place last night.' She squeezed her shoulders inward and gave a faux giggle. 'And would you believe it, he stayed the night.'

'That was quick. He only joined the team a week ago.'

She smiled broadly. 'You know me.' There was an awkward pause, and she looked him straight in the eye. 'I mean you know exactly, don't you, Tony. You stayed in my bed the night of our first date.'

He took a step sideways, away from her, but she edged forward towards him. The hairs on the back of his neck tingled and he struggled to outstare her.

'Morning!' DC Madeline Aria breezed into the room and turned for the fridge in the corner to deposit her lunchbox. She filled an ivy green business suit in a well-tailored but voluminous way. Her auburn ponytail took its cue from her movements seemingly unable to quite keep up. It gave the impression of always being half a second behind as it swung left and right.

27

Tony edged several more steps away, but he never took his eyes from Meredith. Her chestnut bob seemed much more on point than Aria's hair – perhaps even swinging the tiniest fraction in advance of any head movement.

'It really is lovely out there, isn't it?' Aria bustled over to the desks covered in evidence bags. She pulled out a chair and the vinyl seat pad huffed as she deposited her large bulk down onto it. Aria then added two evidence bags to the collection and continued being bright and lively. 'I've just been to meet with the family of victim two.' She leaned back and turned a rosy cheek towards one of the silver grille fans on the adjacent desk, half facing it and half facing Tony. He rotated, and Madeline looked up to him, beaming.

'How do you know who they are? We haven't ID'ed him yet. Have we?'

'Not a hundred per cent, and I was clear on that with them, but Gerard's made a strong suggestion. They've scanned the body, well, the pile of bones, and the dental records match with an army record for a man from Tudhoe.'

'What dental records?'

'Well, this is why it's not a hundred per cent: the army file has a written description of his teeth when he joined up for his national service. No dental X-rays back then, but Gerard reckons the description is detailed enough to make some cross-referencing possible. Anyway, when they found that this soldier lived in Tudhoe, Gerard reckoned to go with investigating it as an ident. Could be a wild goose chase, but it's the best we've got so far.'

Meredith laughed out loud and quite pointedly at her colleague. Tony held up his hand to silence her and asked, 'And was it?'

'Was it what?'

'A wild goose chase?'

Aria looked at him, then to Meredith, and back to him. 'Ah. Don't think so, but it's still not a certain identification. I met with a lovely woman in one of the houses on the front street there in the village, and their family legend tells of how the great-grandfather, Richard Harbottle – Dickie they called him in the army apparently – disappeared off to seek his fortune in America and was never heard from again. The family story has that happening in early 1958, just before the last entry in this notebook from victim two.' She picked up and waved an evidence bag with the older notebook in it.

Tony pointed out that the name and a Tudhoe address was in the front of the book.

Aria nodded wildly, with a big smile. 'Yes! The family reckon they've always lived in Tudhoe, for generations, but they don't have any address details from so long ago.'

Meredith pointed out that the census records should show the address.

'I think we're good as confirmed anyway. The name here' – Aria wiggled the plastic bag again – 'is just written as Dickie H. Got to be Dickie Harbottle. Richard Harbottle. Matching teeth, from the same village, disappears in 1958. Surely must be him.'

Tony nodded. 'I agree. Good work, Madeline. How did the family take it?'

She had only spoken to one member of the Harbottle clan, Richard's great-granddaughter, and the woman had never known him, so the possibility of his skeletal remains being found nearby was more of a curiosity to her than a heartache. However, this apparently reminded Aria of one thing she had not mentioned to her colleagues yet.

'When I spoke to Gerard, though, he confirmed murder for both victims one and two.'

Tony looked at his watch. Despite it being a smartwatch connected to his phone, he rarely used it for anything other than telling the time. 'It's barely 8 a.m. When has he done all that work?'

The DC shrugged. 'I spoke to him bang on seven, when his email said to call.'

Meredith leapt in. 'Oh yeah, I tried at seven, but his line was engaged. I bet he was talking to you then.'

Aria continued with her one-upmanship. 'The other thing I found out was that the cathedral don't have any information about a specific St Cuthbert's Treasure. I went over there yesterday and spoke to a chap whose title is Constable of the Cathedral, and he laughed at the idea. Said it was nonsense and the only such treasures are on display in their visitor galleries – the extra museum thingy out in the cloisters, that you have to pay to get into. He was adamant it's a conspiracy theory of cranks.'

Tony stared back and forth between the two women, eyes wide. 'Well. Um, keep up the good work, both of you. I've got to go see a man about a brass band parade. While I'm out, can you get us two of the big wheelie noticeboards and set up one for each of the victims please. Print out whatever Gerard can send us through and stick it up on them.'

FIVE

Briefly blinded by the sun on the curving drive, Tony pulled up in the grounds of Redhills, home of Durham Miners' Association. The tarmac swept past four light grey statues of the DMA's founding delegates.

The Edwardian baroque building was more than a hundred years old, and very recently refurbished through Lottery funding. Built from union dues and red brick, in the height of the Durham coalfields' most productive years, it looked more like the country estate of a coal mine owner than a centre of trade unionism.

Tony was made to sit in a wood-panelled waiting area for more than fifteen minutes before being called in. The office of the Top Marra was vast, bigger by some margin than the chief constable's. The glory days of Durham coal must have brought in more money than he would have ever imagined.

Up until about two hundred years ago, Durham Cathedral had been the centre of political power – and wealth – in the north of England. Then, from the beginning of the twentieth century, coal had been the black gold in the area, and this had fed huge local steel-making activities too.

The boom years had seen everyone connected to coal mining build small fortunes. The legacies of those good times were still evident all across the county in funds and trusts to support miners' families, land reclamation and historic mining-related organisations. The ultimate embodiment of all these legacies was the magnificent Durham Miners Hall, affectionately known as Redhills.

Barry Black's open-necked, pale blue shirt strained at his belly, and Tony reckoned there was little chance the corpulent man's suit jacket could be buttoned at the front. Black's red face further suggested a life spent supping beer. He guessed his age at fifty years old, but the man did not look like he had ever struggled with a shovel down the pit. *Black in name only*, he thought.

The walls of the office were covered in paintings. One side of the room showed scenes of pithead wheels in rolling green fields, groups of men clad in dark trousers and flat caps, small trucks containing black rocks being dragged along narrow trackways, and ponies either grazing near a pithead or doing the dragging of the coal trucks. Two other walls held a gallery of historic figures from the glorious past: union chapter leaders, marras from days gone by, and strike leaders from nearly one hundred and fifty years of industrial action.

The wall behind "Top Marra" Black's vast desk held two giant sash windows, immense feats of engineering in their own right. Both were closed, and Tony wondered whether they could ever be opened. His mind took one of the pithead wheels from a painting near the door and pictured it near the ceiling to haul up the monster wood and glass bottom halves of the windows.

As he walked across a large Persian rug, bigger than his entire lounge carpet at home, he looked at the man standing behind his oversized desk. Barry Black had a neat bowl haircut, and stared at Tony through large, round glasses.

'Mr Black, I'm Detective Sarg—' Tony interrupted himself. 'Detective Inspector Tony Milburn. I'm taking over from DI Barnes as your liaison for the Big Meeting next week.' He used the common nickname for Durham Miners' Gala in the hope of starting things off well. Having never previously had anything to do with the managers of this prestigious event, Tony wasn't too sure of who or what he might be dealing with.

As the question of what Barry might be like to work with floated through his head, he realised that this whole meeting actually held very high stakes. He would look back through Godolphin's notes and paperwork later. The lanky DI was a difficult man, but his paperwork was meticulous; perhaps the two went hand in hand. Tony hoped that Barnes had not gone demob happy at the prospect of three weeks' holiday in Australia, ignored his bureaucratic obligations, and left the pieces to be picked up by somebody else.

With about two hundred thousand attendees in recent years, the Miners' Gala was the largest event in Durham Constabulary's calendar. Tony's mind fizzed through comparative large events. He didn't know the number of spectators at the Great North Run, but it only had sixty thousand runners. Indeed, the capacity at St James' Park in Newcastle was little over fifty thousand, and that was bigger than Sunderland's Stadium of Light. Durham City's biennial Lumiere festival attracted about quarter of a million visitors, but they were spread over several days.

'Mr Milburn?' Barry had come around his desk to shake his police visitor's hand. 'Are you alright?'

Tony realised he was gripping his own hands together and staring at a piece of wall without a painting on it. 'Sorry. Sorry, just taking it all in.' He separated his hands and gave a broad, non-committal sweep with the right one. He took Black's extended hand and, when they shook, discovered painful pins and needles in his fingers.

'What exactly is it you want?' Black's tone was sharper than Tony had anticipated for the start of this first meeting. He didn't let Tony respond. 'I'm surprised you managed to get past the door – it may have been more than forty years outside these walls, but in here, the atrocities of 1984 are remembered every day. Police are always unwelcome.' This reference to the miner's strike did not surprise Tony exactly, but he realised he had not prepared adequately to navigate the immediately hostile atmosphere.

He paused in the hope of being able to redirect matters, having let the man land his first salvo.

'Rest assured Mr Black, I have real empathy for all the struggles of your colleagues, throughout history. I was a toddler

33

in the Thatcher years, and I'm here to support your event next Saturday. I want to make sure we create a safe environment for everyone, while ensuring it is a great success.'

'"Event"?' The man's tone sounded apoplectic, but his manner was more dismissive than angry. Black turned his back and returned around his giant desk to stand opposite across a gulf of dark oak.

He continued, 'The Big Meeting is called that because it is the biggest celebration of working-class culture anywhere in the world.'

Tony seized on this. 'Oh yes, absolutely. I phased out there a moment ago, as I was trying to think of bigger local events and their policing needs, so I could get my head around what will need to be in place. I couldn't think of anything in the north-east that would rival it.' His own obsequiousness surprised him, but the enormity of this challenge was hitting home, and he needed Black to be onside. 'How does the Great North Run compare?'

'You're thinking too small. No one-day event matches us. Glastonbury, Ascot, Notting Hill Carnival, maybe the Grand Prix, but they're all multi-day events – we pack it all into a single Saturday in July. And we've been doing so for a hundred and fifty years. And the biggest difference, Mr Milburn?' The Top Marra's pitch raised to indicate a question. Tony bit his tongue to avoid the conflict of asking Black to call him DI rather than Mr.

As expected, the question was rhetorical. 'It's all free. There are no tickets needed by our visitors.' He clasped his hands in front of his spherical belly. 'Most folk have been coming every year since they were bairns. We all know each other, and the different pit communities all respect each other. We have no need of any police spoiling the atmosphere.'

Tony knew that there were always arrests at the Gala, but he had to concede that these were generally few and mostly related to drunkenness one way or another. The day was always high-spirited, but friendly – in good spirits.

He replied with a level of doublespeak of which Orwell himself would have been proud. 'I'm fully aware of the high quality of this huge tradition – I grew up not even ten miles from here.' He could see Mr Black nodding with approval. 'But I'm sure you will agree that massive gatherings hold a public safety risk, and we need to be ready to respond if a big issue arises. I could imagine any number of natural disasters that would need sound first-response by trained professionals to see everyone helped to safety.'

The Gala's chief organiser pushed his big glasses back up his nose and leaned forward, his hands on the desk. 'Look, we put up with your lot because of that sort of risk, but let's be clear: nobody wants you there. It's a shame Godolphin's holiday came up right now – he's the only policeman that I've ever come across with any sympathy for the labour movement.'

Tony was blindsided by this view of DI Barnes. He almost laughed out loud at the thought of Penfold saying, probably just as haughtily as Barry Black, 'Sympathetic Godolphin – that's an oxymoron, isn't it?'

Black explained, 'He and I had a plan in place.'

A chink of light – an escape route maybe – had appeared in this gloomy meeting. 'Brilliant! I had assumed that would be the case, and apologies that I haven't yet had time to go over the files he will have left us on this, but I've only just been assigned to liaise with you. Can you give me a sense of the overall plan? I'll check on the details DI Barnes wrote out later, but I wanted to see you in person to make direct contact and get an overview of what was already in place. Any last-minute changes?' He spoke quickly, keen to get it all over with.

The union man stood silent for several seconds looking directly at Tony. His eyes appeared oversized through the saucer lenses of his black-framed glasses. 'The only trouble we ever get is from the gyppos that run the carnival. They're a bunch of thieves, and they're the ones you lot should be watching. Keep your uniforms down by the Racecourse – that's where you'll get any trouble that's going to happen. And that's also the most dangerous spot, down by the river. The odd fella may have had a few during the day, and if they fall in the river, they will need that public safety policing you make such grand claims about.'

Wincing at the offensive term, Tony maintained his own silence for a few seconds, mulling over these suggestions. While the day would start with a brass band parade right through the city, it was true that tens of thousands ended up all over the university sports fields known as the Racecourse. The main cricket and football pitches sided along the banks of the river, and if the hot weather continued, he could definitely imagine a multitude of shirtless drunks going for a swim.

It was also the case that part of the entertainment included a funfair at the eastern end of the Racecourse, but he couldn't remember hearing of many cases of issues with the funfair operators. They were tough carnival folk, that was for sure, but he assumed they made enough money on the day of Durham's Big Meeting to last the entire year and would be foolish to slay that golden goose by being sacked from the event through thieving or any other sort of aggravation.

On balance, though, the idea outlined was a reasonable plan. He wouldn't commit to anything specific so that he could assign some officers all around the parade route too, but by the time of the speeches just after lunch, the vast majority would be on the Racecourse and policing that would be the priority. This wasn't nearly enough detail for a citywide plan, but Tony could bear it in mind when reviewing Barnes' grand plan.

As they took their leave at the wide door of Black's office, Tony's host pointedly stood with his arms behind his back clearly making no offer of a handshake.

'Keep your eyes on those pikeys, Mr Milburn, mark my words.'

Tony winced again. 'It's Detective Inspector Milburn.'

He turned and headed across the waiting area to the main corridor. Tony had done the liaison part of the job, however lacking in actual liaison it had been. *H will be happy that I've pressed the appropriate flesh*, he thought as he emerged into the glorious sunlit grounds.

His heart then sank when he remembered Kathy's request to find out about the shipping containers on Palace Green. He couldn't go back in again now. He'd have to call Top Marra Barry later.

SIX

'Nine-nine-nine, which service do you need?'

'Your Apple Watch has detected a fall at 7.53 a.m. and called the emergency services. Location is 54 degrees 53 minutes 21.0 seconds north by 1 degree 59 minutes 49.5 seconds west.'

The operator muttered, 'Oh, bloody hell,' before bellowing across the call centre floor, 'Boss, we've got another Apple Watch call.' A skinny woman in her fifties raced across the room from her centrally positioned desk and leant in to look over her colleague's shoulder at his reporting screen.

After a few seconds' pause, the initially very loud, automated message repeated more quietly.

The operator asked, 'Hello, caller, can you hear me?'

The emergency services operator and his line manager heard an occasional, quiet moaning or mumbling. All the while, the automated message continued on repeat every few seconds, maintaining a low volume but enough to be heard. The AI transcription software very accurately recorded the message from the watch every time it played, but no characters were displayed on screen to try and represent the moaning and mumbling. Although it was faint, the person sounded as if they must be in significant pain.

Two hours later, on a small grassy hill called Hairy Side, just north of Derwent Reservoir in western County Durham, the responding paramedics handed over the scene to two local coppers from Consett nick. The ambulance had come all the way from Durham City, and they had found the fall victim several metres down an old coal shaft, exactly at the co-ordinates given by his smartwatch.

As DC Diane Meredith drove Tony out to the site, he avoided having to talk to her by texting Penfold. He also called the uniformed police officers who now had control of the scene, once the victim had been confirmed dead.

Almost certainly just to annoy Tony, Meredith called CSI Alfie Johnson on the handsfree in the Golf. They reviewed their date night first, with Meredith pointedly staring forward at the road. Only after complimenting Johnson on his muscular thighs, did she inform the forensic investigator that he was on speaker and this was a business call.

Tony continued to text Penfold, who was driving back down from Thurso. For surf trips, Penfold drove a lime green 1977 VW campervan. His sister, whom Tony knew only as Trident, and who was a computer whizz of the highest order, had installed a voice-to-text device in the van, so Penfold was able to respond to his messages without danger or law-breaking.

Tony took the chance to vent silently, but in the choicest of language, about all the work hassles of the moment, saving particular ire for Meredith. He even impugned her driving. Despite the fact that the paramedics had declared the victim dead, she insisted on racing through the country lanes as if there was an active incident ongoing. She didn't bother with using the blue lights and sirens either, just drove like they were in a rally race.

Penfold replied:

Succubus suffers fools gladly; reaps rewards.

He didn't have time to struggle through Penfold's cryptic six-word stories – he ignored this message and continued text-ranting. In particular, he complained that they were heading miles out to an old mine site – actually just a sheep field with a hole in it – on the grounds that it was the third mineshaft victim in three days. The fact that the first had been there for seventy years did not appear to matter, they had a pile up of bodies and Hardwick had told them to follow it up.

Tony looked at the passing scenery. Ancient trees dangled over lichen-covered stone walls, glaring white in the sunshine. Would this be another treasure hunter who'd lost their footing? Surely it couldn't be another murder. *Is there really a treasure out there that would get metal detector nerds killing each other?*

He pictured the computer screen on his office desk, and the eighteen new folder icons he had copied there moments before getting the order to drive into the verdant countryside. These folders formed Barnes' holiday legacy: plans, risk assessments, staffing deployments, emergency services contacts, highways information, portable toilet location maps, council licence copies, insurance certificates, and on and on and on with all the paperwork needed to plan an event as big as Durham Miners' Gala. Tony had had enough time to read three and a half pages.

MaidMarionettes mentions Hairy Side mine.

Tony didn't have the energy to point out to Penfold that this might just about be six words, but it didn't really constitute a story. Given that Penfold's texts weren't universally written in one of the unusual formats, it wasn't worth trying a bit of one-upmanship on that particular point.

On arriving at the Hairy Side location, Tony was struck by the similarities to the Tudhoe mineshaft crime scene. The phone number that made the emergency call was listed to a Billy Muckle, and a silver Honda Civic parked next to the gate into the field was also registered to William Muckle. A blue and yellow panda car was parked next to the vehicle, so that the police car was actually in the road.

Meredith drove further along to the entrance of a farm and pulled in tight to the hedge at the gate. To get out, Tony had to squash the passenger door into the hedge and suffered a lot of branch scratching as he emerged along the rear wing. The farm's long drive gave a great view downhill towards the huge lake of

Derwent Reservoir. It glinted beautifully in the bright sunshine, almost too bright to look at even through their sunglasses.

Little rain in the whole of the previous month meant that the ground was hard and dry, and Tony immediately stopped worrying about what Kathy would say about mud on his new black leather shoes.

Striding towards the point where the Consett-based officers had cordoned off a ten-metre square with blue and white tape reminded Tony what else he was missing in life. The sheep-trimmed grass was like a lawn, and he pictured himself striding out to bat. This could be an away cricket match between Belmont CC and some local village team like Riding Mill Cricket Club. He imagined passing the club's top batsman on his way back from the crease having been dismissed too easily.

Although football was Tony's favourite sport, both as a player and as a spectator, he also had a great love of cricket. He was eternally grateful to his good friends at Belmont for supporting his occasional and random appearances as a player. Many times, he'd had to leave the field mid-game when his phone had gone off, and he had been called out to a crime scene. More though, he was grateful to the other members of his club for accepting his uncultured, untrained and usually rusty skills with the leather and willow.

When he reached the imagined cricket square at Hairy Side, he could see the gaping hole in the ground, and another of the hinged metal grates that should have covered the hole, just like the one at Tudhoe. He shook his head to dissipate the image of his captain bemoaning the state of the wicket.

The local coppers pointed at the body that was just visible on a ledge a few metres down. The paramedics had been down with climbing ropes but had taken all that gear away with them when they left the police to deal with the scene. This mineshaft had a steel hook embedded in the rock at the surface to act as a permanent piton. However, neither Consett's panda cars nor

Durham's unmarked detective vehicle came equipped with climbing gear.

They could see a man in his thirties, probably, on his side, as if asleep. The bright sunlight reached down to that depth in the hole, but it wasn't nearly as blinding, or even bright, as at the surface. Both Tony and Meredith experimented with taking their sunglasses off and then on again to look in. Neither scenario was perfect.

Meredith shouted down, but there was no movement. They knew the paramedics had already confirmed death and left, but at a distance, it just seemed natural to try and rouse the man.

Tony tried phoning the number that had called the emergency services, and they could see a phone light up in the man's pocket. They could hear it vibrating too, and a tinny tune echoed up the shaft.

'Is that …?' Tony faltered.

The older and taller of the two local policemen nodded. '*Raiders of the Lost Ark*. Getting sick of it now – emergency control have been trying to call him repeatedly.' Tony stopped the call.

The victim was clad in khaki cargo shorts, a dark T-shirt and a fishing jacket with no sleeves but numerous buttoned-down pockets. Most of the pockets bulged suggesting he was carrying all manner of kit. From their vantage point, the body had no visible injuries.

The two detectives had taken up positions on either side of the square opening and Meredith stood with hands on her hips staring down at the likely treasure hunter. The same tune rang out again, but this time somebody was whistling the notes. Their heads all turned towards the sound to see CSI Hunk strolling up the grassy slope with the big toolbox at his side and a beaming grin across his face.

Meredith and Tony exchanged eye contact, and her face creased up into a smirk to reflect Alfie's. He stepped over the tape cordon, dumped his box on the ground and took a gander into the opening. He had brought his own ropes and harnesses, and after their last escapade down a mineshaft, Tony wasn't in the least bit surprised when Meredith suggested she and CSI Johnson gear up and clamber down.

He chuckled inwardly as he thought, *Sure, you two go ahead and get jiggy with it.* It was a pun worthy of Penfold, and he congratulated himself with a second one: *Ha ha, I wonder when the jig will be up for Meredith.*

As Johnson pulled the coiled ropes from over his shoulder, Tony spotted a green campervan puttering slowly along the road and listened carefully to hear its engine shut off just as it rolled out of sight behind a taller section of hedgerow.

'I'm going to check out the car. Send me the photos as you take them, Constable.' Tony lingered on the word *Constable*.

She scowled at him and proceeded to assist Johnson with buckling his climbing harness at the waist.

SEVEN

'Hi there, Scotland no good?'

'Absolutely it was. And the sun never set on the waves. It was brilliant.'

'So, there were waves then? I thought the summertime was never any good for surf?'

'That's why I have to head to pastures new, following any storms over the Atlantic. Thurso has such a good slate reef.'

Tony nodded, his surfing knowledge exhausted. He was grateful to be standing in the shade as the morning temperature topped twenty-five degrees and he still wore a dark suit jacket. The seasoned traveller had pulled up in the shadow cast by an ageing sycamore at the edge of the field. It stood large, heavy with a thick summer coat of green leaves.

The shade also enabled Tony to actually see his phone screen. Photos pinged up one after the other as Meredith hung close to the narrow ledge and Billy Muckle's body. There were numerous extra shots of Johnson's smiling face and blond good looks. She also threw in a couple of her own face and body, casual mistake shots where the shutter kept on clicking as she struggled to maintain stability while suspended on a rope down a vertical tunnel.

Penfold leaned in close, looking down over Tony's shoulder to watch as the images slid on and off screen. Finally, he asked, 'How does this look, compared to the Tudhoe scene?'

Tony stared at the asphalt below the campervan's rear engine compartment, his eyes unfocussed. 'Very similar. I mean the main difference is we've only got one body. And it's on a ledge rather than at the bottom of the shaft. But Billy here looks like he's out on a treasure hunt, same as the other two. And the set-up of that mineshaft, with the metal grille cover, is identical. I can't believe they don't have to seal these up.'

'Can you go back to the first couple of photos.'

He swiped the screen a few times to open up the first image from Meredith and then moved each on slowly, until the surfer stopped him again. Penfold took the phone, gently, but without asking. He squinted closely and then used his fingers to zoom the picture as much as it would go.

'Do you have any images from the Tudhoe site, similar to this?'

He turned the phone back towards Tony, who looked at it for a couple of seconds.

'The CSI took them all, and he did most as video. But I think I've got him going into it from ground level if you want to see that?'

Penfold nodded, and Tony searched his phone's gallery for the relevant video. After a moment or two jumping back and forth between the still picture from Hairy Side and Johnson's video from Tudhoe, Penfold demanded, 'I need to see the Tudhoe site in person.' He paused for a moment and waved over the hedge past the big sycamore. 'I assume you can't let me on to this crime scene?'

'No, of course I can't.' Tony spent a few seconds reconsidering their dialogue. 'Now, you know what? Actually, I can. H promoted me to inspector – acting inspector at any rate – and made me SIO on the Tudhoe murder, which means I can engage consultants of my own choosing, up to a certain budget. I assume you're happy to consult for free?'

Without waiting for the taller man to answer, he continued, 'We'll need to be forensically careful, especially given the pathologist hasn't even arrived yet.'

'I don't want to go into the pit, just have a look from up top.'

They set off to walk back up through the gate by Muckle's parked Honda.

As usual, Penfold wouldn't be drawn on what he was looking for, or what in the photos had piqued his interest. So, *as usual*, Tony tried to observe what the New Zealander looked at and followed his movements wherever possible. And, *as usual*, he spotted nothing, until Penfold had them both kneeling dangerously close to the edge of the hole.

They could hear bright conversation from below, although the detail of the words were lost in the reflecting of the sound waves up to the surface. The tops of Johnson's and Meredith's heads were visible as they swung slightly on the thick nylon ropes. Both wore an orange helmet, and Tony mused on Johnson's thought processes that led to him choosing to bring up a second helmet from the back of the kitted out pick-up truck.

Without words, Penfold indicated that they should lie on their bellies, heads over the precipice. Once again, Tony thanked the universe for climate change and the recent dry weather. He could easily imagine Kathy's sarcastic commentary if he came home with a muddy suit jacket.

'Here, look.' Penfold extended a long arm down the hole to point. The rectangular shaft was stone built all around, like a manhole entry down into a sewer, made not with uniform bricks but rough stones one might dig up in the field around them. Penfold waved his finger around several times, and Tony spotted the rock sticking out of the wall, and then another, and the next. A stairway.

It was uneven and the steps were just a hands-breadth of extended rock at twenty-centimetre intervals. The stairs were identical in colour to the rest of the wall, but once you saw it, the deliberate positioning of the zigzag of unnecessary extra rocks was utterly clear. The original miners had built themselves a way to get in and out without the need for ropes. Tony pictured one of the Victorians in dark trousers and flat cap from Barry Black's office paintings skipping skilfully down the haphazard staircase.

'Wow.' His amazement escaped unbidden.

'Now, check this.' Penfold moved his hand to the first of the stairs and grabbed on to the rock. Tony could see his strong body tense up, pulling hard on the stone. Nothing happened. His friend used his grip on this one support to allow him to lean further in – dangerously far.

His other hand reached the second rock step and pulled on it. This one wobbled and almost came out in his hand. Tony grabbed Penfold's belt. He wore cargo shorts very much like those of Billy Muckle five metres below.

Penfold shouted, 'Below!' and they saw both climbers cower as best they could, hands raised instinctively to protect their helmets.

With Tony supporting Penfold, he managed not to drop the rock and lifted it up for them to examine. A large and obviously recent chip could be seen on the stone, as if it had been hit with a chisel.

'Well, as your unpaid consultant, I would posit that this is murder.'

'How does a chipped stone lead you to murder?'

'You saw how easily it came out in my hand. I'd say we're lucky it was still in place at all. This has been booby-trapped.'

Tony ran a hand across his greying temple, with an uneasy queasiness moving into his stomach. He closed his eyes for fully five seconds and with them still closed asked, 'One question. Why?'

'Maybe there's a treasure down there being protected by the booby trap.'

Tony stood up and his shadow cast across Penfold's face as he knelt with the brick-sized rock in his palm. 'Has everyone gone Indiana Jones mad today? This is an old coal mine with rickety, rusty bars covering it, and a dodgy, very old stone wall holding it up. This is not the palace of some ancient civilisation that made everything out of gold.'

The shadow enabled the New Zealander to look up into Tony's face. He pointed to the fresh chip in the stone. 'I'm sorry, Milburn, but the evidence says the staircase was tampered with. See here.' He pointed to the mudline where the rock had been implanted in the wall. 'This was so close to the wall that it did not happen when your victim fell down and is exactly where I'd hit it if I wanted to loosen it up enough to act as a trap.'

Tony shook his head in exasperation but took a piece of pragmatic guidance from Penfold's hypothesis. He leant over to call down to DC Meredith and CSI Hunk. 'Can you make sure you go right to the bottom of the shaft and search for any evidence that may have fallen down there. Do quite a wide search at the bottom, maybe even along the tunnels a little way.'

'On it, guv.' Meredith's cheeky voice was light and bright. He couldn't see either of their orange helmets, so they must have already descended much further down.

Tony handed the car keys to one of the local policemen and headed down towards the campervan to ride back with Penfold. He wasn't sure about the van as a cop car, but he was settling in to the idea of having Penfold as a colleague rather than some dirty little secret he had to keep from others at the police station.

In numerous past cases, they'd had to liaise in an annoyingly clandestine manner, partly to avoid DCI Hardwick's all-seeing eye, but mostly so that potential prosecutions were never derailed through doubt being cast on the evidence because an unofficial 'consultant' had been involved in handling or even just looking at it.

Tony smiled to himself as he wondered what else he might put on expenses now he had the authority to appoint extra things to the investigation. His smile dropped when he considered the convolutions of this case, which he now imagined might be three murders, including one from seventy years ago. He prayed to the police gods that the cases weren't connected, but feared this prayer was likely to go unanswered.

They had agreed to head to Penfold's house so Trident could be invoked via his private internet connection. She could then let her AI research machines loose to discover why these victims might have been attracted to these mineshafts. Penfold called her en route to set the bots in motion.

Tony attached such a mythology to Penfold's hacker sister that he imagined her in an underground data bunker, surrounded by literal robots typing at keyboards. Not because he believed this was the actual situation, but because she was so good at hiding her identity that he barely knew anything about her. He had only seen her once, driving past in the front of Penfold's other car, the tangerine VW Beetle. Also, the robot vision amused him.

They were headed across country, aiming towards Hartlepool and the surfer's seaside home, when Penfold pulled into a parking area. Michael Dooley's grey Astra had been removed to the forensic warehouse for processing, but the square of blue and white tape up across the field swung gently in the light breeze. It caught the sunlight brightly at times.

'Why have you stopped here? And actually, how did you know to come here – I never told you the exact location of this mine site.'

Penfold turned the ignition off and opened the driver's door. He pointed towards a collection of swings, slides and a roundabout. 'You showed me the scene photos, and I recognised this play area.' His finger swung round to point up the slope towards where the first two victims had been found. 'And now you've put that blue and white beacon up there, everyone knows where it is. I'm thinking we could see if there's any obvious booby trap here.'

They spent half an hour looking around the area inside the tape. A wooden cover had been placed over the opening to avoid any further accidents, and once they hauled it back, they could see the metal grille had also been returned, flipped back over to cover the hole. It remained without a padlock but was so heavy that it would have been a real job for the victim to lift it alone. Even Penfold's surfer's physique made heavy weather of the task of flipping it over on to the grass.

The stone stairway jumped into Tony's vision. It was so obvious when you knew to look for it. The fact that the stones forming the steps were jagged and natural was what had previously stopped him imagining them as an organised part of the wall design.

However, they couldn't find anything to totally confirm foul play. Penfold even clambered a few steps down, with Tony gripping tightly to the collar of his white T-shirt. It had a blue wave across the back which rippled as Penfold clambered and his shoulders tensed. If he fell neither man expected the T-shirt grip would save him, but it did help with balance and stability as he felt for each next step. Two stones were dislodged and slightly wobbly, but not definitely tampered with.

EIGHT

The narrow road that formed a square outside Penfold's old stone home was across the beach road from Seaton Carew's wide seafront path. Promenade Square was full of parked cars – the beach road had been rammed as well – so he pulled the campervan up onto the grass square itself and waved at a woman walking a small dog. She turned her back on the vehicle, and he smirked.

The sandy beach was just about visible beyond the wide esplanade and classic aquamarine railings. After that, the steel blue and occasional cotton wool of surface froth of Penfold's first love could be seen. On such a bright, sunlit day, the sea colours matched his T-shirt.

Penfold put his red-lens Oakleys into a small box mounted above his head and pulled out traditional black ones instead.

As Tony wandered around the flat front end of the van, he watched his friend stretch out of the vehicle and reach both hands up to the sky. There followed a brief collection of tai chi style movements, after which the big, blond man waved a cursory hand towards the beach and said, 'That's why I went to Scotland.'

The sun blazed hot off the sandy lawn, and was intensified in the reflection from the windscreen. Tony moved around to the shady side as Penfold slid open the side door and pulled out a large and clearly heavy waterproof holdall.

Twenty steps later they walked in through the wooden door of the Victorian house. The interior was chilly all year round and Tony felt the sweat on his body immediately turn clammy and cold. Penfold dumped the bag in the hallway, so Tony had to step right over it to follow him to the kitchen.

The coffee machine had already been run – the jug underneath it was full of dark black liquid – and Tony scanned around for signs of the mysterious Mantoro. He spotted a tell-tale saucer of cashew nuts on the counter, but there was no sound from the rest of the house. He wondered how the squat Mexican guy had known when to put the coffee on – Tony hadn't seen Penfold use his phone at all since the call with Trident. *I wonder if he's actually* South *American, not Mexican. The coffee's never anything special though.*

The fridge offered no milk, so Tony made do with the standard mug of black tar that he always had to endure at Penfold's. They both grabbed a few cashews, and he followed his host down the back staircase into the basement lab.

Very white and modern, the large underground space had various workstations around the sides for biological and chemical testing, along with two computers set on large counters. The centre was dominated by a huge worktable, also with a white laminate surface. The wall underneath the wooden staircase down into this scientific lair held a number of tools for all manner of tasks. For many of these, Tony could only guess at their purpose.

The video call with Trident was as unnerving as the lab surroundings. She was represented on screen by a cartoon avatar in a manga style that moved its mouth and made facial expressions as she spoke. It managed this without delay, so the conversation occurred in real time. Tony realised that his imagined view of Trident in an underground bunker surrounded by an army of hacker robots was inspired by the room he and Penfold sat in.

The chairs were like bar stools and Tony found it very difficult to sit comfortably in his. He wondered how Mantoro managed with them. He was short and stout, while the chairs seemed perfectly designed for someone of Nordic or Dutch proportions, rather more like Penfold. Tony pictured the white and chrome chairs on display in the window of a Copenhagen department store. He was not listening to Trident.

'Sorry, could you say that again – I was distracted by nearly falling off my chair.'

Penfold stared at him and Trident chuckled on screen. Tony put his coffee down and stepped off his chair to readjust it in the vain hope that this might somehow fix his bottom to the seat.

Trident had a lot to impart, but how much actually related to the death of the mine victims was less clear. She had researched their lives and cross-referenced their interests, social media activities, purchasing histories, family and friends and a lot of other things. Tony felt it prudent not to ask for any explanations of her processes.

Richard 'Dickie' Harbottle had pretty much no digital footprint. This caused little surprise since he seemed to have disappeared in 1958. Tony expected that there were probably few paper records about the man either. A vision of Trident's robots rifling through filing cabinets made him laugh out loud, and this body movement threatened to throw him off the bar stool again.

Of the other two victims, Trident's summary showed extraordinary similarities. Mick Dooley and Billy Muckle were active treasure hunters. Both men were in their thirties, worked in warehouses, lived with a wife and had no children. Their spare time seemed wholly occupied with chasing lost treasure, whether this be researching the stories of its whereabouts, or actually out on the hunt to find it. This had been a long-term passion for both, with records of their investigations and expeditions – mostly just around the north-east but sometimes further afield – going back years.

At Trident's first pause for breath, Penfold asked if the men had known each other or worked together on any treasure hunts. Despite living less than twenty kilometres apart, and both having a long history of treasure hunting, Trident could find no evidence of them ever meeting. Their past discussions, blogs, social media posts and research generally had them chasing different things at any given time. It seemed that the hunt for St Cuthbert's Treasure was the first time they'd been after the same thing at the same time. It went unsaid that neither man had ever found anything valuable.

Both used several of the same discussion forums and websites for research, but they employed pseudonyms so they wouldn't recognise each other even if they had met. Penfold asked after the pseudonyms they used.

Tony jumped in. 'Don't tell me. Indiana Jones?'

'Well, "Indy", but yes,' the cartoon manga girl replied. 'How did you know?'

'Don't ask. What about Dooley?'

This time Penfold stepped in before Trident could respond. 'Roy Chapman Andrews?'

'Yes! Just "RCA", but yes.'

Tony raised an eyebrow at his friend and Penfold said, with a chuckle, 'Again, don't ask!'

Trident concluded with the best connection she had been able to find. 'Over the last month, they've both used the website MaidMarionettes for a lot of research and had a lot of interaction with its discussion forum about St Cuthbert's Treasure. The blogger that runs the site is very active in its forums and they've all discussed the mine sites where they were found, along with getting on for sixty other similar mines in the area.

'I don't know if you know the story, Tony, but St Cuthbert is supposed to have an incorruptible corpse – it doesn't ever decay. He had a cult-like following in the sort of seventh to twelfth centuries. And they created amazingly beautiful – and valuable – jewellery. His lot were responsible for producing the Lindisfarne Gospels.'

'I did know that – the Gospels are being exhibited in the cathedral this summer. Getting the British Library to lend them out was a bit of a coup, according to my girlfriend, Kathy. They only go on display about once a decade. She specialises in that kind of thing.'

Trident expanded, 'For sure. I mean they're absolutely priceless, along with many things associated with Cuthbert. It was custom for wealthy visitors to the cathedral to bring valuable gifts, and the shrine grew into an absolute treasure trove. There were all manner of silks, jewels, golden boxes and incredible paintings. Somebody even gave narwhal tusks as an offering.

'The treasure hunter world is full of stories and rumours of other treasures from the followers of Saint Cuthbert that have been hidden and lost over the centuries. His tomb has hardly ever been opened. Only half a dozen times in a thousand years. There's stories of all sorts of funerary riches buried with him.'

Tony furrowed his brow. 'So why were these guys looking down mineshafts.'

'Ah well.' Trident's avatar moved its elbows back in an action that looked like a shoulder blades stretch to prepare for telling a great story. 'One well-documented story is of the visit of Henry VIII's commissioners to Durham Cathedral in the sixteenth century, looking essentially to steal church treasures. At the opening of the coffin that time, the commissioners were aghast and scared by the *un*-decayed body of the saint, including his full beard.

'In the mass confusion that followed, the Constable of the Cathedral, who had been forced to open the coffin, is said to have removed a number of valuable items from around the body and hidden them in his own clothing. Two items, which were only ever recorded at that time and have not been seen since, are noted as being "one jewel with value sufficient to redeem a prince" and a "metwande of gold".'

'A what now?' Tony could tell this release of information was something of a game, and he played his part flawlessly.

Penfold answered, 'It's a standardised measuring stick. The "benchmark yard" if you like. So that all measurements in an organisation match up. You couldn't just buy a tape measure back then. This suggests that he had a yardstick – I'm guessing it'd be a yard – made of gold.'

He held out a finger and thumb looped to form a circle, estimating the thickness of a yardstick. Focussed on this hand, his mouth moved quietly muttering elements of a calculation he was doing in his head. 'Say one centimetre. Pi r-squared, yard is about one ninety. Six times ten to the minus six.' He interrupted himself to ask Trident to look up the current price of gold per gram and then continued with the calculation. 'Density is nineteen thousand kilos per cubic metre, so … off the cuff, I reckon that would be just over a kilo of gold.'

Trident pitched in from the computer speakers. 'With the craziness in the US at the moment, it's about eighty pounds a gram, so that wand would be worth over eighty grand.' She added a dig at her brother. 'I haven't checked your calculations, obviously, and we're assuming pure twenty-four carat gold.'

Penfold's head bobbed up and down in jovial agreement.

Trident went back to reading them her notes. 'The familiar pectoral cross brooch or pendant that the cathedral has on display was found in the nineteenth century hidden in the folds of Cuthbert's clothing, still in the coffin. That's the famous circular St Cuthbert's Cross. Rumour has it there were three other such pectoral crosses, plus that wand and jewel, and maybe much more besides, all saved from Henry's commissioners. This treasure was kept by a long line of Constables of the Cathedral, until the Second World War. Fearing a possible Nazi invasion, it is said that the treasure was taken "out of Durham and hid down an old, disused pit".

'Now, the Constables of the Cathedral notoriously never wrote anything down. They're something of a monastic dynasty, and they often came into conflict with the church authorities who're religious about keeping written records.'

'Oh, ha, ha.' Penfold's face was straight.

Trident continued unabashed. 'These days there's a full corporate-style security team for the place, but the role of Constable has been kept on for ceremonial purposes, like looking after the bishop's vestments. More of a curator than a constable.'

Tony redirected. 'So what was the disused old pit?'

'That quote with the location fragment comes from the diary of a man who lived in Durham at the time and had no known connection to the cathedral other than being a member of the congregation.'

'What did he do?' Penfold demanded.

'For a living? Why do you think I would know that?'

'Tell me.'

Trident smiled. 'He was a drayman, for Castle Eden Brewery. Lived in Gilesgate. Not far from your house actually, Tony.'

Tony was a bit lost. 'My house was built twenty years ago.'

'Well, you know what I mean. There was a brewery storage yard up near where Belmont cricket field is now, and Durham City was the biggest market for the brewery.'

He needed some clarification. 'And how is this man involved with hiding the treasure?'

'That I don't know. Well, nobody does. And that's why the exact location of the treasure is a mystery. People have done a load of research about the drayman: why he wasn't off fighting the war, his favourite haunts, family history, anything that might point to his favoured disused pit, or even if he was involved in hiding the treasure or just a busybody writing random stories in his diary. He disappears from the records before the end of the war. There isn't even a death record for him.'

Penfold and Tony spent most of the journey back to Durham lost in their own thoughts, Tony imagining trucks of beer barrels pulled by shire horses carrying fleeing Tudor stewards of the cathedral, and magical un-decayed corpses with golden brooches hidden in the folds of their cloaks.

They even missed the best exit from the A1(M) motorway and entered the city from the north rather than the south. Tony had Penfold drop him at the Market Place so that he could pick up a sandwich in town rather than endure the late-afternoon leftovers in the nick canteen.

He stopped at a kiosk beside Boots that served his favourite Thai-style chicken roll. While they brewed him a really milky coffee to chase away the bitter taste of Penfold's black-only variety, he watched the man who ran the indoor market argue with a truck driver wearing a Durham County Council hi-vis jacket.

He couldn't make out what was being said, but the truck driver had just delivered the third of three forty-foot shipping containers, displaying the Miners' Gala logo on them. A new logo too. Saturday's outdoor market had been finished and packed away more than an hour previously and would not be held the following week on Gala day. Tony's mind whirred. *Hmm, are these the same as the ones Kathy was telling me about on Palace Green?*

The three shipping containers took up a lot of space, but the Big Meeting was the only event they could impact. They lay side by side across the bottom quarter of the Market Place, in front of the entrances to the Town Hall (closed for refurbishment) and St Nics Church. The church was still totally accessible, as were both entrances to the indoor market.

Durham Market Place had a statue of Neptune on a three-metre plinth, along with several sets of steps and a number of stone benches, around all of which the tilt-bed trailer had to be manoeuvred. Tony was impressed at the talent of the lorry driver, who had managed to steer the trailer into the right spot to deliver the third container beside the other two. Only one lorry was still present, so this poor soul had to stand up to the bearded market manager alone. He just kept pointing at his delivery instructions sheet and at the three containers and shrugging.

In the end, the truck driver stuffed a copy of the delivery order into the other man's hand, threw his clipboard into the cab, climbed up after it and pulled away. The market manager was left staring at the big metal boxes. Tony saw him grab at the swing door handles of one of the containers, and wondered if he'd need to intervene as a police officer. The handles wouldn't move, and the bearded man turned and stomped off through the market hall's big archway entrance.

NINE

'Stuff that into your mouth while we walk to the Daily Espresso.'

Tony swivelled round on his heels at the sound of Penfold's Kiwi twang. His roll was half bitten, the takeaway coffee cup in his other hand. He didn't have the mouth facility to query what was going on or why Penfold wasn't on the motorway back to Hartlepool. Penfold had already set off walking up the flagstone pavement in the direction of the cathedral and he scooted to catch up.

When he'd finally swallowed the first mouthful of Thai-spiced chicken, he asked, 'I've already got a coffee; why are we going there now?'

'Meeting Maid Marion.'

'What? She's here, in Durham?'

'Where did you think she was?'

Tony's mind was racing. He hadn't even imagined the host of the MaidMarionettes website to be a real person. He knew she was, of course, but despite her grinning, ginger-haired byline photo at the top of the website, the virtual nature of websites put their authors at a remove from reality.

Penfold's long legs were in overdrive, which meant Tony kept having to add an extra little quickstep into his gait in order to keep up. His mind seemed to be having to race to keep up too.

'Well, I guess I didn't know, but her website is national, even international. So I suppose I just assumed she'd be somewhere else in the country. Everyone's usually far from here!'

Penfold smiled at this. 'Ain't that why we love it?' Tony smiled too.

'But why are we meeting her? And how did you tee this up?'

Penfold explained that part of his sister's online investigations had included emailing the account that owned the domain name for MaidMarionettes. Trident reckoned those contact details had to be in the public domain, and in this case the website was owned privately, and not by some website hosting company like GoDaddy.

By the time he told Tony that Marion herself had replied to Trident's email, and had then been convinced that they should meet, the two investigators had arrived on the threshold of the Daily Espresso just ahead of the 5.30 p.m. appointment time.

Tony stuffed the last of his chicken roll into an already full mouth and threw his coffee cup into the litter bin in the middle of the pedestrian cobbles.

Penfold's favourite coffee shop had a dimness to its interior that was imbued with cosiness. The warm, wooden panelling and smooth jazz background music made it somehow both discreet and convivial. Even when it was packed, conversations seemed to be held in your own little world.

Saturday's crowd was thinning out though, so Tony headed for a table and Penfold went to the baristas. Neither man could see a redhead in the place. In a couple of minutes, Penfold brought over two mugs of steaming black coffee, and was sent back for a jug of milk. Technically the boss in this situation, Tony decided he could have milk if he wanted it.

Marion's smile seemed to enter two steps in front of her. She came in as bouncy as her website photo had indicated. She didn't know who she was meeting, so the men sat and watched her collect a small coffee and a sticky pastry with red pieces adorning its top. Her summery, white blouse could easily be in danger from this sweet treat. Tony cautioned himself to keep his eyes away from the blouse even if a pastry accident did befall it.

She held her phone to the card machine, turned and then scanned the room, looking at the handful of students with laptops, and the few other customers. Her gaze moved to the two investigators for just a moment and then passed on to the old couple on the next table.

Finally, she stepped over to a woman sitting alone on a low sofa reading a book. They spoke briefly and the reader shook her head in apology. As Marion stood tall again, Penfold got up to help her find them. She didn't respond to his rising, or even to his small wave. He headed over and, after a brief introduction, shepherded her back to their table.

Tony stood to shake hands, and Marion apologised profusely. 'Gosh, I'm so sorry. I feel terribly rude – I just thought I'd be meeting Trident. And I don't know why, but I sensed from her email that she was a woman, so I totally ignored you just now. I really am sorry.'

She was bubbly and bright, in a manner that disarmed Tony, given that her face was covered with large areas of scars. He guessed she must have been in a fire at some point. But where he imagined marks like that would make a person highly self-conscious and shy, Marion was the opposite. She seemed to carry no angst about how she looked. Nobody mentioned the scars.

He smiled. 'It's quite alright, totally understandable.'

Penfold added, 'I'll have to warn Trident. She'll be mortified that you managed to glean anything about her from the communication.'

Marion fussed over putting her plate and cup down and smoothed out her long, brown skirt before sitting opposite the two men. She introduced herself as Marion Rufus and asked why they were meeting, as Trident had mentioned a police matter involving her website, but had given no further details.

Tony introduced himself and showed her his warrant card and proceeded to add Penfold in as a "consulting investigator". Marion looked both impressed and agog at being summoned by such important people. Her wide eyes, long nose and handful of freckles gave the impression of a curious puppy, until he explained that two men who had compared notes with her about a lost treasure had both been found dead in mineshafts.

He avoided going on to use the word *murder*, but she already had both hands to her cheeks in disbelief. 'Oh, that's terrible. I can't believe it. Who were they, what were they looking for?'

'We don't have formal identification yet, but we're hoping that you might be able to give us some more information about why they were at the mines.'

Marion's green eyes bored into Tony. 'Wait, "mines"?' She emphasised the *S* at the end of the word. 'They weren't both at the same place together?'

Penfold stepped in. 'Why would you think they'd be together?'

Her head snapped left to look at him. Her voice was higher and wavering. 'Well … well, are you telling me that two people died in separate mine accidents? And both had looked at my blog?'

Tony gave Penfold a look, surprised at his misstep. He tried to keep a soft, friendly tone. 'Yes, I know, extraordinary isn't it. It's partly that coincidence that made us think to ask you what they might have read, or planned, from your site. We think if we know what they were looking for, we might work out what happened.'

Marion's face calmed and she said, 'I haven't brought my laptop, so I may have to send you information later, but I won't be able to tell you anything about these poor men without knowing who they are.' She paused for a moment, thinking. 'Or if you can't work that out, I might be able to shed some light on recent posts on my site about the locations, if you can tell me where these accidents happened.'

Penfold spoke quietly again. 'What makes you think they're accidents?'

This triggered Marion. 'Oh my God, oh my God, what are you saying? No! No! What?' She was making enough of a scene that everyone else in the shop turned to look.

Tony tried to deflect the external interest and regain their privacy. He made a big show of looking around at everyone and holding up a commanding hand. 'It's OK everyone, sorry, we just gave a bit of bad news. Sorry, don't let us disturb you.'

He thought he might make a show of putting a calming hand on the nearest shoulder, where the bulk of Marion's ginger curls spilled down, but caught himself before doing it, in case she recoiled. This could well put everyone else on notice that maybe she wasn't comfortable being there with these two men.

Instead, he gave Penfold another stare and put his hands gently on his own knees. 'Sorry, Marion, I'm sure it's a bit of a shock. We really don't know what's happened at all, except that both men are dead, and they both used your website quite a lot. We just need some help investigating. Whatever you can tell us would be useful.'

Her eyes were welling with tears, and she picked up the napkin that had come with her pastry to press against them. 'Of course I'll do anything I can to help. But I don't know if I'll have any useful information. I'm just an archaeologist with an interest in old things that have been lost.'

Penfold took up a friendlier approach. 'Of course. These men seemed to have had the same love of research as your website displays in spades. They were found, separately, in nearby coal mines and appear to have fallen, hitting their heads on the way down. And it's exactly that coincidence, the similarity of their accidents and the fact that they both happened at nearly the same time that makes us wonder if there's anything more to their deaths. It's total speculation at this point but we do need to investigate. Do you think perhaps there could be some rival treasure hunter who wanted to stop them getting their hands on something? We think maybe they were looking for St Cuthbert's Treasure.'

Tony wondered whether his colleague may have given out too much information about the cases, but he remained silent and observed Marion's response. She nodded slightly and her face lifted.

A pause to collect her thoughts was enough. 'Nearby mines makes sense for the Cuthbertine treasure, as it's thought to be buried somewhere in County Durham. But identifying them might be hard if they haven't used their real names. My website allows people to make commenter accounts just by providing their email address. And with it being St Cuthbert's Friday next week, the traffic in my forums has been quite heavy recently. I've pointed a number of people in various directions myself, but even I hardly ever know who they are.'

'St Cuthbert's Friday? What's that exactly?' Tony looked to Penfold, who gave a brief headshake to indicate he hadn't heard of it either. 'The Constable of the Cathedral didn't mention any celebration day to us. One of my detectives went to see him yesterday.'

Marion dabbed the napkin to her eyes, which were fairly dry by that point. She replied, 'No, it's not his actual saint's day. It's something some treasure hunter came up with years ago. The eighteenth of July is the date when the sources say that the treasure was buried in whichever mine it's in. The Constable of the Cathedral at the time was a very pious man and he reported having a vision during prayer – a prophecy – where Cuthbert came to him and told him the hidden items would be returned to his people on that same date in many years' time. So, it's become something of a tradition for people to go looking for the treasure every eighteenth of July, hoping to be the one who fulfils the prophecy by finding the treasure. This year, that's on a Friday.'

'Sounds daft. Do people really believe in that kind of superstitious stuff?'

Marion nodded vigorously. 'Of course they do. Remember, these are people who are hunting for lost treasures. The whole premise of the search is that it's all based on piecing together ancient texts and rumours. The sketchier the source, the more of a gamble you take following its information, and the greater the reward will be if you find something. It's just like the lottery except that you feel engaged in determining your own outcomes. Am I brave enough to spend time, effort and money following this thousand-year-old treasure map? It might be wrong, or even if it's right, the treasure might have already been found and moved in the meantime. Believing superstitions is an easy suspension of disbelief when the entire premise of your activity is just a fun gamble.'

Tony accepted the point. 'I guess.' Penfold nodded vigorously, very taken with the psychological concept.

She continued, 'In fact, the prophecy goes on: "Until it is finally found on the eighteenth of July, many men will die trying to take my treasure." They call it Saint Cuthbert's Curse.'

They stepped outside into the evening heat of Durham's Saddler Street, Tony shook Marion's hand goodbye and Penfold asked a parting query. 'How did you choose the pseudonym Maid Marion?'

She smiled, glowing in the sun lowering towards the cathedral behind her. 'My mother was a big fan of *Robin of Sherwood*, the 80s TV show, and she says that when I was born, arriving with this hair, she couldn't help herself but call me Marion. Throughout my childhood I styled myself after the woman in the show – my mother made me watch every episode.' All three smiled at this.

Marion shook her curls and said, 'It's like fiery hail raining down on my head.' She strode off down the cobbled street towards the golden-lit statue of Charles William Vane Stewart on horseback.

'Can you get Trident to send through Marion's contact details please. She seems sufficiently well versed in this treasure hunting stuff that we may need to talk to her again.'

'Sorry, no can do.'

'Eh?'

'She would only meet anonymously. Even Trident doesn't know more than "Maid Marion" as a moniker. The domain registry lists "Marion Rufus" and a generic email address. Rufus is hopefully unusual enough that we can find her though.'

They stared after her retreating silhouette. 'Well, as a potential witness of sorts, she doesn't get to make that kind of demand. Tell Trident to send me whatever she has got, please.'

Penfold nodded and corrected himself. 'Actually, I'm pretty sure the domain registry includes a postal address and phone number as well as email. I'll get them all for you, but oftentimes they're dummy listings, coz you get spammed like you wouldn't believe. That database is public access.'

Reaching the top of Old Elvet Bridge, they paused to take leave of each other. Tony pointed down the slope, crowded with the outdoor tables of bars and restaurants at the top end of the bridge. His finger aimed at a fourth Durham Miners' Gala liveried shipping container.

It had been placed against one side of the bridge parapet just at the point where the shops ended and the bridge headed out over the murky River Wear. The place was already full of Saturday night revellers who must have started earlier in the afternoon to judge by the way they were weaving and shouting to each other.

Tony shook his head, wondering about the fleet of delivery lorries that would attempt to squeeze their way past first thing in the morning. He lifted his nose slightly. 'What's that smell?'

Penfold took a loud theatrical inhalation through his nose, and answered, 'Lemons.'

'That's what I thought, just didn't believe it! My sense of smell has never been the same since Covid.'

Penfold nodded. 'There is something a bit artificial about it though. I wonder if one of these restaurants has some sort of scented air freshener. What it really reminds me of is citronella – the mosquito repellent stuff.'

67

'Can't say my nose is really familiar with that.'

'No, I'm sure. I've spent enough time on tropical beaches to be way too familiar with it.'

'No real mosquito problem here in Durham. I'm gonna suggest more likely lemon fresh floor cleaner after some Saturday drunkard's puked up in a corner.'

Penfold smiled at his cynicism. 'Ha, the city's a millennium old, and I bet its residents have been carousing the streets in the same way since it was first founded.'

'You wait till next Saturday and come back here. The Miners' Gala brings a special chaos.'

TEN

DC Diane Meredith raised her chin and breathed deeply. The slight breeze was invigorating. She looked down at the bloody skull. Alfie Johnson, Crime Scene Investigator, knelt and with one gloved hand gently parted the dead man's hair to see the wound more clearly. There was a large indentation where the blood had escaped his cranium.

A uniformed police sergeant bent down to place a large, heavy evidence bag beside the CSI. Through the clear plastic, the three of them could see a rounded stone, about the size and shape of a junior rugby ball. It was smeared with blood.

'That was about ten metres over there.' The local policeman, out of Barnard Castle station, pointed to some longer grass behind Diane. She swivelled to look, and then turned back, estimating that the hilltop pub car park, where their three vehicles stood in a line, was perhaps twenty metres the other way.

'Oh, please don't move anything – I need to photograph the scene exactly as it is first.'

The man nodded. He had left his hat in the police Land Rover, and his hair was almost exactly the same chocolate colour as Diane's, but his curly locks were cropped short enough that they didn't have the same swing and movement as hers did. 'Did it already – I've sent you photos and video.'

Johnson looked at him with a benign smile. 'Thank you, Sergeant Franks. It's great of you to help, but these days the CPS are getting really picky about the composition of scene photos. They reckon that can affect whether or not they win in court. It takes the objectivity and science out of it for me, but they know what they need, so please, if you can, just let me co-ordinate when we move things. Sorry.'

Meredith's new beau was a master of diplomacy; she watched him work the living as ably as he did the dead. Moreover, she thought, his classic, dashing good looks could bend anyone to his will. She engaged the sergeant to distract him from any further thought of argument, although he looked compliant enough after Alfie's request.

'Why have you called me in? I mean you've got detectives in Darlington that are nearer than Durham, and in any case, this is a North Yorkshire Police location.'

They stood on high heather moorland on the eastern side of the Pennines, near the Tan Hill Inn. The dead body had been found a few kilometres south of the A66, as it cut east to west, close to Barnard Castle. The pub claimed to be the highest in Britain, and being south of the Tees it sat in North Yorkshire, albeit only about fifteen kilometres outside their jurisdiction.

The dark-haired sergeant nodded. 'The mine connection. Apparently, that came up on the Holmes computer system as soon as my colleague typed in the basic details.' They all looked at the hole in the ground beside the body that descended into blackness in exactly the same way as Diane and Alfie had seen twice already in the last few days.

Behind the open shaft, the familiar metal grille security gate was also present, but the bars were heavily rusted, with a couple missing completely. The major difference here, though, was that the body was on the ground next to the opening, rather than down in the shaft. He had a similar fatal head injury, but this time it had been caused by a rock – potentially a weapon – up on the surface.

Diane took a step closer to peer into the hole. 'Has anyone been to look down the bottom there? In our other two cases the bodies were found at the bottom. I'm just wondering if he'd been down there, or if he maybe dropped anything that might help us.'

The uniformed officer had his hands stuffed deep in dark trouser pockets. With a shake of his head, he replied, 'Bloke who found the body spotted something on his drone camera.' The sergeant pointed to a man sitting in the back of his police car, behind his colleague. The two were sharing some sort of joke while looking out through the windscreen at them. 'He followed the drone over here to investigate what it was, found the body and called us. Dead body means they send the nearest police, which is us. I expect Richmond will be here soon, but we told them you were coming down, so they may not bother unless we ask for help.'

He paused and stood up to step closer to the hole. Looking in, he continued, 'Anyway, while he was waiting for us to come up, he sent his drone down the hole. Not much to see on the video, but, again, I've sent it to both of you anyway.' He looked at Diane. 'You wanna speak to him?'

'Not particularly. What about you, Alfie?'

He was photographing all points on the deceased's body, sometimes lifting a limb or aiming at the ground beside him, and answered without looking up. 'I don't think so. You guys will take his statement, right? I expect I'll go down the hole myself shortly and see if there's anything to find.'

She took over seamlessly. 'Is this all the stuff that was around the body?'

'Yeah.' The officer pointedly turned his face towards the kneeling CSI. 'Didn't move any of that stuff – it's exactly where it was when we got here. And drone boy reckons he's seen enough TV to know not to touch anything. Said it was why he only sent his drone down the shaft. Not sure I'd be trying to clamber down there if I found this.' He waved down at the corpse.

Diane knelt down beside the various possessions strewn nearby. Signs of a tussle were evident in the way the man's bag was spilled open on the grass. Almost within his reach were a notebook, glasses case, phone. Still in the bag, Diane found some paper maps and a jumper. The man was dressed like a hiker.

71

'Thing to look for in that lot is what's missing?' Alfie had turned to look at her.

She knelt more upright and smiled back at him. 'Is that a riddle? Look for the things that are not there!'

He gave a silent chuckle and a vague nod and turned back to the body. As his blue-gloved hand rifled through the side pockets of the grey combat shorts, he pulled out a wallet and tossed it over to her to put in another evidence bag.

She went through it first, pulling out a driving licence. 'John Bowline. Um, what's that make him? Thirty … and … thirty-eight years old.'

'Looks about right.' Alfie did not look up from assessing the clothing and the ground underneath Bowline.

After sealing the evidence bag, Diane stood up and walked ever increasing circles around the mine opening and the area of the body. She stooped at the spot where the bloody rugby ball rock had come from. There appeared to be a lot of damage to the long moorland grasses, as if somebody had jumped around the place, or maybe crawled around, for quite a while.

The sun shone brightly, but it felt cooler than in the city. Up here, a wind made the air fresher, and she didn't feel stifled and sticky. The view down the long hill towards Barnard Castle was stunning. They stood sandwiched between the North Pennines National Landscape and Yorkshire Dales National Park.

The shades of green cascading down towards Teesdale reminded her of an old duvet cover printed in billows of green colours. She briefly pulled off her sunglasses to check on the exact colours spread down the hill in front of her. The natural wash of greens was even more beautiful. She was amazed that the grass had avoided the browning that Durham City was suffering and wondered if it had rained more up in the hills.

She turned back to watch Alfie at his work and grinned as she saw his broad shoulders flex under the white paper coveralls that never really fit him properly.

Diane stepped slightly further away from the main crime scene and looked closely at one area of squashed stems. 'This looks like a bike came through here recently.' She squatted on her haunches. 'And I think it was laid down here.'

The Barnard Castle copper had been watching them both silently but now seemed bored enough to get involved. 'There's no bike there now, and he's still here. Do you think somebody stole his bike and they fought over it and the thief hit him with the rock?'

Again, without looking up, the forensic investigator answered, 'We've got car keys in the bag here, so I'm not sure any bike was his.'

The police sergeant continued, undeterred, 'Get a lot of cyclists up here on a Sunday morning, so it's not much of a surprise. They often park up somewhere in town for a big ride. The road just here is part of the cycle network.' He pointed across to the strip of tarmac that passed the Tan Hill Inn and had brought them up to this remote spot. 'Maybe we should go inside and see if anyone in the pub saw anything. It's still early in the day, but the staff are here all the time, and it seems odd that only the drone pilot would have spotted him.'

ELEVEN

CSI Alfie Johnson stood up having completed what he could do on site. 'I'm sorry, mate, you're going to have to stay here and look after the crime scene until the pathologist shows up to collect the body. Philip Gerard has texted me that he's on his way, and that was an hour ago, so he should be here any minute.

'Diane, I'll help you talk to the folk inside, once I've dropped my gear in the truck. And I'll need to wait for Philip too, but there's no need for you to hang around after that.'

'Trying to get rid of me?' Diane smiled at him as he shook his head with a grin of his own.

'Actually, I'll use the time while I'm waiting to climb down the shaft and have a look there. I'm really conscious though that you're a long way from the Major Crimes office and the detective work you need to get on with.'

'You're all heart.' She walked back to his side and punched him lightly on the upper arm.

Alfie walked to his pick-up truck, opening several big storage bins built into the flatbed. Each one contained a treasure trove of equipment for tackling any crime scene, large or small, urban or as remote as this one, and with some special stores for things like his climbing equipment, cutting tools, and one box that folded out as a small on-board laboratory. He could match glass colours and confirm blood types, among other chemical testing, all at a crime scene.

Once everything was returned to its appropriate bin, Alfie removed the shoe covers and overalls and gloves, to look a little more presentable for his first visit to a public house with Diane. Even if they were heading in to question people about a murder, he liked to look his best.

Diane admired his cream shirt and blue jeans – simple and effective. Alfie looked good. Cowboy boots extending out from the bottom of the jeans matched his pick-up truck look perfectly.

Walking to the entrance of the pub took them past four expensive looking bikes leant against the gable wall. At a picnic table right outside the door sat four men in full cycling garb, bike shoes and curved, sports sunglasses. Two had a pint of beer and two had a coffee, and all of them had a slice of cake. The four looked to be in their fifties, wrinkled tanned and thin. Diane reckoned they must be out on their bikes all the time.

She took the lead, flashing her warrant card around. 'Morning, gents. You been here long?'

The two cyclists with coffees looked at their flashy smartwatches and started pressing the little screens. One with a beer, dressed in black and red team INEOS-branded Lycra, leaned back to look up at the detective. He pointed at the level of his half-drunk beer and said, 'About this long.'

The other beer drinker added, 'We passed you as we arrived – did you not see us?' He waved a hand back along the narrow, open road, and sounded put out that his neon green shirt had not attracted the attention he hoped for.

'Sorry, we've been a bit busy.' In her turn, Diane waved a hand towards the local policeman who was erecting a square of blue and white tape around the mine opening and the body of John Bowline, which Alfie had covered in a white plastic sheet before leaving him. 'Wondering if maybe you saw anything happen here, but it sounds like you haven't been here long enough.'

One of the cyclists with a coffee, dressed in tight white shorts and white top, offered, 'All we saw this morning was empty countryside. Incredible weather this week. I've never known this area to be so quiet for wind. Normally really hard riding up here, but it's been amazing cycling. Sorry we can't help.'

The one who had thus far been silent said, 'We did see that one woman. On the first lap. You remember, right down the bottom. She was riding towards us from this direction.'

The other three turned to look at their friend, and the cocky, INEOS-clad rider laughed. 'That was a bloke, you weirdo.'

'No, it wasn't. That was definitely a woman.'

The four of them bickered about who they'd seen, with three ganging up on the one who thought it had been a female rider. There was some discussion about the mystery cyclist's height, leg muscles and the fact that their sunglasses and beige hoodie had obscured their face and hung loosely enough to cast doubt on their exact physical stature.

Alfie interrupted, 'OK, look, it doesn't sound like we can get much of a description of them, but could you describe the bike?'

All four immediately agreed on the bike – to a man, they had been impressed by a US import in lightning blue that they knew was so light and strong every one of them coveted it.

'OK, that's helpful. And anything unusual about the rider? Did they have a bag? Any markings or logos on their clothes?'

'Oh, wait!' The more reticent of the beer drinkers suddenly piped up loud. 'His hoodie was all dirty. It had a load of brown spatters on the front. At the time I just assumed it was mud, but there's been no rain for ages. We didn't go through any muddy spots at all today, which is really unusual, that's why I thought it would be mud when we passed him. Never clocked that it couldn't have been mud.'

The two investigators looked at each other, and Diane asked, 'When did you see them?'

The coffee drinker who thought they had seen a woman checked his smartwatch again and, pointing at it, said, 'Would have been seven-twenty-five. I've got all the waypoints logged on here. First lap round, we passed Gilmonby at seven-twenty-five and that rider, he or she, passed us there.' He swiped the screen on the watch. 'Second lap round we were there at eight-forty.'

The other watch-wearer said, 'Two.'

'What?' Confused, she wondered if in fact they had seen two cyclists going the other way.

He pointed at his own smartwatch. 'Eight-forty-*two*.'

She looked at the sky and then felt Alfie's hand pull at her elbow.

He said, 'OK, thanks fellas, we'll try the staff inside and see if they saw anything more.'

As he pulled her pubwards, she pointed at one of the beers. 'You know it's not even ten in the morning.'

A smug 'Yep' followed them in through the door.

The staff inside had been too busy with work that morning to see anything going on outside, but they offered the detective and forensic investigator a welcome iced drink, on the house. They sat side by side on a brown banquette in the cool of the old stone building, and Alfie pulled up some videos on his phone that might interest Diane.

'Abandoned Mine Exploration is an entire genre on YouTube. I've bookmarked a couple from round the county.'

They watched more than ten minutes of footage from various videos, showing men in caving gear wandering across windy fields past the ruins of stone buildings and squeezing down into holes in the ground that never looked large enough.

The commentary on two of the videos included references to them potentially finding St Cuthbert's Treasure down a pitiful overgrown hole. One video even cut to a still picture of the gold pectoral cross on display in Durham Cathedral.

Diane shook her head throughout, repeatedly disputing the sex appeal of men who engaged in this kind of nerdish behaviour. Her left hand rested on Alfie's leg and they sipped their drinks and laughed together.

She had set up notifications on her phone to alert her when new posts were made to the MaidMarionettes website's discussion forum about St Cuthbert's Treasure. Her phone started to ping as a conversation began building in the forum. She opened it up to read what was going on and held her phone for Johnson to read the posts too.

People were already talking about the Tan Hill death. Some of the forum members referred to a user called TheKnottyProblem as being the victim, and there was considerable discussion of Saint Cuthbert's Curse. The handle MaidMarion was in the discussion and posted *"With great wealth comes great danger."* Before Diane put her phone away, they read one user's response: *"I hear that."*

Diane patted his strong thigh and stood up. 'Right, I'd better head back and see what I can find out about this victim. John Bowline … TheKnottyProblem. What a dickhead.' She turned and walked out to her car.

TWELVE

Diane drove slowly down the long hill back towards Barnard Castle, visions of Alfie's gorgeous jawline filling her mind. She knew his good looks and physique would stir up Tony's jealousy. He'd be desperate to find out everything she and the CSI got up to, and she thought through ways to tease Tony. The sun beamed in through the driver's side window, and she basked in its heat.

As she manoeuvred carefully up the narrow hump-backed bridge over the River Tees and into the bottom end of Barnard Castle town, her nostrils filled with a smoky stench. Turning the bend to point the car uphill towards the Butter Market, she leant forward to look as high in the air as the windscreen allowed. A pall of black smoke filled the sky above the high street, drifting over the shop buildings on the right-hand side.

The car's handsfree blared into life, ringing much too loudly. The sudden noise made Diane jump in her seat, and she focussed on keeping the car straight with parked cars on her side of the road and a bus heading down the hill towards her. Pulling into a space between parked cars to let the bus pass, she pressed to connect the call.

'DC Meredith? It's Sergeant Franks here. Listen, I'm staying put at the Tan Hill crime scene, but my colleague is heading straight down into town, and we're hoping you could lend a hand too. The school's on fire and it's all hands to the pump, so to speak. Could you go and join the response team? It's a boarding school and we don't yet know how serious an incident this is.'

The bus's engine noise dropped as it passed, but sirens surged into the air, drowning everything else. A police vehicle with flashing blue lights roared past her and up the steep hill, to turn right at the old market hall that looked like a small stone temple. The Butter Market was now a roundabout and Diane shot up the hill behind her colleague, following exactly in his wake albeit without lights and sirens.

They raced along Newgate, her unmarked car tailgating the blue and green chequered Land Rover far too closely. Ancient trees lined the route, fields on the right and old stone houses on the left. After two hundred metres, they passed the grand entrance and ornamental gardens in front of the Bowes Museum, and the next turning was the driveway up to Barnard Castle School. A chaos of emergency vehicles, running firemen, police, and some people dressed in civvies covered the area at the top of the school drive.

The school sprawled over fields at the edge of the historic market town, and its main building was almost one hundred and fifty years old, solidly built from local sandstone. The black smoke cloud Diane had seen in town was clearly emanating from a dozen windows on the second and third floors of a wing that stuck out to the left of the school's grand central tower. She saw flames inside the endmost two windows.

Two fire engines stood in front of the building, four hose teams fighting the water pressure to point it up and in the windows. A third engine was out of sight further left, behind some big old elm trees. That hidden engine also played two jets of water on to the end of the building, and another two came from a fourth tender which was behind the curving wall, inside the grounds of the Bowes Museum itself, barely separated from the conflagration.

This fourth engine had different livery, boasting it was from North Yorkshire Fire and Rescue compared with the three local engines from Barnard Castle and Darlington. Its star-shaped badge was bright red, rather than Durham county's blue and yellow coat of arms on the other vehicles. Like those other three though, it was squirting two streams of water over the wall and on to the roof of the school building.

Diane abandoned the car halfway up the drive and ran to the top to find someone in charge who could make use of her help in some way.

The nearest vehicles were four open ambulances, with paramedics on standby, trolleys at the ready, but as far as she could tell, they had no patients to care for, yet. A team of four fully suited firemen, complete with masks and breathing apparatus, forced open a door on the ground floor and surged inside, as smoke wafted out past them.

'Sergeant Franks said you could do with some help. I'm DC Meredith – Diane – from Durham City station.' She was addressing a uniformed sergeant she vaguely recognised from the local station. He appeared to be co-ordinating some activities, although the fire crews seemed autonomous, and the paramedics struck her as simply waiting.

An incredible sound, like thunder right overhead, cracked through the air and they both ducked instinctively. Nothing visibly happened.

'Perfect timing. Diane, did you say?' She nodded, and he waved towards a group of soaked civilians wandering around the end of the building that was on fire. They were trying to peer in ground floor windows and calling up to the upper ones, which all appeared to be open. 'This wing is one of the boarding houses. Museum staff from next door were first on scene, and we can't get them away – they're worried about kids being inside.'

'Where are the school staff?'

'The holidays started yesterday. The whole place should be empty apart from their estates team. The head's family live on site in that house.' He pointed across the double driveway and visitor car park to a magnificent, detached house in its own gardens in front of the school. 'But apparently, he goes on holiday on the very first day of the summer break. They reckon it's some sort of magnanimous gesture, leading his staff to take a rest from the year's hard work.

'Anyway, the whole place *should* be empty, but they sometimes have international boarders who stay on for a few days, depending on when their flights home are. So the upshot is we've got no idea who might be in the boarding house rooms. We haven't yet located any school staff, and all the doors are locked.'

He pointed again at the milling group of museum staff. 'But, that lot are getting in the way, and they're really endangering themselves. Can you get them away from the building for me? Be just typical if the whole place is empty but one of them gets killed by a falling roof tile.'

'Of course.' Diane set off to round up the group. Almost immediately, she started getting wet from the spray fallout. She wore navy business trousers, and her brief thoughts of how her white blouse might end up looking like a wet T-shirt competition were banished – she had a job to do.

The eight people – five women and three men – were quickly compliant with her barked requests to fall back. They'd had no response to their cries up into the building and were sufficiently wet that no great convincing was necessary.

Even after weeks of dry, hot weather, the fire hoses had completely turned all the grass and flowerbeds into a quagmire. A river ran down the sloping school drive into the road. Everyone had muddy shoes.

The group huddled with Diane, backs to the old stone wall at the boundary between the school and museum grounds. It had heated up so much in the sun that the stone radiated welcome warmth to their wet skin.

She tried to keep them busy by asking about what they had been doing, how they'd been alerted to the fire, and what anyone knew about who might be in the building. She was scraping the barrel but followed up with questions about their roles in the Bowes Museum. The school and museum had a close connection, and they all knew people who worked in or attended the school.

After a moment or two, the detective constable asked who was left behind to look after the museum visitors. She wondered if this might encourage the group to return to the drier, less muddy, and safer, environs behind the wall. A woman who had presented herself as the gift shop manager said, 'We evacuated. The fire is so close, and our safety protocol is that a fire in the school means we evacuate. So we packed all the visitors off home and then ran round here to help.'

Diane thanked Mother Nature for the hot weather. If she'd had to look after these soaked folk in say February, she imagined the paramedics would have a lot of hypothermia cases to deal with.

'We should have shut the front gates, but the Richmond fire engine arrived and asked to use our hydrant, so they could get this extra angle up to the fire. We've had to leave the gates open.' The woman pointed up over the wall to their left where two arcs of water were flying from the fourth fire service vehicle.

They stood chatting and watching for the next twenty minutes. Diane was bored but understood that she was probably as involved as she could be, given that she was not local to "Barney" and had no knowledge of the school, and she was doing the task she'd been given by entertaining, or keeping an eye on, the museum people. In her mind, she referred to them as *gawkers* rather than *helpers*.

The fire team re-emerged from the building making arm signals to indicate they had found no people inside. The flames and smoke had been doused, and the water hoses were shut off. The wet group watched as various emergency services personnel walked back and forth and discussed matters. More waving of arms, pointing at doors and windows and parts of the building were followed by discussions with two men in suits who had arrived shortly after Diane. She guessed they were probably school staff being instructed in what they needed to do with their building now the fire was out.

MM HUDSON

Eager to get back to Durham, she stepped away from the wall to ask if her assistance was needed any further. She waited patiently as the lead fire officer worked his way through concluding matters with various people with different responsibilities. He talked to the head of the paramedics, and she watched the North Yorkshire fire truck pull back from the wall and head off around the museum's long circle driveway, down and out of the gates, seemingly in a rush to return to Richmond.

As she drove past the magnificent Raby Castle, ten minutes into her cross-country journey back to Durham, Sergeant Franks called again. He thanked her for the support she'd just provided at the fire, before following up with a shock.

The Bowes Museum, something more akin to a private art gallery than a museum, had held its flagship artefact since 1873. The automated Silver Swan, about the size of a real bird, sat on a small silver pond with silver leaves garlanding the edge of the sculpture. It contained an ingenious internal mechanism that played music while the Swan moved its head and neck and caught silver fish from the pond. Franks was reporting that the Swan had been stolen, in the last hour.

Originally made in the late eighteenth century, and literally priceless, it weighed thirty kilograms, mostly of solid silver. It wasn't too hard to move the automaton but, with very delicate internal workings, any repositioning required great care. It had been on display in a second-floor gallery, commanding the centre of the room. The large protective glass case had been lifted off and placed beside the now empty display stand. Only the actual Swan sculpture had been taken.

The museum staff had returned after the fire to discover it was gone and immediately called their liaison officer who happened to be the sergeant she had met earlier that morning up Tan Hill. When they had told him who had refused to let them move from the spot by the wall for more than half an hour, Franks recognised her description.

Diane was confused and flabbergasted. She hadn't seen anything notably suspicious but promised to return in the morning to meet with him and the chief curator of the museum.

THIRTEEN

Acting DI Tony Milburn circled the car park of the University Hospital of North Durham again. He passed Julia Sedgley's white BMW and cursed her for having found a space. It wasn't the only white BMW among the couple of hundred cars spread across the tarmac lot, but her personalised number plate, *4N6*, was unforgettable.

He parked half on the verge, under a line of trees, and from the boot he pulled a hi-vis jacket emblazoned with the word *Police* across the back. This Tony laid carefully on the dashboard in the hope of persuading any parking inspectors that they should let him off.

'Hold the door please!'

Just inside the main entrance, he stuck out an arm to halt the lift's closing doors and, as they reopened fully, Dr Sedgley leapt through, a mass of curly black hair flying everywhere, and a coffee cup looking for all the world like it should spill over him.

'Morning.'

'Ah, Tony, how are you?'

He blew out through pursed lips. 'OK, I guess. Not as bright and breezy as you, on the way to see a body get cut up.'

She smiled. 'Two bodies! Well, I guess I've seen it all before.'

The lift doors opened before Tony could follow up, and they progressed along the sterile basement corridor into the anteroom of Philip Gerard's domain. More greetings were performed as they met with Jan, the pathology lab technician, and then the pathologist himself when he emerged from the compact back office.

Despite being fully clad for a forensic post-mortem, Gerard still managed to radiate the aura of a Hollywood heartthrob. Tony mischievously imagined that they were about to watch "Autopsy:

The Musical". Tony prepared for the pathologist to break into an opening number about the unfortunate body that had been brought into the morgue which he was now prepared for slicing, dicing and chemical testing.

He quickly banished thoughts of how "slicing, dicing and chemical testing" could be made to scan in a musical theatre number, but couldn't stop himself humming quietly. *The toe bone's connected to the foot bone, the foot bone's connected to the ankle bone, the ankle bone's ...*

'Sorry?' Sedgley interrupted, asking what she had half heard. They had moved into the viewing space. Calling it a gallery would be too grand – Jan usually used the term *pod*. Her wheelchair wouldn't fit through the narrow opening into it, but she always needed to assist her boss in the theatre anyway, bagging and photographing and passing tools over.

'Oh, nothing. I always like to lighten the mood a little. Just ignore me.'

Tony would usually hang around in the main "cutting room" as Gerard called it, often leaning up against the lesser used second sink, but with the crime scene manager in attendance, the DI figured he should do things by the book.

'Jan and I tossed a coin earlier and we're going to start with the victim from Tan Hill, most likely one John Bowline.'

While Jan and Dr Gerard began their process, Dr Sedgley asked Tony why Gerard would do a coin toss to schedule his post-mortems.

With the main pathology lab's door closed, the guests in the pod couldn't be heard directly. 'I doubt he did – I think he's just taking the mick.'

She shrugged and pulled out her iPad to show him some pictures. In the tight space, her hair kept brushing the big glass window and annoying her. She fidgeted, unsuccessfully trying to push it back to give her better sight of Tony squashed up against the end wall. The pod had been designed for only one person.

'The grass between the rock and the exact location of Bowline's body suggests he crawled from where he was hit to where we found him.'

She pressed the intercom button to talk through the viewing glass into the cutting room. 'Can you check, Philip, if there's any evidence the victim crawled through long grass recently?'

Jan jumped in with the answer, lifting an evidence bag from the line-up of them on the side counter. 'His trousers do have grass-stained knees. I'll try and extract some trace and see if we can get you an exact pollen identification.'

Sedgley gave the technician a thumbs up and went back to showing Tony the iPad. The next photo was one from Sergeant Franks of the whole scene from the bloody rock in the foreground, across to the body and his strewn possessions, to the dark opening beyond him.

'If he was attacked where the rock is, why would he crawl over towards the mineshaft? And if he was at death's door, why start getting all his things out of their bag?'

In his mind, Tony could see Penfold assessing the questions themselves rather than finding answers. 'Well, if we reckon he crawled from the rock, then maybe there was no assault. He tripped, fell, hit his head, and was then disoriented and crawled over towards the hole, maybe without really knowing what he was doing. Pulling the stuff from his bag, though, I reckon is highly likely – you've got a bad head injury, you go for your phone to call for help, no?'

Sedgley nodded along, mulling over the narrative Tony had posited.

He grabbed the iPad and peered closely at three areas of the image on the screen. Putting aside the nagging thought that he was actually channelling Penfold now, he showed her what had caught his attention.

'Hmm. Three things I'm wondering about: first, look at where the blood is on the rock.' His forefinger pressed on the screen. 'A fair bit visible on the side, but mostly it goes from there around the end and underneath. Not where it should be if he'd fallen on the rock by himself.'

'Right.' She nodded again and looked at him through a hanging garden of uncontrollable ringlets.

'Number two: the mineshaft safety cover is opened up. That means somebody has been over to it already. You've got to assume he couldn't open it in that state, and that nobody went and did so while he was lying there injured.

'And three ... well, three's not so much about this image and the scene, but DC Meredith tells me that this guy goes by the online handle of TheKnottyProblem and is another one of the treasure hunters looking for St Cuthbert's Treasure. In that satchel bag we found maps and notes relating to it, just like with the others, including Billy Muckle there.'

Tony pointed at the second post-mortem candidate for the morning, laid out on a stainless steel table, behind which Gerard was pottering about with various cutting tools and sample bags and the ubiquitous cameras.

Dr Sedgley added an additional conundrum to the mix. 'And don't forget that bike track by the assault location but no sign of the bike.' She pressed the home button on the iPad, cradled the device by her stomach and engaged Tony eye to eye. 'Did you get anywhere finding the mystery cyclist with the bright blue bike?'

He shook his head. 'No, just another one of the many loose ends to try and untangle here.' He pressed the intercom button. 'Have we confirmed the blood on the rock as Bowline's?'

Gerard looked up through his glasses, his safety visor and the viewing window. 'We've run his bloods but got nothing from the forensic team to compare it to yet.' There was just a hint of exasperation in his voice. He was clearly working at full tilt for the investigation and was perhaps put out at the suggestion that he might be slow.

Tony maintained pressure on the intercom push switch so they could all converse, and Sedgley jumped in. 'We've sent some blood from the rock for the same tests. Should be back today I'd hope. Interestingly, we did also manage to find some skin cells on the rock surface too, so hopefully they'll give us DNA. They weren't all in the bloody areas on the stone.'

Tony chuckled. 'They'll probably give us yet another loose end to try and tie up. Additional suspect, anyone?'

They all smiled along with him.

Jan piped up from behind Gerard, holding up a bag containing the victim's khaki jacket. 'All seems very weird to me, grown men playing at being treasure hunters.'

Sedgley responded in defence of metal detectorists. 'I'd say that if you have an interest in history, seeking it out is a pretty decent hobby. I feel like amateur archaeology is more at the root of their activities than just trying to make a quick buck. Anyway, who does it harm?'

Tony and Gerard both turned to look at her. It was the acting detective inspector who spoke. 'Um, well, I've got four dead bodies, all engaged in these *harmless* activities.'

She blushed and tried to take back the ill-considered question. 'Of course, sorry. I guess I'm not counting …' There was a long pause. 'Actually, you're right, we're not even a hundred per cent that these men have been murdered. These could well be accidents from blokes being over-zealous, or maybe even reckless. Sorry, everyone.'

Her cheeks remained bright red. Tony wondered if he was simply imagining it, or if he could actually feel the heat from them at such close quarters.

Gerard smiled and said, 'Dickie Harbottle, Mr 1958, was definitely murdered.'

Tony carried on, 'The other three are pretty likely murders too. Did I tell you about the booby traps we found? Well, Penfold found them, but it's almost a certainty that these men died because of somebody else.'

She shook her head, and Tony could see the two in the cutting room earwigging, even though they were continuing at their work with John Bowline. He maintained pressure on the intercom switch and spent a few minutes running them through the wobbly top rocks in the stone staircases at both Tudhoe and Hairy Side. When he had finished, the post-mortem continued in silence for a few minutes.

Sedgley restarted the conversation. 'But why would you kill multiple treasure hunters at different sites. I mean, assuming they didn't know each other and this was about treasure, I can't imagine more than one finding a big hoard at the same time. So if they were to be murdered for the treasure then surely you just kill the one who's found it and make off with it. How are the others involved?'

Tony gave her further background on the treasure hunter forums where they had probably all had contact, barring Mr 1958, although that was almost certainly a separate incident, a coincidence of location.

He didn't say it out loud but made a mental note that he and Penfold should meet with Maid Marion again to quiz her on whether these men might have worked together in some sort of collective. The breakdown of that kind of loose affiliation might well lead to murder if they found something valuable, which at this point sounded like it could be St Cuthbert's Treasure. Tony wondered what that treasure might actually consist of. If it existed at all. Certainly, the Constable of the Cathedral had told Aria it was nonsense – just a legend. *But the yardstick of gold?*

Gerard interrupted his thoughts. 'Well, that's John Bowline finished. Cause of death was blunt force trauma to the occipital region.' He mimed, pretending to bang his fist into the back of Jan's skull.

Dr Sedgley asked, 'Is that rock the murder weapon?'

'You're on mute.' Gerard laughed, and Tony launched his finger to the button to enable the microphone.

She asked again, and this time, Gerard said, 'Can't say for sure. The shape of the wound is roughly consistent. We found no stone trace visibly in it, but Jan's got some samples of the skull tissue to look at under the microscope. I think if the bloods match, it would be a sensible conclusion to make that the rock caused the fatal injury.' As he spoke, he waved his hands around, pointing over to the evidence bag with the rugby ball rock in it, and then back to the corpse. 'However, I can't confirm it's murder. The scene photos look that way, but that kind of answer is beyond the concluding power of my pm evidence.'

Tony and Sedgley squeezed back out of the viewing pod and met Gerard on the threshold of the pathology suite.

She said, 'OK, I'll chase up all the forensic testing this has generated, but I'm not sure what else we might be able to do to help.'

'No, indeed, it's just a Gordian knot of loose ends.'

Gerard frowned. 'Can you have a Gordian knot of loose ends?'

They all laughed, and Tony replied, 'You can now! And I'm going to need to go and find a Penfold-shaped sword to try and cut them, so I'll have to leave you to Billy Muckle.'

Gerard's eyebrows raised.

FOURTEEN

At 9 a.m. CSI Johnson's black truck crunched across the gravel to park in front of the grand main entrance of the Bowes Museum. Diane Meredith had coerced him into giving her a lift down from Durham City to Barnard Castle and the two emerged from the cab laughing.

The building was in the style of a French chateau, built at the behest of the Francophile John Bowes to be a public art gallery. Long, zigzag stone staircases led down from the front terrace, but after briefly admiring the sunlit ornamental gardens below, Diane and Alfie turned back to head inside.

They were met just inside the revolving door by Alejandra Carrera. Known as Alex, she was chief curator of the museum. The place had been locked up after the school fire next door so that the crime scene investigator could attend to the scene of the stolen Swan as soon as possible.

She had put off Franks until ten in the morning. Mortified about her presence there during such an incredible robbery, Diane wanted to get ahead on this case, before having to give her statement.

Ms Carrera spoke English with the accent of a person whose first language was Spanish. She wore a blue linen suit, and her dark hair fell to the collar of the jacket. She was taller than Diane, who stared around the magnificent lobby – built in the same large stone blocks as the outside of the building.

Without any preamble beyond a brisk 'Good morning', Alex bustled them up a stone staircase with a rust-coloured carpet at least three metres wide, past the first landing and on up to the second floor. As she marched, several stairs ahead, Diane looked at the woman's long, athletic calves with a little envy. The suit's skirt came to her knees, and her legs were bare down to a pair of

Adidas street pumps in a matching blue colour. Just above her right ankle bone, and also colour matched, was a tattoo of a dolphin in outline, a naive line drawing.

When they arrived in a small outer gallery, the wooden floorboards were covered in large muddy footprints, a real dance of feet going backwards and forwards to a lift in the back corner. Their host waved them towards a larger gallery visible through a wide double doorway. The interior of the room was vast but, apart from a lot of old paintings on the far wall, all Diane could see through the door was a grand piano and a big glass cube like a transparent cell.

'Wait!' Alfie held out his hand in a Stop signal and the two women froze. He used the same hand to indicate the footprints. 'I take it the crime scene is in this gallery, is it?'

Alex nodded, mute. She appeared stunned by his commanding tone.

'We need to preserve all this evidence. Can we all step back please to the top of the staircase.'

'I need to show you where they took the Swan. The display case is in here to the left.'

The Spanish curator took a step forward, and Johnson commanded more loudly, 'STOP!'

'Please, Alex, is it OK if I call you Alex? Can we go back to where Alfie said and talk there for a minute. Alfie, will you go to the truck and get some stepping stones so that we can get into the gallery and have a look?'

He raced back down the double staircases, and Diane began quizzing Alex. She hadn't been working the previous day but had spent several hours that evening searching around the building in the vain hope that the Silver Swan had just been moved for safekeeping from the fire, and to look for potential clues.

She had only been in the job for four months and really emphasised to Diane how she was terribly afraid for her job, and for the fact that she had not yet implemented better security measures, despite having spotted several flaws in the museum's set-up. One of the main reasons for hiring her had been her background in Spanish galleries, which was focussed as much on security as it was on conservation and art history. She continuously scratched the back of one hand with her long nails.

Diane tried to be as reassuring as possible, without committing to anything, and was inwardly concerned about the way the crime scene had been compromised by Alex's amateur sleuthing.

Alfie rolled out a long plastic sheet to form a walkway along the landing, through the small outer gallery and then into the main Swan gallery, all the way across to the piano. He laid out a much bigger square sheet to give them a way to walk to the large square wooden plinth that, until the previous day, had held the Swan sculpture.

The mud on the floor was dry and now interspersed with a series of plastic stepping stones. He would photograph all the shoeprints later.

The rectangular wooden plinth had a flat top at about waist height and was two metres long by a metre wide. It was painted in a simple beige with a thin skirting board at its base. It would have been perfect to show off a glittering and intricate silver sculpture.

Behind it stood a much taller rectangular box with four glass sides and a beige wood top with a coving piece that matched the plinth. It would exactly cover the plinth so that visitors could have clearly seen the now absent Swan without being able to touch it.

Diane pushed against the glass box slightly, then a bit harder, and then put her shoulder to it. 'My God, that's incredibly heavy.'

Ms Carrera just nodded and then the radio clipped to her waist crackled into life. 'Alex, I think you need to see this. Are the police with you now?'

She grabbed it and replied into the tiny microphone, 'Yes, we'll be there in a minute.' She lowered the radio and said, 'That's our head of security. He's been looking through the CCTV footage.' She held her hand forward to point Diane back along Alfie's plastic pathway.

He was squatting, already rummaging around in a big grey toolbox he had brought along. 'You go and look at that and I'll get cracking with fingerprinting.'

The curator took a couple of steps and paused. 'We have visitors pressing on the glass all the time. We do clean it every day, but we had many visitors yesterday before the evacuation.'

Alfie looked up at her with a smile. 'I figured as much. My thinking is to see if I can get any prints from right along the bottom of the glass there.' He pointed to where the glass wall rested on the wooden floor. 'The thieves would have needed to lift it from the bottom. At ankle height, no visitor would touch it there. I hope.'

'Ah, good, OK. Thank you so much for what you are doing.'

They descended beyond the grand lobby and on down into the basement. This was very much the bowels of the building, with cupboards and storage space, and Alex led Diane into a security office with several computers whose screens were showing the camera feeds from both inside and out.

A gruff man in a dark suit sat in an office chair at the main desk. He operated the technology to show them four camera views from the previous afternoon, simultaneously on four screens. 'I told you this would happen,' he said without looking away from the screens.

They watched as a fire crew of six men, fully suited up with gas masks and oxygen tanks entered the back door of the museum. This entrance was on the side closest to the school building fire. The men proceeded up the trade staircase and passed the lift Diane had seen earlier, before they streamed into the piano gallery and moved right up to the glass case containing the Swan sculpture.

'What do you mean?' Diane asked.

He pressed a key to pause playback. On screen the Silver Swan looked as if it was in quarantine and the group of men had arrived in full hazmat protection. The seated man swivelled around to look at the two standing ladies.

'I told her not to move our baby from the machines gallery into that big space. It was impossible to remove the glass case where we had it before.'

Alex retorted, 'It was impossible for people to see her too. That squashed up corner could not get more than eight visitors around it at once.'

'That's why it was put there. So nobody could make off with her.'

'No, that is why the thick glass case is there.' The curator's accent grew stronger as she became agitated.

'And look how well that worked out.'

Diane's eyes flicked left and right as the arguments batted back and forth. She asked, 'What security was in place yesterday? Do you have anyone guarding the galleries as standard?'

'You police?'

'DC Diane Meredith from Durham Major Crimes Team'. She pulled out her warrant card to confirm the introduction. 'And you are?'

'Teesdale. David Teesdale, head of security here.'

'Teesdale? Really?'

'I know, don't start. I'm not even from here – I live in Penrith.'

She gave a friendly chuckle. 'Alright, what about guards in the galleries then?'

The security officer leant back in the chair. 'Like I told Sergeant Franks, we should have had four docents patrolling, but with the fire, they evacuated. Which is protocol, but they're supposed to lock the place up.'

Diane nodded approvingly to try and impart empathy with the man's situation – she wanted him onside to gather as much information as possible. 'And did somebody forget that?'

He shook his head. 'Apparently, they were fooled by these bullshit Richmond firemen. They insisted that they might need to get more water from hydrants they said were in here. There's hoses and extinguishers here, but we don't have anything inside that would be any use to a fire engine outside.'

'Oh. Did you not tell them that?'

'I don't work Sundays, and the folks who were here yesterday either didn't know or got confused in all the chaos. They were busy trying to argue the toss with arsey visitors who didn't want to evacuate when they'd paid for their tickets.'

Diane pushed the obsequiousness envelope. 'So have you run security here for a long time?'

'Yep. Been in charge here nearly twenty years.' He hung a pause before adding a bit of needle. 'And we've never lost anything in that time. Last theft here was the jewelled mouse, but that was thirty years ago, before I started. Nothing stolen on my watch.'

Diane sighed slightly to further her sympathy with their loss. 'Until now.'

'Well, no. Until Miss-I-Know-Everything-And-I'm-Going-To-Change-All-The-Security-Procedures rewrites every policy we've got.' He turned his head to Alex. 'I told you we couldn't keep everything safe with you pushing it all into the open.' He turned back to Diane. 'You know she's put half the collection outside cases so people can literally touch things. Some of this stuff is so small you could easily just pocket it.'

'And I told you to keep the gallery doors closed so they have to pass one of the staff to … to …' Alex's voice cracked as she stumbled to find the English word for *exit*. 'To … salir.'

He shook his head again, this time slowly, emphasising exasperation at his new boss's folly. 'And I told you that, in this country, closing all those doors is against the fire code.'

The DC had heard enough of this fractious relationship. 'OK, look, you two can argue about security procedures later. For now, we need to find out who did this, so let's see the video please.'

In a well-co-ordinated movement, the six burly firemen on the small screen worked together to lift the glass case vertically and shuffle it past the Swan on her plinth to put it down where Diane had earlier tried to shove it.

She said, 'Bloody hell, I tried to push that case earlier and I couldn't move it. What do you reckon it weighs?'

Without a pause, the security man replied, '378 kilograms. It's attack resistant triple-ply glass with the middle layer being polymer. You couldn't get through it with an axe, but of course ...' He emphasised his complaint again. '... if you put it in a big space ... you can just lift it away to get the Swan.'

'Well, I'm not sure about "just" lift it away, but it looks like six big firemen together were able to.'

He shook his head again and swivelled back to talk directly to her. 'They're not firemen. This is all a scam.'

'How do you know?'

'Check out the rest.' Teesdale pressed the play button again but looked at Diane and Alex, as they watched the four screens he'd teed up to show the footage from different cameras. The suited firefighters covered the Silver Swan in sackcloth and carefully carried her away from the piano gallery and down the back staircase to the door by their fire truck.

At the vehicle, the entire back end opened, with a ramp down. Two men sidled up, cradling the sackcloth booty, into a big space hidden behind the main body of the truck.

The remaining four wound the hoses on to the side of the truck, jumped in and drove off. She'd seen them fight the flames from over the stone wall for nearly an hour, but in the end, the heist had taken less than three minutes and Diane had been standing less than twenty metres away.

'She only weighs thirty kilos on her own, including the silvery pond with the fish. One man could carry the entire thing, although all the mechanism's pretty delicate, so two of them took her to be gentle.'

Diane was nodding now. 'And of course, the PPE they're wearing is a complete disguise.'

He nodded. 'Yep, bunker gear will you get you in anywhere when there's a fire, and nobody knows who you are. And nobody asks.'

Diane turned to Alex, who was pouting at the screen. 'Where were you yesterday? I don't remember seeing you in the staff group I met.'

'My job is Monday to Friday. I was at home.'

Teesdale needled some more. 'I warned you we needed a senior person here every day.'

'But you wouldn't work Sundays, would you.'

The volume of his voice went up a notch. 'I work every Saturday, and the previous chief curator worked Sundays, but you won't work weekends at all. And, conveniently, you organise the rotas.'

'Alright, enough. Can you put all that footage on to this memory stick for me?' Diane flourished a flash drive and pulled out an evidence bag.

While the computer was copying, it was agreed that Sergeant Franks would be tasked with going down to Richmond to investigate the suspect fire engine that had been badged with the livery of the North Yorkshire Fire Brigade.

They found Alfie wrapping up his work and the plastic sheeting he'd laid. The three headed back down, and out into the heat of another sunny July day. With a quick goodbye to the disconsolate curator, Diane bounded up into the passenger side of his big vehicle.

FIFTEEN

Meredith arrived back in Durham City police station with moments to spare before Harry Hardwick's Monday morning media briefing. The press conference had been scheduled ostensibly to give information about the bodies that had been found, but mostly H wanted to appeal to the public to stop visiting abandoned mines and getting themselves killed.

As the DCI started the briefing, Diane was in the ladies' toilets, adding some touches of make-up. Nothing over the top, just enough to ensure her TV appearance was a complete contrast to the anachronistic old chief inspector.

For the purposes of the media briefing, H had also been temporarily promoted, to Acting Detective Superintendent, but as a result he tripped over his self-introduction. His delivery was much smoother after that, beginning with the basic information that four bodies had been discovered down mineshafts within a few miles of Durham.

He explained that Durham City Major Crimes Team were maintaining control of the investigation as the first two bodies had been close to the city, and all the deaths had sufficient similarity that it would be most efficient for the same team to look at the evidence in all cases. He was slippery about the exact causes of death, and coy about whether or not the men had been murdered.

He did admit they were all men, though – the force's media officer had trained him well to give out some details that would give journalists something to write, while maintaining confidentiality about as much information as possible. He expertly muddied the waters around the question of murder with the phrase "ongoing confirmatory investigations".

H pre-empted the most obvious question by announcing that the identities would not be made public yet, as two were unconfirmed and the families of the other two were still being "supported by specially trained officers". This was a euphemism that could be interpreted as "give the families some time and space and privacy please" but could later be explained as having meant "we're still investigating these deaths".

After the initial slip about his rank, Tony was impressed by H's presentation. It all went downhill from there though. The second part of the media briefing was a further presentation by Hardwick about the perils of entering old mine workings.

He came across as patronising, almost hectoring, while at the same time building up the intrigue surrounding the whole business. By the end, Tony himself was so fascinated about what was going on in Durham's old pits that he too wanted to go and explore.

He stood beside the boss, with Meredith on his other side. They looked at each other and Tony could tell she was thinking the same thing about the prospects of people not heading out to find old pits to climb into. She whispered, 'Let me salvage this.'

He didn't know what she had in mind but was keen for H to stop speaking. When H paused to take a breath, Tony jumped in and introduced 'DC Diane Meredith with more information'.

She was the exact contrast to Hardwick that was needed. Meredith's narrative described going out to find one of the bodies. She was light on exact details and heavy on the harrowing nature of finding somebody unnecessarily dead down a rocky shaft in a lonely field. She bravely held back crocodile tears and described the anguish and shock of the deceased's poor wife. The story was exaggerated or elements glossed over to most effectively emphasise the senseless, unnecessary loss of life and why nobody should put themselves and their families at risk of the same sort of fate.

Tony was pleased that the running order meant people would only remember the parts about avoiding mineshafts. Or, more likely, the TV editors would cut out the growly old man and only air clips of the pretty young detective, so bravely helping people with no thought for the impact the job must be having on her own wellbeing.

That running order was scheduled to conclude with him, as SIO, answering questions from the journalists. This was the trickier part as he was going to need to be elusive about some areas, such as IDs and the gory details. He had learnt many press conferences ago that the most effective and convincing way to approach this was to front up to it.

He answered the first question. 'I'm sorry, Mr Gullon, but as this is an ongoing, live investigation, I can't give out those details. Some parts of what I would say have not yet been confirmed by the forensics and pathology teams, and some parts might identify the victims' families, which we are not prepared to do. I'm sorry to ask you to wait, but you understand that there are timely processes we must follow.'

The questioner would not be put off so easily. 'Are you saying that these deaths could be criminal?'

'I'm not commenting on the nature of the investigations, sorry. There are many ways people come to die, and we have to investigate all of them with impartiality, and sometimes maintaining impartiality requires us to withhold information initially. As you well know in your line of business.' Tony smiled as he said this last sentence.

A man standing at the back had a newsprint lanyard but was also video recording the press conference. He called out, 'Can you tell us about the theft of the Silver Swan from Bowes Museum?'

A buzz raised among the dozen assembled reporters. This was news to them, and it was a big scoop if true.

103

'I can't. I know there was a fire at the school next door yesterday but as far as we are aware there were no casualties from that. That is, of course, a matter for Barnard Castle police to investigate anyway.'

Tony's distraction subterfuge did not suffice for the questioner. He persisted, 'I know there were no injuries, but I'm talking about the Silver Swan. A priceless sculpture, made from thirty kilograms of silver, gone missing, while police and fire crews were in attendance. I believe DC Meredith was on site. What can you tell our readers about that?'

Meredith stepped forward. She wiped her eye in a manner Tony thought might be just a bit too melodramatic to survive the sceptics in the room. 'You're right, I was in the area yesterday morning and when I heard the call on the radio, I just had to stop and help out with the fire. They weren't sure if there were any children in the boarding house at the time, so we all imagined the worst. Luckily, as it turned out, there were no injuries, as DI Milburn has already said.

'However, as I understand it, the smoke was significant and even penetrated the Bowes Museum. Have they've moved the Swan down to the conservation rooms in the basement in order to check that none of its workings were damaged? I really don't know any details, I'm afraid. I'm just glad everyone was safe.'

She put a hand to her heart to emphasise her relief, and Tony again worried it was too excessively dramatic to fly. He seemed to be the only one, though, who was not snowed by her theatrics. There was an audible sigh of relief from those present as they were carried along by her tale. Except the man at the back who had asked the question. He gave a little frown and said nothing.

By this point, the media representatives were becoming restless. They could tell that the best parts of the briefing had finished, and Tony could see a couple of them gathering their things together to leave. One of the local TV news camerawomen was pressing buttons on her machine, which Tony guessed was reviewing the footage taken, and was thus no longer listening to him. Which was a state of affairs the detective inspector was happy with.

He wrapped things up, thanking, but at the same time dismissing, the attendees. He felt that they should give the press conference's mission – to discourage people from investigating old mine workings – further emphasis to finish it off. He needed a soundbite to make sure that was the main message that got through, but the journalists were on their feet, likely to press Stop on their cameras at any second.

Without thinking it through, Tony blurted out a six-word story Penfold had sent him in the small hours. 'Please everybody, stay away from old mine workings. Remember: a fool and his brain are soon parted.'

The audience reacted with a little surprise, but appeared generally positive, their facial expressions suggesting this soundbite could well make either the text or the video versions of their final story.

As he replayed it in his mind, Tony wondered if he'd given away too much information about the nature of the deaths being investigated. His own brain, though, overrode any sensible analysis with the sudden insistence that he count up the words to realise that there were eight, not the classic six.

The newly promoted Acting Superintendent Hardwick collared Tony as they walked upstairs from the media room. H invited him to head to his office, right at the top of the stairs, to recap on the planning for the Miners' Gala.

In the stuffy office, he started with a quick check that DI Barnes's planning documents were all clear and appropriate and that Tony's Friday meeting with Barry Black had gone smoothly.

After some flustered mutterings, in which Tony essentially claimed that all was in hand, H asked what the shipping containers were all about.

'I know, yes, I saw them delivering those to the Market Place yesterday.'

'Market Place? I'm talking about the things up on Palace Green. I was meeting with the vice chancellor of the university in Castle yesterday. There's three dirty great things on the grass up there. I tell you, the VC is not happy at all about us not running that past her first. They own the land you know.'

Tony held his tongue. He had not been involved in any of the planning and thus far had not spotted the information about the storage containers in Barnes's documents. He wondered what he was supposed to do but held back from articulating this. Hardwick was clearly on a roll and would continue anyway.

'What are they doing with the containers? I mean they've got the Miners' Gala logo on them, so they must be in the plans. What are they storing up there? Is it banners or something? I thought the bands and union chapters all carried their banners up to the cathedral in the procession.' He then left an uncomfortable pause for Tony to answer.

'Um, sorry, guv. I've been flat out, but the documentation runs to probably a hundred pages, and I haven't come across any of those answers yet. I'll make it the first thing I look for when I get back to my desk.'

'Yes, make sure you do.' Hardwick did not actually "Harumph" but the implication was clear from his tone. Tony had said all the right things so his boss couldn't dress him down, even though both men knew he was stretching the truth.

'Penfold reckons they smell of lemons, so I've no idea what they're actually storing.'

'Penfold? What's he got to do with it?'

Tony knew the game was up. He'd been wanting to avoid this showdown with H, but it was inevitable, so this was probably as good a time as any. 'As SIO, I've appointed him as a consultant on the mineshaft deaths. We walked past those containers – actually there's one on Old Elvet Bridge, that's the one that smells of lemons – on our way back from meeting with a … witness … a woman who knows all about the treasure hunting fraternity.'

Hardwick's brow furrowed as he processed the notion of a woman in a fraternity, but the DCI was too long in the tooth to be distracted. He came back to the point about hiring a surfer as a police "investigating consultant". 'You're on dangerous ground with that one, Tony. He doesn't follow procedure and you'll be on a really sticky wicket if you lose any convictions because of that. I've told you repeatedly not to involve him. I gave you the acting-up promotion because needs must, and because you deserve it, but you won't deserve it for long if you mess this up. I warn you, Penfold will mess this up.'

With his mouth held in a calm flat line, Tony shook his head and then replied. 'Harry, we've always seen Penfold in different lights. You gave me the authority to take on who I want to, who I need to, and you're going to have to accept my judgement on who I ask to work with us. The one thing you cannot deny is that several times over the years, Penfold has helped us out on complex and confusing cases, and always, always, sees through the fog and spots the right answers. And he won't take any money, so it won't even tax our budget at all.'

'That's what I'm most afraid of. If he messes up, we have no comeback. We can't fire him coz he doesn't work for us, and we can't blacklist him because he's never promised us anything for certain. I tell you, Tony, you're on dodgy ground, and I don't want your career to be taken down because of his arrogant bravado.'

Tony could see arrogant bravado in his Kiwi friend, but he was confident that Penfold was a better investigator than Hardwick understood. They would have to agree to disagree.

SIXTEEN

Jeanette Compton walked across the grass on Palace Green, past three shipping containers brightly painted with scenes from Durham Miners' Galas gone by. Banners flapping, VIPs on the balcony of the Royal County Hotel, a marching brass band, a crowd listening to Nye Bevan on stage on the Racecourse – she examined the murals in detail.

Each picture was signed off in the bottom right with the Durham Miners' Gala logo and Jeanette checked her old-fashioned wristwatch for the date. The Big Meeting was not her sort of thing, and it often passed her by without her even noticing. As a researcher and archivist for Durham Constabulary, Jeanette may well have known more than most people about the Miners' Gala, she just didn't really pay attention to its actual happening.

Detective Inspector Milburn – he was rolling the title around in his mind with a smile on his face – walked up Dun Cow Lane right beside the cathedral, fresh from the city police station and his meeting with DCI Hardwick. Also walking up a cobbled wynd – Owengate – at the opposite end of Palace Green, Penfold carried a takeaway coffee from the Daily Espresso.

They converged on Jeanette as she perused the artwork on the front end of one of the shipping containers. 'They look great,' Tony said. 'The ones in the marketplace only have the logo on. These pictures are glorious.'

Jeanette pivoted round to see the two men arrive. She was quiet and reserved, and it surprised Tony when she used a hand to cover her nose and blurted out, 'Is one of you wearing some terrible cologne?' She looked directly at Penfold. 'Or is that some sort of surfer's suncream with the overpowering smell?'

Penfold stood unfazed, dark black sunglasses hiding anything his eyes might have said. 'Citronella. It's the containers – we smelled the same thing from the one on Elvet Bridge.'

Tony jumped in. 'Eugh. My sense of smell is poor, but that's really bad. Smells like those lemony urinal fresheners. I wonder what they've got in these things.' He paused, looking at the banner procession mural highlighting pitmen's unions, and then pointed at a banner in the picture. 'Do those things need some sort of storage protection like mothballs, maybe? Mothballs smell pretty strong, don't they?'

Penfold smiled. 'You know what? In all my life, I've never come across real live mothballs. Always heard of them as a thing but never needed them or been anywhere that has them.'

Jeanette shook her head and just said, 'Men.' She was in a really outgoing mood that morning.

'Shall we?' Penfold indicated towards the beautiful old oak door of the Palace Green branch of the university library. Above their heads, the single storey frontage was topped with castellations – architecture in keeping with the neighbouring castle and cathedral.

Inside the old stone building, Tony's girlfriend Kathy was chatting with a colleague behind the big reception desk. She came out and greeted them, with an ushering hand signal into the main reference library area, and they stood around a large desk she had reserved for them.

Kathy's hair was tied up in a functional ponytail, matching Jeanette's darker but identical hairstyle, and both were dressed for business, unlike Penfold who had turned up in his usual surf T-shirt and cargo shorts. It was cooler inside the pre-Victorian building, but he was probably the most sensibly dressed for the hot weather. Tony was sweating underneath a smart black suit jacket.

Tony explained to the others more detail about the research activity he'd teed up with Kathy at home the previous evening.

In fact, he handed over proceedings to Penfold, who had requested the library access and the help of Miss Compton.

Tallest of the four, Penfold invited them all to sit down. He proceeded to outline the investigation into the four mineshaft deaths and summarised the information they had about the men and the treasure hunting, as best they knew it so far. He had produced a printed sheet of bullet points for each person, so that they had all the details organised in the order and manner that Penfold considered most useful.

For Kathy and Tony the sheet was mostly for information, as it was to be Jeanette and Penfold who were to spend the afternoon researching, with a strong emphasis on St Cuthbert's Treasure. Since 1948, the cathedral's archive had been in the care of Durham University Library, and the sort of old records that might be of use were kept in the special collections on Palace Green.

Kathy held up her hand to interrupt Penfold's flow. 'You know the cathedral archive has four hundred and twenty-two metres of document shelving?'

He nodded. 'Indeed, but we're mostly aiming to start with early twentieth century stuff, which I believe is fairly well catalogued, no?'

She nodded cautiously, obviously aware that she was going to be the one who would have to go and find any documents they requested. Her response was drawn out, indicating her scepticism about how easy finding documents was, given the cathedral's thousand years of history. 'OK, but what sort of thing exactly?'

Jeanette listened, rapt, as Penfold answered. He indicated a couple of bullet points towards the bottom of his list. 'I'd like to start with finding out the connection between this Castle Eden Brewery drayman and the Constable of the Cathedral during the Second World War. If we can get more information on the drayman's movements, or connection here, we might find out why, or how, he was involved in moving the treasures off site to hide them.'

Tony was intrigued to watch how this exercise would play out. The other three were all extreme, high-calibre intellectuals, and he hoped that this would work in their favour to create an unstoppable research monster. He feared a clash of minds that would all want to go off in different directions. He didn't get to find out though, as Penfold sent him to the cathedral to interrogate the current Constable about his role and that of his predecessors, in order to find out about the wartime safekeeping of precious items.

As he headed for the exit, Tony could hear Penfold and Jeanette thriving in each other's company, working in unison, making a prioritised list of requests to Kathy for documents to pull out from the archives.

Crossing the tarmac corner of Palace Green, Tony baked in its radiated heat. He pulled off his jacket and slung it over a shoulder.

Two cathedral volunteers, clad in Durham's purple robes, met him at the entrance lobby, where they accosted all visitors and tried to point them towards the donations desk. Tony flashed his warrant card and asked to meet with the Constable of the Cathedral. They named a man called Stan Willem, and the oldest of the volunteers – eighty if she was a day – called through to the main office for him, on a handheld radio.

'He'll meet you by the astronomical clock. Do you know where that is?'

He nodded and pointed along the huge nave, past several patterned stone columns the size of ancient oak trunks. 'By the entrance to the cathedral tower stairs, right?'

'Yes, that's right, pet. Wait under the clock face and Stan will meet you in a few minutes.'

His feet clacked on the stone floor as Tony strode along the nave. The place had few visitors at lunchtime on a weekday, so

111

he felt less self-conscious than he might have done making so much noise in a peaceful sanctuary. Turning right underneath the immense central tower, his footsteps were quieter on the large square of black and white tiles at the building's very heart. He passed the intricately carved marble pulpit and headed into the South Transept.

Tony wasn't sure quite where to wait, but he was happy to spend a few minutes admiring the medieval clock. The thing was quite beautiful. It stood four or five metres high on tall wooden pillars, sporting a delightfully ornate clock face with smaller dials, including one showing the phase of the moon. All the paintwork was bright and colourful, as if the latest restoration had been very recent.

Underneath the big clock, the wall was painted with a trompe l'oeil mural. At least it looked like the wall, until one part of the mural opened and a tall man walked through the hidden door. He stepped over and extended his hand. 'How can I help, officer.'

'Ah, good morning, er, afternoon.' Tony was thrown by the similarities between the Constable of the Cathedral and his absent colleague, DI Godolphin Barnes. He wouldn't have mistaken the two, but Stan Willem had a lolloping gait that utterly put Tony in mind of Barnes. 'I'm Detective Inspector Tony Milburn.'

'Yes.'

'I'm Senior Investigating Officer on a case looking into some mysterious deaths that have been discovered in the last few days. I'm hoping you can help me with some background as to why the men may have been at the locations where we found their bodies.'

'Yes.' Willem seemed to be as difficult to engage in conversation as Barnes.

'Can you explain the role of the Constable of the Cathedral?'

'Ah, I can't help you with your investigations I'm afraid.' At first, Tony thought the man was being obstructive, and he couldn't fathom out why that would be. However, Willem had just left a very long pause, before he broke into a forced laugh and followed up with, 'Not that sort of constable at all.'

The detective smiled along with the odd humour and nodded benignly. 'Ha, no, of course. No, we've come across some information about how one of your predecessors, back in the forties, hid some of the cathedral's treasures as a security measure in case of a Nazi invasion. We think that may be linked to these recent deaths, so I'm hoping you could shed some light on this hidden treasure.'

His face became suddenly dark, and Willem answered, 'Oh no, sorry, there's no information about that.'

'You seem terribly sure. Would it be possible to check your records to be certain?'

'It won't help. We get researchers in here regularly, both academics and amateurs, all chasing St Cuthbert's Treasure. It's nothing more than legend, a fantasy. I told your colleague all this last week.'

'I know the evidence is pretty circumstantial, but there seem to be a lot of indirect pointers to it.' Tony wasn't convinced that this was actually true, but he was probing to try and garner more insight about the Constable's unwillingness to assist. Something felt off to his detective senses, but he couldn't identify exactly what. He was worried that it might just be that the man's similarities to Godolphin were making him seem evasive when it was, in fact, his normal demeanour.

'I can assure you, officer, there's nothing. My best guess is that the Constable back then put about the story of hiding the treasures so that any German invaders, or looters, would go looking elsewhere, outside the city. The cathedral itself has many, many hidden nooks and crannies where we could have hidden any treasures we wanted to keep safe.'

A moment of clarity pointed Tony to the source of his concerns: Willem had never engaged eye contact. He was tall but stared into the space over Tony's head in an unnecessarily avoiding manner. Even DI Barnes would look at you when he spoke; he looked down at you, but that was more about his supercilious nature than his height. Mr Willem seemed ill at ease, and it wasn't clear if this was a personality trait, or something else.

He concluded their meeting, looking at the wall behind Tony. 'There is no treasure to be found, and those foolish enough to go looking for it are not the cathedral's responsibility. We want no connection with their activities, and we are not responsible for their deaths.'

The slightly strange turn of the conversation, both in tone and somewhat odd phraseology, perplexed Tony, but he put it down to Stan Willem's awkwardness.

The cool of the great monument had been a respite, and Tony felt the heat intensify as he walked back across the short distance to the Palace Green Library. After reporting to Penfold that there was actually nothing to report from the weaselly man, he headed back to leave them to it and stole a few minutes' chat with Kathy.

She was agog at the working relationship between Jeanette and Penfold. 'They're extraordinary!'

'I know. Didn't I tell you?'

'I've never seen anything like it. They finish each other's sentences and know what the other will say before they say it. She pulled out the right sheet from a document as he was in mid-sentence and handed it to him at the end of the sentence, and it wasn't that he'd asked for it specifically, he'd asked for something that could show him a particular answer. So, she knew the question and how to find the answer before he'd finished the question. It's like they're telepathic.'

Tony just nodded, raising his eyebrows in agreement.

'Do you think there's anything going on between them?' She was a newshound for gossip.

'I've teased him about it regularly, but he just ignores me and moves on to talk about something else. And she simply isn't the sort of woman I'd feel comfortable asking about that sort of thing. Or teasing about it.'

Kathy was in her element, grinning like a schoolgirl at the thought of the gossip. 'I know. She seems like such a formal, mousy sort.' She put her hand on Tony's arm and giggled. 'It doesn't bear thinking about!'

He smiled. 'Stop! Look, I'm going to leave before you say something that embarrasses both of us!'

'I think you embarrass more easily than I do!'

'I know I do.' He kissed her quickly and headed out into the heat for the short walk back across the high pedestrian bridge to the city police station.

SEVENTEEN

The tide was high and, for much of the mile long beach at Seaton Carew, the waves lapped against the sea wall. Promenade Square, where Penfold's rambling old house stood in the furthest corner from the actual promenade, marked the point where the beach started to curve. Here, at the southern end, even at high tide, a wide spread of sand separated the beach road from the water's edge.

Tony leant against the railing and watched Penfold's arms powering his surfboard across the briny foam where a wave had just broken. The New Zealander had effortlessly ducked under the overhanging wave crest and popped up behind, in newly formed white water. The next wave slid towards him, bulging the surface higher and higher, and he turned and windmilled his arms through the water again.

Unconsciously, Tony's body tautened, and he leant slightly further forward, willing his friend's pace to increase. Penfold arched his back in what a yoga teacher would call the Cobra pose, face straining up towards the bright, lowering sun.

Before Tony even realised it was happening, the surfer's feet were underneath his body flat on the surface of the board. He whizzed along the front of the wave's vertical face, outrunning the point that curled over and crashed down, continuously nipping at the tail of his white and black board.

Tony estimated that the overall height of the wave, from the lowest point where the water started to bulge up, right up to the narrow peak, was about the same height as the Kiwi. He was clad from neck to ankle in black neoprene, but in the hot summertime, he could forego boots, gloves and the winter hood.

Seconds after catching the wave, he flew up its face and launched himself vertically up and over its back, diving neatly into the next batch of sparse foam.

This seemed to be the concluding ride, as Penfold proceeded to paddle back to shore, repeatedly gaining a boost as each wave caught up with and passed him. Tony wandered down the wide stone staircase to the golden sand, which glared infra-red heat radiation at him after a whole day of baking. He had changed into boardshorts, T-shirt and flip-flops and wondered if Penfold would even recognise a detective in surfer's clothes.

'Ah, Milburn, you fancy having a go at last?' Penfold dropped the board to the sand and bent down to rip off the Velcro holding his leg leash onto his ankle. This he proffered to Tony.

Tony laughed. 'I think that's a definite case of old dog, no new tricks, I'm afraid.' What he was actually afraid of was being knocked about and hurled under the water by what were scarily large breakers.

Penfold nodded sagely and said, 'An old dog will definitely learn no new tricks if we don't try and teach it any. But you're probably right, for a first go at surfing those waves are far too large. I'd hate to have to explain your drowning to Hardwick.' As he said this, he tugged at the long string hanging down from the back of his neck, pulling the wetsuit's zip down to the small of his back.

'Yes, let's not do that.'

Penfold had an enormous beach towel, in a similar turquoise to the seaside railings that Tony had leant against a few minutes earlier. It sported the logo of Surfers Against Sewage, the very thought of which always made Tony shudder, and he was again pleased that he did not have any desire to head into the North Sea himself.

The towel made a cursory journey over Penfold's head and was then laid out neatly for them both to sit on and stare at the waves. Several minutes of silence followed as Tony revelled in

117

the sunshine, and Penfold stared back at the ceaseless surf. His eyes flicked along the length of each cresting wave, sizing up the possibilities for turns and speed changes.

Tony couldn't help but tease his friend about the tension in the air between him and Jeanette Compton earlier that afternoon. He hadn't actually noticed any tension, but he kept up this suggestion in order to maintain his portrayal that the two were attracted to each other but were denying themselves, and for no particularly good reason given that both were single.

'What makes you think she's single?' Penfold was nothing if not enigmatic.

'No ring.'

'Good Lord, Milburn, watching that press conference I would have put Hardwick down as the anachronism, but maybe it's you.' His hyperbole would often have Penfold exaggerate a public-school voice. The Northumberland boarding school of his youth had given him enough experience to parody a quintessential Englishman flawlessly.

'Oh, did you see it?'

'There were snippets on the local news just now. I tell you, there's nothing better in this world than the BBC. You tell me, though, how have you been getting on with Miss Meredith? She gave quite the performance – pretty much stole the show, I'd say.'

Tony felt his stomach clench. Just the thought of Diane's face had him reeling again. She was brilliant, beautiful and relentless. He felt genuinely afraid of her. Kathy and Tony had lived together for a few years, ever since they shook off Meredith's stalking, but she had never let him go completely. She was always popping up, sneaking her way into his life in a way that was unassailable.

H had been diplomatic and forceful at the same time, compelling her to move to a different station, and for the first year after that showdown, the worry had quietened. Her capability, though, was such that she quickly made it to detective

118

status, and that meant that she could push through her transfer back to the bigger nick in Durham City. With CID mostly subsumed by the work of the Major Crimes Team, she had essentially forced her way back into Tony's life by the back door.

Penfold was about the only person Tony could share these worries with. Even Kathy thought Meredith was simpler than she really was. Tony knew how her mind worked: she could play the very, very long game unfalteringly, and completely under everyone's radar.

'She scares me. I know she has a hidden agenda, a game plan, and it'll be a work of genius, and yet even I can't see the steps in it. She's just started seeing the new CSI, Alfie Johnson, and she has no qualms about telling me all the gory details. I tell her to stop oversharing, and she laughs it off, but of course she has never even mentioned their dates in the presence of others.'

'Why don't you record it?'

'Yeah, I did that before a couple of times and it did hold some water with Hardwick, but even then, what she says to me is never about me. I'd be recording a mildly unprofessional conversation, and it'll be my paranoia that gets the limelight again, not her.'

Penfold didn't respond out loud but nodded supportively. He changed the subject. 'Well, you had the last word on the news segment. I wonder how many fools need to lose their brains before the others take heed.'

'Oh, that made the final cut, did it? I assumed there wouldn't be enough time. Eight words mind you, not six. Can you even count?'

The surfer turned his head to look at Tony, and a small shower of seawater shook from the ends of his fringe. 'Not a six-word story, a reimagined proverb.'

'Answer for everything, eh?'

Penfold twisted his head slightly, pondering. He gave a quiet, chuckling snort. 'Not answers exactly, just facts.'

Tony knew he would get nowhere with this. 'How about coffee?' He stood up and held his arm out indicating up the beach for Penfold to lead the way. The surfer handed the towel to him, picked up his dripping board and balanced the leash over the upper edge so it wouldn't trail and trip them up.

The wet wetsuit had its top half rolled down around his waist, and its legs creaked with every step.

Walking barefoot across the road and along the fifty metres of pavement to his front door did not seem to bother Penfold, despite the fact that the sand, the asphalt and the paving slabs were all very hot, much hotter than the twenty-eight-degree air temperature.

They waved up the esplanade to Mantoro, who was walking a beast of a dog on a long lead. The man had immense black hair, as much of an Afro hairdo as is possible for a Latino. They say owners and their dogs look alike. Tony had never seen Mantoro with a dog previously, but this giant Newfoundland had the same kind of enormous shaggy hair that the short man sported. He asked about the dog and Penfold just shrugged.

He was ushered inside, ahead of his friend, to organise coffee, while Penfold wrestled off the wetsuit in the hallway. A jug of filter coffee sat piping hot on the kitchen counter, and Tony poured out two mugs. He added a bit of cold water to his to make it a drinkable temperature. Penfold needed no such niceties.

A saucer of cashew nuts on the kitchen counter indicated Mantoro's recent presence, and Tony pointed at it questioningly. He was angling for information about what Mantoro might have been doing in the house, but Penfold answered simply, 'Of course, help yourself.'

They descended into Penfold's basement, bright and white, the exact opposite of the sort of cellar one might expect in the Victorian rambling pile upstairs. They balanced on the bar stools at the huge central table, and Penfold started up a display screen on the side wall above the mass spectrometer. He was working from a laptop which was mirrored on the big screen for Tony.

'Trident sends her apologies that she can't join us this time, far too busy with manipulating the Bitcoin market, or some such nonsense that she finds entertaining. But she has sent me a summary of her findings about the social media machinations surrounding St Cuthbert's Treasure. Fascinating.'

'Great, do share.'

Now dressed in his standard outfit of T-shirt, combat shorts and sports sandals, his friend seemed unfathomably oblivious to temperature. Coming down the stairs they had seen a significant drop in temperature, despite all the machinery and servers in the basement. This was after entering the house, which was several degrees cooler than the blazing summer outside. It had been a blessing initially, but now Tony was cupping his coffee tightly trying to eke every little bit of warmth from it.

'Well, there's a fair bit out there on the standard socials, Facebook and Instagram and some, but not really that much, on X. There's a few Facebook groups about treasure hunting and mine exploration, but they've got very little that is consistently about St Cuthbert's Treasure, nor Durham really.'

'I thought you said it was "fascinating"?' Tony mimicked the Kiwi accent badly.

'Patience, Milburn, the good stuff is coming.' He paused to heighten the anticipation. 'The MaidMarionettes discussion forum is the main place where people are talking about Durham mine workings and the old drayman's diary, along with a ton of speculation about what might actually be in that treasure. So, Trident did her thing and found out some very interesting information about all these anonymous users on the forum. There's around thirty regular contributors on this topic. However, only ten or so are genuinely different people.'

'What?'

'There are numerous separate accounts that are actually the same contributor.'

'OK, how did she work that out? And why would anybody bother to do that?'

'Milburn, we've got four dead treasure hunters. We don't yet know the background reason for it, but somebody is clearly manipulating the narrative surrounding these valuables. The how might help us work out who that person is.'

'So, what was it, all from the same IP address?'

'No, no, IP address masking is simple. They're all from servers all over the country. Interestingly, two users are from Durham Cathedral's internet connection. They're not the main player, and parsing their messages with stylistic software suggests they're not the same person. I think the cathedral is just hyping up the Lindisfarne Gospels exhibition. That finishes on the eighteenth, so we reckon they're trying to get a big finish to the ticket sales, I suspect most people have already been to it.'

'Wait, the eighteenth? St Cuthbert's Friday no less. That it would finish then seems like a massive coincidence.' Tony looked Penfold in the eyes.

'I'm not so sure. It's the last day of the school term, and they're doing a bunch of kids' events over the summer, so I think it was just a good calendar moment to conclude. Probably the dates were dictated by the British Library anyway.'

Tony shook his head in disagreement. 'St Cuthbert's Friday. What bigger treasure is there than the Lindisfarne Gospels? There's got to be something in this.'

'I guess it's possible, both the anonymous users from the cathedral are the ones mentioning the Gospels. Their handles are TheDemonDafoe and HiddenTreasures.'

He laughed out loud. 'That's not anonymous! The cathedral's museum is called *Hidden Treasures*.' He stopped for a moment trying to picture the signboard in the cloisters. 'Isn't it?' Penfold was already shaking his head.

'You're thinking of *Open Treasure*, but they changed the name recently. Now it's the inspired and inspirational *Durham Cathedral Museum*.'

Tony looked into the dark liquid in his cup.

'Anyway, like I said, they're not the interesting one. You've got a bunch of others who seem to be legit, just chatting away about research they've done and mines they've visited. You'll remember IndyJones and RCA, and there's TheDetectorist, and LeapingDolphin. Maid Marion is in there busily curating things and connecting people with similar interests or ideas. And then there are nineteen personas that Trident has connected as all coming from the same device. Like I said, many IP addresses but all the messages have the same chip handshaking signature. Indisputably the same person.'

He had never heard of chip handshaking, but Tony could imagine that it would be some tech thing that Trident and few others could hack to identify computers or whatnot.

Penfold continued in a reverential tone, clearly impressed at his sister's research. 'She actually spotted that she should look for the connection by observing the timing of the messages. They've been scheduled using a fairly standard random number generator algorithm. She's got a piece of software that followed the gaps in the timings using a Poisson distribution correction – that's a statistics thing – based on the way people usually converse, and was able to predict in advance when the next two messages would be posted. Then it was a case of mopping up all the accounts that posted at the right time according to the algorithm, and the chip signatures were the corroborating confirmation.' He chuckled to himself. 'Simple, when you're Trident.'

The ins and outs of the process weren't of interest to Tony, and he pursued the thing that would help his investigation. 'So, who is it?'

'Ah ha, the sixty-four-thousand-dollar question. Don't know. The chip is the same all the time, but as the IP addresses are masked, we don't actually know where they are, or indeed who they are.'

They sat in silence for a few seconds mulling over where this led them. Tony piped up first. 'OK, what do the messages say?'

'That's another oddity. They're fairly bland and generic, pushing forward everybody's research about Saint Cuthbert's history and the finding of the treasure and the dynasty of Constables of the Cathedral, and dreaming about the value of the treasure and what a great find it would be. All plausible guff that the rest of the treasure hunters have been spouting too. I get the impression it's just hype.'

'But to what end?'

'Well, exactly! Maid Marion is a good source of information, the one called LeapingDolphin is pretty gung-ho, saying how many mines he's been down, and encouraging everyone to get out there and find the treasure. And then the two cathedral ones talk a lot about the Gospels, with TheDemonDafoe also sounding off about Saint Cuthbert's Curse. The one who's set up multi-accounts doesn't seem to have any particular direction. They don't even say things like "I can find you a buyer if you find the treasures". I just can't see what they're getting out of the whole subterfuge.'

EIGHTEEN

Jeanette Compton stood to take the floor. As a police archivist and researcher, she was rarely called in to join a MCT briefing meeting, but this bright Wednesday morning, she was first on the agenda, presenting the findings of her work with Penfold in the Palace Green reference library.

Penfold was notable by his absence, and acting DI Milburn, chairing the meeting as SIO, thought she looked calm and confident. He was repeatedly fooled by her mousy, librarian's appearance into underestimating Jeanette. As she began speaking, Tony chastised himself. *What even is a "librarian's appearance"?*

He thought of Kathy, now one of the most important librarians in the city, with her shiny blonde hair and blue eyes. As Jeanette started with a bit of context about the importance and celebrity of Cuthbert, and the story of his monks being attacked and chased by Viking raiders, he wondered if Kathy was descended from that Viking stock. *But she's from Leeds, so maybe not.*

After the briefest of historical introductions – knowing her audience well enough – Jeanette moved quickly on to treasure. Discovering what the treasure hunters were likely looking for could help with working out how they had met their ends. The range of possible riches was large, but the strongest indications were for small jewellery pieces – which were mentioned by more than one reference source as being listed in the 1827 inventory by Canon Raine and, again, later in the cathedral's records.

The most famous treasure was St Cuthbert's Cross, a circular gold and garnet pendant found pinned inside Cuthbert's cloak and currently on display in the Durham Cathedral Museum. There were strong indications that three more pectoral crosses, worn as brooches, may have been saved from King Henry VIII's commissioners and kept hidden right up until the wartime concealment.

When she had almost finished speaking, Detective Superintendent Hardwick interrupted, 'But you're saying we simply don't know exactly what treasure items are out there somewhere?'

Jeanette continued in her measured, placid voice. 'The stylistic approach of the Constables of the Cathedral to their documents over the centuries is probably best described as "vague", perhaps even "murky". They clearly didn't want people to know the details, but the church authorities required them to make written records.'

Hardwick persisted, 'Have we spoken to the present Constable? Doesn't he just know all of what we're asking?'

Tony had been leaning against the doorjamb of his office and took a step forward. 'I met with him, and I say that Jeanette's description rather describes his approach in person too. He made all the right noises, without really imparting any information.'

DC Madeline Aria asked, 'Same with me last Thursday, but why would he want to keep anything secret? Nowadays, I mean. Anything like that should be celebrated and put on public display. There's no need to keep it hidden anymore.'

Tony nodded. 'I mean you could well be right. It may be that actually he doesn't know anything more than we do. Like you say, if he knew which mine the treasure had been put down, you'd expect he'd have been out there to dig it up himself.'

The acting detective super brought the meeting back on point with his guttural voice. 'Well, look, I guess it doesn't matter what the treasure is, or even if there is any. These men believe it's out there and somebody seems willing to kill them for it.'

'For something.' Meredith had no qualms about interrupting Hardwick.

He gave her a stare with his dead eye but still asked her to explain what she meant.

'Well, they may be out looking for treasure, but could there be some non-treasure motive for their murders? I don't know quite what it might be, but we seem fixated on the fortune-finding motive here. They're a community like any other, maybe there are jealousies or love triangles among the Indiana Joneses?'

Everybody paused to mull over this thought, but nobody had a chance to think too much, or ask any follow up questions, as Penfold bustled into the room. He had not dressed up for the meeting – shorts and T-shirt, as usual. Most of the folk present, huddled as best they could around the three fans in the open plan office space, looked like they felt a certain envy at his likely temperature.

'Sorry, the waves were back up again this morning, and the tide rises regardless of the follies of men.'

His entry had silenced everyone, and without any preamble, he asked DC Aria to put up a scene photo on the big display screen. She fiddled with her iPad and scrolled through some of the Tudhoe mine scenes to get to the one he requested, showing the 1958 victim in situ in the mud at the bottom of the shaft.

As he strode across the room towards the screen, he said, 'Last night, I had this nagging at the back of my skull.'

Tony worried where this was going, given that this victim, Dickie Harbottle, had his head bashed in, likely before falling – or being dropped – down the mineshaft.

Pointing first at the large image, indicating the corpse's stylised belt buckle, Penfold said, 'This leather and metal belt was one of the few things, along with the bones, to survive seventy years down there intact.'

Harry Hardwick finally got a grip on himself, after seeming utterly nonplussed by the surfer's unruly entrance to the meeting and apparent lack of concern that he should have been there promptly for the 9 a.m. start. 'Excuse me, Mr Penfold. DC

127

Meredith was just speaking about the possible motives for the murders.'

'Ah, I do apologise. Everyone was quiet when I entered. Do you mean the murders including of this man?' His question was rhetorical. Penfold continued unabashed, pointing at the belt buckle itself, which formed a silver-coloured pointed curve, like a double crescent moon. 'We reckoned on this man having disappeared in 1958.'

Hardwick tried another tack at complaint. 'Please come to the point Mr Penfold, we have a lot to get through this morning.'

'It's just Penfold. There's no "Mr".' With that he pointed at his own chest, which appeared to be to emphasise the comment. He held the pose for much longer than was necessary though.

The room was silent, until Tony spotted the connection. 'Shit.'

To assist those who hadn't seen it, Penfold pulled the royal blue cloth of his T-shirt forward to pick out the surf company logo on it. He used his other hand to point back at the display screen. The yellow curving wave symbol on his shirt was identical to the shape of the belt buckle. 'This belt was made by Rip Curl. The company was only founded in 1969, and in fact the range of clothes that includes this belt was only manufactured in the late 1970s.'

H had been giving Penfold the hard stare and kept it up with a dismissive comment. 'Well, we must have made a mistake on the date. Milburn, look into that will you.'

Tony was standing beside the forensics manager, and this instruction made him distinctly uncomfortable. 'Well, sir, Julia is probably best placed to double check on the forensics, and potentially liaise with Gerard about confirmation of the ID.' He indicated Dr Sedgley standing next to him.

She was already shaking her head. 'I can double check on the belt, but we don't have any way to better identify its age than Penfold's research. I mean, I can see from here that that is definitely the same logo.' She directed a question to Penfold. 'Is the logo based on some other symbol? Might the company have chosen something that a person in the fifties could have had on their belt buckle coincidentally?'

'Not to my knowledge. I'll phone Claw Warbrick and ask him how they came up with it. I think the old guy is still alive. What time is it in Melbourne now?' Their unpaid consultant wandered towards the door, tapping at his phone screen.

Tony was surprised at himself: the idea that Penfold could just telephone the founder of a global surf brand somehow did not strike him as incredible but, rather more, expected.

After an extended silence, Tony said, 'OK, let's look at that shortly. For now, though, we need to make some progress with what Diane was talking about. We need motive here. We've got three definite recent murders in different places but similar circumstances and similar victims. Madeline, you've been out to see the families. Can you make any connection between the victims other than their treasure hunting? Did they all work in the same place, drink in the same place, have any common friends or contacts? Is there some other motive we're missing?'

She flicked back and forth through several pages of notes, before replying, 'On it, guv.' She picked up her pen and started scribbling quickly on her notepad. He had wanted her to answer the question but assumed that her response meant she had yet to make any alternative connections.

As Penfold stepped back into the room, he was wrapping up a phone conversation. His New Zealand accent was stronger than normal. '… ha ha, yeah, so stoked you make wetsuits. The North Sea here is eight degrees in winter. Hang loose.'

He put the phone in the side pocket of his shorts and shook his head. 'Nope, that wave logo is something he'd scrawled on the bottom of his surfboard along with some random words including Rip and Curl. He didn't say so, but I suspect they were drunk when they came up with the company name and logo.'

Tony could see Hardwick fuming and jumped in. 'OK, so we've got a bit of a mystery on that fourth corpse. Julia, could you talk to Gerard and see if between pathology and forensics you can work out what's going on there.'

'Pretty obvious, isn't it?' Penfold was in danger of having H force Tony to let him go. Tony shook his head trying to let the man know to shut up. Naturally, he continued, 'It's a set-up.'

Dr Sedgley was intrigued. 'How do you mean?'

'A man vanishes in 1958 – drops off the face of the Earth, even his family don't know where he is. And then he ends up dead down an old mine, at the earliest twenty years later. But in the same village. Where's he been hiding all that time? The community was closer then too. You couldn't hide away from your family in the same town and not get caught out over twenty years. Everyone in Tudhoe would have known him. And if he wasn't there for that time, how did his body end up down that particular mine?'

Hardwick sounded exasperated. 'Do you already have the answer? Tell us what you think.'

'It's not Dickie Harbottle. Somebody has staged this whole crime scene.'

Tony was lost. 'But what for? A disappeared man from 1958, whose living descendants never even met him, appears apparently murdered. What is the goal in staging this?'

Sedgley followed up immediately, 'And do you just mean that older corpse, or are you suggesting the whole double body thing was staged?'

Everyone was surging with questions and confusions. Meredith spoke loudest, silencing the rest, and hers was not a question. 'To keep people away from old mines. This is the motive. Scare people off with deaths at several old pits and talk of Saint Cuthbert's Curse will bubble up, and it'll be like there's a forcefield around all the old mine openings. What better way to have them all to yourself to search for the treasure?' Meredith was excited at her logic. She felt something had just clicked into place.

'Or attract people to the mines.'

Penfold's voice was quiet, but it cut through the jubilant atmosphere that Meredith had built up. She balked. 'What are you on about?'

'The risk is the hype. We've already seen a ton of people trespassing, having to be warned off, or in some cases helped by the various extra police we've deployed to the countryside. What did Richmond Fire Brigade say when Sergeant Franks went to see them about their help at Bowes Museum?'

She visibly slumped, shoulders dropping. Tony tingled at her discomfort, and he had to suppress a smile.

Hardwick had not already heard the answer to this question, and he also needed to be kept up to speed on the Swan theft. 'What was their response, Meredith?'

Tony was positively jubilant inside. Not only had she posited what was probably the opposite of the correct theory, but she was getting her comeuppance in front of the whole team.

She stretched her neck to the side, and her bob swung portentously. She looked the big boss straight in his bad eye. 'They said they had not attended.'

'What do you mean? You saw the engine, didn't you?'

'It wasn't them – the thieves were impostors. They had a ...' She theatrically flicked through her notebook. '... Medium Rescue Pump stolen, eighteen months ago. They thought Franks was calling because it had been found.'

Tony pushed her further, smiling inwardly. 'But what about their current vehicles? Why did they not attend the fire at the school?'

'Both their engines were up the dale assisting mountain rescue with two separate incidents. Although frankly, I think Miss Carrera is out of her depth there. The security was utterly woeful.'

Tony couldn't help himself. 'Separate incidents of?'

'Idiots.' She did not speak further for a few seconds, staring now at Tony. 'Stuck down mineshafts.'

Penfold took over, unwittingly saving Tony from going overboard and fluffing the professionalism needed in leading the briefing meeting. 'So, the outcome of these murders is that a lot of armchair treasure hunters have now been enticed into the field, doing much more exploration than they might otherwise have done.'

'But why?' Hardwick's was the final word on the subject, as nobody had suggested an answer.

NINETEEN

Barry Black, resplendent in black boots, a black donkey jacket over a straining white work shirt, and a flat cap, stepped from the parade procession. Sweat dripped from his scalp as he insisted on keeping the donkey jacket on in the summer heat. The week of glorious sunshine had culminated in humid and overcast conditions, but it was still bright enough for the union man to wear oversized aviator sunglasses.

The enormous snake of brass bands, and union chapter groups from ex-mining villages all over County Durham, had stopped again. His colleagues carried the huge Redhills banner, which shone colourfully, as all the groups headed up towards the cathedral for the Gala service.

Black swaggered over to DI Milburn who stood in the shade of the horseman statue in Durham's flagstone marketplace. Penfold sat on a stone step of the statue's plinth beside Tony. The detective wondered when a donkey jacket had last been worn to work by anyone.

'I trust you've got some polisses down on the Racecourse watching the pikeys?'

His use of the local vernacular for police officers was normal. The pejorative for Travellers, however, rankled Tony.

As if triggered by the man's bigotry, Tony's police radio crackled a message about the arrest of a pair of men on Elvet Bridge fighting over a space to view the passing bands. After the rousing speeches down on the Racecourse, most groups and bands were heading back up towards the cathedral. Some had come into the market square to play and show off some more, and the place was full of people. Plenty of folk would stay picnicking on the area down by the river and the funfair, and the afternoon would get progressively livelier as the day, and the drink, wore on.

Tony removed his sunglasses to look the man straight in the face. 'Good afternoon, Marra Black. We're pretty stretched as it is, monitoring all the street drinking that your paraders are engaged in. And we've got a lot of rural patrols stuck out in the countryside, attempting to prevent any more mineshaft deaths. So not as many boots on the ground as we'd like, but we'll do our best. I don't really think the funfair operators are a significant worry though.'

County Durham's rural police officers had spent the last three days trawling around the countryside, looking out for people who appeared lost or out of place. No more treasure hunters had been found dead, but a significant number had been warned, and in some cases, chased away from old mine entrances. The police had good enough relations with farmers that they had received many tip-offs about where to find people snooping about.

A sudden, chilly wind blew through the crowd.

The principal organiser of the whole Miners' Gala put his hands in the pockets of his jacket and drew himself fully upright. Black was a large man, more fat than tall, and he was about to retort indignantly, when Penfold interrupted. He remained seated, looking across at the man from the highest plinth step, a casualness which Black took as a further affront.

'What's in the shipping containers?' He jerked a thumb over his shoulder to indicate down the Market Place to where the three giant metal boxes occupied a large proportion of the public space.

'How should I know? They're not ours.'

The wind had paused momentarily but swirled again and the sky darkened. Barry Black's hand shot up to hold his cap on.

Tony scowled and turned to look. The massed public leaned against the corners and sides, finding shade and hiding much of the containers, but the Miners' Gala logo was clearly and prominently visible on the top corners above the heads of the milling marras. 'Um, they're emblazoned with the words *Durham Miners' Gala* and that pit helmet logo.'

Barry Black drew in a deep breath, like he was talking to a child. 'I know they are. I've seen 'em, but we didn't put 'em here. I don't know what they're for.'

This did prompt Penfold to stand, and all three men gazed down over twenty metres, at the grey and red shipping containers.

Tony mused out loud, 'Hmm, the guy who delivered these had a Durham County Council hi-vis jacket on.' He turned back to Black. 'You've not had any conversations with the council about public space art?'

Penfold took a half step towards them and lifted his nose up in the air. He also wondered a question out loud. 'But what is it with the citronella?'

Tony could half smell the lemony fragrance, but the square was busy and full of people with all manner of foodstuffs and beers, a thousand smells all whisked together by the churning wind. The odour melange was confusing, and he wasn't convinced he could actually smell lemons. He figured it was an olfactory memory, or assumption.

Black proposed, 'Aren't they refrigerated? Can you hear that hum, or whatever it is?'

They stood trying to make out the exact nature of the continuous but quiet drone that seemed to come from them. There was too much noise to make it out clearly. From all directions, the music of distant brass bands was brought on the fitful air currents, and the crowds in the Market Place were laughing and chattering loudly.

As they had done for hundreds of years, Durham Cathedral's great bells began to chime for half past the hour. As if this was their cue, the nearest brass band re-assembled, and the procession restarted, wandering slowly forward to the strains of

"When the Saints Go Marching In". Tony turned back to see the banner of NUM's Blackhall Lodge Brass Band.

Waving at them from the edge of the march-past, behind Mr Black, Tony could see the woman they had met with the pseudonym Maid Marion blowing hard on a trombone and swinging it up and down in time with the music. As much as was possible with her lips to the mouthpiece, she was grinning, facial scars squashed together, marking white lines between her freckles. The sun had intensified the freckles, and she was clearly having a whale of a time.

Marion's band had exited the market square past the fish and chip restaurant by the time the cathedral's last bell tone sounded. Tony noticed Penfold staring at the tail end of the Blackhall band as it squeezed between rows of bystanders up Saddler Street.

The sky had become like coal. Huge raindrops started to spot the ground.

Before Barry Black could say goodbye and rejoin his group in the parade, a loud metallic grating sound soured the music, louder than the wind. As they watched, the double doors of the three shipping containers all clunked and ground as an internal mechanism swung them open.

Revealed inside of them were a series of shelves, each about thirty centimetres high. These disappeared all the way back, the full length of the forty-foot containers. The shelves were white plastic, and at the front ends, by the door hinge motors, were transparent cylinders the width of drainpipes that came from each shelf and hung down to a few centimetres from the ground. The shelves each contained a seething brown mass that appeared wet and moved and writhed like some sort of giant brown jelly.

Within seconds, frogs the size of fists came falling out of the shelves. Most dropped down the clear plastic chutes, but many also just fell from their shelves on to the pavement. The mass of frogs spewed out from every shelf, seemingly without end. The three men watched spellbound as hundreds and hundreds of the animals jumped, waddled and crawled out into the crowd.

There was panic. The frogs kept coming and everybody jumped about and shrieked. Their ugliness, wetness, erratic and unexpected movements, and incongruity to the scene shocked young and old alike. People ran in different directions to try and get away, causing crushes and screams.

The frogs kept on coming, just as panicked as the stampeding humans, skittering across the flagstones, clambering up on pushchairs, legs, dogs, benches, everything. The unidentified hum or drone from the shipping containers had been the sealed-in croaking of several thousand frogs. This noise now continued in the open air and added to the panic and confusion.

The frogs continued to exit the containers. In less than a minute, the sea of brown amphibians had spread all the way up to where Tony and Penfold stood rooted to the spot, rain landing on their heads. Barry Black had disappeared.

Tony and his friend clambered up the stone plinth as high as they could, and this served as an island to keep the frogs from them, but the whole place was carpeted in the noisy animals. The radio exploded into life, with reports of the same thing happening at all the mysterious shipping containers spread across the city. Durham's central peninsula was awash with frogs and getting wet from the rainstorm. Finally, the summer had cracked.

They scanned the area to see if anywhere in view had avoided frogs, but the only places that looked to be amphibian-free zones were the insides of the containers that had held them. Even the shops, pubs and the indoor market were teeming with them. Penfold was on his phone, trying to establish the species, and doing some calculations.

Tony held both palms out, albeit one with a radio in it, and asked, 'What in the actual f—'

He was cut off as Penfold said, 'One hundred thousand.'

'What?'

'At the very roughest of estimates, I reckon you've got seven thousand frogs per container, and fifteen of those around the city. That adds up to a plague of a hundred thousand frogs.'

Tony's hands dropped to his sides, and he stared out at the chaos all around them.

Dead frogs littered the place, red and bloody where they had been trodden on, but these were vastly outnumbered by live frogs. They bobbed about in the puddles and rivers forming on the pavement, causing upset everywhere they jumped. Many streamed out past the end of St Nics Church on to Claypath, as it curved past the entrance to the peninsula and the UNESCO World Heritage Site.

It was difficult to believe, but those hordes of frogs were being met by hundreds coming the other way, up out of Millennium Place by the theatre. The street was closed to traffic for the Gala, or there would have been a frog massacre.

Moments later, Tony heard the first car crash. That curve of Claypath by St Nics formed an overpass above the wide A690 road. Scared by all the frightened people, frogs on the overpass crowded together, like coins on an arcade penny falls machine, and fell in numbers down on to the road and on to unsuspecting windscreens. With the slick road and windscreen wipers already vigorously sweeping away rainwater, the frogs caused the same chaos with vehicles on the road as they had with pedestrians in the Market Place.

The crashing noise triggered Tony out of his trance, and he leapt into police action. He first radioed for ambulances to attend the four-lane road bridge over the River Wear in case the collisions had caused injuries. He then gave an all-call-signs broadcast to everyone on duty in the city to step up, wherever they happened to be at that moment, and direct people to head back down to the Racecourse. Or home if they could.

Whatever the cause of this craziness, people were in danger in any place thronged with the frogs. A spooked crowd was one of the biggest hazards when policing large events. With frog-filled shipping containers on each bridge, in Market Place, and on Palace Green, the danger zone encompassed the entire World Heritage Site.

Another three containers were on the university science site near the physics building. Penfold said he had also seen three more at the other end of that site, close to the Palatine building, which housed the university administration offices. On Miners' Gala day, in mid-July, on a Saturday afternoon, the university site would be mostly deserted, so the frog swarm there would represent more of a curiosity than a hazard to people. Tony cursed the absent DI Barnes, and the disappeared Top Marra Black, and concentrated on dispersing the crowd as safely as possible.

TWENTY

Durham County Council's pest control division had been denuded over years of government cuts to a two-man service that was hired out to residents to remove wasp nests or lay rat traps. The team to deal with stray animals was similarly barebones, but both vans had appeared at the bottom of Claypath within thirty minutes of the opening of the shipping containers.

Detective Inspector Milburn had expressed surprise at their commitment on a Saturday. They told him that the weekends were always busiest, and they arranged their shifts accordingly. However, turning up was the best they could offer in terms of help. Frogs are not pest-controlled animals, and for such vast numbers, the four men just scratched their heads and admitted they'd never heard of any such thing in all their careers.

As the pest controllers mused and discussed possible ideas for wrangling the amphibious throng, Tony watched a video Kathy had sent him. She worked most weekend days but had knocked off at two o'clock to go out on to Palace Green and into the cathedral service for the Big Meeting. She loved the banners, the parade and the community spirit.

Her video was of frogs disrupting the cool calm of the Anglican religion's third most important church. She could be heard laughing behind the camera, as various bigwigs inside the cathedral tried to corral jumping brown lumps with little success.

The organ, warming up in the hour before the service, could overpower the noise of a thousand frog croaks, but it was clear that the choir would struggle to be heard, let alone the preacher. Frogs hid under pews, in the arms of statues, up on improbably high ledges and, of course, in the font. They had spread throughout the huge nave of stone columns and walls, into the Lady Chapel and St Cuthbert's shrine, and they had followed tourists through the automatic doors out into the rain-spattered cloisters.

Back in discussion with the pest controllers, it was agreed that, where possible, the frogs should be gathered together and removed to the council incinerator – where they normally took roadkill carcasses. Shovelling the live animals into the back of their vans was frustrating work, and nobody wanted to go about the Market Place smacking frogs with a spade.

Five hours later, the frogs had spread wide and were much more thinly distributed. It was possible to walk around and avoid them. Many had found their way downhill into the River Wear.

Luckily, the heavy rainstorm that had arrived at the same time had encouraged the public to leave quickly too. There were several casualties, but all had suffered relatively minor injuries.

Detective Superintendent Hardwick strolled up to meet Tony by the shipping containers up on Palace Green. These sat innocently on the grass between castle and cathedral, with their doors wide open. The vast shelves, each the same size as the container itself, formed trays approximately thirty centimetres deep. Tony remembered the writhing mass of frogs each had contained earlier.

Hardwick's voice boomed across the short distance between them. 'Suffice to say Barry Black is not happy about this. He's asking how we came to allow these containers to be deposited around the city without investigating them at all. The whole Gala day has been ruined. The cathedral service had to be abandoned completely. The bishop tells me the place is still littered with frogs, both alive and dead.'

Tony smiled and shrugged. 'I say we charge the Miners' Gala for the cost of the clean up.' He pointed at the logo, showing the silhouette of a miner's head with a helmet lamp shining rays. 'These things are clearly theirs, although what the whole deal with the frogs is, I've no idea.'

Penfold clambered out of one of the white plastic shelves in the nearest container. He was soaking wet as the shelf trays were all still a few centimetres deep with water, which had formed the captive frogs' habitat for the previous week.

He explained what he had found inside. 'Definitely North American bullfrogs. They're big, and one of the most commonly cultivated agriculturally. This set-up though seems bigger than anything on the internet suggests. Mostly the farming is done in natural reserves, rather than a straight aquaculture habitat like these. The food and ventilation and water that's needed …' He paused, wiped dripping water from his fringe and waved a hand towards the inside of the container from which he had just climbed.

'There's a marvellous mechanism back there. And I don't know what chemicals they've put in this water to keep them from eating each other.' Penfold wrung out the corner of his T-shirt to illustrate a dribble of water presumably containing nutrients and maybe hormones or similar.

Harry Hardwick was unimpressed. 'So, what do we do about it.'

Tony looked to the wet New Zealander for guidance. Penfold shrugged. 'Not much you can do really. I'd get the environment agency in to try and clear as many as possible from the river. They're a pretty nasty, dominant invasive species.' He bent over a little to squint at the interior door handles. 'You might get some fingerprints or DNA from inside one of the containers, which could identify who left them here. Human DNA I mean.' He chuckled, but Tony and Hardwick did not join in.

'That lemon scent.' Penfold lifted his chin, raising his nose to suggest they should all take a sniff. 'Frogs dislike citrus smells, so these containers have been set to open and expel all the frogs at the same time. Whoever put these here intended to cause the chaos that they did. And then they just got lucky that the rain added to the confusion. Does the Miners' Gala have any known enemies?'

Tony looked at his boss who appeared to be gazing at something on the castle walls, until Tony realised he was on the side of Harry's dead eye, which always gave the impression of staring into the distance.

Before anyone could think up some person or organisation that might have a grievance against a large trade union gathering, Hardwick's phone rang. The ringtone was the theme tune from the old western movie *The Good, The Bad and The Ugly*. Penfold and Tony gave each other a silent smile.

He fumbled the phone from his inside jacket pocket and whispered, pointing at the device, 'University vice chancellor.' He tapped the screen and held the device to his head. 'Good evening, Alwyn.' He said nothing more, and her voice was not audible as the phone was pressed to his large ear. The call ended quickly. The only other thing the policeman said to her was, 'Of course, we'll meet him there in ten minutes.'

'Tony, come with me. We need to meet Professor Von Braun over on the science site. There's been a big theft. You though …' He pointed at Penfold. 'Go home and clean yourself up. Get back to work on Milburn's treasure hunter deaths on Monday. We'll deal with this.'

Penfold smiled smugly. 'Of course, sir.'

With no further conversation, Hardwick pirouetted a hundred and eighty degrees and strode off towards the top of Dun Cow Lane at the cathedral's eastern end. Tony was caught out and had to take three very quick steps to catch up with his boss. He left Penfold, still dripping, without even saying goodbye.

'What's the story, sir, that we have to snap to attention for the VC on a Saturday evening?'

'You know who Professor Von Braun is?'

Durham University had a reputation for having one of the foremost astronomy departments in the world. Von Braun

143

famously led the cosmology team, and they were so successful that he was often featured on television news programmes and all over the newspapers for their latest discoveries. The tabloids referred to him as "Von Brain".

The detective superintendent's question was essentially rhetorical – everyone in the city knew of Professor Von Braun. However, he followed up with the detail he was really asking about. 'Don't be fooled, the man is ruthless. He's lived in this town more than thirty years; his manner of stumbling with English and having an overblown German accent is designed to give him the upper hand.'

This gave Tony pause. He had never met the professor but had seen the eccentric academic with the almost comical German accent on TV many times. He thought back through some of the snippets he could remember, wondering what the man's hidden agenda might have been in each case. His memories of them were poor though, as the reporting had always been about some amazing cosmological discovery that quickly left Tony reeling with the scientific details.

'OK, but still, what are we going over there for?'

'They've had a computer stolen.'

Tony stopped in his tracks. They were crossing Kingsgate pedestrian bridge, high above where the river had cut a steep valley over millennia. The detective superintendent did not stop, nor look back, so Tony had to quickstep again to catch up and reiterate his confusion. Avoiding the corpses of frogs on the bridge made it feel like he was running through a minefield, zigzagging left and right.

'A stolen computer is one for uniform. Or more probably calling it in on one-oh-one. Why did the vice chancellor think that it was reasonable to get the two top detectives in the city to attend?'

Hardwick did not turn his head but spoke forward, keeping up the pace as they turned on to Church Street by the student union building. 'Barnes isn't dead, he's just in Australia.'

Tony wondered why the boss was in a mood as ugly as the student union building. He didn't get a chance to apologise or explain that he had meant the two top ranking detectives *on duty*.

Hardwick continued almost without a beat, 'You know they keep simulating the early universe in more and more detail?'

'Yes, I saw Von Braun on the news, I don't remember exactly when, maybe six months ago, talking about it. They had an animation of flying past stars and galaxies.'

'Yes. The computer that's been stolen is the one that runs that project. It's expensive.'

Tony still couldn't see the urgency but walked along matching the brisk pace. In another five minutes, the physics building Tony remembered from the TV interview came into view ahead of them. With wooden panelling all around the outer surface, and a series of weirdly stacked levels, its architecture was striking.

The sound of croaking frogs grew louder again, having quietened slightly on their walk. The footpath past the Bill Bryson Library had fewer dead frogs than in town, and all areas with vegetation swarmed with the brown lumps.

The small car park beside the physics block was overwhelmed by the three shipping containers filling most of the parking area. Their doors were wide open, and the interiors had the same habitat shelving as Tony had seen in the ones on Palace Green and in the Market Place.

The physicist stood at the sliding door in a bank of large windows, frantically typing on his phone. He was surrounded by a frog massacre, more corpses of the amphibians than anywhere else they'd seen thus far.

'Ah, police, zank you. Zis way.' Tony found himself immediately sceptical of the voice. He wondered if Hardwick's intelligence about Von Braun would skew their interpretation of what the man told them. They shared the lift with a frog, and on exiting on the basement level, several more hopped around the corridor.

Von Braun led them to a server room which he opened with his key card. More frogs hid around the various cabinets, each glass door with a multitude of blinking green lights behind it. Immediately, they could see an empty space in the row of cabinets, with a trail of disconnected cables lying on the floor behind where the missing computer must have stood.

The sound of frogs was loud, louder than Tony thought should come from the ones he could see. The ribbiting noise drew their eyes across the room to a broken window high in the wall, which must have been at ground level outside. They were at the rear of the building, and the small vista visible through the window showed the wooded hillside behind the science site.

The professor put his phone away and waved up to the broken window. 'Zey must have entered zis vay. As soon as zey disconnected, ze system sent a message to my phone to say ze simulation had stopped running for a "Power Error".'

Tony's guv'nor stepped forward to inspect the spaghetti of detached cables and the dusty square of floor that had been newly revealed. 'Well, they couldn't get a cabinet this size up and out through that little window.'

'No, zere's no security cameras in here, but the vun in the lobby upstairs shows a pair of men veeling it out to a van. You saw all the dead frogs up zere? Zey must have driven right over them all.'

Tony still wondered what could be so important about this theft but could see a computer cabinet was probably valuable enough for a bit of detective work. He imagined handing this off to Meredith in the morning. That would keep her busy.

He asked, 'Two men, you say. Please send us over the camera footage later, but for now can you give me a quick description of them?'

'Contractors in orange jackets for Durham County Council.' The astronomer jumped ahead to answer Milburn's next question before it was asked. 'Only the back end of the van is visible, but side on, so we can't see the licence plate. A white van. You see the back door swing open and then our computer is gone.'

Tony could see H was pleased he was taking notes of the professor's information. He also noted the occasional slip in the German-English patois. 'And the machine stolen: is it special in some way? Do you know the brand or model? Anything about the cabinet or the hardware that makes it identifiable?'

Von Braun looked hard at Tony, as if he had insulted the man's mother. 'It voz made by Kray. You know the supercomputers? The central chip voz bespoke architecture, built especially for us. It cost more than a million dollars.'

Tony nearly dropped his phone as he typed what the man was saying and the phrase "million dollars" was uttered. He looked at him in disbelief. 'A ... a million dollars?'

The response was a stern nod. Tony looked to Hardwick, who also nodded gravely. Suddenly the involvement of the vice chancellor and Durham City's detective superintendent on a Saturday evening had become imperative rather than questionable.

'And, let me make sure I understand this correctly.' Tony held out his phone and a finger, ready to type to confirm the answer. 'The security in here runs to swiping your campus card and having those hopper windows that presumably are too small to escape out of with a computer?'

The German drew himself up stiffly, his tie straining around the neck. 'Only four key cards open this room. You cannot enter unless you are on the project, or the designated IT support person. Ze door will not even open in fire – ze windows are ze emergency exits. You can leave if zere's a fire, but you cannot take ze computer viz you.'

Hardwick pointed back at the door. 'That lock must record all the card swipes. Can we find out who opened it to let them out then?'

Professor Von Braun nodded, and his face dropped. 'I have already checked the security log. It was my card.'

TWENTY-ONE

Early on Sunday morning, Tony and Kathy had stopped in at the Daily Espresso for takeaway coffee and pastries. They sat on a bench on Palace Green for an alfresco breakfast, right outside the door of the reference library. Tony's job held such irregular hours that they prized little moments for simple pleasures together.

They had enjoyed a number of breakfasts on the same bench, but never before with serenading frogs bobbing about among the pansies in the adjacent flower bed. The metal shells of the shipping container habitats sat abandoned on the grass in front of them. Perhaps as many as two hundred dead frogs lay around the expanse between the castle walls and the cathedral.

Kathy spoke of the river being full of frogs, both alive and dead, as she had walked home the previous evening. A blood red evening sky had been mirrored by streams of red blood in the murky, slow-moving water.

Nothing, though, could take away their enjoyment of the new morning's warm sun and tasty pastries. Both were golden rather than red. Tony wished this was all he had to do all day.

Since her promotion, Kathy's hours had become less "normal". As the chief curator of the university's literary special collections, she had to be mindful of the need to open the exhibitions when the public wanted to visit. Hence, she was scheduled to work every Sunday during the Lindisfarne Gospels exhibition.

The Gospels exhibition was organised by Durham Cathedral, but Kathy had lent them a few special collection manuscripts, out of the library holdings that were her responsibility, to help showcase the Gospels' local connections.

Beyond that, the flow of visitors going to enjoy the Lindisfarne Gospels also increased visitor numbers significantly to the exhibits in Palace Green Library. As the boss, Kathy felt she had to take the hit on working the least sociable hours.

Tony held her hand in the sun with his eyes closed, face raised to soak up the warmth of the morning rays. He opened them with a start as he felt something brush his chin.

'Croissant crumbs, you mucky pup.'

He squeezed the hand he held and let her finish wiping his mouth with the other one.

'Morning, Kathy.' A chipper voice floated to them across the long shadow of the shipping containers. The woman was pale and wore a neat trouser suit, in a similar grey colour to her skin.

Kathy swung her head away from him and squinted in the direction of her colleague. 'Morning, Helen.' She gave a little wave, and the woman arrived in front of them.

Before she could introduce them, Tony sat up a bit straighter and greeted her. 'Ah, Mrs Landrey. How have you been?'

'Oh, you two know each other?' Kathy sounded a little put out.

Tony stood up and shook Landrey's hand. 'Yes, we met on a case a bit over a year ago. I take it you still work for the World Heritage Site,' he enquired.

She nodded and removed her sunglasses. 'Yes, Kathy and I have a meeting this morning on an assortment of artefact-related matters.'

'On a Sunday? How diligent of you both,' he teased. Kathy stood up, pushed him slightly and said, 'We've got an hour before we open for visitors, so you go and do some detective work, and we'll make the magic happen here.'

He watched as the two women pushed back the heavy door and squeezed in the small gap they created. It closed with a clunk, and a nearby frog agreed, with a loud "ribbit". Tony turned to walk straight towards the sun. He also had an early meeting to attend.

Miraculously – it had only taken a million-dollar IT theft – Hardwick had convinced the chief constable to supply the Major Crimes Team with two civilian support staff to cover both the murder investigations and the two high-value thefts. Tony was annoyed that they had still been allocated the Tan Hill body, as the powers that be considered it a connected case.

He wondered how much this had come from pressure on the chief constable by the university's authorities, and how much it was genuinely allocation of police resources based on investigative needs. He scoffed at the very thought. Certainly, North Yorkshire Constabulary weren't jumping forward to offer personnel support for the investigation of the mine death on their patch.

After introducing the two document handlers to Detective Constables Aria and Meredith, the team sat to review where their cases were at and to plan what to do next. This Sunday seemed to be going well for Tony as SIO. He had also been assigned a uniformed officer for the day, to send out on statement-taking duties.

PC Chris Thorpshire appeared right after his shift briefing downstairs and was immediately amenable, eager and professional. Tony wondered how the stars had aligned, and also how long the young man would maintain these qualities before the job made him cynical, lazy and "a workie ticket".

Tony ran the meeting and prioritised the four deaths as of greatest importance. Now they had been established as four murders, and with a multitude of treasure hunters still criss-crossing the county, they needed to stop the murderer before anyone else fell victim. It was too complicated to consider the idea of more than one murderer, given that they had little enough evidence even to search for one.

In his mind, Tony essentially ignored the earliest death and assumed they were looking to solve the recent three. While there was a real blip in the timeline with the early corpse's belt, he assumed there was a forensics mishap somewhere along the evidence timeline.

Moreover, he anticipated that solving a seventy-year-old murder would likely be impossible, so he would aim for solving the possible. *And I'll leave the impossible one for Penfold to solve before breakfast!* He smiled to himself and brought the meeting to order to start on the murders' review.

'OK, Diane, somehow you've managed to work your magic on CSI Johnson, and we've now got the full forensics reports for all the mineshaft bodies, is that right?'

She grinned across the large table at him and replied. 'Yes, we have – it's amazing what men will do for sex. Isn't that right, Tony?'

Everyone but DC Meredith shifted in their seat and stared at their notepads. Tony glared at her and then looked to DSupt Hardwick. The boss knew the full, covered-up history between Diane and Tony, and he stepped straight in. 'Not appropriate at all, Meredith.'

He positioned his head so that he was looking at her with his blank eye. She had learnt not be fazed by it, but he couldn't see her face directly, as giving anyone the dead-eye stare meant looking elsewhere with his working eye. 'Let's just hear the facts please.'

'Of course. Sorry, just a bit of levity to brighten our early Sunday start. Here's where we're at:' She proceeded to lay out the summary of the four murders, mostly for the benefit of the three new members of the team.

Tony hoped that the newcomers would assume Meredith had made a genuine joke, and they would never find out that she was in fact sleeping with Alfie Johnson.

She talked them all through the treasure hunting connections between Dickie Harbottle, Mick Dooley, John Bowline and Billy Muckle, along with the fact that all four had been murdered through blunt force trauma to the skull. While it appeared that two may have suffered those injuries by falling victim to a booby trap, old Dickie Harbottle could have been attacked or just fallen, and Bowline, the Tan Hill victim, had definitely been attacked with a rock to the head.

After much of the basic information had been covered, including details gained from the victims' families, Penfold disrupted proceedings as he entered the room thirty minutes late. 'Apols, everyone, what have I missed?'

Harry Hardwick watched the surfer squeeze in and past Tony to the only free seat around the conference table. Harry's mouth once again hung open as he stared. He was so nonplussed that he followed Penfold's entrance with his seeing eye.

Tony knew exactly where the man had been and was embarrassed at the behaviour of his friend. For Tony's first big case as SIO, all Hardwick would see was an out-of-control DC Meredith, and an equally unmanageable "consultant". He squeezed his forehead and said, 'Sshhh,' then pointed to Diane to continue.

Whatever wiles she had used on the new forensics guy had produced serious news. She built up the tension skilfully like she was directing a movie, so that when the big reveal came, there was an audible gasp in the room. Even Tony felt excited at the news.

'Alfie saved the best for last,' she said, really meaning that she had done exactly that in this presentation. 'He found some trace DNA on the Tan Hill rock, in addition to the victim's. There's no identity associated with it – not in any of our databases. However, that dodgy belt I mentioned—'

'The Rip Curl one from the seventies?' Penfold interrupted.

'Shh, yes,' Tony chastised him.

She nodded and continued smoothly as if there had been no interruption. 'Well, there's trace DNA on that too. Looks like the sharp point on that buckle nicked the murderer, because that blood DNA matches the sample on the rock that killed John Bowline.

'What?' Tony couldn't help his surprise.

Penfold thought it hilarious to reprimand him back. 'Shh!' He waved a hand downwards to hush Tony.

Madeline Aria stepped in with further clarification. 'The beauty of it is that the belt is so unusual. It was pretty easy to find it as a recent sale on neBay. We're in the process of serving a warrant on them to supply us with the name and address of the buyer.'

'neBay?' Hardwick shopped on the high street, and this was an unknown quantity to him.

Aria explained, 'It's an online shop for second-hand – they say "vintage" – goods, based in Chester-le-Street. That's how they got the name: north-east eBay, NE Bay, neBay. That sort of idea.'

Tony was jubilant. 'This is a great break. Top priority, Madeline! As soon as we have that address, we'll pay them a visit.'

Hardwick cautioned, 'Milburn will take point on that once we've got the information, but take care, Tony. Four murders. We don't know who we'll be dealing with. This is a specialist firearms unit job. Let armed response do the raid and be there to do the investigating part once they've secured the suspect.'

Penfold's protestation that the age of the body left a gap, or puzzle at least, in the timeline went unheard in the buzz of excitement that always surrounded a "full kit raid".

Once the initial clamour died down, Meredith continued with more from Johnson's extensive forensics report. Tony wondered if Alfie had actually done all the lab testing, or if Diane was simply giving him all the credit. Dr Sedgley ran a strong team, and he assumed that they'd all have contributed to the graft. He couldn't deny that the amount of forensic work delivered was huge and had come fast, and he pictured Diane pulling Alfie's strings to get what she wanted.

She said, 'The digital investigations have also yielded fruit. They've managed to break into all the phones and the various computers gathered for evidence from the victims' homes. Following up on movements and contacts in the metal-detector-nerd world has also produced some interesting connections. Aria?'

Madeline's presentation on the big screen clicked through a variety of screenshots of emails and forum posts, as well as some texts and WhatsApp messages. It mostly reiterated the initial findings Trident had discovered earlier, but these new sources legitimised the inclusion of her findings in a way that should be admissible in court if it came to that.

The summary reported that the three modern victims had all communicated with each other in disjointed and seemingly disconnected conversations about various hoards and hoaxes within County Durham. In recent weeks, the focus on St Cuthbert's Treasure had become intense, and the other players in the conversations included those Trident had previously listed.

There were a number of websites dedicated to their hobby, but the MaidMarionettes site seemed to have been the main discussion forum. There was a chatroom for just about any treasure one might hunt for in Britain, and these men had chased many of them.

The focus on St Cuthbert's Treasure had also urged them on to try and find the hoard before the prophesied date, with some sort of idea that they could beat the clock and get the loot for themselves this way. It all seemed ludicrous to Tony.

The golden nugget from trawling through all the forum discussions was that Aria had pieced together meetings for each of the men with unknown suspects, each one at the mineshaft where they were found. When she listed the usernames of those meeting up, Penfold confirmed that they were all pseudonyms for the same multi-user person that Trident had identified through the handshaking algorithm connection.

Tony was forced to confirm to the room, including the detective superintendent, that their knowledge that this was the same person could not be produced in court, but hopefully once they found this person, that would become a moot issue. H was not impressed but, like everyone, he was intrigued. All the recent victims had arranged a mystery meeting at the location they were found dead.

Hardwick looked at his watch, an old school beast of a machine strapped to his left wrist. 'OK, Tony, where are we at with the computer chip theft? I need to update the vice chancellor on our progress in an hour.'

Tony frowned. It was barely more than twelve hours since Professor Von Braun had reported the loss. He responded sarcastically. 'Well, I trust we'll be able to convince CSI Johnson to work on Sunday as well and get the forensics of that scene all cleared up today.'

DC Aria stepped in to help Tony. 'I've been sent the CCTV footage and the key card logs for the room. There's not much more than what you found out initially from Von Braun, but he's coming into the station shortly, so we can find out a bit more about how his card came to be the one used by the thieves to get out with the chip.'

Hardwick had become distracted. He closed the meeting. 'OK, good, thanks Madeline, you keep following that up and let me know anything you get asap. Tony, see if Dr Sedgley can get a CSI down there today. The rest of you, let's keep getting all our ducks in a row for when we get that address for the belt suspect. Oh, and Tony, I want to see Barry Black in my office first thing tomorrow morning. I want to know exactly what the hell that frog fiasco was all about.'

Tony smiled. 'My pleasure.'

TWENTY-TWO

Just as Tony set about confirming task assignments to each person in the room, his phone rang. Kathy's picture flashed up as the caller, and he let his phone vibrate on the table as he finished off his instructions. He'd only left her an hour earlier, and she knew he had the briefing meeting.

He stepped into his office to call her back and had barely closed the door in time when her voice shrieked around the small space. 'Get here now, Tony! The Shakespeare's been stolen!'

He froze, clicked off speakerphone and lifted the device to his temple – he had to hold it a little away from his ear as she wailed painfully loudly. 'It's gone, Tony. How can it be gone?'

'OK, can you calm down a little so I can understand what you're saying? Take a breath and sit down and tell me what you're talking about.' He caught Penfold's eye through the glass of his office's main partition wall. The New Zealander could see something was off and opened his eyes a little wider to ask if he should join him. Tony replied with a slight shake of his head and held up an open palm to say *Wait*.

Kathy repeated that the rare first edition compilation of Shakespeare's plays had been stolen, again. Everyone in Durham, and in library circles globally, knew the story of its previous theft and miraculous recovery in Washington DC. The last thing Kathy could have imagined, as she took on the new role curating all the rarest manuscripts, was that it would be stolen again.

Tony could hear the tears in her voice as he urged her repeatedly to sit down. He exited his small office and, without a word, Penfold stood up and followed him out to the stairwell to descend two flights of old wooden stairs to the public foyer at street level. 'I'm on my way, sit tight for five minutes.'

Penfold must have gleaned enough from his demeanour to know they were heading back on to Durham's peninsula, to the place where Penfold and Jeanette had spent Tuesday afternoon researching the Cuthbertine legends.

After about fifty metres of pacing up the hill and round the side of the student union building on to Kingsgate Bridge, Penfold ventured a quiet question. 'Is she OK?'

'It doesn't sound like it. She says the Shakespeare folio has been stolen.'

'Oh, shit, really? Again?'

'Exactly. It's probably the one manuscript she needed to keep safe above all others. And it was her big plan to put it on show when the Gospels were also in town. All her idea. A way to cash in on all the extra visitors to Palace Green. That was her first major action in the new job. She couldn't stop telling me what a clever idea it was.'

They continued apace up the cobbled lane and marched towards the long stone library with its ornamental castellations, entering straight in, even though the library was not yet open for visitors. Helen Landrey met them just inside and waved them through to head down to Cosin's seventeenth century library.

At the far end of the space, beyond a variety of fancy books from various periods through the ages, Kathy sat on a chair by the wall, agog. She gaped at a large display case with an empty plastic bookstand inside it. The case appeared undamaged but was completely vacant. She looked dazed and confused, also vacant.

'Kathy,' Tony called as he walked towards her.

She continued staring at the illuminated acrylic box. Without turning from it, she raised a hand limply to indicate the empty case.

Penfold had come to a halt just inside the exhibition area and put out an arm to stop Mrs Landrey too. They watched as Tony tried to break his girlfriend out of her shock. He bent forward to give her an awkward hug and tried to put himself between her and the object of her fixation. Kathy responded to his questions with grunts, and eventually Tony waved the other two over to join in a discussion that might rouse her.

Landrey explained that this was indeed the display case that had held the first edition compilation of Shakespeare's plays. Dating from 1623, the book had been purchased by Bishop Cosin not long after publication and was one of only a few surviving from that original print run. She also stated that she had seen the book in this display case less than twenty-four hours previously, when she had popped in after the Miners' Gala's morning parade, before heading into the cathedral.

Kathy regained coherence and joined in the conversation. 'It was here when I left at two. It's always the last thing I do – walk right around this room before exiting back up the stairs. The same routine every time I leave.'

Tony ran fingertips through his short hair, the more brown, less grey part, on the top of his head. Slow hand movements, thinking how to proceed. He pointed at Penfold. 'Call Sedgley, will you?'

The Kiwi nodded and stepped away to phone for a forensic investigator to join them.

Helen Landrey had a small responsibility for the materials in Palace Green Library: the curator of the World Heritage Site was more of a co-ordinator across university, cathedral and council, providing UNESCO expertise wherever possible. For the Shakespeare folio though, the buck stopped with Kathy.

Tears ran down Kathy's face as she stepped forward, key held out to try and unlock the empty display case. Tony grabbed her wrist and gently applied a force backwards away from it. 'Don't touch. We need to preserve any forensic evidence.'

Her head dropped, her red-streaked face shrouded by straggly strands of hair. 'Of course, sorry.' It was barely a whisper, but they all heard her voice crack. Kathy stepped back and sat down again, now fully sobbing.

Penfold returned. 'OK, so it was definitely here at two o'clock yesterday and had gone by ten this morning. The sign in the reception area says you close at 5 p.m. Given the frog chaos yesterday afternoon, did your colleagues maintain that timing, or did they close up early?'

The mundanity of the question, diverting her away from the stolen object, helped to engage Kathy without upsetting her further. She lifted her head and looked intrigued. 'No, you're right. Hildebrand was the last staff member here. She sent me a message at about ten to four saying the council pest controllers had finally removed the last frog, and they'd decided to close then to avoid any more getting in.'

Penfold tilted his head to one side. 'Frog o'clock was two thirty, and yet the council pest controllers had managed to arrive and clear them all out of here within ninety minutes. That seems amazingly efficient.'

Tony agreed. 'Yes, those two pest control vans in the Market Place only arrived at three, and they worked down there the whole time.'

Penfold continued gently, 'Kathy, are there any cameras in here?'

She nodded meekly and stood up. 'They feed direct to a folder on my office computer.'

Tony spoke in a similarly quiet voice. 'Could you show us what happened yesterday afternoon?'

The four of them moved back upstairs and crowded into Kathy's little office behind the bookshop sales desk. She was deft with the mouse and the video began playing in a matter of seconds. The other three looked over her shoulder at the display screen, which was split into four rectangles. Three cameras inside the building and one watching above the main door fed to the same video file, so all the surveillance footage they had was playing at once.

'May I?' Penfold asked, his hand hovering over the one Kathy was using to control the mouse. She slid hers away and he skimmed it back and forth, clicking occasionally. On fast forward from two thirty the previous day, they watched a slapstick comedy of frogs rushing into the building, scaring visitors and staff alike, who jumped and screamed and ran in different directions.

While the humans rushed comically at four times normal speed, the frogs also jumped, staccato, all around the place. Barely ten minutes after their ingress, four men followed, clad in the same uniforms and hi-vis vests Tony had seen on the pest controllers in Durham Market Place.

'I recognise him.' Tony pointed at the top left quarter screen showing a man with long hair in a ponytail. 'He's the driver I saw delivering one of the shipping containers outside St Nics Church.' By the time his finger had pressed on to the screen, the man had skipped off at four times pace.

They watched him move into the exhibition hall, carrying a big, square laundry bag type container. He held the lid up as his mate grabbed frogs and dropped them into the carrier. From the height of the camera, the frogs could be seen clambering over each other in the bottom of the giant bag.

The two did a good job of quickly gathering up all the amphibians in the room, even if at normal speed it would have taken nearly twenty minutes.

'There!' It was Penfold's turn to stick a tanned finger out and point at the men on screen. With his other hand, he clicked the mouse to pause the action. All eyes were on the frozen pest controllers in the top right corner. The men were rooted to the spot as they stooped for a frog behind the Shakespeare folio, clearly visible in its display case.

Penfold clicked for the videos to run on at normal speed. It was slick, like a three cups street scammer, but clear for all to see. The man Tony recognised as the lorry driver slipped up the acrylic case lid and dropped the Shakespeare book into the carrier with the frogs. It wasn't obvious from the footage exactly how they had opened the lock on the case, but the movements were so quick, everyone assumed they had a copy of the key. Without a break, they continued sweeping the space to gather up more frogs.

It took a further forty minutes, but they dutifully removed every last one, before having a brief laughing conversation with Hildebrand, the final staff member on site. She followed them to the door and exited immediately behind the men.

The outside camera showed her taking her leave of the men who clambered into a white van with the livery of Durham County Council.

'And I recognise that van too. It looks just like the one described by Von Braun at the science site. Have you got a USB stick so you can give me a copy of that video, Kathy? The file will be way too big to email it to me. I'll get it to DC Aria so she can compare with what we got from the chip theft.'

Kathy scrabbled around in a drawer and pulled out a flash drive to copy the video for him. They all waited in silence as the computer detailed its progress with the copying. The quiet became awkward and Tony was relieved to hear Julia Sedgley calling around the vestibule area for somebody to meet her.

He planned to hand over Kathy and Mrs Landrey to show Julia the area she needed to examine, while excusing Penfold and himself to get back to the station to throw this extra case into the mix in the MCT office. But Kathy insisted on chatting to the two men before they left.

She took them back down into the old library room and over to the empty but well-lit first folio case. As they descended the staircase behind her, Kathy pulled her hair back with both hands and, slipping a hair band from her left wrist, slid it up the gathered hair. She turned back to them, her blue eyes still moist, but with a steeled, brave face. Stepping to Penfold, she took his hands in hers. The physical contact made him start, but he didn't turn from her gaze.

'You will find the Shakespeare, won't you?'

He remained silent.

Tony could see her fingers squeezing his hands for emphasis. 'Penfold, I need you to promise me you'll work on this night and day.'

A slight tilt of his head pre-empted a cautious answer. 'Milburn will tell you that I am only commissioned to investigate the mineshaft murders. I came along just now because it's you, but this case is not within my purview.'

Kathy shook her head, and the blonde ponytail swung from side to side. 'Whether you investigate officially or unofficially, I don't care. But find it for me please.' She let his hands go and walked away, giving Tony a brief kiss on the cheek as she passed.

'What the hell?' he said, once she had left.

Penfold shrugged and said, 'I'm going to head home for a surf. Need to get in the water while it's still hardout.'

With that, he followed Kathy out of the exhibition space and left Tony fuming. Kathy's entreaty to Penfold rather than to him, her very own personal detective partner, had dumbfounded Tony. He stared at the doorway.

I solve burglaries for a living. Hey! I'm the bloody detective here! He was shouting inside his own head. Out loud, he followed up, although nobody was there to hear. 'And then that layabout just slopes off to go surfing. Well, she can think whatever she likes of that arrogant prick. He's not going to find her precious book in the North Sea.'

Tony strode out of the building without even looking at anyone.

TWENTY-THREE

'Thank you for coming in today, Mr Von Braun. Hopefully we can get all the information we need from you in a short interview.' Tony used the title "Mr" quite deliberately. He hoped to rile the professor into giving something away.

There was no reason to suspect Von Braun in the theft of the million-dollar computer chip, but Tony had seen DI Godolphin Barnes get the most surprising results through his abrasive approach. When the idea of being rude to the physicist made Tony feel a little wobbly, he reminded himself that their only real clue thus far was the use of the professor's own key card in the theft. So they could justify putting the thumbscrews on.

As DC Meredith showed the academic to a seat opposite where the two detectives would sit, Tony's mind pictured her putting a literal thumbscrew on to one of his big German digits. He saw the stony face grimace with each turn she made of the wooden screw handle.

Meredith started the video recorder, and they introduced the interview to the camera, listing participants, date and time, and location, and finished with an emphatic statement that this was just to establish information and Von Braun should not consider himself a suspect. Utterly implicit was the opposite idea, that he was most definitely a suspect.

The astronomer clearly appeared out of sorts in the surroundings but had the air of a man confused by the policing approach rather than concerned about hiding all his secrets.

Meredith was to begin, and she would be playing good cop. Tony was terrible at playing bad cop, but she had insisted she would use her feminine charms to convince the man to spill any beans that might be hidden in the jar. Tony knew only too well the power of her womanly wiles.

She spoke. 'Professor Von Braun, we need some preliminary information please. Firstly, can you detail exactly what has been stolen. Itemise it all as best you can, and where possible give us a sense of the value of each item please.'

She passed him a pad of paper and a pen. 'If you can write the list down but also say them all for the camera please. This will help a lot when we get to court. Thank you.' As he followed her instructions, Meredith complimented his "beautiful handwriting" and his "amazing command of English, when it's not your first language". All was delivered with body language that one might more likely expect in a strip club.

She made Tony feel uncomfortable. He shifted in his seat on the professor's behalf. He knew she was play-acting, but she went beyond the pale. He also noticed that she had positioned the video camera carefully, so that her most unprofessional bottom-presenting and chest-puffing actions were out of the view of the camera. He shook his head in amazement, but nobody spotted the slight movement.

She followed up by asking Von Braun to list the people who had key cards that would access the basement server room from where the computer had been taken. He dutifully wrote the list, concentrating more on the paper and pen than Meredith's unnecessary stretching and preening. His own name was last, but he added in parentheses after it *"(card used during the robbery)"*.

She leant too close to him and pointed at this annotation. 'And do you have any idea how your card came to be involved? I mean' – she gave him a lascivious grin with her back to the camera – 'I'm assuming you didn't steal it, did you?' Her voice was coy and cheeky.

'Of course not, don't be stupid.' The man was straightforward and logical, essentially immune to Meredith. This impressed and amazed Tony – nobody resisted her.

Moreover, he feared for the good professor. Rejecting Meredith was an extremely dangerous game. Tony himself had suffered three months of stalking when he had dumped her and taken up with Kathy. It was a scary period, and only Kathy's strength and brains had seen them through it. Working with the Crazy Cow, as he and Kathy called her, remained difficult, but after several years, and at Hardwick's insistence, Tony simply had to get on with it. He never stopped worrying about her hidden agenda though.

Tony decided it was time for bad cop to step in. He wasn't good at it, and they weren't even really in a situation that called for interrogation techniques. Greasy Godolphin appeared in his mind, like a devil on the shoulder, urging him on to be brusque.

'Are there any personal circumstances we need to know about? Anything in your life that might have caused somebody to target you, either to take what you have, or to put you in the frame as the thief?'

'I'm not sure vot you mean.'

'Come on Von Braun, you're a man of the world. Do you owe anybody a lot of money? Or maybe there's a jilted lover, or a jealous husband?' Before he could stop himself, Tony's mouth continued in full Barnes mode. 'Any drug problems we need to know about?'

The physicist exploded. 'Are you two mad? Vot is zis, crazy police day? First ve have Detective Constable Pole-Dancer here, and zen ze lead detective accuses the victim of being a drug addict.' His ire amplified his accent even beyond its normal "first language is German" sound.

Tony hated himself in that moment, but he knew the drill, as did Meredith. They both remained silent, waiting for the man to slip up. If he was going to, it would be in that anger. However, Von Braun shut up abruptly. He looked up to the small window high in the wall and then pulled his phone from the inside pocket of his sports jacket.

'Please no phone calls during the interview.'

Their suspect, as much as he was a suspect, nodded and set the phone on the table. He had returned to being the cold, logical physics professor, and his better English accent was restored. 'Ze only person I can think of who might have had access to my key card is my girlfriend. We've been together only four months, so I don't know very much about her background. She's a museum curator and she's Spanish. I know very few details about her history before we met.'

'Oh, and all of a sudden you think she's ripped you off for a million-dollar chip?' Tony continued his sarcastic bad cop routine, but Meredith jumped in, her characterisation lost.

'Wait, is your girlfriend called Alex Carrera?'

'Yes. How did you know zis?'

She leaned over and whispered into Tony's ear how she knew of Ms Carrera.

Tony also changed his demeanour immediately. 'OK, Professor, this is significant. There was a huge robbery at the Bowes Museum, where Alex is the curator. She is head of security policy there. Did she tell you about that burglary?'

'I have not seen her for ten days. She went to Spain for something with her family.'

Everybody paused for a minute's thought. Tony was first to speak after working through some ideas. 'OK, if we imagine for a moment that she is involved in the theft of your computer chip, and you haven't seen her for a while, how could she have used your card yesterday to exit the server room? And then get the card back to you almost immediately so that you were able to show me and Detective Superintendent Hardwick around the lab at about eight o'clock?'

'Yes, I have not seen her. She cannot have done zis yesterday.'

Meredith asked, 'Is it possible to copy the cards? Could she have made a copy of your card some time ago and used it yesterday?'

'I assume ze technology is available to copy key cards. But Alex is in Spain.'

'Is she? How do you know for sure?'

He nodded. 'Of course. I do not know zis as a certainty. She video called me from a place that looked like Spain, but I do not have five sigma level evidence.'

Tony nodded. 'OK, can you write her name and contact details next to your list of key card holders. And if you know the contact details for anyone else on that list, add them too please. And then if you can give us your key card too, we'll get our digital forensics team to look at it.'

Their interviewee scowled, presumably imagining all the places he would be unable to enter if he gave them his card. He dutifully complied, unclipping a photo ID of himself, printed with the purple shield logo of Durham University, from the black lanyard he wore like a narrow tie.

Meredith wanted to be sure there was no mix up going on here. 'Can you tell me of any distinguishing marks we could use to confirm identification of Alex? Scars, birthmarks … tattoos?' She lingered on the last word enough to push Von Braun to go straight to a description of the line drawing dolphin tattoo on Alex's ankle bone. Meredith nodded at Tony. It was definitely the same person.

Distracting him, Tony's phone vibrated on the table in front of him. As standard, its screen was face down, so he lifted it to read the text message from Penfold.

Darkweb sells takeaway chips, cheap as.

In a measured and slow manner, he returned the phone to the table.

'It seems that your computer chip is already available for sale. You told me yesterday it was bespoke, made for you. How special is it? By which I mean, who might buy it?'

Von Braun did not seem fazed by this new information and stroked his grey goatee while mulling over the question. In the end, he looked directly at Tony and pushed his lips out in ignorance. 'Sorry, I am no expert in IT. I wrote a proposal for what we needed it to do, but ze supplier took zat information and produced a chip zat could do it. It voz very good at ze task, too. My researchers wrote ze code for ze simulations and ze computer crunched zose numbers quickly and efficiently.'

Meredith butted in. 'Bitcoin miners?'

He shrugged. 'Maybe. As I say, I don't know vat else is possible with it. We paid a lot of money, but maybe zat is just ze cost for a big, powerful chip and it vasn't so much, um, "tailor-made" is it?'

Tony could tell this was going nowhere useful. 'Right. Can you put the manufacturer's name on that paper too please. Do you know their contact details?'

'I have paperwork on my office computer. I vill email you later.'

Tony was uncertain as to whether he had interrogated this man enough. They had a couple of leads to follow up from this conversation, but he was unconvinced that he had eliminated Von Braun as a suspect. The intertwining of this case and the Bowes Museum Swan theft was a big deal, but the astronomer had been helpful to a fault and seemed to have no concern that the police were interrogating him. *Germanic sangfroid?*

Diane straightened out Tony's confusion with an old school question. 'Where were you yesterday, Professor?' She was all smiles, but the over-sexualised body language was gone. The act was left behind and she was back to being DC Meredith.

'I vas attending ze Gala. I play saxophone in the university brass band.'

Tony and Diane looked at each other with an unspoken "Really?!"

She continued, 'And what about when the frogs were released. With that and the rainstorm, the whole thing broke up early. Which was before the robbery at your building. Where were you then?'

'I vas already in ze cathedral. We stayed and helped ze volunteers to keep ze frogs out from ze Lindisfarne Gospels display rooms. I wish I had gone to try and keep frogs away from my computers. Maybe I'd have seen ze robbers.'

Tony asked, 'Did you have your key card with you then?'

'Yes, I always carry it.'

TWENTY-FOUR

'Perfect, let's go and see the Tan Hill murder site.'

Penfold was breathing heavily and dripping wet in the early morning sunshine. Tony had never previously seen him surf in just boardshorts and a wetsuit shirt. The hot summer was changing things everywhere.

Tony turned to face up the beach, indicating they should go and get Penfold dressed for work. He knew that in fact that would turn out to be shorts, T-shirt and flip-flops, but there was no professionalism argument that would have any impact on how Penfold approached life.

As they walked, Tony countered his friend's suggestion. 'Um, no, we're going to the Bowes Museum to investigate this report. Carrera was reported missing by her work an hour ago, so we need to go there and see how this fits in with the two thefts and Von Braun.'

The sand on the beach just south of Hartlepool glowed golden in the bright sun and crunched beneath Tony's work shoes. They dried quickly as the two walked away from the water's edge, leaving white salt stains on the black polish.

Penfold walked barefoot and the dry sand stuck to his skin in a fine patina. He said, 'I thought I was only commissioned to investigate the murders?'

Tony had foregone a tie given the weather forecast, but even at ten fifteen in the morning, his suit trousers felt sticky around his thighs and the jacket hanging over his arm uncomfortably hot. He wrestled internally with the knowledge that Kathy had given him clear instructions to get Penfold on to the case of her missing folio.

He decided that if you can't beat 'em, join 'em, and came back with sarcasm. 'I'll tell you what, we'll go up to Tan Hill and get an iced drink at the pub. You can have a shufti at the crime scene, although I can't imagine there's anything left to see there, and then we'll both stop in at the Bowes Museum where you can act as an observer, make notes for me and that sort of thing.'

Penfold was smiling as they crossed the beach front road and headed around Promenade Square to his house for a quick change.

While he waited in the kitchen, Mantoro emerged up the basement staircase and chatted to Tony.

'How's it going, Tone?' The man's accent was very American, although he was actually from … . Tony realised he knew no more precise provenance for the man than an entire continent. His round face was scarred from an acid explosion during drugs manufacturing in his previous life. That had killed Mantoro's brother, and Tony decided he probably wasn't too surprised that the guy didn't talk much about those earlier times.

'Sweaty! I imagine you saw plenty of weather like this back home?'

Mantoro was shaggy in all directions, including a bulging dark moustache under his round nose. He smiled, creasing some of the scars, and Tony's mind was taken back to the Daily Espresso and the scars on the face of the ever-smiling Marion Rufus.

He drawled in reply, 'Man, I lived in a shipping container in the jungle for six months. You ain't seen sweaty heat!'

'I bet it didn't come with a thousand frogs in it?!'

Mantoro's bright face broke into real laughter. 'Man, I heard about that. Crazy stuff! Did you ever find out what it was all about? Some stunt by the miners or what?'

'We're still investigating.'

'You know what time we found was the best to do a big heist back home?'

Tony shook his head, intrigued. 'Um, on a public holiday? Christmas maybe?'

172

Mantoro continued grinning, and shook his own head, like a lion shaking its mane. 'Mardi Gras. Chaos on the streets, people everywhere, and all the police out controlling the crowds.' Without any leave-taking, he turned and descended the basement stairs again.

The detective and his civilian consultant investigator clambered out of the black police Golf on to the gravel right in front of the grand Bowes Museum building. David Teesdale met them at the revolving door. He was smartly dressed in a tight security guard outfit, all in grey, including a peaked cap. Their car had been air-conditioned inside, but the short, sunny walk had made Tony hot and sticky again. The inside of the chateau was refreshingly cool.

After leading them down into the basement security office, Teesdale jumped straight into impugning his new boss. 'I knew she was trouble. She's just gone off the reservation completely now.'

'Your call said that Ms Carrera was missing. Can you tell us exactly what you know, why you are reporting her missing?'

'After the Swan was stolen, she was getting some real heat from the trustees, a full investigation of everything she'd done since starting four months ago.'

Penfold interrupted. 'Sorry, I need to take notes of this information. Do you mind if I just record everything you say?' He held up his phone, already recording.

'No, of course not, happy to help. I'm not saying she's involved or anything, but I knew she was never up to this job.'

Tony then interrupted, redirecting Teesdale on topic. 'Sorry, you were telling us why you want to report her as a missing person.'

'Missing person? I'm not sure that's what I mean exactly. After she'd been grilled for most of Monday and Tuesday, she went off sick the rest of last week. She doesn't work the weekends, and we've heard nothing from her this morning. She's not answering her phone, or email, and should have been here at eight. She only lives three streets away, so I went to her house to, er, check she was OK, and she's not there. There's a couple of letters stuck in the letterbox, and she has milk delivered, which is still on the doorstep.'

'Milk delivered?' This concept distracted Tony.

Teesdale explained, 'Traditional little town with lots of dairy farms nearby. I reckon most people in Barney get their milk delivered on a morning.'

Penfold moved them on. 'So, it would appear that she left suddenly, unexpectedly. But she didn't tell anyone here about going away?'

The head of security did not reply, just shook his head.

'We met her boyfriend yesterday and he says she had to go back to Spain for some family thing. You didn't hear anything about that?'

'That grey-haired German bloke? Seemed a bit of a cold fish if you ask me. I couldn't see what she saw in him. Must be twenty years older than her. And she's pretty fiery at times – they struck me as total opposites.'

The old cliche that opposites attract fluttered through Tony's mind, but he said nothing.

Penfold pursued a more direct way of finding out about her disappearance. 'She's new in town, so I'm assuming her house was a rental, I don't suppose you know who the letting agents are?' He turned to look at Tony. 'We could get them to let us in, milk on the doorstep sounds like there could easily be the possibility that she's hurt, so we should get inside.'

Tony scowled at the idea, and Teesdale followed his lead, frowning too.

Penfold ignored them and pursued this. 'Any idea?'

The security guard clearly thought it could only get his unwelcome new boss in more trouble if the police snooped around her house and quickly offered her up. 'The house is owned by the museum; it comes with her job. Our estates team have a spare set of keys. And you're right, we'd better make sure she's safe. I'll have to come with you though, as a matter of protocol, you understand.'

All three knew that the whole idea was stretching the limits of any protocols, but they quickly left to go and investigate the little cottage.

Teesdale unlocked the front door and called her name loudly and repeatedly as they went in. Four more letters sat on the mat behind the door. The place was silent and still.

Tony joined in calling her name and added 'Police. Are you OK?' each time.

The house was made of local sandstone blocks and Tony guessed it must be more than a hundred years old. It was the odd one out in the street, surrounded by council housing from recent decades. It also provided cool against the thirty-degree heat outside, until they entered the kitchen where the sun streamed in the large back window, heating the room up like a greenhouse.

In unison, the men put a hand to their nose as the stench of decomposition hit them all at once. Nothing was visibly out of place or disturbed, and everything looked neat. Fully furnished, but it did not appear lived in.

Kitchen units extended from the sink, in front of a back door with two large, frosted glass panels in it. At the end of the units, the waste bin had a flip top lid that was not airtight, and as Teesdale pushed it timidly open, the smell did not change in intensity, but when he leaned forward to look beyond the bin, he jumped back with a strangled 'Oh!'

Penfold's arm raised, and he pointed at a small rivulet of dried blood just visible as it extended from behind the cupboard units, soiling the large inlaid coir mat.

Tony took a step forward so he could see round the dark green cupboards.

On the back doormat, they found the source of the smell: a dead kitten.

The cat's throat had been slit open.

'Oh my God, she loved that cat. She never shut up about it at work. Constantly showing off pictures of it on her phone.' A pool of blood stained the doormat underneath the now stiff body of her beloved animal. Maggots wriggled in its fur, mostly around the eyes and the bloody wound, with a few in the dried blood around the body.

'Everyone, stand still!' Tony held out both arms with his palms facing the other two, like a traffic cop with a pair of oncoming vehicles. 'This has just become a crime scene. As best we can, we need to go back to the front door without touching or disturbing anything until we get forensics here.'

As they tiptoed back down the hall, Tony dialled up Julia Sedgley to send them a crime scene investigator. He requested Alfie Johnson as he had already examined the scene of the Swan theft and had met Alex Carrera.

By the time Johnson arrived an hour later, they had despatched Mr Teesdale back to his office to send them all the details he had about Alex, plus two photos of her: the one from her job application, and the one that had been taken for her ID badge.

Her olive skin and wavy, dark brown hair spoke of a Moorish ancestry in central Spain. The image on her ID badge further confirmed that heritage – her full name was listed as Alejandra Rae Carrera.

Penfold and Tony were already togged up in paper overalls, shoe covers and hats, along with the blue nitrile gloves that meant they shouldn't contaminate the scene at all. They followed Johnson's lead regarding the process but spent most of their time searching the place for clues about the missing woman, rather than worrying about the kitten that Alfie had to examine.

CSI Johnson also examined the house for any trace evidence that might suggest what had happened to the museum curator. He found nothing. None of them found anything useful.

'In my opinion, this place has been forensically cleaned. There's no fingerprints anywhere, except yours, Tony. But more than that, there's no DNA evidence anywhere. No hairs, not even in the shower drain. Bleach on all surfaces – more than you'd use to clean the place.'

Penfold asked, 'Was the kitten put there to cover up somebody hurting Alex? If they couldn't get the blood out of it, and the mat is inlaid into the flooring so they couldn't remove it, is that a forensic countermeasure?'

'I haven't tested it yet, obviously, but that blood at the back door is going to be from the kitten, I'm sure. There's not enough for it to be from any significant human injury, and it's pooled exactly as I'd expect from the cat's injury and where it's lying.

'The maggots are consistent with a possible time of death from four to seven days ago.'

TWENTY-FIVE

'Her car is missing too. It's not at the cottage, so we've put a message out for all units to keep an eye out for it. A little, red Renault hatchback.' Tony was leaning against his office doorjamb, as the MCT brought the superintendent up to speed on Alex Carrera.

'So, do we think she's been taken? Killed? Or is she involved in the robberies?' Acting Detective Superintendent Hardwick supported his question with a beady look from his good eye. The dead eye stared off towards Penfold.

In the background, Meredith sat at the big desk surrounded by evidence bags of items that they had collected from Alex Carrera's cottage. Alfie Johnson had already checked them for fingerprints and had taken away the items most likely to offer DNA. He hadn't left them confident of finding any though: the house was bizarrely empty of personal objects like hair or toothbrushes.

Meredith piped up from her seated position. 'She didn't strike me as particularly competent, given the responsibility of such a valuable collection at the Bowes. My money's on her having run off back to Spain in fear, after having lost the most valuable item in their collection.'

Penfold said, 'That would explain the absence of her things – the house didn't even have any clothes left behind – but by all accounts, she loved the kitten, so what happened to that? And why the extreme cleaning of the rest of the place? If she's just running away, they knew she lived there.'

Tony rejoined, 'Yes, and being Von Braun's girlfriend is too much of a coincidence for me since his key card was the one used for the burglary. Guv, I'm worried she's been taken. Some sort of gang pressuring her for the information they needed for both thefts. There's no indication at her place that she was hurt. Johnson reckons only the cat's blood was present.'

Harry Hardwick had been silently taking in all the various theories. 'The place was bleach cleaned. Might that be something you'd do after killing her there?'

Penfold countered, 'But why take her body away?'

Nobody had time to consider this question before Hardwick's mobile phone rang. The university vice chancellor seemed to have him on speed dial. After a few brief words, apparently offering no actual information, he primed Tony to join him to go and visit her immediately.

'And you,' he said, as he pointed at Penfold. 'I know we've picked up a lot more work here, so I want you to focus entirely on the mineshaft murders, and we'll cover the burglaries and disappearance of Miss Carrera.'

He continued, 'I'm going to take over as SIO on the robberies. Tony you'll remain heading up the treasure hunters, but I'll need you to work on everything. Meredith, you continue sifting through those things.' He gave a peremptory wave at the half dozen evidence bags. 'And let us know if you find anything. Where's Aria?'

Tony answered, 'She went to see about getting a warrant to push neBay for that address. She reckons they're dragging their feet.'

Without any more words, Harry headed for the door, leaving Tony to give Penfold a quick shrug and chase after the boss.

The two policemen entered the double wide glass doors as they slid open with a brushing sound. Durham University's Palatine building, mostly clad in timber and with arching, wooden columns like flying buttresses, looked like the Ark as Noah neared completion of his giant boat.

Inside, they had entered at one end of the internal winding "street" that the architects had been so proud of, and there was a confusion of people milling around twenty metres ahead, beyond the circular reception counter.

Hardwick and Tony advanced and were met by the vice chancellor just before they reached the crowd, who were all talking and pointing at the empty white wall that stretched high to the vaulted glass ceiling. A large square cordon formed of yellow and black tape held back the onlookers from one blank section of wall. The whole corridor wall was white and blank. Tony wondered what the fuss was about.

'Oh my God!' H exclaimed and pointed up at the wall before the VC could say anything.

Tony felt like he was the boy in "The Emperor's New Clothes". He wanted to shout out, 'People, there's nothing there!'

'Yes.' The vice chancellor was stony faced. 'Come and take a closer look.'

Tony's mind was racing. *What the hell are they on about?* As they walked nearer to the cordon, people stepped aside. On reaching the tape, approximately three metres from the wall, Tony could make out a small, yellowy outline where it appeared a picture had previously hung. He struggled to see it clearly, as it was high on the wall, and the bright sun outside streamed in through the ceiling glass, making the wall almost blinding.

'It was stolen over the weekend.'

Tony asked, 'Forgive me, I've only been in this building a couple of times.' The Palatine Centre abutted the Bill Bryson Library, where Kathy had worked for many years prior to her current job. In all the times he had met her at work, there had been little cause for them to enter the central administration building. 'What was there that has been stolen?'

Harry whispered, 'The Picasso.'

'Yes, well the most valuable one at least. We still have some more in the archive. It was a gorgeous cubist image of a bull and a matador. Orange and black, just stunning.'

'How much are we talking?' Tony was now on his toes, scanning the empty space.

'Perhaps we should talk in my office. Security will keep people back until your forensic team arrive.'

The lift to the third floor opened on a luxuriously carpeted corridor and they crossed to the expansive office at one end of the building. The view from the panoramic window took in Durham Cathedral and Tony could just make out bits of the castle poking up behind the many roofs of the colleges along North Bailey.

Their discussion revealed that the missing artwork had been purchased for £1.1 million but was currently insured for over two million. Tony held his tongue and turned to face the glass to avoid saying anything he would regret.

He knew Kathy's salary, her pay as one of the most important curators in the university. He was also aware of years of strikes by the lecturers' union, and more recently, a long and bitter dispute with the union of the catering staff across the colleges. The students themselves were currently embroiled in a rent strike against the high costs of studying in the town.

How could the university justify spending a million pounds on artwork for the corridors? He compared it with their other big loss on Saturday: the computer chip theft. That could be considered a reasonable research expense. Probably – Tony was acutely aware that he did not know anything about the market forces for such an exclusive integrated circuit. *But a million quid on art?* He wasn't even sure you could study fine art at this university. He certainly couldn't think of an art department building, and he prided himself on knowing the city centre's geography intimately, as a policeman ought to.

As if reading his mind, the vice chancellor told them that the Picasso had been an investment: a way to keep the value of the university's financial reserves increasing. Fine art, she claimed, was one of the fastest rising investments available. Press and student scrutiny had exploded when a freedom of information request had revealed the overall cost of the art collection.

'We felt that putting the Picasso on display would go some way towards appeasing that public opinion. It was difficult to get across the concept that our financial advisers reckoned this was a better way to protect the reserves than having a bunch more zeroes on our bank account. An institution of this size needs millions in contingency money that we simply don't use. Working out what to do with that money is a perennial headache.'

Tony felt like saying, "Best bet, probably, wouldn't be to leave it lying around in the corridor of the central admin building."

Instead, he asked for the name and contact details of the person who could supply them with CCTV footage for the building and surrounds. That office was on the ground floor, not far from the now vacant Picasso display site, so he excused himself to go and co-ordinate gaining that video footage along with meeting the crime scene investigator. He didn't envy the forensic challenge of attempting to find evidence that had not come from the scrum of onlookers.

The head of security wore a dark three-piece suit and insisted that the painting could not have been more secure. The mounting was in a state-of-the-art polycarbonate case, well above ground level, in a busy space that even had passers-by on Sundays. Half the workforce had a key card that would open the building after hours but, with the security office just metres from the Picasso and staffed twenty-four hours, nobody had imagined that the painting could ever be surreptitiously removed.

The acting detective inspector earned his promotion in that security office. He directed the stiff-suited man to search the video footage beginning at two thirty on Saturday afternoon. He had a sneaking suspicion he knew what they were about to watch.

Sure enough, frogs began to ingress the building and steadily scared away the few people heading to or from their offices.

After a brief scurrying up and down by the two members of university security on shift at the time, including several clumsy minutes where one attempted to use a broom to sweep the frogs back to the door, several other men arrived.

These were dressed in the white pest control overalls with Durham County Council hi-vis vests. In a new move, compared to the other robberies Tony had watched on CCTV footage, they hid their robbery by cordoning off the critical part of the corridor. A giant white tent marked *BIOHAZARD – Keep Out* was erected in front of the Picasso wall, and then an additional tape cordon extended around the tent, even larger than the barrier the university had put in place that morning.

Two "pest controllers" stood at the ends of the corridor waving people back if they approached. The camera had no audio, so the sounds of tools could not be heard on playback. A number of large toolboxes went into the tent, including an extendable ladder, so Tony could easily assume what must have gone on.

Less than fifteen minutes after they had arrived, the area had been cleared of frogs, so the cordon and the tent were dismantled and removed. As the men disappeared out of the front entrance doors, the blank space shouted out of the screen that the robbers were getting away. Just visible through the doors was the same van Tony recognised from the other robberies. White and marked with the council's pest control livery, it sped away towards the A181, which passed along the side of the building.

'OK, pretty much as I expected, although the tent's a new thing.'

'What, you seen this before?'

Tony ignored the question and asked for the footage to be transferred on to one of the evidence USB drives he now carried. As the computer was counting up the percentage that had been copied, he asked an additional question. 'Can you tell whose key card opened the doors when they first entered? I assume the building wasn't generally open on a Saturday, like it is today?'

'Ah no, you're right, with the timing on the video, we should be able to get that exactly.' He fired up a database on a second computer and cross-matched the timestamps for the entry of the robbers. 'OK, that card was issued to a K. Stoneman. Just give me a second ...'

Tony's legs rocked underneath him, and he grabbed hold of the edge of the desk.

'Yep, here's the personnel file. It has that as a Miss Kathy Stoneman. She's a curator in Palace Green Library. I'll print you a picture and her address.'

On the screen, Tony's girlfriend stared at them from a digital image of her ID badge. He could barely answer. The printer was quiet, but it was louder than him as he mumbled his thanks and grabbed the sheet of paper. He turned to rush out and was in the corridor before the guard called him back.

'You've forgotten the USB drive, Inspector.'

He grabbed the flash drive from the man's fat hand without a word and ran away along the bright white indoor "street", exactly as the art thieves had done two days earlier.

TWENTY-SIX

Following the loss of the Shakespeare folio, Kathy had accepted Tony's insistence that she take a day off. The shock of the whole affair had made her shaky and nauseous for most of Sunday evening.

She hadn't been scheduled to work the Monday anyway but had assumed she'd need to meet with a variety of university bigwigs to account for the security failings with the missing book. It was unusual for Tony to insist on anything in their relationship, but given her upset, he'd put his foot down. Kathy had not been fit to resist him too hard.

On returning to their suburban home, he abandoned the car on the driveway and ran inside to find her on their cream sofa with a cup of camomile tea, reading the latest Stuart Turton mystery. The blinds were closed but the windows were slightly open, and she had two fans blowing. The ventilation made the room pleasantly cool.

He put his hand to his chest in relief, before bending down to give her a kiss. This brought a smile, and she tapped her phone screen to see the time.

'How come you're here so early? Surely there's a ton of investigating to do? Wait, has something happened?' She leapt to her feet, standing on his toes in the process. 'Have you found it?' The ache in her voice brought a tightness to his chest and he had to admit there was no progress in finding the lost Shakespeare.

She sat down hard, and her book dropped to the floor.

'Where's your key card?'

'What? What do you mean?'

'Your uni ID badge, the magnetic card that opens the doors. I need to see it.'

'You came past it in the hall. It's hanging on the key hook, same as always.'

He marched out to find her lanyard dangling from the hook she always left it on. Returning to the lounge, Tony pulled the crumpled paper from the security office out of his jacket pocket and compared the card with its printout. He'd known with certainty when he first saw the image on screen, but this confirmed that it was the same card in his hand as the one the university computer had recorded as opening the Palatine building for the theft of Picasso's matador painting.

He slumped down beside Kathy and dropped the ID card and its paper facsimile on to their walnut coffee table.

'What's up? Why have you got a printout of my campus card?'

'I think you're in danger.'

'What? What are you on about?'

He turned to face her and took her nearest hand in his. 'You remember I told you about the disappearance of the curator of the Bowes Museum?' Kathy nodded. 'And her dead cat?' She nodded again, dumbstruck. 'Your key card was used to open the Palatine building on Saturday, and they stole the Picasso painting from the lobby there.'

Kathy's blue eyes widened in horror. Her voice was barely audible as she repeated, 'What?'

'Could you go and stay with your brother in Leeds for a while?'

She sat up straight, stiff like a mannequin. 'Stop! What are you talking about?'

Tony wasn't a hundred per cent sure himself quite what he was afraid of, but the coincidences were too much, and Alex Carrera had vanished. Spanish authorities said she had not entered the country, and her phone had not connected to any network for over a week.

He inhaled deeply, exhaled briefly and laid out his concerns. 'The Bowes Museum woman was in charge of the security for the Silver Swan, and it was stolen. She was seeing Professor Von Braun and his key card was used to enable the robbery of the astronomy department's million-dollar computer. She's now disappeared, and her kitten was murdered.

'You were in charge of the Shakespeare book, and it was stolen. Your key card was also used to enable the theft of the university's Picasso. The similarities are too close. I don't want to come home to find you missing and Flint dead on the doormat.'

As if on cue, their tortoiseshell cat sauntered in and jumped up on to the sofa. She ignored the two humans and curled up at the other end of the milky seat cushions.

Tony could sense Kathy's tension. He could see conflict passing over her features.

'I can't leave Durham now. How would that look? I'll be suspect number one in the folio theft. If I'm not already.'

Quietly, almost under his breath, Tony said, 'You're not.'

'No, I have to get back to work and help with figuring out what went wrong in our security systems. I'm sure there's a ton of paperwork to complete about the robbery too, quite apart from helping your lot get their act together and recover it. Have you spoken to Helen Landrey yet? She's an expert on the recovery of stolen artefacts.'

'I don't think you quite understand how serious this is. Nobody's seen Miss Carrera for days. I fear that we will find her body in the River Tees any time now. I saw her kitten with its throat slit. Her house was bleached clean. These criminals are not messing around. Of course we'll throw everything into finding the Shakespeare, I'll send Meredith to see Landrey tomorrow. But for now, please will you pack a bag.'

Kathy swayed away from him. 'I don't think you understand how serious I am. I can't just run from my responsibilities.'

The determined and capable woman he had fallen in love with sat in front of him, defiant and strong. He realised that he should have known this would be her response.

'And bringing the Crazy Cow into this only makes me more angry. Keep away from her, Tony.' This sentence ended with a little more hesitancy, and although it was barely detectable, he was sure he heard a quavering in her voice.

'Don't worry, I keep her at arm's length all the time.' He added an unnecessary qualifier, 'She really is deranged.' Realising this would more likely increase Kathy's anxiety, rather than quelling it, he stood down a little on his stance of sending her into hiding. 'I understand you need to work through it all with the uni authorities and will most likely need to be at the library to do that. But I am worried for your safety. How about this: can we make sure that you are never alone? I'll accompany you to work and home again, and can you make sure there's always somebody with you in the library?'

She nodded slowly, taking the idea in.

Tony continued, 'In fact, I wonder if you can ask the university security office to station somebody at Palace Green Library all the time?'

Her head movement turned to a more convinced shaking. 'They'll never have enough staff to do that. They'll just say we have to close until it's all sorted out.'

He spoke quietly, fully expecting a negative response. 'Maybe you should close. Just for a short while.'

Kathy did not jump down his throat, as he half expected, but she would not countenance the idea. She argued that the library building would be much safer for her, especially if the doors were open so that the public could just walk in at any moment. Any thugs who came in would never be certain that they'd be able to avoid witnesses. She claimed it was possible to lock the front door in its open position during their opening hours, so there was no danger of that safety net being closed off.

Tony knew he had gained all the concessions he could hope for, and promised himself he would pop in to visit her regularly every day.

It was time to change the subject, so he asked about what kind of takeaway she might fancy for their tea. Kathy was not in the mood for food, and once she told him so, he was at a loss for what to talk about next.

The last thing he wanted to discuss was any police matters. The number of serious crimes on his plate seemed ever increasing and little progress was being made. They were gaining a great deal of information and physical evidence related to the four major burglaries and the four coal shaft murders, but none of it seemed to be throwing up any useful leads.

He felt like he was stuck at the bottom of one of the mineshafts, just stuck in the dark. He could see the dead body on the ground beside him but couldn't move anywhere. For a moment he could hear Kathy calling from the drift beside him, but he couldn't see her as that passage was pitch black. He looked at the corpse and it wore Dickie Harbottle's Rip Curl belt.

Tony emerged from his daydream in the kitchen beside the kettle, which was full and heating. Kathy was tugging at his belt asking if he was OK. The kettle clicked off and he saw he had already set out mugs with teabags in them. 'Mmh, yeah, sorry.' He pointed at the cups. 'Want a cuppa?'

'No thanks, I've still got half of my camomile. You sure you're OK?'

'Yes.' He smiled unconvincingly. 'Just thought of something I need to check with Madeline Aria. Put the TV on, and I'll be back in a sec.'

He thumb-typed a message for DC Aria:

Any progress getting those delivery details for the belt purchase?

That's our best lead right now.

189

Before he had finished putting milk in his tea, his colleague replied:

> First thing in the morning. Judge just signed off the warrant, and my contact at neBay insisted they'd send me the details as soon as I presented the warrant. She only works 8-4 of course.

Tony sent a thumbs up. He was in the middle of typing a reply – that he would meet her in the MCT office at eight in the morning – when Penfold sent a text:

> Maid Marion springs
>
> Daily Espresso breakfast;
>
> Update incoming.

He amended his meet with Aria to be nine o'clock and reassured himself that she'd need a few minutes at least to contact the legal liaison representative at the internet sales company.

In reply to Penfold he asked for the coffee shop meeting to be at eight and further asked if the surfer could just get on with it and tell him the update, rather than sending cryptic haikus. The curt reply told Tony that he had misunderstood, and the update was coming from Marion, at breakfast, which was already slated for 8 a.m..

It was difficult to tell in a text message, but Tony assumed the patronising final missive was sarcasm:

> And the first line means Marion is paying for breakfast.

He shook his head. *We can't let a witness pay for our breakfast. Come on man, that's the first thing they teach in anti-corruption school.*

TWENTY-SEVEN

The mellow jazz background in the Daily Espresso suited any time of day and Tony was glad to step out of the early morning heat into the seriously air-conditioned cold of the small coffee shop.

Penfold leapt up from a round table across from the entrance door and shook his hand. 'Morning, Milburn. I trust you're in good form?' He only ever called Tony by his surname, but the greeting was much more exuberant than was normal.

He smiled. 'I'm fine, thanks. You sound pretty chipper.'

Penfold leaned in and quietly imparted, 'I have a good feeling about this meeting. I'll be honest with you, I've rather struggled to make much headway with these cases. Or the various parts of this one case. I am convinced the four dead bodies are linked somehow. Most likely the same murderer.'

He pointed over to the bar where Marion's bright red summer dress dominated the morning queue. 'I suspect any one contact on the forum that has communicated with all Dooley, Muckle and Bowline is highly likely to be their murderer. Not quite sure how the Harbottle skeleton fits in, but any breakthrough will be a great start.'

As Tony watched Marion's tall frame standing patiently, he thought that the treasure hunter community they were dealing with was likely so small that they'd all have had messages with everyone else included in them. It would be "like finding a nerd in a haystack" he smiled to himself.

Before he could dispute the idea with Penfold, Marion turned around. She was about to be served and waved to Tony, her hand signals asking what he might want. She clearly didn't want to call across the room and disturb all the other patrons, nor did she dare to step from the queue to come over and ask him directly. Such a move would have then required her to either go to the end of the long queue, or to attempt to push back in at the front. It was a classically English dilemma.

Bugger. They didn't have time for him to wait in line as well and Tony was starving. He convinced himself they could get past any possible impropriety by giving her cash to cover their food and drinks.

He shrugged in an overly polite, also very English, manner, as if suggesting *Oh, anything you'd be so kind as to buy for me*. He supplemented this with a drinking action and then also pointed at the croissants lined up on the glass display case. He concluded with a thumbs up gesture and a mouthed "Thank you."

The two men sat down and waited for Marion to return with a tray of coffees and pastries. Tony explained that they would need to get the information from her as quickly as possible. They had to get to the police station to organise the raid on whatever address Aria got hold of for Harbottle's mysteriously out of time belt.

Penfold pointed out that although the body had been found in nearby Tudhoe, the belt delivery could have been from anywhere in the world. All they had was an internet archive page of the sale auction being closed. The two men mulled this over, staring at the dark wood tabletop.

A tray landed in their eyelines, with a clanking of china and cutlery. 'Oops! You two seem utterly morbid.' Marion was bright and chattering as she flopped down into the third chair at the table. Putting a hand to her chest she said, 'Oh gosh, I was about to joke "Did somebody die?" but of course that's why we're here. How insensitive of me. So sorry.'

Penfold waved away her apology, and Tony proffered a stiff twenty-pound note for their breakfasts. She left it on the table, untouched and unmentioned.

'It was great to see you at the Miners' Gala. Have you been playing the trombone for long? It was very professional.' Penfold sounded like a teenager talking to a girl he had a crush on.

She played along, dutifully blushing and making light of his compliments. 'Oh, a little while. I'm not sure you could hear me at all among the cacophony of our band. What happened with all those frogs though? That was crazy. Was it one of those weird storms you read about where frogs rain from the sky?'

Ignoring her amphibian questions, Tony moved the conversation along. 'Penfold tells me you have some more information about the treasure hunters whose bodies we found. I take it there's been some discussions on your blogsite about them?'

'Yes of course, sorry, listen to me blathering on about a plague of frogs.' She tucked her hair behind both ears, an action to collect her thoughts. 'In fact, the conversations have been much more focussed on St Cuthbert's Friday coming up. There's a lot of excitement that the treasure will be found on that date.'

Tony was making notes. He usually used his phone for this job, but he was far quicker with a pen and notebook. Scribbling quickly, he noted the things she said and on a separate page created a list of actions for himself to follow up.

The first action on that list had come from her question about the source of the frogs. *"Find delivery source of shipping containers."* Back on track with the treasure hunter problem, he added *"Email all Durham stations??expand their rural patrols??"*

The question marks indicated his uncertainty that there would be any capacity to further increase the movement of panda cars around Durham's country roads. This had already become a standing order since John Bowline's body had been found, but it was a Herculean task. The number of disused mineshaft entrances in the county far outnumbered the police officers on shift at any one time. *Like a hundred to one, or maybe a thousand.*

Penfold asked, 'What about mutual connections between the three men who died? Did you find anyone who had a lot of chat with all three of them?'

193

'Yeah, I mean tons of people. Well, the whole forum has about four hundred user accounts, but only about thirty that regularly contribute, so that active group of thirty-odd basically all talk to each other at some time or another.'

'Sure, makes sense, niche interest group, I suppose.' Penfold was nodding and smiling, supporting her every word. 'What about offline? Did any of the conversations talk about meeting up in real life?'

'It's not common. These folk aren't loners, they nearly always go on the hunt with somebody else, but they tend to already have a search partner that they go out with. Same pairings all the time.'

'And no conversations that broke that mould?'

'You know what, there was one person, with a lot of accurate information, who reckoned their research had produced a whole lot more, and they were looking for partners to help them follow the clues they'd uncovered. They didn't reference the mine locations where you found the bodies, and they talked to a lot of other people, but they did talk to the three who were killed.'

Penfold smiled, and it was infectious. Marion couldn't help but smile along. He said, 'Come on, spill the goods. You've been building up this big reveal, let's hear it.'

She closed her eyes and nodded in admission before pulling a slip of paper from her little cloth bag and laying it in front of Penfold. 'The username is LuvCuthbert. Here's the details I have, but it's just a name and email address, as you only have to fill in an online form to join the forum.'

Penfold's phone had two little fins attached to the back, shaped like the tail fins on a surfboard. These enabled it to stand upright on the table as he slid a finger gently up the screen. The surfer's blond head bobbed, and he pointed at the screen, although nobody else could see. 'Yep, that's one of the multi-user accounts.'

'Multi-user?' Marion's voice held a note of confusion. 'What do you mean? And how do you know the usernames on my forum. Have you been looking through it?'

'It's a long story.' Penfold held up his hands, with a soft, little smile that could have reassured the passengers on the Titanic that nothing was amiss.

'Still nothing on that from Trident?' Tony felt this was sufficiently cryptic that it was OK to say it out loud in front of Marion.

Penfold's response was bland but drawn out. 'Noooo, I'll chase her up on it.'

The policeman looked at his watch. 'Thanks for coming to see us, and thanks again for breakfast, you really didn't need to, but we have a lot of investigating to get into this morning. I hope you won't feel short-changed on the breakfast if we have to leave now.' He rose from his seat.

'Oh, gosh, no, of course.' She sat upright and gave an awkward thumbs up at the idea.

Penfold looked across to his friend, bemused. His eyes flicked back to their witness. 'Was that all you had to tell us?'

She nodded. 'Um, yes. LuvCuthbert arranged to meet with all three of the dead men. That was all I'd found out.'

Tony sat back down again. 'Wait, you didn't tell us he was going to *meet* them all. What were the details of that?'

She blushed again. 'Sorry, yes that was the point. Did I not actually say so? Trouble is, they swapped phone numbers and agreed to take the messaging off my forum and organise it by phone. So I don't know any more than they were keen to meet.'

Penfold was fully attentive again. 'Do you have those phone numbers?'

'Oh gosh, I'm awful at this. Sorry, I can transcribe them when I get home, but I didn't realise it was important enough to bring them now. Sorry.'

On his actions list, Tony scrawled *"Digital forensics check phones for LuvCuthbert messages"*. He said, 'Please do. If you can send them through as soon as possible please. That phone number might be the break we need to solve these murders.' Tony wasn't sure if this was true, but they had virtually no leads on the mineshaft deaths, so anything would help.

They parted company on the street outside. Marion was headed up to the cathedral; she had secured a ticket for the Lindisfarne Gospels exhibition. She pointed at a squashed frog in the gutter as she left them, and sang with a smile, 'It's raining frogs, hallelujah, it's raining frogs, oh, fro-o-ogs.'

At these lyrics, Tony took Penfold's arm and said, 'I've got an idea. This way.'

He explained that he had seen the manager's altercation with the delivery driver who had dumped the final shipping container out front. Two minutes later, they climbed to the mezzanine level of Durham Indoor Market and entered the management office.

The two pokey rooms making up the "management suite" held a desk each along with a variety of other mismatched furniture items, all cluttered with boxes and papers. The bearded manager sat behind one desk, struggling with his computer, poking the keyboard with one finger at a time.

He barely appeared to be listening, but once Tony had explained that he was investigating the frogs and the shipping containers, the man leant over and pulled a sheet of crumpled paper from a waste bin behind him.

Tony flattened the paper out on a small square of empty desk space. It was the delivery note for the third shipping container outside. 'Can I take a photo of this?'

The man shrugged. 'Keep it, I don't want it. It wasn't even delivered to us. We don't own the Market Place, as the driver was at great pains to tell me.'

'Milburn, didn't he claim they knew nothing about this?' Penfold leant over Tony's arm and pointed on the form at the authorising signature space. In a smart hand, the name *Barry Black* was plainly signed.

'He did.'

The manager was gamely prodding his keyboard again, staring at the display screen, so Tony and Penfold left without another word. They split up as Penfold had "some things to do back in the lab".

As soon as Tony arrived back in the police station, DC Aria presented her boss with the invoice for the purchase of the old Rip Curl belt.

He headed into his partitioned office and texted the delivery address to Penfold, who immediately called back. 'Are you sure that's the right address?'

'Oh, um, I think so, hang on.' He looked at the neBay order details form and confirmed, 'Yes. Yes, there's even a picture of the belt. It's not covered in mineshaft muck in this picture, but that buckle is unmistakable. Castle Eden Manor, Castle Eden. The only name on the order is the single letter "M" – I can't believe they accept that kind of anonymity for placing an order. Do you know the place?'

'Not directly, but that's the same address as the domain registration for MaidMarionettes.com.'

'Oh shit. Do you think she could be involved?'

'Well, she didn't murder Dickie Harbottle. His skeleton – or whoever's skeleton it is – has been dead longer than she's been alive. Albeit not as long as we're being led to believe. So that corpse is deliberately misleading, and she's involved in that subterfuge. Or at least, somebody at the same address she used to set up her website. Which seems too much of a coincidence to me for it to be another person.'

Tony was nodding excitedly, now imagining the flame-haired Miss Rufus elaborately putting together a sort of dummy corpse. 'And she's the only one we know of for certain who has had contact with all of the modern murder victims.'

Penfold laughed. 'Come on then, Milburn. What exactly is modern murder?'

'You know what I mean.' Tony rolled his eyes. 'Anyway, ask Trident to double check that for us if she could.'

Penfold was curt. '*I* can check that. I told you, the domain registry is public.' He paused for a moment, and Tony wasn't sure if it was for effect. He finished with 'So to speak.'

'Well, what about this as something for Trident instead: does she have access to some sort of tattoo image database or anything like that? The police databases are a bit disjointed and hit and miss when it comes to identifying tattoos.'

'I can certainly ask her to search out whatever she can. What are you looking for?'

Tony tapped his phone screen a couple of times to pull up his notes on Alex Carrera. 'It's the missing woman from the Bowes Museum. There's one thing we did get on her, although I don't really know how this might help find her, but maybe could give us some sort of lead, who knows.'

He swiped his screen to move onto a photo of a sketch that Diane Meredith had drawn of what she had seen on the stairs in the Bowes Museum. 'She's got a tattoo of a dolphin.'

There was silence for a full five seconds. 'A dolphin tattoo?' Another constricted pause. 'Wh-where is it?'

Tony assumed that the phone connection was going in and out as Penfold's voice wavered.

'On her ankle. I'll send you Meredith's sketch of it.'

There was another long period of silence after Tony had clicked to send Penfold the image. The surfer finally asked, 'Do you remember the noms de plume of the various people in Maid Marion's discussion forums?'

'Um, maybe. Indiana Jones, or sorry, Indy. And did you say CRA? Um, WillemDafoe or something. Oh, I do remember TheKnottyProblem. Who else was there? Anyway, so what?'

'I'm thinking of LeapingDolphin.'

Tony laughed out loud. 'You mean some connection to the tattoo? Carrera's not connected with the mineshaft murders – she's somehow connected to the Swan and the chip thefts.'

Penfold paused again. 'I think we're going to discover that she's heavily connected to everything.'

TWENTY-EIGHT

The large barn had two brick walls nearly ten metres high and two open walls consisting of several separate columns, and steel girders that served to hold up the roof. The sun beat down and twenty or so uniformed police officers cowered in the shade that, at four in the afternoon, only covered half of the floor space.

Tony could smell straw and manure. The farmyard odours reminded him vividly of finding Michael Dooley and Dickie Harbottle in the Tudhoe mineshaft twelve days earlier. He felt hot and sticky again, his stab vest's Velcro fasteners holding it tight against his chest. They were barely two miles from the beach at Blackhall Rocks, and the salt in the air muted the stink of horse manure slightly.

Sergeant Baz Bainbridge was the lead on their raid on Castle Eden Manor. This was the next property over from Hesleden Hall, where the police had gathered to prepare themselves for a potentially violent sortie across the fields at the Manor.

That address had received delivery of the belt found on a dead man, and DNA on that belt had also been found on the rock used to kill another man.

Bainbridge, built like the proverbial brick outhouse, already had a black eye. An old school Geordie copper, he was also a keen amateur boxer. It was, nonetheless, a surprise to Tony that the sergeant's current injury had not been sustained at the hands of his wife, Carrie.

The two had a very physical relationship and Baz regularly turned up to work on a Monday with injuries. Tony had met Carrie at numerous social events, and there was no question of domestic abuse – the two were equal partners in their altercations. She and Baz got drunk together and fought; it was their thing.

'Reet, let's gan!' Bainbridge called the massed officers to order. Tony stood off to one side, next to Detective Constable

Meredith, and at this turn of the sergeant's local dialect, he took a half step to leave. By the time Tony realised the man had meant "Let's get started [with the briefing]" rather than the more usual meaning, "Let's go!", he found himself awkwardly close to Diane. She did not move away to give him any more space. If anything, he reckoned she leaned in even closer to him.

Bainbridge continued, 'This'll be a difficult raid. We divvent knar if we're headin' into an empty building or if we'll meet a gang of dangerous criminals. None of the databases give wor any clues. The council tax is paid by a Marion Rufus, who is also listed in the land registry as owner of the property since early last year. And she's also the named owner of the website where our four murdered men met online and arranged their visits to old pits on some sort of treasure hunt.'

A pair of portable whiteboards on wheels had been set up in front of the few hay bales stacked against one of the barn's solid walls. Bainbridge stood between these boards.

On his left were pictures of the four dead men, along with notes of basic details about them and a map of the north-east, with red stickers showing where their bodies had been found, and a blue one where the police now stood. The byline photo of Maid Marion from her website had been stuck on this board too.

The second display board held a close-up map of the area, along with the blurry satellite images of the two adjoining properties that were available on Google Maps. Most prominently, an outline plan of the ground and buildings had shading and coloured arrows to indicate the planned movements of various groups of police, including the dog unit, the forensics team and the MCT detectives. The latter team consisted of Milburn and Meredith who would follow up after the property and any suspects had been secured.

Hesleden Hall, the adjacent property, was a rambling smallholding. Along with the barn, there was a residential house, some dog runs and a large well-appointed stable block. The place was owned by a horse-riding friend of DSupt Hardwick, and the boss had pulled in a favour to allow them to base their raid preparations in this barn. The location would also enable them to approach Castle Eden Manor across the rear fields, which they hoped might ensure some element of surprise.

Just outside, in the baking sunshine, stood a host of police cars, along with an ambulance, a police van ready to transport anyone they arrested, Alfie Johnson's huge pick-up truck and Penfold's lime green campervan. Penfold was under instructions to wait at this hard-standing area for the raid to be completed. If the place showed up anything that could inform his investigative work, Tony would call him to join them, but Hardwick had been explicit about "keeping the civilians safe".

The New Zealander knew how to pass time in hot weather, and he had immediately endeared himself to the rank-and-file officers by bringing a giant coolbox filled with all manner of iced drinks and offering them round while everyone was waiting.

Bainbridge had explained the plans for the movements and responsibilities of the various teams and asked if there were any questions. Tony had not seen him edge his way in at the back between the paramedics, so he was surprised when Penfold piped up, almost invisible in the crowd, 'Why do we have an armed response team here?'

Baz knew Penfold and his position, or lack of it, in the hierarchy. He looked over to Tony and wiped the sweat off his shaven head. 'As I just said, Roads and Armed Response are acting as backup. They'll set up the first roadblock on the long, shared driveway out to Mickle Hill Road.' He turned and pointed to the big map.

'Sorry, yes, I understood that. What I mean is why do we need firearms at all. I've met Miss Rufus, and she's a waif of a woman. I expect you'll find her watering flowers in a summer dress.'

Tony judged that Marion Rufus had quite a bit more strength to her than a "waif", but he let it go. Sgt Bainbridge shrugged positively. 'Let's hope you're right and this all falls into place easily, but we've got four dead men, one hit hard with a heavy rock. Worst of all, we've got very little intelligence of any sort about what's going on at the Manor. It's quite possible this woman has been coerced by a gang of thugs.'

'Hope for the best, prepare for the worst,' Tony concurred.

Penfold shook his head and wandered back out of the barn towards his campervan.

The second canine unit crackled over Bainbridge's radio. 'We've strolled the length of the walkway past the property and there's no sign of anyone.' Two police officers, acting as a couple in plain clothes, had walked their Alsatian dog along the Castle Eden Dene walking trail, which went right beside one fence line of the Manor's fields.

Before the sergeant could respond, they followed up with more information. 'There's a number of vehicles though. Several white vans, the front end of an articulated lorry and what looks like a fire engine. Hard to see the last one as it's mostly behind a building when you look from the walking path.'

Tony leapt forward to his colleague. 'Wait, what? A fire engine? Tell them we need more detail on all the vehicles, but especially the fire engine.'

Bainbridge relayed the request but instructed them to remain hidden and use binoculars.

'You're going to have to delay, Baz. At least until we know what is going on here. Those vehicles sound like the ones used in the big robberies – the Swan at the Bowes Museum and all the ones on the day of the Miners' Gala.'

The hand slicked over Bainbridge's scalp again. 'Ahl reet. What are ye thinking?'

'Well, those robberies were done by a crew. On the CCTV at the Bowes Museum there are definitely six of them. Some big

203

blokes like you too. Between them they lifted a really heavy display case. The other ones were probably only two men per robbery. At a guess that could be the same six doing three jobs at once, in pairs.' Tony paused, not sure himself where he was headed, nor what they should do with this information.

Meredith jumped in. 'Look, we've got a ton of poliss here.' She swept her arm around the barn space to indicate the twenty or so colleagues, sweltering in their thick protective vests. 'Maybe bring forward the backup teams so we've got greater numbers in the first assault, but I see enough people here to take down a team of six, even if Maid Marion is added in as well. We've got two dog teams and four armed officers. This isn't Waco, we've brought plenty of numbers. Let's just get on with it.'

Her sentiments were supported by a general grunting and nodding of approval. Tony felt they could be rushing into things, without having planned it carefully enough. While there had been no violence used in the robberies that now seemed to be connected to this address, the items stolen were worth millions of pounds, so one had to assume the thieves would be well-armed and prone to violently protect their spoils and their liberty.

Bainbridge held up an iPad, showing Tony a photo from the reconnaissance dog walkers. The logo of North Yorkshire's Fire Brigade was clearly on the side of a big red truck next to a big stone building.

Looking out of the barn, in the distance over the top of a screen of tall trees, Tony could see the old Victorian chimney pots on the building.

He nodded and addressed the assembled colleagues. 'That's definitely the truck used in the robbery at the Bowes Museum. We may be raiding the place for stolen goods worth millions of pounds. Take care of yourselves and each other.'

More quietly and directly to Sergeant Bainbridge he said, 'I think Diane's right. We're here, and they could well be tipped off if we wait around. I agree: up the numbers in each team, and approach from more directions, as much as our numbers will allow.'

As the ranking officer on site, Tony was effectively directing things, although the protocols kept Bainbridge as official commander of the raid.

In ten minutes, they were off. The detectives were now assigned to be closer to the entry team than in the previous plan, and they had specific responsibility to cover one identified possible escape route up a small stream. The watercourse was tree-lined and jammed in between the fences of two open fields. The nature of the available cover meant that Tony and Meredith had to approach the back field hiding in this vegetation, basically walking in the stream.

The hot weather that Durham had enjoyed – or endured – for nearly three weeks meant that the stream was practically dry. Thunderstorms three days earlier had made the ground underfoot sticky mud and Tony's shoes were ruined as soon as they set off.

The need to keep hidden as they covered over a hundred metres in the vegetation gave Meredith the perfect opportunity to squeeze close to Tony, and she took the opportunity. Every so often, she would catch her footing on a low branch, or a particularly wet area of mud and stumble into him. Each time, she had to put her arms around him or grab at his clothing to catch her balance. By about halfway to the back of the big house, he could take no more of it.

As quietly as he could hiss at her, Tony said, 'You walk in front, and I'll follow. You keep stumbling because we're too close to each other.'

'Don't give me that, you're loving every moment of it. I can feel your muscles tense and thrill each time I touch you.'

She wasn't wrong. He knew that his body did tense up every time she touched him. He hated – feared – being alone with her like this. The stalking that he had endured from her still left him in a state of anxiety whenever she was near. Her behaviour walking along this stream bed was exactly the reason for that angst.

He didn't respond but waved her to go on in front of him. With a Cheshire Cat grin, she skipped two or three steps ahead. Plain clothes officers did not wear bodycams, but silently behind her he set his phone to record audio.

Meredith proceeded lightly, stroking the occasional leaf and stooping to smell the yellow flowers of marsh marigolds. In the heat, insects were thriving and the oasis of dampness they were following held swarms of flies, bees and other insects. Tony was uncomfortable in so many ways.

They stopped as instructed at approximately thirty metres' distance from the fence of the building's rear garden. The stream appeared to go right through the garden and Tony could see a pair of back patio doors clearly through the fronds of the leafy bush they hid in.

Without looking behind her at him, Meredith crouched and continued gaily imparting the tale of her date the previous night. Tony couldn't help but picture CSI Hunk as she talked of a relaxed evening at his place, watching a movie until things got hot and heavy on the sofa. She had no filter and chattered on about all manner of very intimate activities.

Tony whispered close behind her, 'Sshhh.'

His concern that she might give away their position – most of the windows in the house were open – was misinterpreted as being about the content of her chat rather than the volume. 'Oh gosh, I'm sorry, Tony.' She turned her head and gave him a smouldering look of concern with big, brown eyes. 'Listen to me prattling on. It must really hurt you to hear about my sex life with other men.' She patted his hand, and he shook hers off.

'Just be quiet and pay attention to the house. We're only a couple of minutes away now.'

She looked at her phone, confirming the time, and they could both see that Bainbridge had not yet sent the "Go" command message. They faced the back yard of the house again, Tony slightly behind his DC.

Without turning, she breathed, 'You know I'd give up Alfie for you.'

'Please, Diane, stop! You and I are not a thing. We haven't been together for years, and we are not getting back together, ever.' He had to keep his voice quiet, despite wanting to shout at her to pack it in.

'Your words tell a different story from your eyes, and your body language. I can see you want me every time we're near each other.' She reached an arm back and slid it up his thigh to press her hand gently against his crotch.

Tony batted her hand away, took a step back and his voice became loud. 'Stop this!' She turned her head and put a finger to her lips to shush him. Quieter again, he said, 'Give it up! You and me, never again, not ever. Stop this shit!'

From her crouch, she patted his knee. 'That witch has put a spell on you. Don't worry, though, I'll put a stop to it. We'll get through this, Tony. Together we're stronger than her.'

Just as the words slipped from her lips, their phones buzzed, vibrating in Meredith's hand and, simultaneously, in Tony's stab vest front pocket.

TWENTY-NINE

The temperature must have been over thirty degrees, and the vest made Tony hot and sweaty. They had received the same group message from Sergeant Bainbridge:

GAN!

They heard shouting from the front of the house and saw the plain clothes dog team emerge from a bushy area of vegetation to their right. Meredith had already vaulted the fence beside them and sprinted off across the field. Tony followed, giving her a five-metre head start, and they headed for the back of Castle Eden Manor.

Doors could be heard cracking under the weight of battering rams, and more shouts from the police warned the residents that they were coming in. Tony and his DC climbed over the wooden fence and, along with the dog team, spread out as best they could across the garden. Their focus was on the rear patio doors, but they needed to be ready to sprint into action in any direction.

With multiple windows open on all three floors of the house, the shouting progress of the officers inside could easily be followed. After nearly ten minutes of boots stomping up and down stairs and police shouting to each other throughout the property, Tony heard his name called.

Looking up, Tony could see Baz Bainbridge leaning out of an upper floor window. 'Aahl clear inside. Come on in.'

Their arrival at the front door coincided with CSI Johnson pulling his pick-up truck to a stop just at the bottom of the large staircase up to the porch. 'It's a bit like a mini Bowes Museum,' he joked, pointing up at the fancy house built of local sandstone.

Meredith turned to Tony and silently mouthed the word "Sorry". His stomach knotted and he lost concentration on what to do next. *She's absolutely mental.* There was no chance for any further chat, as Johnson quickly handed over packages to get them all dressed up in paper coveralls and booties.

A couple of dozen sets of police issue boots had already gone charging around inside, so any crime scene would not be forensically "clean", but they had not yet been informed about what had been found inside, so Johnson insisted on all the correct protocols for the three of them.

The vestibule inside the front door held a classic wooden hall stand with a big mirror. A wide staircase with very skinny banister spindles rose up from the black and white tile floor. Sergeant Bainbridge descended the last two stairs in a single big step to appraise them of the situation.

'Hoose is empty – of people at least. A lot of ahld furniture, but mostly it seems not to have been lived in. Or not much. The place is pretty huge, and most rooms don't appear to have seen any action in a long time. You're gonna wanna gan into the master bedroom though. There's like a whole disguise set-up there. Make-up mirror and wigs and stuff. But the really big stuff is in the main reception room. That's up there too.'

Alfie Johnson confirmed, 'So you reckon first floor's the only place any suspects might have been? The only place I need to be examining?'

'Well, nar. There's also five vehicles outside.' He turned more directly to Tony. 'Pretty sure they're the ones involved in the robberies.'

Bainbridge's radio squawked at him as a colleague spoke. 'Something interesting in the bigger brick outbuilding, Sarge. Not sure what it is exactly, but it's not an original part of the building.'

'Shall we?' Tony indicated the front door.

Ignoring the chain of command, Meredith said, 'Right then, Alfie, you and I will go and look at the hair and make-up thing in the bedroom.' Without checking for any confirmation from

Tony or Bainbridge, she set off up the stairs and immediately fell on the bottom step that the sergeant had jumped over earlier.

'Aye, lass, you need to wait till you're telt. We also found several booby traps around the place. I got two injured constables, and that step is the first of the traps. Nothing too dangerous there though. Y'alreet?'

She picked herself up off the floor, uninjured. When she pushed on the stair carpet with the palm of her hand, they could all see it spring back at her like a catapult. 'Seems like a bit of a waste of time. Surely you put it midway up the staircase, so people properly fall down.'

A voice intoned from the doorway behind them. 'Depends on whether you actually want to hurt an unexpected visitor … or just be warned of their arrival.' Penfold stood on the threshold.

'Ooh, don't come in please, Mr Penfold. Not until you've got coveralls and, um, flip-flop covers on.' Johnson was holding up his palm in a Stop gesture.

'I tell you what,' Tony interjected. 'How about we head over to that strange find in the outbuilding, and Meredith and the CSI here can go up to the bedroom.' As he followed Penfold back down the stone steps outside, Tony smiled to himself. He felt this last comment had played Meredith at her own game. Nobody else might catch it, but she'd know what he was meaning.

As they approached a square, single storey building made from Victorian brick, Penfold pointed up to the small chimney. Several wires from the main house were suspended across and met the roof at the base of the chimney. 'See that white cable. Much thicker than the rest. I expect that'll be for heat lamps, ventilation and pumps.' A policeman stood at the doorway. With no chance of shade, sweat dripped down his face.

'You think this is a cannabis farm?'

Penfold turned and looked at Tony like he was a madman. 'No. No, I don't. I think we're going to find frog spawning habitats inside here.'

They stepped past the guarding PC without a word and entered the dim outbuilding. The degraded brick exterior belied a modern, lab-style interior. A large plexiglass window with a narrow corridor along the front of it was all that could be accessed from the entry door. At the end of the window was an airlock style door that they could see enabled entry into the main body of the space. Shelves of white plastic, just like Tony had seen inside the shipping containers, filled most of the lab. They were like giant troughs with a few centimetres of dirty water spread over the several square metres of shelving. This was repeated every thirty centimetres from floor up to ceiling.

Hanging above each shelf was an array of lamps, and at the far end of the room, large ventilation fans had been recently installed into the gable wall. They could see the brightness outside through the grills and fan blades. In the opposite corner, they could see a control panel attached to the wall underneath the fans. It had numerous switches and lights and handles.

'OK, so you were right – this has got to be an industrial frog farm. That's definitely the same kind of set-up as in the shipping containers. But this place isn't big enough. We had fifteen containers around Durham, and this building is as big as, what, two maybe?'

Penfold waggled a finger and led Tony back outside. They squinted at the brightness, and both quickly reinstated their sunglasses. Behind the block, Penfold halted and pointed at the large concrete farmyard. Five rows of three rectangular spaces marked the ground. The large rectangles showed slight scrapes on the concrete but mostly were a lot cleaner than the areas between them.

'I suggest, they part-reared them inside, from spawn to tadpole or maybe even slightly older. Then they transferred them into the shipping containers and completed rearing them inside. And from here, the lorry drove them over to Durham last week.' He did some quick calculations of road travel times to the city, along with loading and unloading of a shipping container onto a tilt-bed truck and trailer. 'If you worked flat out, with only one truck cab, you could probably deliver fifteen containers in two days.'

'I saw the third one being delivered to the Market Place at the end of the day on that Saturday we met Maid Marion, so maybe they did it on Saturday and Sunday?'

'Possibly.'

Tony's phone made a sound like a tolling bell, and he pulled it out of his stab vest to see what Meredith had sent. His jaw dropped and he turned the phone to show Penfold. The sun was too bright on the screen and the taller man took the device and had to step around to shade it with his body. No surprise registered on his features.

'Am I seeing that right? Isn't that Marion's hair?'

The photo showed a wig of curly red hair, exactly the style and length they had seen on Marion Rufus.

Penfold smiled slightly. 'At the address registered to her website domain, does that bewilder you?'

Confusion filled up Tony's mind and was then quickly chased away by ire. Penfold was an incredible help in investigations, but he could be as supercilious as DI Barnes at times. *Thank Christ they're not both here*, he joked to himself. Holding his anger in check, he calmed down before speaking.

'Bewildered, no. But I am confused at quite what we have here.'

Before he could continue, Penfold interrupted, 'Misdirection, Milburn, plain and simple.

'The plague of frogs created chaos all across the city, and under that cover, she was able to orchestrate a series of high-value robberies. They've walked out with million-pound – and higher value – objects in broad daylight. The frogs are a quite brilliant move. Not likely to cause significant casualties but they occupy a lot of security resources, infiltrate all manner of locations, and spread complete disorder. People running around in the manner of a public emergency. But a low stakes one. Fantastic cover for other crimes, as long as you know the chaos is coming. Clean-up crews are not merely expected, they are wanted. Security staff and police are otherwise occupied. It's very clever.'

'That makes total sense, I can see what you're suggesting. I mean it'd take a huge organisation to set all this up, but we've seen it actually happen, so that's a bit of a moot point until we catch them.'

Penfold gave a stifled chuckle, without opening his mouth.

Tony continued, ignoring his friend's apparent amusement at the idea of catching the gang. 'No, what I still don't really get is Marion's involvement. How is she connected to all this? I mean the wig and the website address seems to be telling us that this is her place, and the frog habitat and these ...' He wiggled his hand towards the rectangular marks on the ground in front of them. 'This all tells us that the frog diversion was set up from here, but the MaidMarionettes website incited the murders of the treasure hunters. And they're nothing to do with the robberies. What's going on with them?'

'It's more misdirection, Milburn.' Penfold stopped abruptly, pulled off his sunglasses, and stretched his body up to its full six feet two inches. He peered into the middle distance, over the wooden fence at the edge of the concrete, looking into the adjacent grass field. 'Is that a body?' He started to step towards the paddock, and Tony leapt into action.

The DI ran all the way over and stood up on the bottom wooden stringer to scan the field. It was old and rickety, so the whole fence line wobbled for a moment, and he clung onto the top of the nearest upright.

The grass was short, like it had recently had livestock grazing it, and there was plenty of sheep dung to corroborate this.

Nowhere could he see a body, living or dead, human or animal. He turned back and the farmyard was also deserted.

Beyond the brick outbuilding, as the driveway led back around to the front of Castle Eden Manor, he could see a few wandering police uniforms and some parked vehicles. Penfold was not visible anywhere. Behind his sunglasses, Tony scrunched his eyebrows together and started walking back over to where the shipping containers had once stood.

As he neared the edge of the frog building, Penfold stepped abruptly from around that corner. 'Last Saturday, many police officers went out into the countryside to stop people falling down mine openings in fields. Just now, you went looking for a body in a field, and while you were doing so, I vanished. And took your phone with me.'

He held up Tony's phone and passed it back to him. 'The murders are all misdirection for the robberies. Sucking up police resources, on the day of the year when you were at your most stretched anyway.'

Tony stopped and stared, trying to get his head around the fact that there was no dead body, that Penfold's theatrics were to make a point. The point itself though was the really mind-blowing thing.

'Are you suggesting that somebody committed four murders in order to make it a bit easier to get away with stealing a book, a painting and a computer?'

'No, not quite. The Swan theft from the Bowes Museum was also a part of this. And there are only three murders. Whoever Dickie Harbottle's body actually is, they were definitely already dead. So maybe three murders and a grave-robbing.'

THIRTY

DI Milburn had turned his radio volume back up, and it squawked his name, requesting they return to the main house. Upstairs, to see "something really interesting". DC Meredith was the caller, and she must have finally made it safely up the booby-trapped staircase.

On entry, there were now a series of metal squares to act as stepping stones across the property hallway. Up the stairs, there were pieces of green plastic taped to the carpet, in a sequence to indicate where it was safe to tread.

At the top of the stairs, a vast landing gave onto a number of rooms, all with police and CSIs flitting about securing and searching. The team of white-suited operatives all looked the same. It was difficult to pick out the identity of individuals in the bland paper coveralls with hoods covering hair and most of each face.

Through one doorway, they could see a person dusting a dressing table mirror for fingerprints. It had a set of lights all around, just like in a theatre dressing room, and Marion's curly, ginger wig hung on a mannequin head.

'In here, guv, you gotta see this.' Diane Meredith stood in the doorway of a room at the opposite end of the landing. Beyond her, the light from a huge window made it hard to see anything clearly and she appeared as a silhouette. Tony toyed with the idea of putting his sunglasses back on but felt it would be weird, and refrained.

She turned and they followed her in. 'We've dubbed this place the "War Room".'

Penfold and Tony paused to scan the place and consider the various areas of the room, each with its own planning purpose. It was difficult to take it all in.

Behind the large white door, Alfie Johnson was on his knees taking photos of the fingerprint dust on a machine that appeared to be for producing ID cards. It had a stock of white plastic blanks the size of credit cards, which fed through a narrow printer. Beside the ejection tray stood a separate machine, the sort of thing hotel receptionists use to programme key cards.

CSI Johnson held up a metal wire rubbish bin with a few test runs dumped in the bottom. With his gloved hand, Tony reached in and pulled out an image of his girlfriend printed on one of the cards. It was smudged and there was no writing on the card, but he identified the Durham University purple shield in the corner.

Tony turned to show Penfold, but he had moved and now stood staring at an electronic display board. Without looking away, the New Zealander moved his head down and sideways, then back up and then repeated the action. As he did so, the digital image of an Ordnance Survey map of the area shifted up and left. Newcastle scrolled away off the top, so that the Hartlepool area sat in the centre of the screen.

'Fascinating this, Milburn.' He remained transfixed but pointed towards the screen. As he did so, the image zoomed in, and Tony recognised Seaton Carew and the area where he often met Penfold at the beach. 'The sensors monitor your head and eyes and gestures and move the map to show what you're looking for. Remarkable.'

'Very nice. Does it tell us anything? Anything marked on the map?'

Penfold couldn't take his eyes off the screen and his voice was slow. 'Yeeaah.' He raised a hand to point at a red blob. 'There are pin markers on the mine sites where we found the bodies. This is Tudhoe mine entry.' He wiggled his head, and it took a couple of tries to scroll the automated map onto the next red pin. 'There's Hairy Side, next to Derwent Water there. And finally … the Tan Hill Inn and a marker on the last mine crime scene.'

'OK.' Tony paused and stared at the map for a minute. 'So, this is where Rufus registered her website. We've got information plotting the locations of the murdered treasure hunters, and we've got the frogs and trucks by which all those Durham robberies took place, as well as the rogue Richmond fire engine for the Swan theft.'

'If you look over at that model, you'll see the heist locations marked with little flags.' Penfold waved his hand over towards the window, accidentally triggering the map to swivel and zoom again. 'Bah.'

Tony walked away, smiling. The triple-wide bay window was large enough to hold a full-sized snooker table which had a wooden cover over the top of the whole playing surface.

On this was built a replica of the City of Durham of such quality that any model railway enthusiast would be jealous of the variety and detail of the buildings and the famous peninsula's natural surroundings. Even the loop of the River Wear that enclosed the World Heritage Site was accurate in its topography and beautiful in its colour and ripples. A little plastic coxless four sculled their way under the middle arch of the meticulously modelled Prebends Bridge.

On the Prebends Bridge deck sat a mini shipping container with the pit helmet logo of the Durham Miners' Gala. Tony scanned the model and spotted the other fourteen containers, exactly as he had seen them in real life.

Penfold appeared at his side and pointed to a mini flag on a cocktail stick. It appeared much as one might see spiked into a cube of cheese at a party from the 1970s or 80s, but this one was spiked into the castellated roof of Palace Green Library. Tony was astonished by the veracity of the sandstone colour used on the library building. He also knew that Kathy's library had no flagpole on it in real life.

The tiny flag here looked just like the pub sign of The Shakespeare on Saddler Street, with a portrait of the bard in a green jacket. He bent forward to examine the model pub and saw that the sign was indeed similar to the flag image, if not identical.

Neither man spoke, they just stared in wonder.

Tony's eyes followed as Penfold's pointing finger swung to the right to highlight the mad architecture of the physics building, adorned with another little flag. This flag's image showed a rectangle with eight tiny bent legs sticking out the sides, like an angular looking beetle. After a moment he worked out that it was a picture of an integrated circuit – a computer chip.

The finger continued a little further to show another flag flying from the half-built Noah's Ark that was the Palatine Centre. It took Tony a few moments of staring but knowing it was the Picasso that was stolen, he quickly worked out the two tiny, dark blobs were a bull and a matador.

He moved his head in a slow shake of disbelief. Penfold's finger was not finished though. He dragged it across Tony's eyeline, to point to the narrow stone roof that formed a square around a lawn. This was attached to the side of the model cathedral, at its south side. In one stretch of this roof stood another little flag. The picture on this one looked like a tile with lines across it and little splashes of colour here and there.

Turning his head from side to side, Tony scowled and asked, 'What is it?'

'If I'm not mistaken, I'd say that is a page from the Lindisfarne Gospels.'

'But they haven't stolen the Gospels. Have they?' Tony imagined some subtle switcheroo whereby the Gospels on display in the cathedral's exhibition were in fact fakes, the real ones having been taking during the chaos of the frogs swarming.

'Maybe you should call Mrs Landrey to confirm.'

Diane Meredith had spent the last several minutes tapping away at an open laptop that sat centrally on a desk in the far corner of the room. She swivelled the comfortable office chair around and tried to slide it away slightly. The wheels were defeated by the plush carpet that covered the floors throughout this level of the house.

'You should look at this, guv.' Tony continued to examine the incredible detail and accuracy of the Durham model. She persisted, louder. 'Guv!'

'Yes, sorry.' He took a few steps towards her voice before finally pulling his eyes away and taking in what his detective constable was indicating on the laptop screen.

'This is logged in to the MaidMarionettes website discussion forum and has admin privileges. And' – she clicked an alternative tab – 'it's got several usernames all logged in and able to make posts. From here you could have what looks like a discussion between loads of different people.'

'And then there's this.' Meredith clicked an icon on the desktop and a photo file opened. It showed Alex Carrera tied to a chair in a dingy room. 'Oh, wait, hold on. I'm pretty sure I've seen that room downstairs. It's like a pantry off the kitchen. That chair's still there, but there's no sign of Carrera.' She turned and left, towards the stairs.

Tony slowly scanned around the whole room, again taking in all the different parts of this command centre. 'War Room. Yes, indeed.'

'Guv.' Bainbridge stood in the doorway looking at the DI. 'There's something else out here.'

Penfold was engrossed in poring over the model city, and Tony followed the sergeant out to a large cupboard which also opened on to the landing. Most of it was occupied by a filing cabinet. It was cream metal, with two big drawers, a standard office job from the days when physical files were the norm.

The top drawer was fully open, and Sgt Bainbridge pulled out the first hanging folder and laid it across the open drawer. The papers showed that it was a personnel file. The first sheet had a CV including a photograph.

'I know that guy!' Tony was so surprised at his recognition that he almost shouted.

'Who is it?' The beefy cop was looked downwards slightly to engage eye contact.

Tony shook his head and picked up the paper. 'No, sorry, I don't know him. I've seen him. He was one of the pest controllers in the CCTV footage of the stolen Picasso.' He put his forefinger to the name headlining the sheet and read out loud, rolling the name around his mouth. 'Darren Fairburn. Darren. Fairburn.'

The remaining sheets in the folder included a criminal record printout, some screenshots of news website reports, and a couple of grainy CCTV stills. All of them related to Mr Fairburn and his past. The man was seemingly responsible for, or at least had been a part of, some audacious and high-value robberies over the years.

Without turning away from reading in the dim light of the cupboard, Tony called, 'Penfold!'

'What have you found?'

The New Zealander was immediately behind Tony, who jumped with a start. Turning, he exhaled heavily. 'Jeez, creep up on a guy why don't you?' He had the dark green folder open in both hands and passed the whole thing over before reaching in to find the next folder.

Bainbridge also took another file out. 'Same sort of thing. This one's is a bloke called Peter Beardsley. Haha, not that one though.'

Tony replied, 'What? I've got Alan Shearer! What's going on here?' They compared photos, which looked like passport pictures but were definitely not the two old footballers named.

They dived into the filing cabinet to check on the next two files.

'Mark Knopfler! Clearly not the Dire Straits guitarist though.'

'I've got Winston Churchill!' Bainbridge stabbed a stubby, gloved finger at a small photo printed at the top of another CV style page.

Tony looked over to the papers Penfold was perusing. 'I don't recognise the name Darren Fairburn though, who is that? Was he one of the band members of The Police?'

Baz shook his head, 'Nah, man. Sting, Stewart Copeland, Andy Summers.'

Penfold chipped in. 'Probably Fairburn was the only one stupid enough to tell her his real name.'

They continued to look through the files and found a crew of six men, all with a similar history of various types of robbery and each seemed to contribute varying skills. Fairburn, they guessed, might be a real name, and his specialism appeared to be as a getaway driver.

After they shuffled them all around and everybody had seen all the files, Penfold mused, 'All the printouts are the same. Same ink shades, same paper. Like they were printed at the same time, in one run.'

'So?'

'Well, that's not how you build up personnel files. You gather all the bits of information and collate them together, piecemeal. These have clearly been stored on a computer and then printed out en masse.'

The sergeant was called downstairs, and Tony took up the mantle of interrogating Penfold's thoughts. 'But why would you do that? These days you just keep the files on the computer and use them from there.'

'Exactly. Why would anyone do this?' He gripped the folder and papers he held like a tray and pushed them forward as a pointer towards the filing cabinet in the cupboard.

'What are you doing? I haven't photographed anything in there yet!'

Tony and Penfold folded up their sheafs of papers and returned them to the cabinet. 'Don't worry, Alfie, it's all back in the same order.'

Alfie continued to scold them. 'But not exactly as we found them. No pictures for the court from exactly as they were left.'

Tony could see Meredith loitering at the top of the stairs. He imagined her revelling in this spat between the men.

'Look, there's no way we can investigate this after you've processed everything. There's so much here it'll be mid-September before you're done. Why don't you call Julia to send some more help over?'

CSI Hunk took a glance over his shoulder to Meredith before he replied. 'I can easily process everything here myself, if you keep your dirty hands off things until I've dealt with them. You follow me and only look into things when I've photographed them in first locations.' The final pronouncement was punctuated by a staccato air-stabbing finger. 'You. Follow. Me. Got it?'

Tony smiled as he noted Johnson's voice was just a little louder with Meredith now in earshot. He bowed his head in mock subservience. 'Yes, boss.'

THIRTY-ONE

Tony stood in front of the big desk and played the audio recording. Diane Meredith's voice breathed into the air. Acting Detective Superintendent Harry Hardwick leaned back in his office chair, his face up, looking towards the suspended ceiling. A thread hanging from one ceiling tile fluttered in the weak draught of the small wall fan.

He had been here before. Reporting his colleague to the boss for sexual harassment and assault had gotten him in hot water in the past. Meredith had always had the unspoken, albeit loudly whispered, backing of the other police officers in their nick. Few people believed Tony's tales that he was the victim, most believing the exact reverse. She had always engineered things so that he had struggled to fight the sticking mud.

Though they were again working in the same CID office, her stalking activities had all but disappeared, until the last week. Now, Tony found himself back in Hardwick's office asking to have her removed once again.

The sounds of the countryside predominated the playback. He and Diane could be heard talking in the field before the raid, and much of their conversation was clear. However, as it was audio only, the device's microphone could not capture the moments when she touched him.

As she had been facing away from him much of the time, and with their whispering voices, it was impossible to tell how close she had put herself to him. Moreover, that closeness could have been put down to the operational need to remain hidden in the restricted cover of the vegetation, and to the need to communicate quietly.

Hardwick pressed the screen for the recording to play again and closed his eyes. Tony had seen this look before, and it wasn't good. Having had to present evidence of harassment previously,

223

he was all too aware of the need for it to be iron-clad. He-said-she-said cases rarely ended well for the victim. He knew this from trying to convict rapists, as much as from bitter personal experience.

Even the times her recording talked about getting back together with Tony could, at worst, be classified as unprofessional. He realised that she had waited until they were definitely away from any cameras. Her words were carefully crafted to sound like the innocent wishes of an excited colleague, still high from the stimulation of meeting a new boyfriend. This audio "evidence" presented almost the opposite of sexual harassment. She positively revelled in Alfie Johnson and sounded like she only wanted to help Tony out of a jam with his current girlfriend.

Did she know I was recording?

His legs failed and he crashed down into the chair opposite Hardwick.

Tony's longtime boss sympathised and explained what he already knew. The only time they'd managed to make Diane alter her behaviour, he and Kathy had compiled a full dossier of evidence of months of stalking behaviour. Until Tony could provide something concrete, Hardwick would not even call her into his office.

The superintendent understood Tony's difficult position and agreed he would monitor her and do his best to "fix" their working patterns, but the threshold for discrimination was low. He could not end up in a situation where it was Diane calling in her federation rep to take Hardwick and Tony to task. If she gained that upper hand, they would never make anything against her stick.

He agreed to get a camera installed in Tony's office, but they wondered how easy it would be to do so covertly. Diane was probably the smartest cookie in the station – such a thing would almost certainly be noticed by her.

Tony stepped slowly down the staircase back towards the Major Crimes offices. He felt sick, and it wasn't just because of the heat outside Hardwick's office. His stomach dropped further on reaching the doorway and seeing the hive of activity with Diane at the centre. He couldn't go in.

He descended all the way down to the canteen, grabbed a cup of tea and a chocolate bar and sat in a corner trying to compose himself.

'Now then, Tony. You look a bit down in the dumps.' PC Bob Smith had been a copper in Durham for nearly forty years. Smith was a giant of a man. However, he carried his bulk quietly, his own personal nuclear deterrent should anyone think that they might get their way through being physical.

He played rugby for the same club as Madeline Aria, both making the first team for their respective genders, albeit Smith played at veterans' level. Tony realised that he'd often seen Madeline in the chair he now sat in, sharing a cuppa and a chat with old lag Bob. Tony's mind was scrambled. He felt uncomfortable as if he were sitting in somebody else's seat.

'That obvious, huh?'

Bob chuckled and sat down opposite. 'Aye. No need to explain though, we all go through things from time to time. I guess it'll be all the shenanigans from yesterday's raid. Real shame about Jamie's leg.'

Tony nodded mutely. He was silently pleased that Smith was off in the wrong direction, but the issues from the raid went beyond Meredith's inappropriate behaviour. The booby trap injuries from the day before did weigh heavily on his mind, despite their sergeant's entreaties for Tony not to worry.

Bainbridge had been low key about the injuries to two of his men during the forced entry phase. After Tony had discovered that one had a broken wrist and the other had been impaled by a spike and lost a fair bit of blood, this knowledge had plagued his thoughts all night.

Firstly, he worried that, as the ranking officer on scene, he should have immediately gone to speak to the two casualties and checked on their welfare. It had not been his raid to plan, and booby traps are a rare eventuality, but he felt a pang of guilt that he had not thought about warning the officers involved. He knew rationally that he couldn't possibly have foreseen the existence of traps, but he blamed himself for the omission, nonetheless.

To try and put things right, he had telephoned the two officers first thing. Both had been instructed to remain at home for at least the rest of the week. Each one spoke brightly to Tony, thankful for his call, which neither had expected.

They were both of the opinion that they had suffered from the sort of risks that are part of the job. The first, the man with the impaled thigh, even joked that if he wanted to be able to knock down doors, he had to expect that occasionally he'd get knocked back. The calls did little to assuage Tony's feelings of self-reproach.

His conversation with Bob Smith was mercifully interrupted by his phone vibrating. A text told him that Darren Fairburn had been arrested in Newcastle and had just arrived at Durham police station for questioning.

'Gotta go, Bob. Might just be a chance here to put somebody away for hurting those two.'

Smith showed a broad smile, and his giant hand, wrapped around his teacup, raised in farewell as Tony scraped the plastic chair back and headed towards the canteen's double doors.

In the custody suite, Sergeant Andrew Singh was checking in his latest guest to a delightful single room. Fairburn was a seasoned professional, and his solicitor arrived at the same time and made sure that Singh followed protocol to the letter. They requested thirty minutes to consult before any interrogation.

Tony corrected the solicitor, using the word *interview* instead of *interrogation*, and asked the custody sergeant to bring them to Interview Room Two at that time. Interview one was available, but Tony knew that, in room two, the sun would be shining through the little windows straight into the eyes of the criminal and his brief.

This gave him time to talk with Madeline Aria, and also to call the interview consultant at Durham Police Headquarters. The three of them together came up with a fairly open-ended strategy for the interview. They had some connections between Fairburn and the planning of the robberies, and the CCTV footage in the Palatine building would definitely put on the pressure.

Tony wondered if this would be enough to push the man into flipping on the rest of the crew. The criminal fraternity were notoriously unwilling to give evidence against each other. They viewed time in prison as an occupational hazard and would be unlikely to be recruited on to a crew again in future if they were known as a snitch.

At the appointed hour, Tony asked Andrew Singh to move the prisoner and solicitor into the room and sit them down and then wait. The plan was to have them sit in the hot rays of the sun for a good few minutes before he and Detective Aria breezed in and began the "interview".

The room was like an oven despite a dilapidated air conditioning unit. As Singh passed them on the threshold, Tony could see beads of sweat rolling down his temples from the edges of his turban.

As expected, the interview consisted of a series of "no comment" answers to virtually every question. The still from the CCTV footage of the Picasso theft did little to shift the intentions of the suspect. His solicitor continually demanded they give him water and take a break on account of the extreme temperature.

Tony and Madeline were also sweating continuously and feeling the heat. When Diane Meredith appeared at the door to tell the DI that they had something he needed to see, everybody breathed a sigh of relief that they would get a break from the room.

The two followed Meredith up to their office and she led them to her computer and an email from CSI Johnson. His boss, Julia Sedgley, was copied in, and Tony assumed this was the reason it was formal and to the point. Meredith read it out loud for them all.

'Fingerprints for Darren Fairburn found on a tyre iron (murder weapon) at the scene of a murder last week. Four victims found in a burning car on an old airfield south of Middlesbrough.

'Colleagues at Teesside University forensics labs confirm a good match – conviction quality. Two other burning cars nearby at the scene but only one with bodies.

'No other leads on that crime scene. Cleveland Police asking for Fairburn to be held, pending their interviewing him.'

Tony stared at the white polystyrene tiles of the ceiling. 'Get in the queue, lads,' he muttered to himself.

THIRTY-TWO

They reconvened in Interview Room One with a good-cop claim that they had moved to give Fairburn and his lawyer a cooler environment. In reality, DC Aria had told Tony she would likely pass out if they had to endure room two again.

Even this larger room was hot and stuffy as it was in the basement of the city centre building. It also had a couple of small, high windows, which again did not open. The basement was the only part of the building with air conditioning, but its effectiveness reflected the paltry budget that had been put towards it.

Tony started sweating as soon as he sat down, and he had instructed Aria that if either of them used the word *tropical* this was a cue that they needed to leave the room. Fairburn had on the shorts and T-shirt he'd been arrested in and was likely suffering less from the conditions than either of the detectives, or his solicitor, who wore the uniform of a business suit. Andrew Singh had provided each person with a bottle of water from the canteen.

The detective inspector switched on the video cameras and introduced everyone in the room for the record. 'Right, Mr Fairburn, let's make this as quick as possible and we can all get out of this greenhouse.'

The suspect smiled and responded, 'Why don't we all just leave now then? I already said all I'm going to say.'

Tony took the lead. 'Well, you might want to reconsider that as we've just been sent through some new evidence, and that puts you in even hotter water than this room.'

'Yeah, yeah.'

Aria had a folder of documents and shuffled through to find a printout of the crime scene photo that Johnson had forwarded on from his colleagues in Cleveland. She turned it round so that

229

Fairburn and the solicitor could see charred bodies in a burnt-out BMW.

Fairburn sucked in his cheeks theatrically. 'Ooh, that doesn't look too clever. What's it got to do with me?'

Tony paused for a considerable few seconds to raise the tension. 'For the tape, DC Aria has just shown the suspect a crime scene photograph from Dunsdale Airfield, close-up on the bodies of the four men inside the car. Although they may look like they died in a fire, in fact the driver had his skull split open.'

Aria presented a second photograph, showing a black metal bar lying alongside an L-shaped forensics ruler. She said, 'I am now showing the suspect a photograph of the murder weapon recovered from the scene. And now a close-up of the murder weapon with the fingerprint dusting clearly visible.' She grabbed the next photograph and laid it beside the first two, all facing Fairburn.

'OK,' he said. 'So what?'

Tony held another pause and then pointed at the fingerprints close-up, on the last image. 'That, Mr Fairburn, is your fingerprint. Carelessly left on the tyre iron, sorry I should say "on the murder weapon", which itself was carelessly left beside this vehicle as it burned.'

'What? No!' Fairburn's freckled face jerked up to look at Tony and then to Aria and then sideways to his solicitor, and then back to Tony. 'No, I never killed nobody. I don't do violence. I'm a driver. I only take part in jobs where nobody gets hurt.'

Tony tapped the fingerprint dust in the photograph. 'Your prints on the murder weapon. All forensically proven to a level the CPS assure us will be an easy conviction.' He was inflating the truth a little, but CSI Johnson had used the phrase "signed, sealed and delivered" in his email.

Calmly, the lawyer put his hand on Darren's arm. 'This is a new and sudden change of situation for us. Could I have a few minutes alone with my client please?'

DC Aria gathered up the photos and Tony pressed the button to stop the video recording. 'Of course. Perhaps as part of your conversations, you could mention that the CPS also told me they would look very favourably on any information Mr Fairburn can offer us that helps to convict on any of the crimes he has also been party to here in County Durham.'

It was fewer than five minutes when a polite knock from the inside of the door of Interview Room One called the two detectives back inside. Fairburn and his brief clearly knew how the game was played.

'My client has agreed to help you prove he did not murder anyone.' Tony began to laugh out loud, but the solicitor continued, 'By helping you prove who did murder those men in the car. He has a lot of information in that regard.'

Tony pushed his luck, half-bluffing on the hand he had. 'Well, that may help him with matters at Teesside Crown Court, but as I said we are interested in robberies and murders here in Durham, and we have evidence of his involvement with these too, so we're going to need information on all of them if we're to recommend anything to the court behind us.'

He referred to Durham Crown Court, which stood in a two-hundred-year-old neoclassical building of ashlar stone, just around the corner from the city's police station.

The solicitor nodded. 'I believe we may be in a position to help you there too. For the record, my client has committed no murders, indeed, no violence of any sort. Mr Fairburn is a peaceful man who sometimes finds himself working with some unsavoury characters.'

'I think you can get off the high horse and just tell us everything you know about these robberies.' Tony passed over a handwritten list: *the Silver Swan at the Bowes Museum, a high-value computer chip from the physics building at Durham University, Shakespeare's first folio from Palace Green Library, Picasso's painting from the Palatine Centre.*

231

Fairburn outlined essentially what they had already pieced together about these heists, with a few extra details slotted in gaps they had, and some where they didn't even know they had gaps.

The crew of six men and Miss Rufus had lived at Castle Eden Manor for well over a year to prepare it all. They learnt how to breed frogs by the thousand and did reconnaissance at the previous year's Miners' Gala. One of the gang was a consummate pickpocket and had "borrowed" Kathy's campus card in order to copy it.

At one point, Fairburn surprised everyone in the room. 'Marion also met you … I was her driver for the meetings at the Daily Espresso.' He accurately listed both dates and times when Tony had met with Maid Marion. 'She didn't look like that really though – she is an incredible master of disguise. Her hair's dark really.'

Tony wanted to move the conversation on as quickly as possible. He remembered chatting casually with her over coffee, and he felt an extra level of sweatiness on his legs. They itched and made him shuffle in his seat.

Fairburn wasn't particularly set on discussing it more and continued with the general duties the crew had undertaken in Marion's employ. The men had also been tasked with sourcing the various vehicles and shipping containers, painting them up with new livery and maintaining them to a high standard. The tyre iron in the crime scene photo looked much like one that Fairburn had used to fix a tyre on the fake pest control van.

They had burgled a house in Washington, Tyne and Wear, and took a bunch of old papers in a big box. That was all Marion had wanted and all they took. Torn and worn with fancy printing on them. He wrote down the address and Aria photographed it to investigate any connections.

Stranger than this, they had burgled an administrative army building in Catterick, but in that case, they had put a folder into a filing cabinet but taken nothing away. He reckoned that they'd done that job without detection at all.

Mr Fairburn consistently held his line that he, and the other robbers, were non-violent and had not involved themselves in any activities that included brute force. Only Marion was prone to violence. He kept presenting this as if from some sort of moral high ground, but Tony suspected the man was just a coward. He wondered how the guy fared during his spells in prison.

It dawned on him that perhaps Fairburn was scared of Marion. But although she was more athletically built than the "waif" Penfold had described her as, Fairburn and the other men in the personnel files they'd discovered all seemed like traditional criminal thugs. It seemed to go against the grain that they would be scared of her.

'Please tell us, then, just how four men came to be murdered around old mine workings if your crew are all pacifists.'

'I'm telling you, she did it all. I was the driver, and I had to take her places and be ready in case we needed to bug out of there quickly, but I never got out of the car on those jobs.'

Aria asked, 'Could you take us through these meetings step-by-step then?'

'They were remote places. Fields well off the road. She got me to park up, and she'd head off to see someone she'd already arranged to meet there. I never saw her take a weapon, but she wasn't shy about telling us the details. Said she helped them break open the mine entrance and then shoved them in, so they fell down screaming.'

'That's it? You didn't wonder what the hell it was all about? Why was she doing it?'

'She said it'd get you lot out of the way for the robberies. Same as the frogs. I mean she wasn't wrong – everything we stole: it was like scoring against Sunderland. Piece of cake!'

DC Aria had doodled a picture of a stick person on a bicycle. Tony saw it and asked, 'Did they all happen like that? We've got four dead bodies, but only three down a mineshaft.'

'No, you're right. There was one down near Barnard Castle where we put her bike in the back of the van and I dropped her off a few miles from the actual meeting place. She disappeared off on the bike and came back with quite a bit of blood on her hoodie. She didn't explain and I didn't ask.'

'OK, that accounts for three of our bodies. What's the story with the skeleton? Did you see that at all?'

'Oh, bloody hell, the skeleton! Took us hours to get that down there, in the middle of the night. We had to lower the bones one at a time and she was down the bottom with a plan of how to reconstruct the whole thing, so it looked like it had always been down there. She was really pernickety about how it should look, with the weird clothes and belt and maps and stuff.'

The detectives looked at each other and did their best to avoid giving away how confusing this information seemed. The crime scene photos of Dickie Harbottle down Tudhoe mine didn't look like anything strange, just like a bloke who'd fallen down there seventy years ago.

Tony chose to apply extra pressure with something where he knew they were in charge. He again placed down the photo from Dunsdale Airfield, showing the bodies in the burnt-out car. 'Riddle me this then: how did the driver in this car die from a blow to the head with the tyre iron with your fingerprint on it, if you didn't do that to him?'

'The bitch did it to frame me for all this.' He passed his hand over the photo and the list of stolen items to encompass basically all the crimes they were investigating.

'I don't know who those thugs are, but we met them at the abandoned airfield. Her and our whole crew, all together. We went along in numbers because that was a scary group. Russian, we reckoned, but definitely somewhere funny from Eastern

Europe. They bought the Silver Swan. I helped put in the back of this SUV.' He pointed at the photo of the burnt-out BMW.

'In return, they gave us two massive holdalls of cash euros. She knew it was likely to be a set-up, so just as the exchange happened, she'd arranged for a pair of vehicles full of petrol to crash into each other pretty close by, on the airfield. No lights on, and far enough across the runway so they just sounded like nearby road traffic.'

He clapped his hands together and tried to voice a sound like a bomb going off.

'The explosion was incredible, and just as she'd told us in the briefing, it distracted this lot long enough for us all to get away. We had two vehicles, and she drove herself. As soon as we set off there was no looking back – just meet back at the farmhouse after midnight. We each got a fifty-thousand-euro payday that night. In the end, was supposed to be fifty K each, for each of the objects. We all expected a cool quarter of mill by the end.'

Aria interrupted, 'That'd get you to a tropical island, I imagine.'

Tony heard the codeword and extracted them from the interview. 'I expect we're all feeling the heat. Let's take five minutes, and I'll buy us all a cold drink from the vending machine. Can I get you two a can of pop or something?'

THIRTY-THREE

In the cool of the canteen, as Tony waved the Major Crimes' bank card at the vending machine's contactless panel, Aria wondered aloud, 'Something doesn't add up, guv.'

'Ha, which bit. This whole thing is off the wall in my book. And I've seen some strange cases in my time.' The inspector felt he sounded much older than he wanted to be.

'The payoff. He said they'd all get fifty grand for each of the objects they stole.'

Tony jumped ahead, guessing incorrectly at what had her confused. 'Well, six in the gang, that's three hundred grand to pay them, per item. But every item is worth more than a million pounds, so even if you take off all the costs of setting it all up, I reckon she's on to a tidy profit. And the Swan is worth way more. How much do you reckon would be in two holdalls of, say, hundred-euro notes?'

'That's not what I'm getting at. He said that he'd get quarter of a million. That means they stole five things. Is it possible something has been nicked, and the owner hasn't noticed it gone yet? Surely nothing that valuable vanishes without being missed for a week.'

Tony tried to put the payment card away without dropping the two slippery cans he was holding and ended up juggling them hand to hand. Aria intervened by grabbing a can, so he only had two things to deal with. She gave him a quizzical look, but all he could do was shrug. 'Let's ask him. Get him on the back foot a bit first and then make him explain his calculation. Maybe he just can't count.'

They re-entered and distributed the drinks.

Aria restarted the questioning. 'So, if the deliberate crash distracted them and you all took off like bats out of hell, how'd these blokes end up dead and their car on fire?'

'I don't know for sure, but I've got a bloody good idea. She was the only one on her own after we split, and she's the only one who could've taken this and planted it there.' He lifted the photo of the crowbar by the yellow ruler.

'I can't wait to see her face when you've arrested her. Stupid cow thinks she can frame *me*.'

The solicitor interjected, 'This, detectives, is where we expect the full leniency of the court to appear. My client has information that could enable you to catch Ms Rufus and the rest of the crew.'

Tony over-exaggerated an inquiring look at his colleague and said, 'Sounds intriguing. Let's hear it.'

The miscalculated money had been momentarily forgotten but immediately became clear.

'They're going to steal the Lindisfarne Gospels on Friday.'

Aria responded, 'That's a big claim. Given that the frogs have all been rounded up now, how are they going to manage to get past what I assume is bank vault level security?'

Darren Fairburn laughed briefly. 'Bank vault level? You're joking, aren't you? I wouldn't deposit my kid's pocket money in that place!'

He went on, 'We spent a good while doing reconnaissance on the museum and the security, and Marion reckons this Friday is the best time for it. Final day and all.'

'OK. What's the plan then? And is the plan not scuppered since the police raided your hideout yesterday?'

He answered the second part first. 'No, we abandoned Castle Eden on Monday afternoon. She set off with a new lorry I stole last week. All the rest of us were to split up, each drive between one and two hours in different directions and then meet up again this morning for the briefing. She reckoned forty-eight hours would be enough time to get us all prepped for the heist. Reckoned it was safer if we didn't all know the plan in case anyone got nicked.' He chuckled. 'Guess she was right on that score.'

Tony looked at the solicitor. 'You expect us to take that to the CPS and ask for some sort of deal?'

Fairburn continued, 'Well, I can tell you the meet location. She was picking us all up again after scattering from the manor house. The meet time was four hours ago, but they're gonna have to be storing the truck somewhere. The way she made me prep the inside storage racks, I'm certain it's for the Gospels.' He wrote out a What3Words location that Rufus had made them all learn by heart.

Tony shrugged. 'For the sake of argument, what if this location is abandoned? It sounds like you want us to catch this murderer, otherwise you're on the hook for the murders. But we'll need more than this to do so.'

'It's definitely Friday. And it's definitely the Lindisfarne Gospels. More than that I don't know, apart from the details of the truck and, well, you've already got details of the six of them that are still out there. Come on detectives, even I could catch them with that information.'

He scribbled the make, model and colour of the box truck for them to be on the lookout for. He even knew the registration plate it had carried when he'd seen Maid Marion drive off into the distance in it two days earlier.

DC Aria looked at the paper, lifted it off the table to turn it towards the suspect and his lawyer. 'M4IDM? Really?'

Fairburn shrugged and replied, 'She's an oddball all right.'

The detectives left the other two to wait on Andrew Singh to show Fairburn back to his room. Detective Superintendent Hardwick then joined them in the Major Crimes office to be put in the picture.

On their way up the stairs – it was far too hot to contemplate using the lift – Tony texted Penfold his own cryptic six-word story:

Recce, no interaction: help.uses.best M4IDM

He smiled to himself that it was actually seven words. *That's poetic licence that is, you smug git!*

Madeline Aria hugged one of the creaking fans as she searched the Automatic Number Plate Recognition databases for hits on the lorry's registration, and Tony explained to the Major Crimes Team that they had an opportunity to catch the mineshaft murders gang.

Meredith and Hardwick had been watching the interview with Fairburn via the CCTV feed. DC Meredith had already googled the meet location and reported it was a sand and gravel quarry between Castle Eden and Hartlepool.

Hardwick asked if the aggregates pit was still operational, and she offered to place an order for a tonne bag of footpath gravel for the superintendent's garden. 'The website makes it appear very much like an ongoing concern.' She turned to Tony and asked, 'Why would they meet there?'

It had taken Penfold barely twenty minutes to reach the security gatehouse at the quarry, from where he rang Tony, who put him on speaker for the team to listen in.

'Your information was good quality, but a bit behind the wave. The guy on the gate here says that truck did arrive this morning, driven by a woman.

'He made some comments about her good looks but was more intrigued by her "crew" – his word. Five men arrived separately, all in taxis, and climbed on board before she drove up to the gate.'

The detectives looked at each other. Harry Hardwick asked, 'So what did they want? Or what did they do there?'

Penfold answered, 'He's not sure. He won't let me in as I don't have the right paperwork, but he says Marion did have the necessary papers to get them all on site. He described her as the boss, and reckoned the men were probably her construction crew. He's stuck on the gate the whole time, so didn't really get a good view of what they got up to. But he reckons they didn't go near the office, just parked up, climbed in the back, and had a lot of conversation, including looking over a big paper, her finger popping all over it. Probably some construction plans, he guessed.'

H gruffly interrogated further. 'And it's definitely them?'

'He has to note down the registration plates of all the vehicles he lets on site. I saw his sheet: M4IDM.'

The superintendent jumped up. 'Right, I'll call some local poliss to seal the place off, and we'll get head down there straight away too. Do not engage them Mr Penfold, you're not trained for it, and you're not authorised to.'

The New Zealand accent came over the phone's speaker again. 'Hold on, guv.' Tony knew the word *guv* would not be a part of Penfold's vocabulary and assumed he was being sarcastic again. 'That's what I meant by "behind the wave": they're not here anymore. They came in at ten o'clock and were gone by half past. They all left together in the black truck, and they didn't collect or deliver anything. Just seemed to meet up and talk about some maps they showed each other. But there's nothing to see here now. The gate guard can't even remember which direction they turned when they left.'

Hardwick slumped back down in the blue office chair, like the heat had taken everything out of him.

THIRTY-FOUR

The car was so hot Tony and Penfold opened all the doors and stood in the shade of a tree for ten minutes in vain hope of it being cooler afterwards.

After fifteen minutes of the sun baking through the car windscreen, heavily overpowering its ailing cooling system, Tony pulled into the circular drive at the front of the Durham Miners Hall almost underneath Durham City's railway viaduct. The high arches were an incredible feat of Victorian engineering. Made from stones half a tonne each, it also hailed from the glory days of Durham's coalfields.

At nearly half past four on a Wednesday, the detective hoped that Barry Black would honour the appointment he had made with Black's secretary earlier that morning. As they stepped around the car to head in, Penfold grabbed Tony by the arm. He pointed towards the edge of the building where a large blue Volvo was nosing forward, the driver scanning the car park. Despite his large sunglasses, Black's bulk was unmistakable as he tried to lean forward, right up against the steering wheel.

Penfold walked back across to the grand entrance gateway and bent down to retie his shoelaces. With this roadblock in place, Tony walked halfway towards the vehicle and stopped in the shade of a large oak tree. He took off his own sunglasses and gave the large man a little wave, accompanied by an equally cheeky grin. He pointed at his watch and mouthed "Four thirty appointment?"

The Volvo's electric front window slid down with a hum, and Black moved his head nearer to the opening. He called over, 'Sorry, I can't stop, I've got a branch meeting to get to. I know Vicky told you to come along, but she didn't know I was attending the other meeting.'

'I'm sorry, Mr Black, we must speak with you now.'

The noise of the handbrake ratchet being pulled on echoed out of the car. Black's movements were laboured as he peeled off the seatbelt and then levered himself up and out of the door. Tony stood his ground and was happy to wait as the Top Marra stepped slowly across the tarmac drive and grass border. As he came to a halt in front of the detective, sweat was glinting in his sideburns and a big drip emerged on each cheek, sliding a wet trail down his jowls.

'Apologies for holding you up, but we'll be as quick as we can. Under the circumstances.'

Penfold arrived beside Tony and stood silently, hands in the pockets of his shorts.

'When we spoke to you on Saturday, you insisted that the Gala did not organise those shipping containers bearing your logo and the sort of murals I would expect your union chums to be very proud of.'

Black's eyes could not be seen through his dark lenses. 'No, indeed. I trust you can see that it would be stupid of us to set away all those frogs and ruin our own event. There's no question of an insurance fiddle or anything neither. The event has little income, so we don't insure against a cancellation halfway through the day.'

Tony was intrigued at the machinations of Black's mind, but he put that in the bank for later and pulled a piece of paper from his trouser pocket. He unfolded it and flattened the sheet against his own chest.

'Maybe we'll come back to that. For now, though, perhaps you could explain this delivery note please. As it happens, quite by chance, I saw the driver hand this over to the manager of the indoor market a week ago Saturday.'

He handed the page over to Black, who scrutinised it with squinting eyes. Reading out loud, the union man confirmed the delivery item, 'I'm not sure what you think I can add to this.

"*Three times forty-foot shipping container as public art installation.*" I mean that definitely describes the object. I don't know whether or not you can include the frogs as part of the art, mind.'

'Please look further down and confirm who authorised the delivery.'

Black's eyes widened and he lifted the paper right up to his face. He lowered the sheet and looked Tony in the eyes. 'I'm not sure quite what kind of trick this is supposed to be, but this is exactly the sort of thing I was talking about when we met last week, and I told you that here we don't trust the police, or any part of the government.'

'Please confirm, Mr Black, that it was you who authorised the delivery of the shipping containers of frogs that disrupted the city on Saturday.'

'That is a lie!' The man's voice was raised to booming but not quite shouting.

Tony smiled. Quietly, he asked, 'Is that your name on the line marked *Authorising signature*?' Black scowled at the policeman. 'And before you reply, I should mention that I have also checked on the confirmation letter you sent to DI Barnes, which has your signature in ink on it.'

Barry Black scrunched the paper as he shoved it back into Tony's chest. His voice sounded both strained and restrained. 'It may look like my signature, but clearly it's a forgery. As I already told you, it would be stupid of me to disrupt the Big Meeting that I organised and was the highlight of my year. What possible benefit could it have for me?'

Tony looked at Penfold and they both gave a small grin. 'Well, as I'm sure you already know, during the time when the frogs had everyone distracted, the same crew who delivered the shipping containers stole three items worth more than a million pounds each.'

This information had not previously been released to the public. Tony worried that he might have made a mistake to tell Black, but making the man squirm would be worth any fallout from the top brass.

An additional bead of sweat ran down his forehead and Black pulled a greying handkerchief from a trouser pocket to mop his brow. They all stared at each other for several seconds. Black blinked first, saying, 'This conversation is over.' He turned and waddled back towards the Volvo.

Back in the VW Golf, the two investigators mulled over their thinking on Barry Black's involvement in the robberies. Tony didn't think the man clever enough to be involved, but Penfold pointed out that to rise so high in a trade union required political nous and manoeuvring. He did agree though that these kinds of smarts were not the kind that helped in a complex series of crimes like the ones involved here.

Tony said he would ask Julia Sedgley to engage a graphologist to compare the signatures they had for Black. Deadpan, Penfold countered that they might get it done much more quickly if DC Meredith were tasked with asking Alfie to get the comparison made.

THIRTY-FIVE

Another hot morning woke Tony up at six, sunlight baking the bedroom curtains. He made a coffee for Kathy and left it on her bedside table. With a small kiss on her cheek, he said he was heading to the station to continue searching for the stolen Shakespeare folio. Barely awake, Kathy's hair half covered her face, but he could still make out the smile she gave at his kiss.

The coffee did its intended work, and Kathy was up and ready for their walk to Palace Green in less than thirty minutes. As they parted, on the threshold of her little office, Tony saw the brave face and squeezed her hand. 'We're gonna catch them. Tomorrow.'

In the Major Crimes Team office, even at seven in the morning, desk space in front of the creaking fans was the prime real estate. Madeline Aria had secured two fans, one arranged on each side of her, and Diane Meredith was huddled in front of the third. Tony set himself up with his laptop on a desk just in front of DC Aria so that he got as much as possible of the air spilling around her.

They had opened all the small windows, but it was debatable whether these actually brought in hotter air than if they kept them closed. While the days since the storm on Saturday had been hot, Thursday had added a layer of humidity. Just centimetres outside the sphere of influence of the fans, the air became muggy, stifling.

Seemingly oblivious to the heat, the two civilian administrators sat at desks they had commandeered for the duration of the investigations since Hardwick had managed to secure their services through the chief constable.

Helen Landrey, Durham's World Heritage Site curator, came in smirking. She concluded her conversation with Penfold with the single word, 'Priceless.' Tony couldn't tell if they were discussing the value of one of the stolen items, or if the surfer had told her a funny joke.

Penfold was the only one dressed for the weather. Everyone else wore work attire, as lightweight as they could manage, but nonetheless business clothes of different varieties. DCI Hardwick bustled in and immediately removed his jacket, leaving a crisp white, open-necked shirt and the dark trousers of his suit. He was followed by PC Chris Thorpshire who had been assigned to CID again and would be assisting on the Major Crimes Team for their next operation. The constable was in uniform but, in the station, that meant he could also try to keep cool in a shirt with no jacket, hat or stab vest.

Harry Hardwick rapped a fist on the nearest table and everyone fell silent. Only the three fans dared to interrupt his introduction with their whirring and clanking. He scowled at the noisiest one but made no suggestion that someone should switch it off, and it was too hot for anyone to take the initiative to do so.

'Good morning, everyone.' Multiple mutters of "Morning, guv" overlapped in reply. 'We're joined this morning by Helen Landrey, whom I think you all know. We concluded our meeting yesterday with an understanding of where we're at with investigating both the murders and the robberies. All signs point to a single, but complex, series of crimes. The bodies left in the old pits appear to be a calculated distraction, designed to divert police resources and improve the odds of the thefts succeeding. However, Mrs Landrey has brought to my attention the social media propaganda surrounding the idea of the treasures being recovered on "St Cuthbert's Friday". We wondered why anyone would continue the hype beyond the date of those thefts last Saturday. The hype is continuing I take it?'

Detective Constable Aria had been following the online build-up carefully. 'Oh, yes,' she replied. 'The MaidMarionettes website has been offline since our raid on Tuesday, but all the other socials have increased activity. There feels like a real crescendo coming for tomorrow. I've counted over sixty people saying they're going to head out to a mine then. Some as far afield as Wales.'

'Bloody idiots,' carped Hardwick. 'Anyway, this ongoing activity doesn't make sense, unless there is some criminal purpose to it. Helen has pointed out that the cathedral's exhibition of the Lindisfarne Gospels is also due to end tomorrow. Our informant's intelligence says they'll be attempting to steal them, and that the crooks are hoping we'll all be out of town patrolling various coal mines so that they can attack the exhibition more easily.'

The superintendent continued, 'Well, we're not going to let that happen. No, we're going to put a plain clothes surveillance operation in place in the cathedral all day tomorrow. My understanding is that the British Library's security requirements for the Gospels exhibition are far superior to those that were in place for any of the four items stolen already.

'That is both good and bad. It means it should be easier for us to protect them, but it also raises the stakes for the thieves. They're going to have to break through several layers of security.

'Before we work out the details of how we will conduct this operation, I'll hand over to Helen to explain the various security systems that are in place, both human and technological.'

Mrs Landrey had a presentation set up on the display screen on the room's long wall, and she pressed a remote clicker to start her piece. Eight slides outlined eight levels of protection that had been insisted upon by the Gospels' owner, the British Library.

The first she explained involved ticketing that required an online sign up, with tickets then delivered to a postal address. She had already liaised with the National Crime Agency to sift through their intelligence databases and flag up any "interesting" ticket applications.

It was too late to send uniforms to all the addresses connected with these dubious ticket holders, but the automated entry system could flag up when any of these tickets were scanned at the turnstiles. Meredith suggested that they would be better served simply following these ticket holders rather than alerting them with undue attention from the guides or police.

Everybody had an opinion on her proposal, but it was held over for later; Landrey suggested they should hear all the security protections before trying to decide on any courses of action, especially given the limited number of bodies at their disposal. Hardwick had already prepared her for their staffing restrictions.

The layout of the supporting exhibits in the cathedral's museum space had been designed to slow down any smash and grab exit. The displays were in the Durham Cathedral Museum, on the first floor, with access via two stone staircases, one end for entry, and the exit stairs at the other end. Similarly, the exhibition spaces included an outer room that one had to pass through to get to the inner sanctum where the most precious items were being shown.

Physical obstacles made for a simple security measure that villains often failed to account for. It became clear that Helen Landrey was an expert in the details of past museum heists from all around the world.

After explaining some of the background checks that were undertaken of the exhibition's staff, and the slightly off-topic conservation needs of the Gospels, she moved on to the final slide.

As St Cuthbert's Friday coincided with the closing of the exhibition's six week run, they had to consider the possibility of a robbery being staged during the breaking down of the displays and the transportation back to London of the various elements that belonged to the British Library. The black box truck, *M4IDM*, suggested the same.

H considered this the most likely approach by any professional crew. He also suggested that this helped Durham

Constabulary on the grounds that as soon as the high-value items were handed back into the custody of the team sent up from London for transportation it was no longer on their watch. Tony wondered if a career in this job inevitably made people cynical.

Landrey dismissed Hardwick's comment as unhelpful, and, as their UNESCO liaison, she was the only person in the room he could not shut down. Tony saw Penfold smile as Hardwick gave her his dead-eye stare, and she continued unaware of what she was supposed to take from the look.

After the security briefing, they pushed several tables together and sat around as a working party to hammer out the details of the plan. Hardwick had important matters to attend to and appointed Tony as the lead on Operation Oswald.

He was happy that the boss was entrusting him with more and more responsibility, but a project like this was unusual, and he knew he would need to defer to Helen's encyclopaedic knowledge of possible heist approaches to ensure they covered all bases.

It was at this thought that he realised Hardwick must have some of the same political nous they'd imagined in Barry Black. If a successful robbery did occur, the buck now stopped with (Acting) Detective Inspector Milburn. *The sneaky bugger*.

Jeanette Compton knocked at the open door and took a step inside the Major Crimes office, looking at Penfold. 'Ah, Jeanette, pull up a pew. Milburn, I texted Jeanette to join us, given her knowledge of the cathedral's geography.'

Tony had no objection, the more brains the better, and Jeanette was a constabulary employee. Looking around the table, he knew this group had a great range of knowledge and experience to prepare a top-notch protection plan for the Lindisfarne Gospels. Hardwick also nodded positively at her introduction to the room as they passed each other.

Tony picked up the reins. 'Right, Operation Oswald. Helen has explained the layout and systems we'll be dealing with. Let's put together our plan.'

He instructed DC Aria to tell them about any online hype relating to the Lindisfarne Gospels rather than St Cuthbert's Treasure.

'First up, the LuvCuthbert user account on the MaidMarionettes forum: the digital forensics team found conversations with the same phone number in all the victims' mobiles. One of them had added the number as a contact called LuvCuthbert, so we're pretty certain that's the connection that Ms Rufus told DI Milburn about.' Aria nodded towards her boss, and he nodded back.

She carried on. 'They do all have WhatsApp messages arranging to meet, and the times and locations are consistent with when and where we found the victims. LuvCuthbert's phone number is a burner SIM, and the purchase details give the address as Castle Eden Manor, so it's basically the same dead end.'

Tony cocked his head and said, 'I wouldn't call that a dead end, that's confirmation of our murderer. We just don't know who that is exactly.'

Penfold shuffled in his seat and shook his head but did not interrupt.

'Please go on, Madeline. What about the Lindisfarne Gospels and the treasure hunters?'

She responded with a measured explanation that this angle had received minimal coverage in the treasure hunter groups.

One of the first points agreed was that they would ask any station that could stretch to sending a uniform patrol around some of the better known mine sites to do so. The criminals should believe that the police were taken in by the misdirection ploy.

In the cathedral, the on-site security guards should also continue to work as normal. Indeed, the decision was made that the cathedral would not be informed of Operation Oswald. The possibility of an inside job was sufficiently high that they could not risk any leak of their plans.

Tony suggested they could go one step further by having Helen give a special security briefing to the staff and guards. Her talk would highlight the end of the exhibition as a moment of vulnerability and mention the high-value thefts during the Miners' Gala. This briefing would also serve to tell any criminal infiltrators that no additional security was being added. The undercover police presence would never be mentioned.

When it came to assigning undercover roles and locations, Penfold pointed out that he and Tony had both met Maid Marion. Whoever she was, she would recognise them.

Similarly, Alex Carrera had shown Meredith around at the Bowes Museum, so Meredith, too, couldn't work that close to the main surveillance target area. The general mood was that Carrera had run off, that she was in the wind, and her exact connection to the Swan theft had not been established. Fairburn had not heard of her by name, but that robbery had gone exceedingly smoothly.

Personnel were at a premium, and they put together a hodgepodge rota of faces not known to the criminals, who could pass through the exhibition room repeatedly to keep an eye on the other visitors without any one of them being there noticeably too long.

The tickets were on a timed entry system every thirty minutes, so this monitoring could easily be achieved with a rota of DC Aria, PC Thorpshire, the detective super, Jeanette Compton and Landrey herself. Though, these last two were not trained to work in such a field operation as this, nor did they have the necessary official police appointment to do so anyway.

The solution was that they would be eyes and ears, with one part of their rota also stationed in an operational HQ. At any sign of suspicious activity, they would radio Milburn, Meredith or PC Thorpshire to apprehend suspects as they descended the exit stairs.

Helen would use her position to commandeer the Chapter House for the day as the HQ room. It could be shut off so even cathedral staff would not be aware of what was going on. Stan Willem was to be brought into the loop, and he would be tasked with telling the staff a tale about the room being closed for maintenance all day.

The three remaining "faces-known" personnel would patrol the other parts of the nine-hundred-year-old old monument, especially the nave, cloister garden, Galilee Chapel and the back exit area around the cafe and bookshop.

Historically built to protect itself and the Prince Bishops' wealth, as much as to praise God, Durham Cathedral had two pinch points for exiting: the main North Door, nearly always used for visitor movements, and the gatehouse exit from the college on to South Bailey. A third pathway from the cafeteria exit back out to Palace Green had conveniently been fenced off for repairs to the sandstone brickwork on the west end of the building. Thus, they needed to protect only two routes where a thief might leave the area with any booty.

Tony couldn't leave the office during the operation's preparation work, so he sent PC Thorpshire to drive Kathy home.

After two hours of settling on patrol routes and rotas, everyone was relieved at the chance to descend to the nick canteen. The basement room was noticeably cooler but suffered from little movement of its air, and the kitchens at the far end did not help. The humidity seemed to crank up a notch cancelling out any benefits of the lower temperature.

People bickered over the portions of wilting salad leaves, complained about how little ice was put into the water jugs, moaned at the limited selection of ice creams available, and threw their hands up in dismay on finding that all the soft drinks had sold out. Summer thunderstorms were building.

THIRTY-SIX

Tony survived the afternoon with a wet handkerchief in his hand, constantly dabbing his forehead. As soon as was feasible, he dismissed his group to go and prepare their individual responsibilities. They would meet at seven in the morning in the Chapter House to put Operation Oswald into action.

He arrived at home just after eight with a takeaway curry. As he was laying the foil containers out on the kitchen counter, Kathy took umbrage at the meal.

'Curry? Why on earth would you think that was a good idea on a night like tonight?'

'What are you talking about, what's special about tonight?'

'The weather. The last thing I want is a big hot meal. What I really want is Viennetta. Why didn't you bring Viennetta?'

'Don't be ridiculous, that's not a meal. Anyway, you didn't make any suggestions – I had to choose something to get us.'

'But why curry?' Kathy's voice was a childlike whine.

'You know they eat spicy food like this in places like India because it's hot. Makes you sweat and you cool down.'

'Eugh, God, no. The thought of it is making me ill.'

'Look, I've spent all day at work, there's no food in the house, so I sort out tea, and you just complain. Why didn't you choose something? You didn't answer my messages.'

She had a sheen of sweat on her smooth face and sat down carefully. Tony was in no mood for hassle. He dumped a plate of rice and chicken tikka masala in front of her and threw a silvered bag containing a naan bread down next to it. Grabbing his own plate and naan, he slumped down in the chair opposite her.

'I can't. I just can't.' Kathy pushed the plate away towards the middle of the oak table.

'God, you're so ungrateful.'

Tears came to her eyes, and she shouted at him. 'I got fired! Are you even looking for the first folio? Or just spending your time ogling that Crazy Cow?' She leapt up and stormed out.

Stunned into silence, he watched her leave, unable to process what to say or do. A feeble attempt to speak was many seconds too late. 'Wait, fired?' His voice was a quiet croak. *How is this my fault?*

Tony was ravenous, but he knew his meal would have to wait. He tore off a strip of naan and stuffed it into his mouth as a stop gap.

He found Kathy on the sofa, elbows on her knees and face in hands, sobbing. Tony knew his girlfriend was a resilient woman, and on the few occasions when he had seen her like this, he had learnt to resist his strong urge to hug her. In the heat and humidity, all thoughts and actions seemed to move slowly, like they had to push their way through the thick air. This sluggishness probably helped him refrain from jumping in with both feet, as did the mouthful of food that he was struggling to masticate quickly enough.

After pulling off his shoes, Tony sat down on the sofa. He chose a spot far enough along the cream fabric that she would know he was present but was not pushing his way into her troubles. He was there for her, for when she wanted to talk to him. This slight pause gave him a chance, too, to finish chewing the naan bread and swallow.

As her tears and sobs continued, the awkwardness of nobody speaking tore him up. He was desperate to offer support and to help solve her problems. However, as a seasoned interrogator, he also knew that her reaction was mostly psychological. Their conversation and progress would be stronger if they'd both had time to work through the clouds of stress, or distress, fogging their minds. He held his hands together calmly and ignored the sweat pouring down his back.

Several minutes passed, and Kathy's tears stemmed, her breathing quietened, and she wiped her face a few times with the backs of her hands. 'I got fired, Tony.' She was barely audible.

'I don't quite get how that could happen. I know the Shakespeare is really valuable, but the university would have to go through a long process to blame you enough to force you out. It was only stolen five days ago.' He didn't know exactly what the disciplinary process might be within the university, but he had seen the Police Federation reps in action often enough to know how difficult it was to get rid of somebody employed in an institution like that.

He thought back to a meeting with Hardwick and Meredith and her federation rep. That had been one of the worst situations he had ever found himself in. Wrongly accused of wrongly accusing her and being berated by the rep – a colleague he had thought of as a friend, who had been totally taken in by her and wilfully refused to even consider the evidence he had brought to the table. If Meredith could get away with stalking and harassment, there was no way Durham University could sack Kathy for the criminal actions of somebody else.

'What did they actually say to you? And who told you?'

'Well, they redeployed me back to the Billy B, but it's effectively a sacking. That curatorship was the ultimate job. I've been a librarian for ten years already. I worked so hard for that promotion.'

He remembered the day she'd danced into the kitchen singing about her new job. She had been alight with excitement, blue eyes bright and hair flying around, as she twirled and sang.

Understanding flooded Tony's brain. After her promotion from the university's Bill Bryson Library to curate the special collections, he could see how being "redeployed" back to the Bryson library would crush Kathy. He could also see how the university powers would react with a knee-jerk scapegoating to protect the reputations of those at the top.

She started breathing loudly, quick sharp intakes. Kathy put a slender hand to her chest and her eyes were wide. She looked like she was choking, but Tony could see her chest moving in and out, albeit rapidly. She rasped, 'You must find the folio.'

'Well, of course.' Her appearance worried him. 'Are you OK?'

She looked up at him, no inhaling or exhaling visible. 'Find it, Tony!' At her shout, he jumped back along the sofa so far that he felt cool material under his bottom, a whole seat's distance further away from her. Her soft eyes looked dark and angry.

'I will. We're working on it. We've got some really strong leads.' He wasn't sure of the veracity of this, but if they were to catch the crew trying to steal the Lindisfarne Gospels, the Shakespeare book would surely be found.

'Stop saying "we"! I don't want to hear about her. You can't be too bloody upset, if you're still spending all day with her.'

He tried to look her in the eyes, but they were malevolent dark fires that he hadn't seen before. The last time she had been this angry was when they were battling against Meredith's harassment. At that time, though, they had been fighting her together, hand in hand, Tony and Kathy against the world. In this moment, Kathy's vitriol was aimed directly at him.

She knows Harry's hands are tied. What is this? He spoke very quietly. 'I'm on your side.' The words fell on the sofa between them. Her difficulty breathing had been replaced with seething. 'Are you too hot? Should I get the fan?'

This time she really shouted, 'Don't be so bloody patronising!' Her face was flushed bright red, and she pointed at him, her voice still loud. 'Go and use your new bloody rank to get everybody out searching for it.'

He couldn't see what she might expect him to do beyond what he was already doing, all day, every day, in thirty-degree heat. He snapped and shouted back at her, 'This is not my fault!

I didn't steal your precious bloody book. We're out there doing everything we can.'

Kathy jumped up. 'Oh really? Well, if you aren't going to help me, I'll go out there and look for it myself.' She stormed out of the lounge.

In a matter of seconds Tony heard the front door slam. He muttered, 'Course you will.'

His curry was cold, which might normally have been acceptable, given the hot weather, but he just poked and pushed it around the plate, nibbling on naan as much as he could manage. Even his beer seemed fizzy and tasteless. It was still cool though; he pressed the bottle to each cheek and enjoyed the condensation sliding down his neck.

Tony prepared Kathy's meal, to go in either the microwave or fridge when she returned. He assumed she was walking around the block to blow off steam. He went upstairs and set the shower to as cold as he could stand. The chilled water on his salty, grimy skin felt wonderful.

As he towelled dry in their bedroom, Tony looked out at the vaguely darkening sky. The blue was no more, and the sun filtered through hazy cloud just above the rooftops across the street. As he scanned the little neighbourhood around their home, he heard muffled voices entering through the open window above his head.

He looked down, nosy at which of his neighbours was out gossiping at well gone nine at night. The trim lawns and well-arranged drives and paths gave the place a lovely suburban feel. He spotted the old woman who lived with her son three houses along the road. She had her small pug on a lead, presumably out for its nighttime necessities before bed.

He dropped the towel. The woman stood in the road at the end of his driveway to attend to Kathy. A boulder sat in gravel between the ends of their drive and the footpath from the front door. She was sitting on the boulder, her back to the house, shoulders slumped, hair bedraggled, and her arms resting on splayed legs.

The pug sniffed Kathy's toes, as the woman leant forward, obviously attempting to be supportive in the face of Kathy's anguish. Now that he could see her mouth moving, the woman's words that came through the little window made more sense.

'I'm sure he'll sort it out for you, pet. You say he's really good at solving crimes – he'll come through. It'll be OK.' Kathy leant forward to stroke the small dog, who flirtatiously lay down and exposed her belly.

As he rushed around the bedroom trying to quickly pull on shorts and at the same time find a T-shirt, he nearly toppled over. What he would have found funny normally just made him angry at himself, and at the bedroom. He had to get outside and make things right with her.

By the time he opened the door, Kathy was standing and saying goodbye. She turned and stepped slowly along the paving slabs towards him. He gave a sort of apologetic wince and mouthed the word "Sorry". She responded with a dismissive wave of her hand and her mouth formed a flat line attempt at a smile. The exterior temperature and humidity immediately engulfed him. Sweat prickled on his brow again.

As the lady walked back along the street, she called, 'Why don't you text that Penfold and tell him you got fired. That should put a rocket up his backside. He'll get working doubly hard on the investigation, I'm sure.'

Tony's stomach dropped. She'd been telling the woman that Penfold was the great crime-solver, not him. Despite all his cooling down and calming alone-time, Tony's hot anger shot up again. It choked him, so he couldn't speak to her. His intentions of happy hugs and apologies were smothered by muggy heat. His brain filled with the image of her entreating Penfold to solve the theft.

Before she had made four steps towards him, Tony bolted back up the stairs. He slammed the door of the spare bedroom shut and stayed in there all night. Kathy never attempted to communicate with him, and she was gone from the house by six when he got up and went into their room to find some clothes that would not scream "Undercover Cop".

The night had been a sweaty, restive pendulum, where Tony's thoughts swung between anger at Kathy, shame at his anger at her, sadness at their conflict, and reconsideration of all the evidence for the crimes that Operation Oswald would hopefully put to bed. He was not looking forward to meeting Penfold in the Chapter House for the operation's final preparations.

THIRTY-SEVEN

Penfold always looked the part of a holidaymaker and had not had to wear anything unusual to work undercover. Tony looked like a geography teacher on a Saturday. He sported grey walking trousers, with the legs zipped off so they became shorts, and a black T-shirt from a music festival on Newcastle's quayside that he and Kathy had attended three years earlier.

The DI had stepped out of his house in flip-flops before realising how useless they would be if he had to run after a crook. A quick change later, and he wore white socks in trainers, completing the weekend teacher vibe perfectly. He had been grateful that Kathy had not been at home to laugh at his outfit. Although he figured that such sartorial incompetence should help his undercover persona to be convincing.

As he entered the circular stone room of Durham Cathedral's Chapter House, technicians were just completing the temporary installation of the police communications and surveillance system. This included several screens grabbing the feed from various CCTV cameras around the giant, old church. The techs handed each person a fancy little in-ear radio device. These connected everyone but were pretty much invisible once inserted in the ear. The domed room, made famous in Harry Potter movie scenes, now looked like a CIA surveillance station in Moscow.

Tony took in the remaining clothing choices. While detectives always worked out of uniform, they followed an unspoken dress code of smart work attire, always chosen to enable swift movements if anything kicked off. To dress in civvies and have no possibility of being mistaken for police took quite an eye for both fashion and sociology.

Detective Superintendent Hardwick made for a very impressive summer racegoer, his cravat and Panama hat truly making the outfit.

Madeline Aria clearly had little variation in her wardrobe to select from – she appeared to be channelling primary school teacher, with forest green trousers, flat shoes and a thin sweater in a similarly mossy colour.

Unsurprisingly, Diane Meredith was looking to create a stir. A summery bra top left arms, shoulders and belly on show, and her lower half was covered by tight leggings that matched her top. She wore Converse high tops on her feet, and too much make-up on her face.

I think we'll have to call this mode, Summertime Skin, Tony thought, as her look accosted his eyes. She gave him an overt and aggressive wink, as she popped a piece of bubble gum in her mouth. Diane was a method actor.

Helen Landrey walked in with Stan Willem, the Constable of the Cathedral, and he nearly dropped his clipboard at the sight of DC Meredith. He had met her before and recognised the police officer. 'I'm sorry, detective, but even Mary Magdalene wouldn't get into the cathedral in that outfit. If you go to the volunteers at the reception desk back in the nave, they have shawls to lend to visitors who arrive inappropriately dressed.' Despite addressing her directly, he never met Meredith's eye.

She was dressed much like many visitors to the cathedral and almost certainly wouldn't stand out. In high summer, it was common for a proportion of female visitors to be wandering around with loaner shawls, to maintain the respectability required in a church.

Hardwick chipped in, 'Oh, brilliant. That will actually add to your cover, Diane. No poliss is going to try and come into the cathedral half-dressed and have to borrow a dressing gown.' Nobody in the room could tell if H was serious that her disguise would be improved, or if he was giving her a dressing down for looking so chavvy. Meredith blew a bubble with her gum until it popped with a loud crack.

Roles, rotas and patrol routes had been established in the planning phase and Tony ran through a cursory recap. He then huddled with the Constable of the Cathedral and the security guard to brief them directly. These were the only two employees of the cathedral who would know of the police operation.

The recently departed technicians had given weight to Willem's storyline that the Chapter House was undergoing maintenance for the day, but the real hope was that the last day of the exhibition would keep all the guides and volunteers busy. They shouldn't have a chance to worry about anything out of the ordinary and expose the police operation by asking too many questions.

To this end, the Constable suggested that Hardwick, with his Panama hat and cravat would likely be a very memorable tourist – he asked if a change of clothes was possible or if the boss could do less frequent tours. Tony agreed.

Begrudgingly, the superintendent removed both items, after which he looked like a plain, easily forgettable, tourist. He pressed the cravat into service as a handkerchief and mopped his sweaty forehead.

In the plans, PC Thorpshire was scheduled to monitor the CCTV feeds and relay monitoring suggestions via their closed radio network. He had turned up in shorts and a T-shirt printed with a Saltire and a slogan espousing Scottish independence. His extremely short hair might not help, but Tony reckoned the shirt would deflect anyone from the notion of him being police. Tony decided Chris would be switched into the rota on every third patrol that had originally been allocated to Hardwick and Meredith.

The thick stone walls in the Chapter House made the room bearably cool. The temperature quickly rose outside the door in the cloisters around a square, open lawn. The sky was bright blue, and the sun already hit much of the grass area. Even at just before seven in the morning, and even in thin summer clothes, the heat out there was stifling.

Penfold had disappeared and returned just as Tony was re-organising the patrol patterns for Meredith, Hardwick and Thorpshire. This job mostly involved the young police constable teaching H how to use the surveillance screens. There was a console of buttons with two inbuilt joysticks to enable panning and zooming to follow suspects.

Hardwick was a good copper, but he was very much a pen and paper man. However hard he tried, the superintendent always seemed to pan when he wanted to zoom and zoom when he wanted to pan. In the end Chris wrote on Post-it notes, labelling each joystick, and stuck them to the console.

Penfold carried two large paper bags branded with the logo of the Daily Espresso. Each bag contained some takeaway drinks, crammed in to avoid wobbling and spilling in the bags. On top of the cups, the upper half of each bag held a variety of pastries. He set up a buffet on a table by the door and announced that everyone should help themselves.

This breakfast largesse annoyed Tony. That Penfold had done this off his own bat was a friendly supportive gesture, but the operation lead should have thought to provide refreshments – something Tony felt irritated with himself about. The man was undermining his authority, even if only he and Penfold actually knew who had organised the breakfast.

The heat was getting to him again, and he bit into a croissant so as not to utter the cross words his brain was itching to hurl at Penfold. He remembered the arguments with Kathy the previous night and his shirt felt itchy with sweat. This day would need emotional control – the heat would raise hackles too easily.

He took out his phone and messaged Kathy.

> Sorry for last night. We're on an operation in the cathedral today which with luck will lead us to the folio. Hope you're OK. x

He toyed with signing off with an emoji of a love heart or blowing-a-kiss but didn't feel that they were in a good enough place to do so without getting her back up. The simple "x" would have to send the intended message.

The cathedral opened at eight, but the museum in the cloisters did not have its first timed visitor entry until ten o'clock. Helen Landrey was impressed at the operation HQ they'd set up in just an hour and commented on how there was no indication of it outside the door.

The wheeled display boards had been brought over from the Major Crimes office and one now held a large plan of the cathedral and surrounds. She used this to reiterate to everyone the high-risk areas, the places restricted by ticket admission, the bottlenecks for movement, and the two exit points from the cathedral.

Tony's patrol areas were shaded in purple, and others in various colours overlapped, so that the entire floor plan of the ecclesiastical estate was covered. At the side, encoded with the same colour scheme, each police officer's timings were listed, always a minimum of two of them at any one time, wandering the chapels, nave, cloisters, cafe and museum. All of the opening hours were covered, and in a few places, the original assignments had been scribbled out and Chris Thorpshire's name added in pencil.

The second display board was set up as a motivator more than anything else. It held photos of each crime scene: each mineshaft murder victim, and each robbery location, Carrera tied to the chair, with a close-up of her tattoo, and the head shot photos from the CVs of Marion's gang, along with her photo from the MaidMarionettes website.

Tony leant against a white-grey stone pillar, arms folded across his chest, staring at the paper list, trying to learn his timings off by heart. In the end, he pulled out his phone and took a photograph of this latest iteration of the rota.

'Spotted the hole in the surveillance cover?' Penfold had sidled up beside him and was also looking at the colourful printed sheet.

'What, no. Where?'

'No, that's good. No holes in geography or time, then we've done all we can.' Silence fell between them for a moment, as both men continued to read and re-read their names and patrol times. 'Although no plan survives first contact with the enemy.'

Tony nodded at this truism. 'Well, hopefully we've got backup systems in place to bring everyone into play when needed.'

Hardwick had also appeared alongside Tony, and he said, 'Armed response unit has just confirmed they're in place in the cathedral maintenance yard.' This put a police presence in a location where they could block off the archway exit from the college as well as the maintenance corridor from the cathedral interior out to the college area.

Penfold shook his head. 'I still think armed response is overkill.'

Wiping his brow, Hardwick turned his head so his dead eye stared guilelessly at Penfold and said, 'Overkill is kind of the point. If these criminals are willing to kill just to misdirect us, they're not going to think twice about violence if they're cornered in this place. No use bringing a truncheon to a gunfight.'

'I disagree. If you bring a gun, you *make it* a *gun*fight.'

Tony countered. 'Correct, except that you make it a gun*fight*. Until then, you're just getting shot.'

The big boss addressed the room conclusively. 'Everybody be careful out there. These artefacts are not worth losing anyone for.' He stuffed the cravat back into a trouser pocket, turned and left the Chapter House, the heavy wooden door creaking closed behind him.

THIRTY-EIGHT

Tony paused inside St Cuthbert's shrine, looking at a headless statue holding up another head. He carried a small guidebook for Durham's World Heritage Site. It told him that this was the head of Saint Oswald being held aloft by Saint Cuthbert. How the statue of Saint Cuthbert had lost its own head was not clear.

Oswald's real head was apparently also in St Cuthbert's tomb, at Tony's feet, despite the then King Oswald being killed forty-five years before Cuthbert died.

The detective thought about the Tudhoe mineshaft. Mick Dooley and Dickie Harbottle's corpses lay together in that muddy tomb, despite Harbottle dying many years earlier. The similarity struck Tony as weird, poignant, pointed.

Keeping to his cover as a tourist visitor, he turned his phone up towards the roof and tried to get a shot of the shrine cover. The spectacular embroidered canopy showed Jesus and some symbols. The huge square cloth proved very difficult to fit into the screen on his small phone and he made a show of taking a photo but didn't worry too much about the actual outcome.

Leaving Cuthbert's small chapel, Tony's ninth patrol came near to its conclusion. He stood in a quiet spot in the Chapel of the Nine Altars and broadcast a rallying cry to his colleagues. He knelt on a rainbow kneeler and spoke as if muttering a prayer quietly to God. His invisible mic picked up every word and relayed it into the ears of the rest of the team.

The detective inspector reminded everyone of the need to guard against boredom. After an early start and hours of wandering their various designated areas without incident, it would be easy to miss something. As Helen Landrey had warned in her part of the briefing, museum guide boredom accounted for a significant proportion of thief escapes.

267

He smiled at the thought that an all-seeing God might react to his reminder by keeping extra alert for sinners. He hoped the others in his surveillance team would be suitably pepped up.

Penfold replied sarcastically to say he had been asleep and thanks for waking him. Hardwick then came on, his voice giving away his relish at the chance to admonish Penfold. 'Let's keep this channel clear please. Operational comments only.'

The line went silent but, in his mind, Tony could picture Penfold having to bite his tongue to avoid making some further insufferable remark.

To return to the surveillance HQ, he had to pass through the full length of the nave. As he approached the black and white tiles in front of the Quire, Tony spotted Kathy near the chapel for the Durham Light Infantry. He could see the back of her head, blonde hair cascading over a thin blue sweater. She seemed to be taking in a collection of miners' banners that were hung to one side.

He walked quickly under the central tower, the vaulted roof nearly fifty metres above his head. *What do I say to her? I can explain the operation, but we've seen and heard nothing unusual. We've caught nobody, not even had need to question anybody. I'm no further forward with the folio than I was last night.*

The quiet atmosphere of the place of worship stopped him from calling to her. He waited until he had arrived behind her and reached a hand to her shoulder. 'Kathy, what are you doing here?' It was a pretty lame question. Her workplace was on Palace Green so she often visited the cathedral, but he was worried she was ignoring their agreement that she should avoid going out alone.

The blonde head turned towards him, and he jumped back, as if receiving a static shock from her sweater. It wasn't Kathy. 'Oh, I'm so sorry, madam, I didn't mean to startle you. I thought you were my girlfriend.'

'I wouldn't tell her that you're mistaking random women for her.' The woman's advice was accompanied by a generous smile, and she turned to stroll towards the Neville family tombs. As she walked away, he could see that, although her style was just like Kathy's, she had a slightly more athletic build, a few centimetres taller. He smiled at her back. *Oops!*

On returning to the Chapter House, Tony discovered a very sweaty Chris Thorpshire sitting with a cold can of Diet Coke. He had completed a seventh tour of the exhibition of treasures and felt over-heated.

The first-floor museum was encased in stone walls, but was outside the main cathedral, in one of the buildings off the cloisters. The heat and humidity had again built heavily through the day, and Tony was relieved that his patrolling assignments had avoided the suffocating room containing the Lindisfarne Gospels. He could understand why the exhibits needed humidity-controlled display cases on a day like this.

'Anyone of interest on your rounds?'

'Nothing at all, guv.' The young man shook his head and pulled out his phone. 'I've noted down all I saw up there, but it's just tourists. Lot of Americans, lot of Chinese. I followed one guy briefly, as he seemed to be alone, and you don't get many going solo. But he just left. Read some of the signage, had a really good squint at the pectoral cross, but didn't touch anything. I passed him on to Landrey at the exit turnstile and she followed him out to the North Door and he left.'

'Essentially the same story as the whole day then?'

'Aye.'

Penfold's little backpack of refreshments sat on the adjacent seat but there was no sign of the Kiwi himself. *Must be out on his last patrol.* Diane Meredith was stationed at the CCTV screens, conscientiously attentive to the lack of action.

Tony tapped his phone to see the time – *15:56*. The last timed entry tickets had been allocated to start at three thirty, and

Detective Superintendent Hardwick would be on that patrol. The museum was to close at four; the main cathedral building much later at eight, but public access to the Lindisfarne Gospels would no longer be available in just a few minutes' time. Tony stepped behind Meredith to view the display monitors. Over the miniature radios, he asked if anyone had anything to report.

On screen, he could see the boss dabbing his face with the cravat that had made him look so dapper at eight in the morning. He was feigning interest in a stone obelisk with a cross at the top. Helen Landrey was in the corner of the museum, watching the room, and the only two tourists remaining were being chivvied to the exit by a guide in a flowing purple robe.

Tony climbed the stone staircase to join Hardwick and Landrey. 'Helen, can you do a sweep of the room and make sure everything is in its proper place, please?'

She nodded and set off around the cases, dismissing the guide to leave them alone in the exhibition. The man paused, staring at H and Tony like he thought they were two tourists. In the end though, he apparently accepted she would deal with these two unknowns.

The two men waited patiently, sweltering. The museum's main exhibits room was the old monastic dormitory. Tony perused the leaded windows and the huge wooden bookcases crammed with old theology books behind glassed doors. Overhead, the magnificent, medieval wooden roof was supported by gigantic horizontal beams, each one an actual oak tree trunk.

In five minutes, Helen finished her scan of the museum. 'Unless they've managed to switch out with a very good copy, everything is as it should be.'

Tony shook his head. 'Substitution is not their MO – this crew just take the stuff. Quickly, while your eyes are elsewhere, but they don't mind you noticing that it's gone. If it's all here, then they've missed their window.'

Hardwick wiped the silk cloth hard across his forehead and countered, 'Still got to get all this back on the lorry to the British Library. Until they sign off that it's in their care, we remain vigilant.'

The DI laughed. 'We probably should remain vigilant even after that.'

Helen held up her phone. 'I've been told that the lorries have arrived in the maintenance yard.'

Tony squinted and said, 'Let's make sure that it's the legit lorry. Let's not get done over by some impostors.'

She continued to hold up her phone as a prop for her next answer. 'Yep, that protocol is in hand. Before we load up, I'm going to video call the head curator at the British Library and show him the lorry driver and his team, face by face, so he can confirm they're the people he sent up from London for the Gospels.'

She began to point around the room, explaining to the two detectives how the exhibition would be dismantled, which parts went on the high-value items lorry and which parts went in the ancillaries' transport.

The interruption was loud in their ears. Stan Willem, Constable of the Cathedral, shouted that he had seen the dolphin tattoo. He gave a brief description of a blonde woman in jeans and a blue sweater. He was following the woman discreetly from the Galilee Chapel but needed police backup to actually stop her.

Willem had not realised that the tattoo blow-up on the display board he'd seen in the Chapter House belonged to Alex Carrera, who had dark hair.

From her position in the Chapter House, Meredith followed up immediately. 'Got her on camera. She's almost at the nave exit. Who's on patrol there?'

Tony was already running down the stairs, and he heard Hardwick puffing steadily behind. As they sprinted along twenty metres of flagstone colonnade beside the Cloister Garth, the sky was black with clouds. Fecund raindrops spattered over the marble of a medieval stone water fountain in the centre of the lawn.

'I'm just pulling the North Door closed now.' Penfold's voice sounded over the airwaves, calm and conclusive.

'You're doing what?' It was Willem.

The New Zealander casually replied, 'There's now no exit this way. So we can't lose her.'

As Tony entered the main building from the cloisters, directly across the nave, he could see the last chink of darkening light cancelled completely as the giant doors came together, the Sanctuary knocker on their outside clanking as Penfold crashed them shut.

The Constable of the Cathedral was puffing as he spoke. 'You can't close those doors – they must remain open throughout the day.'

Penfold ignored him. He waved to Tony and pointed down the nave. 'She's headed towards the east end.'

Tony confirmed, 'Stan, did you definitely see the dolphin tattoo? Where was it? A dolphin for certain?' It didn't make sense that she had vanished and then turned up here.

'Yes. On her ankle. Um, right ankle.'

Hardwick and Tony had come to a standstill in the nave, just inside the entrance from the cloister. As they turned, Tony saw the woman he'd mistaken for Kathy cut across from the centre of the cavernous space, over to their side, about forty metres away. She was heading in the direction of the astronomical clock.

'She's not going for the tower, is she?' Hardwick asked nobody in particular. He and Tony set off running again. Stan Willem was in the hunt too, but his spindly legs seemed unable to run at any pace.

Still calm as anything, Penfold was following them at a jog. 'I sincerely doubt it. That's Marion. She's not one for capture, nor for suicide.'

They rounded the corner into the South Transept, just as the door in the trompe l'oeil mural was sealing shut. The four men bundled through and into narrow corridors leading back to the outside.

Further along the alley, another aged door hung open with the cloisters visible beyond. The stone arches in Norman design held no glass, and they formed a peristyle all around the Cloister Garth lawn. The sound of heavy rain spattering on the narrow roof of the cloister walkway echoed loudly.

Sprawled backwards over the knee-high ledge at the base of one arch, Meredith was picking herself back up, blood streaming from her nose. Her head was wet from having been stuck out into the heavy rain. She held a hand to her face and moaned that the suspect had punched her. With her other hand, Diane pointed around the colonnade in the direction of the gift shop.

PC Thorpshire's voice came into their ears. 'I've got her on camera. She's gone through the cafe and gift shop and out to the external toilets.'

Willem said, 'There's an exit to the college there, and on out to the Bailey.'

Thorpshire responded, 'I'll radio the armed response team.'

As the posse raced out and round into the tree-lined college grounds, they paused to scan for the fleeing woman. The rain caused a sudden chill, and Tony squinted against the drops smacking his face. The cul-de-sac of old houses formed around a central green exited on to South Bailey through another big arch made from the same old stone as most of the cathedral.

Reaching this point, they met four uniformed officers with automatic weapons and cloth caps with black and white checks. The armed team had sprinted down the maintenance yard drive, but their instructions had been seconds too late. Out on the newly re-cobbled road, they saw Marion's saturated figure disappear around a curve towards Prebends Bridge. The four men in plain

MM HUDSON

clothes and four uniforms ran after her, but it was treacherous going, the slick cobbles slippery underfoot.

As they reached the old city gateway, the road became a wide footpath which then split into four directions. There was no sight of their suspect, so they had to split up. One gun and one unarmed set off along each route. The day was black.

Tony ran northwards along the riverside path. Above him, on the high route along the River Wear, right under the cathedral walls, he could see Penfold and a uniformed officer weaving a search pattern to try and see into all the undergrowth around them. Tony slowed down and told his colleague to do the same.

Wind howled along the narrow river valley, cut deep below the plateau of the World Heritage Site. The hairpin bend in the Wear was thickly vegetated on both steep bank sides. Green trees and bushes, heavy with summer leaf, shook and groaned as the wolves of the wind chased through the sodden woods.

Over the surveillance team's radio network Penfold called, 'Got her!' It was only because his radio receiver was right inside Tony's ear canal that he could hear the other's voice.

THIRTY-NINE

He looked up the bank. Straight above him, twenty metres up a steep tree-covered slope, Tony saw Penfold waving down. Apart from his gun-toting support, the Kiwi stood alone. No suspect with an arm twisted behind her back; no fight ongoing; no sign of her. He waved again, indicating that Tony should come up to their position.

The DI started scrambling straight up the muddy bank, but with rivulets of water streaming down, he slipped and fell repeatedly. The officer with him fared little better, and the two of them took five minutes to get up to the path where Penfold stood.

Tony rubbed his hands on the asphalt to clear the mud off, wiped them on the metal handrail for something of a wash, and attempted to dry them on his shorts. This made no difference as his clothes were soaking wet too.

He shouted to be heard over the storm. 'Where is she?'

Penfold spoke calmly in reply, 'Don't shout, Milburn, we can all hear you fine with our super spy radios.'

A disembodied Hardwick barked, 'Yes, normal voice please, Tony. Where are you? Have we captured the suspect?'

Diane Meredith's voice percolated through, sounding as if she had a heavy cold. 'That bitch broke by dose. Bake sure you brig her back here. I want five bidutes alode with her id the Chapter House.' Tony smiled, more at the thought of Meredith's broken nose than at her request.

The superintendent shut her down though. 'Quiet, Meredith! Milburn, where are you? Do we have the suspect?'

He stared at Penfold, eyes imploring him to explain why he had broadcast her capture to the team. Penfold pointed through the protective handrail at the edge of the high path. He indicated a metre or so below to a stone cylinder.

Tony wiped the water from his forehead and shivered, the wind now making his wet shirt cold. Reminiscent of the ones he had seen recently at the abandoned mineshafts, a grate of iron bars lay propped open at the side of a hole, which descended into blackness in the middle of the stonework. A rock sat next to a smashed padlock.

He spotted the damp pile of yellow that Penfold was pointing to. A wig of long, blonde hair hung, caught on a rusty corner of the metal grate. 'Is that …?' Tony stared at Penfold.

'Another one of Marion's disguises, yes. Looks like she caught it in a rush to get out of sight.'

'I spoke to her, inside. Maybe twenty minutes ago. I can't believe it.'

Penfold nodded with a grin. 'Yes, we could all hear you. Don't worry, we won't tell Kathy.'

Hardwick interrupted, 'Enough. We need to catch her. Where are you?'

Tony looked left and right and, wiping the continuing rain from his face, also looked up to the steep walls at the back of the Palace Green Library building. 'We're on the upper path, just below where Windy Gap comes out. She's gone down an old mineshaft. It must be horrible down there in this weather. I can't imagine why she chose to hide down there.'

He climbed down to the wall and leaned over to look down the hole. Rusted metal rungs in the wall formed a ladder. The mud was slippery underfoot, and he held on to the grate that hinged up and would normally cover the opening. The wig felt greasy with rain, as the wind flapped strands against the back of his hand. He called down into the dark. 'Marion, you can come up now. There's no getting away.'

Into his ear, he heard the croak of Stan Willem. 'There are no mine workings on this side of the river, that's an old well. It's called Saint Cuthbert's Well, and … oh, no!'

'What is it, man?' Hardwick could be heard puffing as he spoke. The two of them appeared further along the path, neither running effectively, but both making the effort. The superintendent was looking sideways at Willem as they approached, and he worked one hand in a circle to tell the man to impart what worried him.

'Only the Constables of the Cathedral know this, but St Cuthbert's Well is named that because it has a secret passage from the cathedral. It's an escape route for the monks in case of attack. Hardly anyone knows about the passage. That's the kind of knowledge that's kept and passed on between us. She's gone back inside.' He was staring at the ground between them all.

'Misdirection,' Penfold said quietly. 'She's got us all out here while the Gospels are unguarded.'

Helen Landrey came over the radio into Tony's ear. 'Er, they're not. I'm standing in the exhibition room right now, and you've still got three police in the Chapter House who can get up here straight away. I can see the Gospels displays. All remain as they were.'

DSupt Hardwick took charge. 'Right, Thorpshire, get up there to support Mrs Landrey. Meredith, I want you on the camera screens. Tell us as soon as you see her. Mr Willem, where will she emerge inside?'

DC Aria spoke to all. 'Diane's not in a good way. I've got first aid going on her nose, but she's definitely concussed. Pretty woozy right now. I've sat her in a chair and removed her earpiece so she won't try and get involved.'

'Understood. Aria, you stay with her, but watch the screens, please. Willem! Where?'

'Um, I've never been in the passages myself, but I'm pretty sure there's two possible exits, one in the Great Kitchen, and one in Saint Cuthbert's shrine. They're both covered over with furniture though.'

Penfold said, 'The Great Kitchen – she'll be going for the Gospels, and the kitchen's right downstairs from the museum room.'

'Let's not get caught out.' Hardwick made the remaining assignments. 'I'll head back up, topside, and check out Cuthbert's shrine. Milburn, you and Penfold go through the passages to stop her returning this way. Willem, are you OK to go with them and give directions?'

The man looked scared and somewhat daunted at the prospect of the dark hole, but he nodded. 'Will do.'

'Good man. Armed response team, return to your vehicle and be on standby. It doesn't look like we're dealing with an armed crew here, the woman was carrying nothing as she ran from us.' Without another word, the older detective set off through the rain towards the alley called Windy Gap.

Tony climbed up on to the circular wall and let himself down on to the metal steps bolted into the well casing.

'Watch for booby traps, Milburn.'

'Well, sure. But she has just come down here herself.'

Penfold and the lean Willem clambered down and followed him into the dank, tight space. They all had phone torches lit but had to keep putting the phones away in pockets to take the rungs with both hands.

About four metres and a dozen steps down, they reached the point where a passage led off into the wall. The well continued down and the occasional falling piece of old stonework made a loud plopping in the reservoir below.

The escape passage had been well-designed, however many centuries ago the monks had put it in place. The space was large enough to stand and walk, or run along, and had been lined with stone to prevent collapse. The dark loomed a couple of metres in front of the phones' bright bulbs, but they could move at a brisk pace.

Arriving at a fork in the tunnel, Penfold and Tony cut right, towards what they guessed must be the Great Kitchen exit, while the Constable of the Cathedral turned left to go and meet up with Hardwick in the shrine.

Thirty seconds later, another ladder of metal rungs rose up towards a bright opening in the roof. They paused and signalled to each other to be quiet on ascent. Tony had no idea if they might encounter the woman in the room above, but best not to broadcast their arrival just in case.

They were close to the top of the ladder, Tony in front, with Penfold right at his feet, when the metal grate, which had been up, fell and banged down, just centimetres from the crown of Tony's head.

Marion stood on the bars looking down at them with a broad smile. 'Gentlemen, so glad you could join me.' She wore black shorts, a long-sleeved black T-shirt, and over it all hung the purple robes of a cathedral guide. Without the blonde wig, or the red one, her hair was very dark and straight. It matched much better with her brown eyes, and also with the photo they had of Alex Carrera.

Just above Tony's face, a blue dolphin leapt over her ankle bone. Below him, and so quietly that Tony could only hear through the amplification of the radio earpiece, Penfold said, 'Calling all cars. She's in the Great Kitchen. We can't get to her, as the tunnel exit is blocked by a metal grate, and she's standing on it.'

Why does he have to make a joke of everything, even at a time like this? Tony restrained himself from looking down at Penfold, but he realised that Marion was actually looking past him at the surfer. She wore a smile just like those he'd seen so often on Penfold.

While her eyes were on Penfold, Tony eyed up where he might grab her if he launched a hand upwards through a gap between the metal bars. Before he could implement this plan, Marion crashed to the floor, her chest pressed against the grate.

There was wrestling above, and Tony grasped a piece of purple robe that dangled down next to his face. He twisted his fist to wrap a couple of layers of it around his hand, forming a strong grip.

With more rolling around and grunting overhead, he realised Marion had been rugby tackled by DC Aria. He hung on tight to the cloth, but after a moment it went loose. The clasp had popped off and fell down, hitting Penfold on the forehead. It bounced down to clatter on the dark floor below.

Tony looked back up and the space was well lit again. He heard Madeline groaning both directly and through his radio. The grating was clear, so he pushed upwards, and it lifted, hinged above the ladder. As he climbed slowly, unsure of the situation above, he saw his DC with a cut above her eye socket, and a bloody candelabra lying close by.

He bent down beside her and determined that the injury wasn't too serious. Marion was gone though. Looking out into the cloisters and cloister garden, Tony could see nobody, and the heavy rain made such a noise on the roof that there was no chance to hear her fleeing footsteps.

'I can't see where she's gone. Is anyone on the CCTV screens right now?'

Jeanette Compton replied, 'I don't think Diane is on comms right now, but Chris is on his way down the stairs. Helen and I are guarding the Gospels.'

Penfold came up out of the dark hole, his hand held out. 'This was what had fastened her robe.' He held up a brooch type clasp, dull yellow in colour and round, with the St Cuthbert's Cross in the middle. Four red gemstones sat around the outer circle at the ends of the arms, and a larger one was set in the centre of the cross.

'That's not …'

'No, the St Cuthbert's Cross in the museum isn't nearly as complete as this. I think this is one of the missing pectoral crosses.'

'Saint Cuthbert's Treasure?' Tony was spellbound.

FORTY

Another moan from Aria snapped Tony out of his confusion. They helped her up and back around to the Chapter House where the first aid kit had been left open on a chair. DC Meredith sat in front of the computer screens, but she had a bandage held up to her still bleeding nose, and her other hand pressed on to her forehead, pain writ large across her features.

Hardwick bellowed in their ears, 'Have we got her location?'

PC Thorpshire replied, 'There's nothing on the screens. I can see you, sir, at the North Door, but she must be avoiding the cameras. We've only got four views.'

The superintendent commanded, 'Right, I've closed this door again, and I'll stay here to make sure she can't get out this way. There's only two exits, so if we cover those things we'll find her. Thorpshire, get on the radio to the armed team and get them to block the college arch exit. Two stay there and two start searching back into the cathedral from out there. Milburn, you and Penfold start searching inside the main building.'

The Constable of the Cathedral came echoing into their ears. 'Can you come and help me in St Cuthbert's shrine please. The exit from the tunnel is blocked.'

'Right, you two, start your search along the nave to the shrine and help that man out. He can assist with the search. Thorpshire, get on to the station to send more uniforms for the search. This place is huge – tell them we need everybody. And I mean everybody. Get on to the panda commanders to come back from that nonsense in the countryside.'

As they walked along the south side of the nave, the place was deserted. Penfold held out the pectoral cross for Tony to examine. 'Well, the existence of this, suggests she may well have found St Cuthbert's Treasure.'

Willem answered from underneath the Quire, in the tunnel. 'My torchlight is not great, but it was stored down here. I've found several cases that have been broken open, and they're empty. They're old and wooden with the word *Cuthbertus* inscribed on the lids. That's Cuthbert in Latin.

'The Bible lectern has been positioned right over the tunnel entrance. If you can shift that, I can get up and out.'

H took charge over the radios. 'Don't touch anything down there. I'll call the head of forensics to get her team to check those chests out for fingerprints and stuff. That new CSI Johnson is good down holes, isn't he?'

Penfold raised his eyebrows to Tony at Hardwick's comment. They had climbed the handful of steps into the small square shrine dedicated to Durham Cathedral's principal saint. Cuthbert's tomb formed the centre of the space. Tony remembered the huge colourful cloth suspended overhead from his final patrol.

They spotted the wooden frame with a carved eagle, wings spread, on the top. The bird was the height and size of Tony's torso as he approached the lectern. On top, the large book looked seriously aged. Ragged and without a cover, the uppermost page had a contents list penned out in fancy calligraphy. It looked fragile, so they had to be careful.

The two men together were suitably circumspect in shifting the heavy reading station sideways enough to reveal the grate covering a hole in the stone floor. Blinking at the sudden light, they saw the skinny face of Stan Willem looking up. He climbed the metal ladder, and they helped him up out of the hole.

'I'll get the guides to bring ropes and close off this area until you've done whatever police work needs to be done down there, but it looks like they got away with St Cuthbert's Treasure.' He pointed down at the series of wooden trunks lined up along the side wall of the room below, all with their lids open.

Willem had not stood up from kneeling and was looking back down through the opening. His voice caught and Tony thought he might be hurt. The two helped him to his feet and uttered some reassuring words, which Tony delivered unconvincingly.

As they stepped away from the hole, Willem stopped and pointed at the lectern. 'Where's the Bible?'

'What do you mean? We just pushed the eagle aside. We haven't removed anything.'

'The Bible we keep in here – that's not it. It's only a Victorian specimen, big leather-bound thing, but that's not it.' He was pointing at the book they'd taken pains to be careful with.

Tony looked in detail at the contents page on the top. He read to the others. 'Catalogue. Comedies, Tragedies, Histories, *The Tempest, Two Gentlemen of Verona*. This is Shakespeare, not the Bible.' He looked at Penfold, eyes wide with excitement. 'Have you ever seen Kathy's book? Is this it?'

The New Zealander bent forward to lean over the eagle's head to see the book. 'I haven't, but that does look very much how a first folio might look like. But hadn't Durham's one lost the front few pages in that previous theft?'

Before Penfold had even finished, Tony was video calling Kathy. He turned the camera for her to see what they had found, and she screamed.

'Tony, Tony, that's the folio! … But wait, it's different. Can you pick up that catalogue page?' He followed her instruction, and the page lifted off in his hand, it wasn't attached. He handed it to Stan Willem so that he could try the next page. That came off too. He lifted page after page until he found one that was attached. The first page of the play *The Tempest* began the parts of the book that were still all in one piece. 'Oh my God, Tony, those are the missing pages, where did you find them?'

'Can you come to the cathedral right now? You'll need to talk to Julia Sedgley about what forensic processing she can do without damaging the book.'

'I'm already getting my shoes on.' She hung up.

After four hours of searching, with a dozen reinforcements, there was still no sign of their suspect. With a comically large bandage taped across her nose, DC Meredith was still a bit wobbly on her feet. She had insisted on helping to find Marion and had been scouring the CCTV footage.

She called Tony into the Chapter House and Penfold followed to see what she had found. One of the four camera angles they had included a good view of the cloister walkway past the Great Kitchen to the base of the stairs up to the museum.

At the critical moment, DC Aria was seen to charge in through the door. The next movement captured by the camera was Tony sticking his head out the door to have a look left and right, before returning to the room to help the then stricken Madeline Aria. PC Thorpshire then ran past to get back to the Chapter House, but there was never any sign of Marion, or indeed any unknown person.

'She never left the Great Kitchen!'

Penfold and Tony bundled back around the corner into that room. The place was another grey, stone-walled space. Spacious and dimly lit, it had a number of proportionately large items of furniture – wooden benches and tables for refectory style dining – showpieces to give tourists an idea of monastic life.

Both sides of the long room included grand wooden sideboards. It was conceivable that a person could crouch in the shadows at the end of one of these and hide.

Tony darted around the place trying to find the woman, but there was nobody. After vainly opening some cupboard doors, he eventually wandered back towards Penfold who had not moved far beyond the threshold.

The New Zealander simply pointed at the floor. He was indicating the metal grate and the open hole they had both climbed out of hours earlier. 'There are three exits from the cathedral, but we only covered two of them.'

Tony knelt to look down the hole, more in exasperation than any sense that he might see her.

They returned to the Chapter House to find Harry dismissing everyone. Julia Sedgley was there and DSupt Hardwick proceeded to give her a list of places that needed forensic examination with a suggested order of importance. Having noted them all down, she said, 'This will take a long time. You realise we'll need to close the cathedral for weeks.'

Stan Willem stood in a corner. His voice wavered slightly as he argued, 'Not possible. The cathedral authorities will never allow that.'

Hardwick retorted, 'You closed for a week to film that *Avengers* movie. Don't give us that nonsense!'

Penfold stepped forward. 'You said earlier you'd never been in the passages. And you also said "Only Constables of the Cathedral know" about the passages. And then you said "*Hardly* anyone knows about the passage." You're the only Constable of the Cathedral right now. So, who else knows?'

Willem put out a hand and steadied himself against the solid wall. Penfold turned a spotlight from the tech desk to shine on and illuminate the gaunt figure. Tears were on the man's cheeks. He was visibly shaken and struggling to stand.

Hardwick strode over and pressed for an answer. Willem broke down, mumbling that his life's work had failed – St Cuthbert's Treasure had been stolen.

While the superintendent huffed and puffed, wanting a simple name for them to chase after, Penfold questioned lightly, teasing the full story out.

Willem had watched over the half dozen caskets for forty years, since the death of the previous Constable. Every four hours, he had entered the passage from another entrance at the base of the cathedral tower staircase. He had the only key to that hidden door. Nobody else knew of its existence, and the main duty of the Constable of the Cathedral was to watch vigilantly over the treasures.

Because of the duties of Operation Oswald, this had been the first day he had been unable to get away and complete his regular inspections. He had thought he was protecting the treasures that were in the museum, but had failed to protect those that a predecessor had hidden eighty-five years previously.

The story of the wartime drayman had been circulated as a cover to distract people away from the real hiding place. When Marion had approached him two years earlier, he had spotted a way to increase the visibility of that cover story via her website.

The enthusiasm with which Mr Willem had engaged the charming Miss Rufus had been his error. At some point, her conversation had caused him to give away the detail of his four hourly checks. Although he had revealed nothing of the secret passages, she must have realised he couldn't travel far for those checks without failing in his other duties.

As he spoke, Willem continued to break down further, until they had to physically restrain him from hitting himself in the face. He became a blubbering wreck and there was no more information to be had. He had never had any contact details for her beyond the website, and his story put the police in no better position to find Marion or her crew.

FORTY-ONE

Tony put his phone in the car's glove compartment and got out to try and find Penfold on the beach at Seaton Carew. There were five surfers in the water, just across from the Norton Hotel.

The promenade itself was wide and constructed from modern tessellating cobbles. Hartlepool had long ranked as a deprived area, and the kilometre or so of pathway had been paid for in the glory days of pre-Brexit EU funding. Tony struggled to see any improvement in the local neighbourhood fortunes as a consequence of the quite delightful, "new" promenade.

He remembered the old railway advertising poster, a reproduction from the early twentieth century, that hung in Penfold's hallway. *Visit Healthful Hartlepool-by-the-Sea* it proclaimed. Under normal circumstances, Tony would have agreed that the sea air was bracing. In the enduring heatwave, the flat cobbles radiated so much heat that it was truly uncomfortable.

Descending the wide stone staircase to the sand came as a slight relief, but the dry sand above the high tide mark also emitted intense heat. The air stank of a fetid, fishy, seaside odour, mixed with hot diesel. He could see three container ships plying the horizon.

The surfers in the line-up sat astride their boards on a becalmed water surface. The sea rippled slightly, but it was only every few minutes that a surfable wave would come through. Tony removed his sunglasses just long enough to wipe sweat from all around his eyes and nose, before quickly replacing them. The air from over the sea was a little fresher, and he moved, quite unconsciously, on to the cooler wet sand nearer the water's edge.

The next wave showed as a slight convexity in the surface that slid inexorably towards Tony. It was a long straight line rolling directly towards the beach, lifting the water maybe fifty centimetres at each point it passed. When the depth reduced enough that the wave crested to break, it was slightly larger, but still less than waist high for a standing surfer.

Two men and a woman attempted to catch the passing wave. The woman stood but collapsed into the water within a second. One man failed to get his board going with the weakness of the wave, but the second started to glide inwards.

After his board had gained some momentum, Penfold stood, feet together dead centre on the middle of his board, facing forward. This was not the crouching, side-on stance Tony associated with surfing. At one point the Kiwi even put his hands on his hips, bored, as the board slipped ever closer to grounding out in the sandy shallows.

Moments before this happened, he stepped casually off the board into ankle-deep water and skipped forward a couple of steps, before stooping to pull off the leg leash and lift the board up.

Tony had never seen this board before – it was absolutely gigantic, a least twice the height of Penfold himself. When he flipped it horizontal and up under his right armpit, the thing looked like a ladder in an old, black and white comedy movie. He would never be able to turn around without knocking over fruit stalls or small children.

'Milburn. Good to see you!'

'You seem in a bright mood. How so? Correct me if I'm wrong but I'm sure you've told me before that waves like these are no good at all. I'd expect your mood to be foul, no?'

Penfold laughed, which in itself worried Tony. The man was typically dry, deadpan or just plain cynical. Whole-hearted laughter seemed out of character.

'Quite right, Milburn, but two things have changed that today. Firstly, I've just invested in this longboard.' He waggled the surfboard slightly but not enough to endanger other beachgoers. 'And it has proven itself spectacularly successful. As you say, waves like this offer little or nothing … to a shortboard. Even young Cerys there couldn't catch anything today. Now, I've never been one for longboarding, but the surf here is so unpredictable – for which read generally small – that I thought I'd go back to basics and have a go with it.'

'And?'

'Wonderful. I mean you saw my last ride there. With minimal effort even the smallest wave can be ridden on this baby. There's no turning to be had, for sure, but this morning has taught me of many other nuances. I'm glad my mind is open.'

'Lovely. I'm pleased for you. But I meant "And what's the second thing?"' Penfold's obsession with surfing, especially during work hours, was increasingly annoying to Tony.

'Ah.' With his free hand, Penfold tapped a wet finger to his dry nose. The contrast highlighted that Penfold's hair was also completely dry. Tony could see that the waves were not crashing about the place, but for a surfer to land on shore with a dry head was something new to him.

This slight distraction didn't keep Tony from getting hot under the collar. The New Zealander started to walk up the beach, leaving the detective sweating in the bright sunshine. He took a few quick steps to catch up. 'What do you mean "Ah"? I don't expect my civilian consultant to keep things from me. Come on spill it.'

Tony had no idea if the second thing might be relevant to Operation Oswald, but he had a sneaking suspicion it would be. Penfold was always most coy when he felt he was a step ahead of everyone else. He was infuriating, and in the heat as they walked over the grass of Promenade Square, Tony could feel himself close to exploding. Penfold's stride was too big and fast though. He could never quite get into a position far enough in front to give him command of the situation, before they arrived at the front door.

In the cool of the house, Penfold shot upstairs to change, and left him to regain control of his anger. He headed down the kitchen staircase to Penfold's main workplace, his basement lab.

Once again Mantoro was there, swivelling around on one of the too-small bar stools and working on a laptop. He gave Tony a big grin, bright white teeth shining out from underneath his extremely bushy and very black moustache. 'My man,' he drawled. 'Another great day in paradise!'

'Blimey, is everyone in Seaton Carew on pep pills today?'

'Just cashews for me. Want some?' Mantoro's usual saucer of cashew nuts had been replaced by a large bowl of the nuts, at which he waved a strong paw.

Mantoro was not a young man, but he still radiated a taut strength from his stout frame. Tony imagined his past days as being a cartel enforcer in Mexico or perhaps El Salvador.

But the South American rarely gave away more than intriguing titbits about his personal history. Most of what Tony had in his head about the man had been developed through interpolating Mantoro's skills and knowledge with those Tony knew were used for criminal activity. Smuggling high-value contraband came across as Mantoro's principal area of expertise.

Before he had a chance to quiz Mantoro about possible sales routes for the stolen items he was currently responsible for chasing down, Penfold hustled down the stairs, whistling. It was not great whistling, but it wasn't random – he was clearly attempting some tune that he could hear in his own head.

Tony picked a couple of nuts from the bowl, held them up to show Mantoro and said, 'I tell you, there's definitely something in the coffee here today. Everybody is so unreasonably cheerful.'

'Who's put something in my coffee?'

'Nah, nothing, boss. Tony and I were just shootin' the breeze about cashews.' Again, Tony was intrigued with his use of the word *boss*. He couldn't fathom out their relationship at all.

Penfold launched himself into one of the high stools stationed at a computer terminal so that it did a full pirouette before he plonked his coffee on the white laminate surface beside the mouse mat.

The detective inspector gave a laughing exhale and said, 'Come on then, there must be something. You summoned me here with a cryptic haiku, and you're both acting like you've won the lottery.'

'I've been playing chess.' Penfold tapped the mouse, and the computer screen woke up. The display was also repeated on two giant TV screens hung on the long wall of the cellar, opposite where Tony sat.

The screens filled with a chess game already half completed. At the top of the screen, playing the white pieces was the name *Penfold* and a small collection of black pieces off the board, the ones he must have taken already. A similar graveyard of white pieces sat at the bottom of the screen, just above the word *Marina*.

'What on Ear—'

Penfold cut Tony off in mid-gawk. 'I know, incredible, isn't it?'

'She's still alive? How?'

Penfold's face took on a mask of confusion. 'What do you mean "How"? Why would you think she wasn't alive?'

The criminal they spoke of had vanished underwater a few years earlier, and her body had never been recovered. The case had been huge: a kidnap and murder as cover for a gold heist. Marina's disappearance had been as much of a shock as her crimes themselves.

Tony turned to Mantoro for help. The man raised his eyebrows giving an unclear message, so Tony persevered. 'Well, you were there. I dived into the freezing water at Hartlepool docks to try and save her and nearly drowned myself. I hate to admit it, but if Meredith hadn't rescued me, I'm not sure I'd have survived. We searched the water all night and for two days afterwards.'

'Never found a body though, did you?'

'I know you couldn't believe she was dead, but I went in the water after her, and I can't see anyone surviving in there. It took me more than a whole day to get back to a normal temperature.'

On the screens, a black knight came to life and, in a delightful animation, whinnied and jumped over a pawn to land in front, threatening a white bishop. Penfold nodded in approval at his opponent's tactics.

He turned away from the screen with his coffee in his hand. 'Look, Milburn, her identity is clear. Endangering misdirection is her absolute MO, right? She kills a few people in countryside locations, so that police resources are diverted away from the valuable items she wants to steal. Add into the misdirection nothing less than a fire at a boarding school, and then a city centre in chaos from a plague of frogs, and you have set up the perfect opportunity for the high-value thefts we've seen.

'Items like the Swan, the folio, Picasso and computer chip are exactly her sort of targets. Especially as distractors from the pièce de résistance – Saint Cuthbert's golden yardstick and, what was the phrase … "A jewel enough to redeem a prince" was it?'

'Yeah, sure, but this is not evidence.'

'Patience, young Padawan, all will be revealed.' Penfold was smiling broadly.

Tony didn't need the big reveal, his subconscious had sifted the information, and he saw the definitive connection in his coffee's surface shimmer. He pictured the criminal, Marina, standing proud on the deck of her white boat: tall, athletic and defiant. He could see how her build matched Marion Rufus, but that didn't make them the same woman.

His mind's eye scanned down the image of the woman on the boat and he saw the tattoo. Marina had carried the identical blue line image of a dolphin on her ankle. He cursed that he had not immediately connected the dots when he had seen it through the Great Kitchen grate.

He nodded slowly. 'No wonder Alex Carrera's also missing. There never was an Alex Carrera. She was Marina too. Bloody hell.' His final comment was more wonderment than curse.

Penfold waved at the chess screen on the wall. 'She's engaging me with this, but I fear it's mere taunting. "Catch me if you can" kind of stuff. The communications that send her moves have Trident completely baffled – Marina remains hidden in the aether.'

FORTY-TWO

Two days later, at their favourite table for three in the Daily Espresso, Kathy sat next to Tony and squeezed his hand. Penfold sat opposite, with a long black Americano in his hand. They were all still buzzing with the excitement of Operation Oswald.

Tony asked his friend, 'Come on then, spill the beans. When exactly did you know Marina was behind it all?'

'The belt.'

'What do you mean?' Kathy had heard Tony mention bits and pieces about the mystery of Dickie Harbottle's remains and the surf company belt from the wrong era for his skeleton.

There was a slight flicker of Penfold's eyebrows. 'That body had to be a set-up, but to what end? A Rip Curl belt – only available in Australia and the US, at the time it was made – on the skeleton of a County Durham soldier down a Tudhoe mineshaft. And a more recent body that would almost certainly bring Milburn to the mine. That whole scenario screamed that it was a message for me.'

'But why a message from Marina?'

'The set-up is so complex, I've never heard of anyone else going to such meticulous lengths. It wouldn't surprise me if it's not even Dickie Harbottle, but that she went as far as to insert fake dental records into his old army file.'

'Fairburn's break-in at Catterick. I bet they put his dental records into the army's historical archives.' Tony looked Penfold in the eyes. 'She also killed the other three just for the sake of some sort of smokescreen. She's properly psychopathic.'

Penfold conceded a slight nod of his head. 'I assume she merely helped them onto booby traps. Something didn't work out with the Tan Hill dude though, and she clocked him with the nearest rock to hand.'

'His name was John Bowline, and he left a pregnant wife.' Penfold did not seem to catch on to Tony's anger at his straightforward analysis of the murders. He could never understand how the man managed to be so cold.

Kathy was wide-eyed. 'Really? I mean I know they got away with some incredibly valuable things, but was all that necessary?'

'Of course not. No, she likes to show off. Just look at the whole frog breeding programme. She wants us to know just how incredibly talented she is at all manner of criminal activities. The high-value thefts are merely to finance the whole grand performance.'

'So, the return of the Shakespeare was just another stage in the show?'

Tony explained to Kathy how Fairburn had told them of burgling a house in Washington and stealing some old papers. The address was that of the original thief of the Shakespeare.

Kathy commented, 'Surely the police had searched his house?' She was met with shrugs.

Penfold answered, 'He was actually imprisoned for handling stolen goods. He definitely took the folio to the Shakespeare library in DC, so presumably had those front pages at one time. Who knows how the police missed them.' He sipped from his coffee before continuing. 'I guess Marina figured returning the folio to you, with the lost pages added, was a sort of quid pro quo for the goodies in St Cuthbert's Treasure.'

Tony asked, 'Do you still have no leads about where she might be? The electronic messaging for that chess game didn't give you any clues? We need a quid pro quo for the murders.' Tony grimaced, intending to indicate to Penfold that he was in danger of being as callous about the dead men as Marina herself.

'No, Trident found nothing. Did your investigations get anywhere with any of the paperwork around the vehicles, or Castle Eden Manor itself?'

The detective shook his head. 'No, but that's a huge load of work. It'll take a good while and it's all bureaucratic paperwork. Painstaking.'

'I'm sure Barnes will be keen to get on to that when he gets back. And Meredith. How long is she off for?'

'As long as possible,' Kathy interjected. 'Seeing her with that bloody nose was almost as good a feeling as seeing the folio back in place. But recovering the extra pages, that topped it off. Best. Friday. Ever.'

'St Cuthbert's Friday did see treasures returned then. Well, some at any rate.'

She smiled. 'Not exactly Cuthbertine treasures, but I'll take it.'

Penfold chuckled. 'No, Marina will take those.'

Tony scowled at Penfold's casual appraisal, or even praise, of the woman's criminality. 'We still need to solve all this, Penfold. Forget the stolen items, four men are dead.'

'Only three by her hand, but you're right, I will redouble my efforts to track her down.'

'I'm sure you will.'

***

Author's website:
mileshudson.com

Join the Marras:
friendsofdurhamminersgala.org